But now you're here and I'm hungry to destroy you.

Eat you up and taste the demonic shade of your blood.

Because even if I don't want you, I can't help but crave you.

CU01507804

–

Editing and Proofreading: Amy Briggs
Cover Design: BooksMoodsCo

FATED

LIZA JAMES

TRIGGER

Trigger Warning: This book confronts potential triggers such as sexual assault, rape, blood and violence. It also contains scenes in which sexual content is explained in explicit detail. Recommended for ages 18+.

BLURB

LUNA

I never asked for this. I never wanted this.

But I've been forced into this life I never knew existed. How do I begin to comprehend the reality of Fallen Angels?

I'm surrounded by my worst nightmares and greatest fears, but I'll be damned if I let them control me.

You've consumed me without my permission. Made a home inside of my blood without my asking.

Now, I'm lost to you in every sense of the word and I'm unsure if I want to find my way out.

———

ELIJAH

I never wanted you.

I could have lived my entire existence without you and been content.

I prefer my soul embrace the Demon, corrupted with darkness and refined with humanity.

———

Spotify Playlist:
https://geni.us/fatedplaylist

CHAPTER ONE

CHAPTER ONE

Luna

EVERYTHING SURROUNDS ME IN DARKNESS, SWALLOWING up my senses and causing a thick fog to envelop my mind. The musky scent of wet cement, mold, and infinitely empty rooms fills my nose. I haven't the faintest idea of where I am. I was blindfolded the minute I was taken outside the small, quaint coffee shop I work at in downtown Brooklyn.

I remember working the late shift, closing the shop and locking the narrow glass door. At the time, my back was turned to the quiet street behind me and I was ignorant to the shuffling of heavy feet as two incredibly large men crept up without my knowledge.

I should have known better. This isn't the first time I was involved in a dangerous back alley incident. It's been seven years since that destructive night happened. I've been slacking off and letting my guard slip far too much recently, the result of refusing to let my mind linger on those revolting memories. I force them back—whenever they rear their ugly little heads—intentionally choosing not to relive them.

There are moments I wish I hadn't survived that night.

And that's when I drive them back down and remind myself that there had to have been some momentous reason that I'm still alive.

There has to be more than this.

Yet here I am, terrified and following what I can only assume is a line of other young women. I can hear their sniffles and cries as we walk down a dark, narrow hallway to what is presumably going to be our death.

So, maybe it was all for nothing after all.

The cold chill in the air brushes along my exposed shoulders from the loose, burgundy tank I had worn to work. My intentionally distressed skinny jeans are now easily compared to the rest of my body, also distressed and torn up from the outside. My hands are tied grotesquely tight in front of my waist as I clutch onto the thin fabric of whomever I'm following. I believe she's doing the same as well. Maybe we're hoping to find solace and comfort in the simple fact that we aren't alone in this nightmare.

As we continue to walk, I quickly assess my injuries. My long, dark, chestnut hair is matted to my forehead in what I think is my own blood. Thin strands fell from my messy top knot when I was grabbed. The men smashed my head against the cement wall when I tried to escape. Their large, calloused hands snaked around my waist and tightly gripped the back of my neck. I knew in that moment I wouldn't be able to evade another incident like this again. You can't be *that* lucky twice in one life.

Seven years ago, I let the fear take over. I cried, begging them to free me. I remember all too well how that ended. So, now, I'm silent. Even as my insides tremble in anticipation of what exactly I'm headed into. I bite my tongue and push forward. In my mind, I've been envisioning countless ways to break free from this line. I ache to release my reddened, sore hands from their knots and tear the blindfold away from my swollen eyes.

I tried once, when we first arrived at this undisclosed location. I was yanked out from the back of a vehicle. One man clung to me forcefully from behind, his long fingers digging into the skin at my shoulders. When I lurched forward, intending to catch him off guard, I broke away, but another man was already ahead of me.

He shot out and gripped my hair in his fist, yanking me toward him while my scalp stretched and tore from his hold. I gasp before biting my bottom lip so hard I tasted the metallic tinge of fresh blood inside of my mouth.

I didn't want to shout, yelp, or cry out in pain, giving them any sort of satisfaction at my expense. No, I was never giving someone that gratification again. I would never beg for my freedom or to be saved. If I was going to die, I would do it with my chin held high, staring into the eyes of whoever was fucked up enough to do this.

I'm suddenly shoved forward roughly, stumbling into the girl in front of me as she cries out in fear.

"Quiet, bitch," a loud, masculine voice shouts behind us.

"It's okay, we'll get out of this," I whisper as I dip my lips closely behind her head, trying to offer a slice of reassurance while she cries. It doesn't help, she doesn't stop and the others in line start crying as well. I can *feel* the tension growing around us. It's thick and black, like long vines winding around our middles and wrapping around our throats. The anticipation of what is happening is a toxic poison infiltrating our lungs.

Human trafficking? It's the only logical explanation I can think of. We're getting shipped overseas and being forced into slavery of whatever kind of debauchery they prefer.

I hear the fearful protests before those large hands land on my shoulders and tear me away from the line. If I have to guess —which I am—we're being lined up horizontally now. I feel a trembling shoulder brush against my own, my sight still completely blinded by the rough black cloth tied around my face.

Drip.

Drip.

Drip.

The steady sound of water dripping in the background hits my ears. I'm not sure if we're underground now, but I don't recall any staircases. *Was it raining outside?* Fuck, I can't remember and right now my mind is racing frantically with whatever we're about to uncover.

Suddenly, my knees smash into the cold ground below as I'm shoved down from behind and forced into a kneeling position. If anything kicks me into a small, uncontrollable panic it's this. I've been here before, forced onto my knees when I never should have been. This moment alone sparks the memories I've buried in my subconscious, back up and to the forefront of my mind.

No, no, no. Not again.

I take a deep breath in and then exhale.

In.

Out.

In.

Out.

One by one, our blindfolds are ripped off of our faces as we blink away the darkness and attempt adjusting to the dim lighting. My hands are still tied, so I bring them both up to my face and struggle to rub the fog out of my sight. My eyelashes have caked together in blood, clumped from bottom to top so that it's nearly impossible to fully open my eyes again. I feel tears prick to break free, not from fear, but from being strained against the fabric for so long.

At first, I glance to my right, quickly taking count of how many other girls are with me. Four or five of us in total. We're all knelt down, each of our hands tied together and each of us bleeding from one place or another. A couple of the other girls look a little rougher than I feel, obviously having taken a harder hit when they put up a fight while being abducted.

I knew better though. The harder you fight, the harder they hit. Last time, I'd fought until there was nothing left. No energy to push forward. No voice to yell out anymore. I screamed and cried and begged, hoping anyone passing by could hear me. But it was wasted, and in the end, I was left alone. Finally, alone.

So, now? I don't beg. I don't cry. I simply don't give anyone the ability to have that much power over me anymore. Until this moment. Until I was caught off guard relaxing for the briefest second.

I turn my gaze back to the front and realize we're in a small room, hardly bigger than the bedroom in my little apartment near the Brooklyn Bridge. The walls are discolored cement slabs, some covered in graffiti and others splattered in a dark pigmented material that I refuse to try and identify.

Instantly, the drip begins again, so loud in the heavy silence it catches each of our attention and throws my eyes to the corner of the room. A few girls scream, most of them break out into a sob as we realize what's in front of us.

I stay quiet, my eyes trained on the dead man who is ruthlessly hanging upside down from the mold covered ceiling. Fear keeps me rooted to the floor, unmoving, unflinching, hell even unblinking, as my mind attempts to process what is happening.

How the hell did I find myself here?

His throat was slit, the blood spilled down and over his chin, covering the eyes that are now too swollen to fit inside his sockets and have fallen out. His skin is blue and purple, veins inflamed and sickly while his thick blood soaks what hair he has and slowly, ever so slowly, drips to cold floor below him.

Drip.

Drip.

Drip.

Not water. Blood.

CHAPTER TWO

ELIJAH

Fuck. I need to get out of here.

I'm usually quicker than this. But something is nagging at me from the inside, pulling at my intentions and diverting them in ways I can't explain. I was supposed to get in here, get an eye on Amelia and Danner, and then get the hell out. I know she can't feel me now—not since the bond was severed—but if she sees me, everything will be wasted.

Amelia and Danner have been lurking through the city lately. Vanishing and reappearing in perplexing places. We have eyes on them constantly, but we're having a difficult time understanding their motives and solidifying any patterns.

That's why I'm here tonight. Ideally, to gain insight on their intentions and what they've been working on. I'm the best candidate because I know where she lives due to our history. She hasn't moved nor has she kept her whereabouts a secret, and I believe that makes her even more dangerous.

It's been seven years since she took everything from me, ruining and leaving me for dead after I had so blindly accepted we were created for each other.

What a fucking joke.

With her disturbingly long, snow white hair and her milky, pale skin, I was instantly pulled under. I surrendered to her large, glacial blue eyes. I gave her everything—my entire being, along with my heart—for an exchange I assumed was of equal value. How the fuck can you be bonded by blood with a person and *not* become attached to them? How could she feel my every emotion, how could I feel hers, and yet still be so blinded by my love for her?

If I'm being completely honest with myself, I fucking knew it was coming before it happened. I can deny the feelings all I want, but I felt the distance in our bond. I sensed the way she began pulling away and I picked up on the tiniest spark of a flame when she met Danner. But I ignored it, slowly cutting off my own emotions with alcohol, and numbing whatever bond we had left.

Still, no amount of alcohol or drugs can drown out the agonizing physical pain of severing a bond. Nothing will ever compare to the loss of someone who has been ingrained into your DNA, into your veins and the very cells of your being. Nothing can prepare you for having a limb torn from your body while you're expected to simply shake it off and move forward.

It's why I vowed never to initiate a blood bond again. I will gladly fuck my way through New York with baseless one-night stands and hook ups. I will never give anything more than a casual fuck to another woman again. Not because I'm still hung up on Amelia—hell no.

Simply because I will maintain the control over my own life, preserve the hold and responsibility I have over myself. No one will get that piece of me again because that means giving away a portion of my control.

I'll never allow this to happen again.

Now, as I mask myself in inconspicuous colors and slowly make my way through Amelia's seemingly innocuous mansion down to the cellars, I'm thankful for what happened all those years ago.

Because Amelia Traverse is a fucking psychotic train wreck. One that desperately needs to be locked up, if not killed all together. Now that she has bonded with Danner—a fellow Thronie who has devoted himself entirely to her cause—she's been infuriatingly difficult to nail down.

She believes she should be the Queen of our race, ironically claiming to be committed to justice and the fair distribution of power. This belief is what got her here in the first place, but only if that distribution of power means she wields all of it. She doesn't care about our people, or the war we are fighting outside of her ridiculous quest for reign.

The race's capital is nestled tightly into the center of downtown Manhattan. It's based in the old white, neo-gothic cathedral and is constantly overrun or attacked by the cambion demons that have tried to defeat us. Right now, the cathedral is our most important asset—housing all of our intel, organizations, master lists of allies and assumed enemies—yet we're in a constant war to defend and protect it.

Instead of joining with us to help us preserve what is rightfully ours, Amelia is focused on overthrowing and obtaining all of the control she can with Danner by her side. She hasn't built a powerful enough command to successfully overthrow my brother yet, but she's constantly working on it. She's strategically engaged behind the scenes, in the dark alleys and isolated corners of our race where she can gain a footing. She's weaving herself in the lonely strands of their minds in order to manipulate them to her betterment.

See, we all Fell at one point. We all lost our right and privilege to stay where we were created and flourished from. We all made mistakes—ones that some of us regret, ones that I never will—that have the same outcome. They cost us our precious positions in Arcadia above.

We're Angels. Fallen and forgotten by those of most importance, but never released from the constant war raging below. The demons work to pull us just a little farther under, until we're serving and slaves once again as Aeshma—wrath demons designed for war.

But for an entirely different deity.

CHAPTER THREE

Luna

I sense something, a low simmering boil within my blood. It's incredibly mild and nearly indiscernible, but I feel it all the same. What I don't understand however, is where it's coming from.

I'm not angry, no. I'm scared—yes. Anxious? Absolutely. But this is different, I'm craving something in the slightest of ways. I've never done drugs, nothing hard anyway. But I imagine this is what a recovering addict experiences—that nostalgic sentiment of needing a fix but knowing you can never have it. A reminiscent yearning of something more, but also something unobtainable at the same time.

Instantly, all of my senses begin firing smoothly again. It's faint, but everything begins lighting up on alert. I feel the fog clearing from my mind, but not enough to truly give me the energy I need to get out of here. It's as if my body is becoming somehow more attuned to the situation, an invisible string of strength slowly leaking back into my small frame.

I suddenly realize there are two people leisurely standing in front of us, leaning against the wall as their eyes rake over our bodies. The woman is small, about my height, standing at five-foot-three, but that's where the similarities end. Her hair is the complete opposite of my own. Where mine is long and dark, thick with uncontrollable natural waves, hers is bone straight, long to the point of hitting her waist and stark white. It's thin and free of a single stray hair, parted directly down the center and framing her stunning ice blue eyes.

I blink a few times, processing the way her gaze literally pierces the darkness. Her skin, a soft milky white, naturally glows in contrast to the dimness of where we are. Instinctively, I can't help but compare myself to her and I don't even understand why. But I'm taking note of how my skin has just a bit more color than hers and envisioning how my own eyes are a dark chocolate brown rather than her stark blue. She's beautiful in a way I can hardly fathom even though I'm staring directly at her.

I've never been considered outrageously stunning, and certainly not even in the same league as the woman in front of me. I have my good days, like everyone else but I'd say I fall under the average category of beauty. My figure is full of curves and I'm bustier than I'd prefer, but I have always loved my hair, mess and all.

Her eyes linger on me, scanning me from head to toe as if she's sizing me up against her as well. So odd, this invisible exchange happening between us. But I realize that in my gut, I impulsively know that she is not to be trusted. There is something evil lurking in her gaze.

That same toxic poison of tension I felt from earlier? I can practically see it leaking from her pores, rooted in her being, and infecting everything around her.

The man next to her is massive, well over six feet tall and eerily lean. Narrow hips lead upwards to his slightly wider chest and broad shoulders. But there is something simplistic about him. From the way his dark eyes watch each of us before turning their attention back towards the woman, I can tell he is following her lead. The dismissive air around her is practically tangible, tainted with an unnerving amount of confidence. She looks like she couldn't care less to be here but is unfortunately stuck with the necessary task.

He raises his hands in a smooth, lazy motion and lifts the wiry strands of his dirty blond hair up, securing them into a tight knot on top of his head. They are both dressed in entirely black outfits. His, a long, leather trench coat that shrouds most of his body. Unfortunately, I have a sinking feeling that coat choice was intentional, as he's easily able to hide weapons underneath it on his lithe body. I can barely make out his ripped black jeans that peek from the bottom of his jacket, tucked messily into a pair of black army boots.

She on the other hand, showcases her weapons proudly. A pair of small but obvious handguns secured to each of her hips and a long, blinding dagger that is nestled tightly against the outside of her leather-clad thigh. The very one I imagine was used to slaughter the poor man hanging in the corner. There's a chance I can see blood smeared across the blade, but my eyes are swollen and it's too dark to know for sure.

She sports a tight, thin, black tank top that hugs her tiny frame seductively, displaying her figure in a way that has me feeling oddly defensive. I can't define the reasoning behind these illusive emotions she's pulling from me, as if I have anything to defend from her other than my own precious life at this point.

I focus on leveling my breaths and stilling my body to hide the fear that's bubbling up inside my stomach. I'll never share that with them though. I narrow my eyes and lift my chin, using every ounce of control and strength I have left over to keep the trembling at bay.

The man steps forward first, slowly making his way from one end of our row to the other. He stops at the girl next to me, leaning down and brushing his thumb across her bloody, swollen bottom lip. Her eyes squeeze shut on a whimper as she shrinks back from his impetuous touch.

A small smirk plays on his lips before he releases her and steps towards me. Coming face to face with him causes a bolt of anger to shoot through my chest. I tilt my head up defiantly, daring to meet his eyes with my own as he crouches down into my space. His hands rest casually on his knees as he silently rakes his gaze over my body, processing whatever it is he's seeing within me.

"You. What is your name?" His cold voice infiltrates the dense cloud of tension that suffocates us, slicing through my skin and chilling my bones.

I lift my chin even higher, refusing to answer his question. He deserves nothing from me. The corner of his mouth rises in silent appreciation, clearly enjoying the fight I'm offering him. His long, thin fingers reach forward and gently trace my jawline, leaving goosebumps exploding across my skin as I fight to maintain my falsely calm state.

"Did you hear me, little one?' His voice is now gentle but dishonestly kind as those same fingers grip and dig into the base of my throat. He jerks me towards him, closing the gap between our bodies so that I'm flush against his. I feel the warmth of his breath as it falls against my lips when he speaks. "I said, what is your fucking name?"

In moments like this, when you're caught in the midst of a

seemingly life or death situation, time passes far too quickly. My mind races in a matter of microseconds, considering how to respond and whether I should play along on the off chance that I could survive. So, I do, whether it's the right decision or not.

"Luna," I choke out, gasping for breath beneath his sadistic touch. I dig my nails into my aching palms to the point of drawing blood, I can feel the warmth filling my hands as they strain against my lap.

"Lu-na," he repeats, intentionally uttering my name slowly, letting each syllable roll off of his tongue as it moves so disgustingly close to my face. Just when I feel I'm about to lose control, when my vision becomes hazy with lack of oxygen, I hear her voice break through the room.

"Enough." The only word she speaks, on a command, and his grasp is immediately released. Uncontrollably, I fall forward as I gasp for air, trying to catch my breath before sitting upright.

I spit at his boots as he stands and meet his eyes once again. The undeniable strength and heat in my blood giving me the odd ability to continue fighting this undoubtedly deadly situation. He laughs, the sound loud and shrill as it cascades around us. His large hand swings back before crashing against my cheek. I fall backwards, my shoulder smashing the concrete as my head whips back and makes contact with the hard ground as well. Everything is ringing so loudly in my ears that I barely hear the cries and shrieks from the girls next to me.

For a brief moment I close my eyes, allowing myself a second to simply exist in the darkness. I wish it would swallow me whole and keep me here so that I didn't have to face my past demons or whatever hellish situation I've found myself in now. But a soft voice reminds me what my reality is. The vague sense of encouragement and power course quietly through my body as I regain my vision and face my captors once again.

The woman has stepped forward now, standing side by side with the man as they center themselves in front of us.

"I'm sure you are all confused and scared. It's an unfortunate situation you find yourselves in tonight and I truly am sorry that you all had to be the collateral damage for a war you know nothing about." Her expression seems genuinely kind as she speaks. I can *almost* feel remorse in her words as if she was sincerely uttering the truth. But the casual and relaxed stance she holds tells me otherwise. I can sense a liar when I see one and I'm not fucking stupid.

"Lies," I grit out between the clenched teeth of my sore and swollen jaw. Honestly, I'm surprised by my own courage at this point. With each passing moment I'm realizing that I must not give a shit about my own life anymore. I've dealt with this once and handled things in a completely different way. But it was a way that left me on deaths door, abused and painfully living the rest of my life in an absent and vacant manner. Not truly thriving, but numbly existing from day to day, which I suppose compels my current behavior.

Her head sharply twists towards me. Those bright blue eyes widen slightly, appearing surprised by my voice speaking against hers. "Excuse me? Do you have any idea who you're speaking to, dearest Lu-na?"

I glance to the young woman next to me when I feel her shoulder softly nudge into my own. Her eyes are brimmed with tears as she silently pleads with me to keep my mouth shut. Poor girl, she has no idea that we're not getting out of this alive. A sudden wave of regret fills my stomach as I remember the words I spoke to her earlier, encouraging a small pang of hope at the idea that we'd survive. I should've known better than to offer false hope to another person, but back then, I truly thought there might be a way to escape.

I was wrong though, it's clear now that their intentions are

16

to kill us. In this small, windowless room at an unknown location, surrounded by anonymous people who are now bonded together by this single act of chaos and destruction.

I exhale an apologetic sigh at my nameless friend before turning my gaze back toward the woman in front of us. "I don't need to know who you are, or why you're doing this. It's crystal clear that your minds won't be changed and that there is some strange, twisted reasoning behind this impending slaughter. But what I do know, is that you're lying. Spare us the false sympathy at your actions and simply own them. If you're going to kill us, be a fucking woman about it and say it."

Without a word, the woman with snow white hair steps closer to me. Each movement forward is an intentional declaration, I can feel it twisting and burrowing underneath my skin as I keep my eyes on her.

Her gaze never leaves my own, but her friend steps forward, his hands lifting upwards and directed towards each of us. Immediately, all of the women next to me stand at the exact same moment, their bodies completely in sync with one another as if tied together by an invisible string. I choose to rise with them, delayed by only a brief second but one that doesn't go unnoticed by both the woman and man in front of me.

A flash of intrigue shimmers in our captors' eyes before their walls of control quickly slip back into place. Each of the girls next to me are clearly confused by what is happening. Their faces show mixed expressions of fear and apprehension.

"You are correct, you stupid, fragile girl." A sad smile drifts across her face as her cold hands lift and rest on either side of my slender neck. Her thumbs graze softly across my cheeks, tracing the lines of my nose and then my eyebrows, as if she's memorizing the soft curves of my face. "You unknowingly speak to your Queen with such disrespect, a fault I will choose not to hold against you. You have no idea, after all, the kind of blood that flows through your veins. You have no knowledge to give you the strength you need to fight back. No, you're weak, little Lu-na. But you already know that, don't you? You know you've never been strong enough to fight back. You've only ever let those around you take and take and take, failing to defend yourself when you needed to most."

I try to focus and make sense of what she's saying, but her words cut through me in ways that are destroying the shield of strength I had managed to erect around me. She couldn't know what happened seven years ago. I never told anyone, I never went to the police or my family. By family I only mean my younger sister. We've been alone for most of my life, never knowing who our biological parents were. We jumped through the foster system until I was old enough to emancipate myself and take care of the both of us. Now, as a twenty-seven-year-old woman who manages a coffee shop and photographs families for a living, I've found myself in an irreparable position. I can only hope my younger sister by two years—Stella—will be able to move forward once she realizes I'll never be showing up at her apartment unannounced again. She's strong though, stronger than I've ever been. I have to remind myself of that and believe she'll be okay.

"Have you ever had anything to offer anyone? Anything of value within yourself? I don't think so. That's why everyone you know has left or taken from you in one way or another." Tears sting my eyes as the impact of her words spiral through me. She doesn't fucking know me, yet everything she says rips through my mind and poisons my heart. "It's okay, sweet one. There's nothing wrong with simply providing a shell of a life for someone else's cause. Nothing wrong with being so exceptionally, unexceptional. So, you are correct. I am going to kill you, each of you, and I do not feel any remorse over that fact.

You are simply a means to an end, an unfortunate casualty in the name of war."

I have no words, no ability to form any sort of remark back to what she's thrown at me. Because in the matter of mere seconds, she's stripped me of each of my darkest fears and brought them to light, exposing them not only to everyone around me but also to myself. She's pulled every memory that I've worked my ass off to forget back to the surface and shoved it to the forefront of my mind in a way that has completely silenced me.

And it's in that moment, the one where I lost myself to that night seven years ago, when I'm suddenly surrounded by the sounds of gasps and cries from the women beside me. Their voices rip me out of my memories and back to reality as I glance around and realize each of them is struggling to breath, clutching and scraping at their own throats before they fall back to their knees.

What the hell is going on?

CHAPTER FOUR

ELIJAH

I KNEW I SHOULD HAVE LEFT. THE SECOND I CAUGHT SIGHT of Amelia and Danner stepping into the back, gated entrance of her mansion, I should have turned my ass around and gone back to the Capital to report. It's as if my body is moving on its own, my mind screaming to turn around and not risk everything we've worked for, but some innate genetic predisposition within my body is literally refusing to follow through.

A low, deep yearning called me to follow Amelia down into the depths of the mansion. I could hear their steps and hushed voices and in order to stay on their tail I followed at a distance until I patiently waited for her and Danner to disappear around the dark corner ahead of me.

I was surprised to find the small, cold and dingy room at the end of the narrow hall. I can't understand why they would be headed to such a low place themselves. Amelia usually assigns prisoner tasks to the few guards she has for handling. She doesn't like getting her hands dirty, not unless she had to.

Now, as I peer in silently behind a veil of darkness from the hallway, I watch as a small row of young women are forced to their knees. My heart thunders in my chest, anger and disgust coursing through me as they each finally notice the dead man hanging loosely in the corner. No doubt they are all terrified, surely they have no idea what they've walked into. No one does, Fallen Angels live in plain sight, keeping our identities and pasts a guarded secret. It's worked surprisingly well. The humans around us usually don't notice the slight differences in our DNA, why would they? We all look the same on the outside, for the most part.

While they struggle with simple physical hardships, we practically glow in comparison. Healthy, silky hair. Clean, clear skin. We crave exercise and adrenaline, making it easy to keep our God-like bodies in ideal condition. We were designed mirroring perfection, after all. It allows us to be admired by humans, but we intimidate them as well. So, while they have no idea how different we are from them, they usually don't seek out relationships with us either. Makes things easy.

My eyes immediately fall to Amelia, noticing how her small, thin body easily moves forward to address her captives. I internally wait for some sort of emotional response to rear its head at me, remind me that I was once in love with her. But it never comes, in fact, a wave of disgust rolls through me instead at the reminder that I was once so naïve and ignorant to let my foolish feelings attach to that.

A small, but strangely confident voice breaks through the room and injects directly into my blood. A shock of electricity erupts in my chest and spirals through each of my limbs, igniting my fingertips in a way that causes me to physically wring out my tattoo covered hands. I can't see any of their faces, but instinctively I know which body the voice belongs too.

On the very left end of the row, a small woman with thick and wild dark hair lifts her head to challenge Amelia's surprised gaze. I watch their interaction, not hearing exactly what is being said but completely enraptured by the unknown woman's body language. She's kneeling, in a completely submissive position but the aura around her screams everything but.

Unbelievable strength radiates from her core, I can feel it flowing through the room and electrifying the air. Danner steps forward and uses his influential talent to control the women to rise up from their positions.

And that's when I see it. Immediately, confusion and appreciation lick across my body, because I believe I'm witnessing someone who is potentially immune to Danner's abilities. She stands, just as the others do, but she does it of her own volition. She's just a brief second behind everyone else. She has unknowingly given them a vital piece of information she should be protecting. An odd sensation of affinity interrupts my thoughts as that unfamiliar craving continues surging through my form.

I should leave. Logically, I remind myself of this. Especially now that such strange and foreign emotions are plaguing my mind. I shouldn't care, hell, I don't care about these people. It's not my fault they have ended up in this shitty place. But my feet refuse to move, my body refuses to shift even slightly towards the exit. No, even if I truly wanted to leave, I'd never be able to. Not until I knew that this unknown creature in front of me made it out of Amelia's grasp alive.

Instantly, each of the women in the room begin gasping for air as Danner simply steels his intense gaze on them. I know what he's doing, he's killing them through suffocation. Stealing their oxygen and leaving them to die a vile death. I don't understand their reasons for killing these humans off, but I'm sure it has some sort of grounding in her desire to obtain the throne.

My eyes zone in on the nameless woman on the left. Danner has come to stand behind her small figure, his snake-like fingers sliding around her waist while one hand wraps tightly around the base of her throat. Amelia's eyes are like fire, the heated blaze sparking her features into sharp and distorted angles. Whether it's from fascination, or anger, I do not know. But I do know that if this girl is immune to Danner's influence, there is absolutely no way she will be allowed to leave alive.

Danner throws his head back in a fit of maniacal laughter as he drags her body flush against his own. Amelia watches with a sadistic amount of appreciation coating her features, enjoying the show of her bonded mate stealing the life of someone who holds an undoubted amount of power over her.

Unexplainable fury builds in my gut and eats at my organs as I watch Danner's hands seductively caress her bewitching figure. "We'll have to do this hard way, I see. But I appreciate that in a woman such as yourself, little Luna. It's been a while since I've had to conquer a true challenge."

Luna.

I hear his words this time, while my body and mind awaken in indescribable ways I've never experienced before. Hearing her name sends an influx of adrenaline surging through my chest. All of my senses have sparked to a new level, not incredibly higher than before, but enough to hear his words and feel the incredible power warring in the room ahead of me. My vision is slightly clearer, time slows by just a fraction of a second as I step forward, letting the dim lighting illuminate my massive stature as I reveal that I've been lying in wait.

I am risking and possibly ruining everything I've worked for.

To intervene on behalf of a faceless girl I know nothing of.

"Amelia."

CHAPTER FIVE

Luna

THE GIRLS AROUND ME ARE DEAD. CLEARLY, AS THEY LAY scattered around the room after fighting to catch their own breath. Fear finally rushes through my mind and overwhelms my body, effectively replacing the false confidence I was so sure I could fake through this. I don't understand how this awful and evil man standing behind me did it. While his cold and chilling fingers glide over my skin and possess my throat, I struggle to decipher any logical explanation to this entire experience.

His words barely register as they skirt across my ears. His lips brush the shell of my ear, sending a breath of chilling air slithering across my neck. I don't know what he's saying, but the feeling of his grip growing tighter and tighter across my throat is overtaking my mind and body in a way I can't control.

"Amelia."

A new voice. A masculine, deep, radiating voice booms from behind us and envelopes me like a thick blanket of heavy velvet. It replaces the cold chill behind the revolting man's fingers, with something much more sultry, akin to the scorching heat on your skin in the middle of July.

For the first time, I see a clear spark of fear light the woman's eyes in front of me. *Amelia*, it must be her name. One she never offered to the likes of us, discarded, valueless people who were a simple means to an end for her.

Immediately, I'm twisted around in the same arms of the man I wish so desperately to escape from. His grip on my body has grown incredibly harder. I'm practically bolted to his chest with a strength I didn't realize someone of his lean stature could hold. Amelia stands to the right of me while the grip on my neck remains, continuing to constrict my airway just enough to barely keep me conscious.

I meet the new arrival's gaze in an instant. One that scorches through my skin as his emerald green eyes quickly rake over me. A strange sensation of kinship flourishes in my chest, as if a thin tether between the two of us is connected. I can't explain it, but suddenly that fix I needed as a hypothetical addict comes breaking back to the surface of my mind.

Amelia steps away from me and toward the man ahead of us. A feeling of defense builds in my mind as she nears him. It doesn't make any sense, this unfamiliar feeling of, what? *Jealousy?* It can't be that. There's nothing to be jealous of. I have no idea who any of these people are.

As she closes the distance between them, I'm given a quick moment to process the man who interrupted my impending death. He's tall, astonishingly so. Taller than the man who I'm currently pressed tightly against. He's also much broader and wider than anyone I've ever met before. His thick arms showcase his bulging muscles as they cross casually in front of his chest. He's wearing a black, long sleeve thermal that clings to his defined pecs before it falls over his low slung, dark denim jeans. His legs are just as impressive, solid and clearly tense with restrained power.

I notice his tattoos next. They're everywhere, trailing out from underneath his sleeves and leading to each of his fingertips. They even peek out from under the collar of his shirt, rising up his neck before stopping at a clean line under his sharp jaw. His dark hair is long on top, informally pulled back into a small knot while the sides are shaved close to his scalp.

He's attractive, in the most demanding and sensual way possible. I shouldn't even realize this right now, but when his light, forest green eyes leave my gaze to meet Amelia's, the distinct feeling of disappointment uncontrollably wells in my gut.

"My Elijah," she whispers.

Elijah. Her Elijah? The knowledge of his name evokes something within me, something ambiguous and possessive that I can't seem to place.

Her voice shakes with a slight tremble that shocks me. I feel the man behind me tense at their interaction. I can't help but think that these two must have a past, and if he's with her, then my last shred of hope at escaping this place has been destroyed.

Her small hand reaches up to gently rest against his cheek. His face is completely stoic, showing no signs of what his thoughts or intentions are. Slowly though, he uncrosses his arms and reaches for her hand, briefly taking it in his and pulling it away from his face. He leans forward, his soft, full lips mere inches from hers and I find myself anxiously shrinking away at their potential kiss.

"Don't. Fucking. Touch. Me." The words leave his mouth on slow, deliberate intervals. The ice dripping from his voice is unmistakable and I fight away the odd feeling of relief that washes over me.

She laughs, a sweet giggle at his remark as she quickly turns on her heel and marches back towards us. She snakes her fingers into the thick strands of my hair, gripping and pulling tightly so that I'm pinned between both her and her partner.

"What the hell are you doing here, Elijah? Come to watch the show? I've missed you." She yanks my head towards her, and I swear I feel parts of my scalp tear under her unrelenting grasp. I refuse to cry, or yelp in pain so I bite the inside of my cheek to keep quiet.

"I haven't missed you, Amelia." He turns his attention towards the man behind me. "How are you, Danner? Still as sickly as ever I see. Preying on young women was always your forte." His tone drips with venom as he bites the words out through his clenched teeth.

Amelia releases a bitter laugh and I can practically feel the tension rolling off of her body in waves. She's uncomfortable, clearly unsure of where this is headed. "Leave now, Elijah and I'll allow you out with your heart still beating inside of your worthless chest."

A deafening silence falls inside of the room, heavy and smothering between each of us. The smallest pang of fear sparks in my chest at the threat of his death. I'm a lost young woman, caught in the midst of something I know nothing of, experiencing feelings and emotions I don't understand and there's nothing I can do about it now. Danner's grip on my throat has relaxed just slightly since Amelia holds my head firmly towards her. I'm conscious and present but I straddle the mental line of wishing I wasn't.

"Why are you doing this, Amelia? This wasn't you before." He completely ignores her threat and chooses to challenge her with this clearly loaded question. I understand now that they definitely have some sort of past between them and if I wasn't mistaken, I'd say that I see it mostly in Amelia's eyes. I can practically feel the war between hate and love blazing within her.

"Because it has to be done. You've never understood the importance of what is at stake. You've never cared about the throne until now, never cared to rule when it was just the two of us. Why now?" She's pleading with him in a tone that spews toxic anger and fury.

"There was never a threat as dangerous as you before now. You have no right to that throne, Amelia."

"And you do? You disowned your right to rule when you turned your back on your own race."

Amelia pulls me out of Danner's grasp and into her own. Even with her slight figure, I'm surprisingly banded so tightly against her. There is a heat radiating from her skin, soaking through mine and infecting my body with whatever poison she can control.

"My intentions with the throne are none of your business. And you've failed to answer my question. Why these women, *suilean gorma?*" I hear the slight accent in his voice for the first time but have no idea what he's just called her. From the moment of hesitation within her body, I can only assume it's a term of endearment and Danner takes a step to close the distance between us. His tall body comes flush behind mine as he reaches for my wrists and grips them tightly, pulling them up and over my head to hold me against him.

"Enough!" he shouts into the darkness and Amelia's guard quickly slips back into place.

"These women all have the Angel race in their bloodstreams, they each had the potential to stake a claim to the throne. But they would never be able to rule. They would never be strong enough to maintain our stance against the cambion demons, let alone the entire demonic rule below. They had to

be taken care of for the safety and well-being of the rest of us."
Amelia's other hand rises to my cheek and her fingertips drift
down my cold skin. She trails them along my jaw line and even
further to caress my collarbone. Goosebumps break out across
my shoulders in response to her icy touch. "This one is
different though. She has the blood of Archophys and Estera
flowing through her veins," she pauses, turning her gaze back
towards Elijah as she speaks. "Did you know they were Fated?
It's true."

I have no idea who or what she is talking about. They
clearly have the wrong person. I am a simple young woman
who was thrown into the foster care system growing up. It
would be my luck that they incorrectly abduct the wrong
person and I'm stuck here in this fatal situation.

"Impossible," his voice cuts through each of us as Amelia
whips her head back towards him.

"Must I prove it to you? Honestly, I'm surprised you
haven't put all of the pieces together yet. Don't you feel how
long you've known her? Please understand, once I show you,
I'm going to have to kill you as well."

Known me? Confusion flashes in his eyes for a brief
moment, his lips turning down in a slight scowl as he tenses.

A sadistic smile plays across her lips as she reaches for the
long, thin blade nestled against her thigh. I instinctively stiffen
my body, mentally preparing myself for my looming death, realizing there is no way I could ever escape this disastrous circumstance. But I will stick with my initial plan, I will never let them
see me break. I won't beg or cry or ask for mercy. I will die with
my head held high, staring them in the eyes when they take my
life.

"Amelia, I am warning you now. I am taking the girl and I
am leaving, do not force me into hurting you in the process."

His voice is clipped, short and intensely commanding with each word.

She ignores him as her blade lifts to rest on the side of my throat. She pierces the thin skin below my ear just slightly at first, until she begins dragging the blade downwards, slicing and flaying me until blood seeps from the wound and flows down my neck from the shallow wound. I refuse to cry, but an uncontrollable whimper falls from my throat and I bite my tongue to hold it back. My eyes impulsively shut as the feeling of wet, thick blood falls over my chest and between my breasts, soaking the shirt that so ironically matches the color of my own blood. It's as if it disappears, having happened and so quickly forgotten.

I force my eyes open immediately, lifting my chin higher when my gaze meets Elijah's once again. His body is restrained, a silent killer as he watches the scene unfold in front of him. Amelia's fingers slide to my neck, effectively touching some of my blood and rolling it between her fingertips. When she turns her hand towards Elijah, I realize the color is drastically different than when it was on my own skin.

On hers, the color changes to a midnight black, absolutely no hint of the deep red it was once before. She laughs humorlessly as she eyes her own fingers, relishing in the fact that she was indeed, right about her conclusion. Danner joins her, reaching around me to grip her face and bring her lips to his. I'm caught between them as they smile into each other in this brief second of celebration. In what is the slowest moment of my life, Danner releases her face to grip my own from behind, twisting my neck in a searing pain so that I'm angled towards Amelia.

"It is time, my love," he says as Amelia's hands rest against my blood-soaked neck.

"It is, sweet Luna. You have been a delicious surprise." Her hard lips crash against mine in a powerful kiss. Immediately, I feel my body begin losing something instrumental to my survival. I have no control over the way she manipulates me, forcing my mouth open to hers as her tongue enters and strokes my own. It's not an enjoyable kiss in the slightest, instead it reminds of that dreadful night seven years ago where I was forced into things I never wanted to experience. But instead of having the ability to fight back, my energy and strength is being pulled from my body in electrical waves.

I go completely lax against Danner as his arms snake around my waist to hold me upright. I have no stamina left to maintain my own stance. I can feel the edges of my vision going hazy and dark. I'm going to pass out, I can feel the heavy wave of obscurity quickly approaching.

In the last second, I vaguely hear the sound of bodies slamming against others. I collapse to the cold ground below as both Amelia and Danner are ripped from me and my head cracks against the cement in a powerful blow.

Finally, after wishing and begging to be alone seven years ago, I'm left alone now.

But it's the first time I have the smallest inkling that maybe I don't want to be alone after all.

CHAPTER SIX

ELIJAH

"I don't fucking care what you're doing. I'm headed to your place now, fucking get there and be ready for us!" I shout into the small Bluetooth speaker of my Jeep. I'm trying to stay calm talking to my brother, but I need his fucking help and he needs to be there.

I glance behind me, for the millionth time, to make sure Luna is still breathing. But I know she is, I can feel it, as if I've known her my entire life. It's coming out of her in shallow, quick breaths that have my heart racing unexplainably.

She's there, lying on her back while blood stains her body in countless different places. Her hair is a tangled, thick mess of blood and sweat all rolled into one. Her shirt is torn and caked with it as well, plastering it to her stomach while she lays there unconscious.

"All right, I'll be there brother," he finally responds. I can tell he's confused. I haven't shown this much interest in a single person for years. But I can't explain it to him, I have no idea why I'm doing what I'm doing. All I know is that the quicker he can fix her up and get her on her feet, the quicker she can leave and get out of my fucking life. I don't need this and I sure as hell don't want it.

My mind spirals with the information Amelia claimed. It doesn't make sense, Luna's supposed parents. Or the fact that she mentioned how I've known Luna for longer than I realize. Nothing tangible about her is familiar, I have no idea who she is outside of the mess I just pulled her from.

After taking on both Danner and Amelia at once, I realize now that I suffered a few more injuries than I initially thought. I'm pretty sure Amelia stabbed me somewhere in my lower back—wouldn't be the first time—and Danner was quick to try and choke me to death without laying a finger on my throat. Fucking coward. He's always been afraid of me.

Thankfully though, I caught them off guard enough to land a few solid hits myself as well, until her guards heard the commotion and interrupted our little encounter. I snatched Luna up off the ground as quickly as I could and took off while Amelia struggled to regain her footing from my blows. I was never into hitting women, ever. But Amelia is a warrior—we all are—and in that case, I don't discriminate.

I race through the crowded streets of New York until I'm a decent distance outside the city and well into one of the small, surrounding towns where it isn't full of tall, close knit skyscrapers. Instead, this is a quaint little area with homes that have larger property lines, scaling hills, and local shops. I love this area, close enough to the city when I need it, but far enough away to give me the privacy I crave. My brother and I both live out here, in separate homes, but near to each other nonetheless.

When you've Fallen, and you find yourself shamelessly

living in a world you simply observe from afar, you seek the closeness of anything familiar. For a while, that included Amelia for me. I sought out the relationship, her connection, and the fact that we had both Fallen and were struggling to find our footing in this world.

Now, however, the only relationship I keep near is my brother's. Even then, we aren't as close as we could be. I've realized the farther I push everyone away, the less I have to worry about and the fewer responsibilities I have in caring about someone else's safety or well-being. I don't owe anyone anything at this point, other than the servitude and protection of my race. Which I will willingly give, as long as it is needed.

As a Seraphim Angel, I was naturally in line to obtain the throne when I first Fell almost two decades ago. But I refused it, I didn't want it and I didn't want the responsibility of ruling over a mass race of Angels. I never questioned that decision until Amelia began showing interest in the throne herself. As time has passed, I've seen the destruction and chaos she leaves in her wake, and see that it may be time I stake my own claim.

I'm realizing that I need to take back what is so wickedly being destroyed. Our people need a ruler now more than ever, and the stand-in has always been my brother. He's younger but has reluctantly taken on the throne because I disowned it.

Truthfully, I've always believed he was the better choice as King of our race. Nathanial has always been driven by his need to help and support others. He doesn't discriminate whether you're human, Angel, or Demon. He simply wants to provide for and save those that he can.

A loud crack of thunder breaks me out of my thoughts as I round the gated entrance into our community. There is a storm approaching, nearly black skies grace us above and I can't help but question whether this is a sign, a slight communication from those who are still observing from their rightful stations in Arcadia.

This particular neighborhood has homes spaced farther apart, giving each owner a sense of privacy. Green lawns that have been manicured to perfection and large, full pine trees provide shelter and seclusion where we need it most. My brother lives on one far end of the community while I live on the other. I quickly pull into his circular driveway, parking in front of the large, elegant brick home nestled tightly against the trees behind.

I open my door and race to the back seat, checking once again for Luna's breathing. I rest my fingers gently against her throat, searching for a pulse. For a moment, I can't find one and terrifying frustration overtakes my mind. I didn't waste all this effort, all this time, as well as exposing myself for her not to survive this.

But instantly, it's as if her heart kicks a little harder, reassuring me and letting me know she's still there, even if barely so. I quickly but gently lift her into my arms and race up the steps to my brother's door. I kick it open immediately, refusing to spare even the short moments it would take for him to answer it. He's already in the foyer, his eyes wide with confusion and apathy.

"Please tell me you found this woman on the streets in the city, maybe behind a bar, or at a restaurant." His eyes are pleading, he knows what I had to do to get her here.

"I found her in the city. Maybe behind a bar or at a restaurant," I deadpan as I step closer to him so he can look over her. His eyes never leave mine, but a flash of disappointment breaks through them.

"Motherfucker. We're fucked, you know that right?"

"I don't give a shit what we are. I need you to save her, Nathanial." For a moment, we stand in silence as his gaze searches mine for the answers we both need. I don't have them, and his understanding proves that he knows me better than anyone else. He turns on his heel and moves up the staircase to his study. I follow him closely, Luna still unconscious in my arms as my mind races with unanswered questions and impossible fears.

CHAPTER SEVEN

ELIJAH

I LAID HER DOWN ON THE LONG, BLACK LEATHER COUCH that sits in the corner of the room. Nathanial is a doctor, the best I know on both human and the Angel race alike. If there is anyone who can help Luna, I knew immediately it would be him. He's standing over her, checking her vitals and gathering the information he needs. He's already closed the wound on her neck and the one on the back of her scalp, both which seemed detrimental to her survival. He forced me to sit still while he quickly stitched the knife wound on my own back, but I wouldn't let him look into any of the other shallower injuries. His attention needs to focus strictly on Luna.

I can tell that he's tense, though not as much as I am. The lone fear lagging in my mind is that she is beyond saving. Her breaths are still shallow, but are now creating gravel-like sounds, as if there is liquid building in her lungs.

"Hurry, brother," I growl, pacing back and forth inside the

small room. The ceiling is too low for my standards, as I stand slightly taller than Nate. For the most part, houses don't usually accommodate my size well. I had to remodel most of my own home for it to fit my liking. Taller ceilings and larger furniture were a simple necessity for my space.

"Elijah. I don't know what I can do. She's too far gone. I already closed the injuries that may have been fatal, but Amelia stole her spirit. She has no strength to fight the rest of the way back." He won't turn to face me as he speaks and I'm sure he's already confused and unsure of my current state. If he's going to tell me that there are no other options though, I need him to look me in the eyes.

I knew exactly what Amelia was doing when she kissed Luna, her seductive touch equal parts both toxic and deceit. When an Angel falls, most manifest a certain ability, or strength amongst humans. Amelia's ended up being the perfect weapon to use against others. With a simple kiss, she can absorb the very essence of your being, leaving you frail and nothing but a shell of your former existence.

I round the couch so Nathanial and I are both standing on either side of Luna. I look down first, noticing the way her chest heaves and falls in short, quick bursts. Her skin has paled dramatically, and her lips are beginning to turn blue at the corners. My heart slams against my chest at the unfamiliar need rising within me to fix this.

"Tell me again," I say, forcing him to look me in the eyes.

"There's nothing I can do, brother." He speaks the words quietly, meeting my gaze reluctantly with his soft amber eyes. I stare at him for just a moment, willing his phrase to change and for different words to leave his mouth. Turning around abruptly, I smash my fist into the wall behind us. My knuckles crack through the dry wall and leave reddened sores on my own hand, ones I barely comprehend in comparison to the emotions warring inside of me.

"Elijah, why does she mean anything to you? Who is she?" he challenges, reminding me that I have no fucking idea why she means anything to me at all.

I scrub my hand over my face, wracking my mind for another option. "I don't know, Nate. I don't fucking know. All I know, is that she can't die. I can't explain it, I don't have answers for you." I begin pacing the room again, realizing that we are running out of time quickly. My heart is beating erratically, my breaths beginning to mimic Luna's and a chilling sweat has already broken out across my skin.

The chalky sound of a cough bubbles up from Luna's throat and my eyes dart back toward her. I move to her side immediately when I see the slight tinge of blood slip out from the corner of her mouth.

Fuck, fuck, fuck.

There is another option, one I didn't want to acknowledge because the thought of it sears through my blood furiously. I can't do it, but I know the only person who can.

"Bond with her," I choke the words out of my own mouth. Nathanial's head whips to me as shock lines his features.

"No." He speaks a single, simple word that fills me with undeniable rage towards him. If he refuses, I'll hate him for letting her die. If he agrees, I'll hate him for keeping her for the rest of our lives. There's no winning in this situation, I realize that. And the fury builds in my stomach because of it.

"Yes. It's the only way she'll survive Nathanial."

"Absolutely not. First, I have not chosen her for myself. Second, I am not bonding with someone that you so clearly care for. That would be torture, brother. How can you ask this of me?" Agitation and surprise lace his tone. Another break of thunder cracks around us. We're getting closer to the end. I feel whatever is left of her leaking out of her own body and into the open air around us.

"Do you think I want this? Believe me, I fucking don't. She will learn to love you and you, her. I have asked nothing of you before now, I realize this is unfathomable. I will give you anything, brother." I hate every single word as it leaves my dry mouth. I am asking him to give me everything, truthfully. I'm asking him to give up everything for a woman neither of us know. It doesn't make sense and I fear it never will.

He watches me in silence as I see his mind turning over every single possible alternative route to change this. I know what he wants to demand, I see it working to the forefront of his mind.

Don't say it, don't even fucking think it.

"You bond with her," he states clearly.

"I can't and you know this," I refuse, plainly and simply. I've refused for seven years now and I will not place myself back into that position again. Creating a bond and living with one is distressing enough when both partners are not devoted to the other. But severing a bond? It's a miracle when an Angel survives it. Nothing compares to the excruciating pain of literally tearing your other half from your body.

I would never be able to give her what she needed out of this kind of commitment, because I simply don't want to. Nathanial would. He may struggle at first, but he would, and she would love him the same.

"You can, but you choose not to. If I do this, you cannot hold it against me for the years to come. You will have to live with this decision and know that it was you who demanded it of me," he states his terms and even though I know I will not be able to truthfully adhere to them I nod a quick approval if it means saving Luna's life.

He looks disappointed at my agreeance but sits on the edge

of the couch next to her and takes her wrist in his larger hand. My brother and I have similar builds, both wider and taller than our fellow Angels. We come from the Seraphim line and while there aren't many of our precise kind left, we stand out amongst the others. It's another reason why our ancestral line was chosen to bear the throne.

I watch as he removes a small, thin blade from his brown leather bag on the floor near his feet and places it gently against her soft, milky skin. A thread of tension begins pulling in my chest, mildly at first but wrenches tighter as he drags the blade down her wrist in a shallow cut, just enough to draw a bit of blood and then flips his own arm to do the same to himself.

Briefly, I consider telling him about her blooded roots, but impulsively decide against it in case it changes his mind to follow through with this. It's a selfish decision, but I never claimed not to be a greedy asshole. He slowly slices his own wrist, applying pressure against his skin to draw a clear line of blood. I feel a lump building in my chest and working its way up my throat as I watch him flip his wrist over and place it atop hers, aligning their wounds and integrating their bloodlines.

Even the smallest act of watching them bleeding together affects me. If I could just understand why this matters, I could control it to my own benefit. The lack of answers is gnawing at my bones and eating away at my mind. I'm plagued with such desire and without any understanding at all.

I shut my eyes, refusing to watch as the words of our people are whispered out of his lips. It's a language I haven't heard spoken in years, Enochian. I intentionally avoided using our native tongue when we Fell, severing just another reminder of the place that shunned us for such absurd reasons.

He speaks quietly, and pain laces his voice as each word is spoken. We're both hurting with this choice, surprisingly so, and I wish I could understand why that was the case.

I wait anxiously, listening for the sound of her breathing to level out and any sign that his blood is working to heal her. But nothing comes, in fact her breath continues its rough and ragged pace. When I open my eyes, I notice how both of their bloods have dripped and slid down her wrist, mingling but not connecting in the way that the blood bond should trigger.

"What's going on?" I ask in frustration. We're lucky she's even survived this long.

"I'm not sure. But she isn't accepting the bond. I can't do anything if she won't receive it, Elijah." He pauses for a moment, clearly searching for the answers in this circumstance. "Leave the room," he states.

"No, absolutely not." My head darts toward him as I process what he demands of me. He must be a fucking idiot if he thinks I'll leave her here while she's dying.

"Yes, her blood may not be able to accept the bond with you so near." He doesn't look at me as he says this, as if he's revealing something I should understand. It shouldn't matter who is around for the blood bond to be initiated and completed.

"I'm not leaving, Nathanial. She doesn't know me. My presence means nothing in this moment." I plant my feet firmly next to him, crossing my thick arms across my chest and refusing to move.

Finally, he turns to look at me before speaking. "She may not know you, but her blood might. If you both are Fated, she could never bond with me while you are near."

I watch him for a moment, silent tension building around us at his revelation. It makes no sense, in fact, it's impossible. "No. There hasn't been a Fated couple in decades. That cannot be the case here," I state the words logically, briefly remembering Amelia's comment about Archophys and Estera. If they were Fated, they would be the first in nearly eighty years.

In my gut however, I feel a spark of acceptance at this possibility. It would explain why I'm so drawn to her without knowing a damn thing about her. It would explain why I can't seem to pry my body away from hers while she's so near death. But it has been decades since a Fated couple emerged from our race.

At one point, the Fated were rulers and warriors of the Fallen. They were ideal monarchs because their abilities were enhanced, or new abilities resurfaced when paired with their other halves. They were difficult to kill because one partner could heal and protect the other from nearly every injury and vice versa. They protected our race and served with strength, dignity and passion. There was a myth that each Angel had a Fated partner, but they were nearly impossible to find, so it was rare when couplings emerged.

Suffice to say, a Fated couple contained an innate connection that ran even deeper than the blood bond. Something eternally and infinitely ingrained into the soul, not simply the DNA. They say it was His way of giving us one last gift, even after we Fell and were disavowed from Arcadia.

Once the Demonic realm realized the bond between the Fated was indestructible, they began separating couples and killing them off, one by one. Throughout the years, the Fated had to go into hiding, removing themselves from the positions within our court and unable to show themselves at the Capital for fear of destruction. That was when the Seraphim Angel's began ruling over our kind and our ancestral family sat at the throne.

Eventually, even the Fated in hiding were found and slaughtered. Soon enough, it became even more rare that a Fated couple ever emerged, and if they did, they were quickly killed until there weren't any left again. Since those attacks so many years ago, we haven't seen another Fated come forward.

"Leave the room, Elijah." His harsh words cut through my

mind as I turn and stalk out. I don't go far, I round the door and stand outside in the hallway, listening to every ragged breath she takes. In and out. In and out. Quiet, bitter sounds lace her soft voice and it cuts me to the bones not to be nearer. I'm torn equally between innately needing to be close to her and never wanting to see her again.

It's an ironic punishment truthfully, handing me my Fated when there is no way I would ever accept her.

Fucking Hell.

Or Heaven, actually. Fucking Heaven.

CHAPTER EIGHT

ELIJAH

SILENCE.

More fucking silence as I stand out here and wait for my brother's voice, or more painfully, Luna's.

"Anything, Nathanial? Anyfuckingthing?" I growl through the thinly plastered wall separating us.

A beat before he answers, "No. She's not accepting me. There's nothing I can do now." His voice is resigned, succumbed to the fact that this is how she will end. I step forward and dart back into the room in order to see for myself. Once I reach them, I crouch down on my knees, hesitantly lifting my hand to her wrist in order to examine their connection.

I lay my large, calloused fingers against her soft skin and a sharp jolt of pain hits my chest when the slick coldness of her body reaches mine. It seeps into my skin slightly, and I know if we were bonded how much more I would feel her distress, her pain, the icy chill of her body letting go.

My thumb brushes against her blood and I have to shut my eyes as the slick heat inoculates my own, sending rushing waves of fear, pain, and attraction all flowing through me. No doubt her own emotions over the last twenty-four hours. The fact that I alone, can feel this through the simple act of stroking her blood tells me that Nathanial is right.

She has to be my Fated.

Instantly, my brother rips my hand away from Luna's wrist and turns it towards himself. He eyes my hand curiously, realizing now how her blood has turned into a deep black against my skin. He flips his own wrist, scrutinizing her blood on his skin as well for the same characteristic.

His eyes dart towards mine, accusation simmering in this iris's, "What is this?"

I briefly consider telling him that she possibly has the blood of both an Angel and a Demon running through her veins if what Amelia claimed is correct. But I choose to ignore him as Luna begins violently coughing once again. For reasons unfamiliar to me, I know deep in the pit of my stomach that this is the end for her. I feel her essence escaping her body with each passing second.

Without warning or control, I greedily take Nathanial's blade and roughly cut down my own wrist, uncaring to make it clean or shallow. I flip my arm over and force it on top of hers as I quickly speak the words that should trigger our bond.

"Ol, Elijah, Seraphim Angel c Arcadia, allar ol cnila de yours g sibsi.

Ol darbs de a etharzi c ge congamphlgh ca el."

· · ·

47

I speak the Enochian words that uncomfortably scrape against my throat on the way out. I hate this connection to our past lives. I've worked to build a completely separate and new existence here on Earth since I Fell. But I say them anyway, declaring them to our blood and claiming the bond for ourselves.

At first, nothing happens. My own blood simply coats her arm and creates a red wave against her stomach where both our arms are stiffly resting. I close my eyes, dropping my forehead to lay on her shoulder as I chant the words like they're the last prayer I could ever surrender. I'm warring internally with what I'm allowing and what I never wanted to experience again. But the choice was taken from me the moment I set foot in Amelia's mansion tonight and felt the need pulling me under.

I quickly glance up again, realizing that still, her blood is not accepting of mine. A bitter growl erupts from my throat as Nathanial rests his hand against my shoulder. "Focus, Elijah. Focus not on the covenant, but on the innate bond you feel even without her blood."

I force my mind to target the emotions I experienced at the mansion, before I ever laid eyes on Luna. I pull up the deep yearning I felt as I stalked through the halls of Amelia's home. I absorb the unexplainable tether I felt to Luna when I entered that room and saw Danner's arms wrapped grotesquely around her waist. I relish in the hatred I experienced when Amelia's lips fell to Luna's and I instantly knew that I needed her with me, away from them and safely hidden.

I target the notion that while I have easily denied every single emotional connection over the last seven years of my life, I was unable to deny this unknown woman even the simplest of actions. Simply not knowing her, ignoring the draw I felt to her very core was impossible.

Finally, *fucking finally*, I feel it. The smallest integration of our blood in a quick second. Just one cell to the other, minute, barely noticeable until they each begin working together. In a seamless moment our blood assimilates, harmonizing as one while everything pulls upwards and simply stops flowing out and over her small body. Instead, they move together, working together, building and healing together as one entity.

As our blood connects, I realize hers quickly transforms into that black, inky substance that fuses perfectly with my deep red. As one, we create an undeniable masterpiece, even I can see that. It's a twisted sequence of dark and light, evil and good. We're an impossibly imperfect blend of things that should never unite. Yet here I am, feeling wholly complete for the first time in my life.

One inherently good and one intrinsically evil.

An Angel and a Demon.

Unfortunately, at this moment, I'm not sure whether I'm the good in this union, or the evil.

CHAPTER NINE

Luna

I GASP AS THE FIRST, FULL INVIGORATING BREATH OF oxygen fills my lungs.

I'm alive.

I'm not sure how long I've been out, but I relish in the feeling of warmth radiating against my skin. I've felt cold over the last twenty-four hours or, oddly enough, I've felt cold my entire life compared to now. It's like I'm experiencing the intense sun on my skin for the first time. It's addicting, truthfully. A searing blaze that ignites inside my chest and spirals out into my limbs.

Hell, I'm feeling the best I've ever felt and considering everything that's happened since I was taken outside the coffee shop, I expected to feel a little worse for wear. I begin with my fingertips, testing out the movements and slowly working up towards my elbows and shoulders. I gently attempt to move my head and open my eyes but the lights above seem strangely bright for what I'm adjusted to after so much time in the dark. I close them again, open again, close, open, waiting for everything to acclimate so I can figure out where I am and how to get out of here.

In an instant, the warmth that I now realize was so instrumental to my comfort, is gone. But, I know it's near, like the heater had been up against my body but now pulled across the room. I know it *exists*, but no longer for me.

Lifting my hands, I softly push the heels of my palms into my eyes, rubbing away the exhaustion and discomfort while I attempt sitting up. A large hand hastily lands on my shoulder for assistance and I feel an odd pang of jealousy scorch my chest, but it's just as quickly gone.

"Be still, you've been through a lot over the last day," the voice says. It's a man, but not the one who I met in that awful place with my captors. I open my eyes and process who is in front of me. He's large, almost as big as Elijah from earlier. But while Elijah had dark, long hair on top and was covered in tattoos, this man is a clean cut version. His golden hair is long on top as well, but still an inch or so in length on the sides. His is a bit messier, clearly pulled at or mussed with tension. I don't see any visible tattoos under his pristine, white, button-down dress shirt. But his sleeves are rolled up and cuffed tightly, revealing a set of strong, sinewy forearms.

A hit of possessiveness that isn't mine bolts through me and instinctually my eyes dart to the corner of the small room I'm nestled in. I'm overwhelmed as I try to make sense of where I am and who I'm with. But when my eyes land on Elijah's, an unfamiliar wave of relief washes over me. He leans against the doorframe, his thick, muscular arms crossed tightly around his chest. His dark, distressed jeans still cling to his powerful thighs and one black biker boot is casually crossed in front of the other.

I press my hand against my heart, absently massaging a mild painful tick that has started there. "Who are you?" I ask, bringing my eyes back to the man in front of me.

"My name is Nathanial. Elijah is my brother." His voice is low, a gentle tone laced with uncertainty.

"Did you—" I pause, trying to find the right words to describe where I came from. "Did you find me where I was? In that place with, what were their names? Amelia and Danner?" I'm not sure who brought me here, or what happened after I passed out when Amelia kissed me. Nathanial opens his mouth to speak but is abruptly cut off.

"I found you and brought you here to my brother." Elijah's snarling tone rips through the room and Nathanial's face falls with disappointment as he turns to face his brother.

"Elijah, no need to be so aggressive," he snaps admonishingly. Elijah looks like he's going to argue so I quickly jump in between the two before things spiral.

"The other girls I was with, are they safe too?" I ask tentatively, I have a feeling I know that answer, but I need to hear the truth from them.

Nathanial looks to Elijah with surprise, clearly unaware that there were more people taken captive. "The others were dead before I could intervene," he deadpans. The lack of emotion he shows both infuriates and confuses me. I feel an odd sense of connection to him, yet a massive wall is erected between us.

"I don't understand. How were they killed? How did that happen?" I lift my hands to my eyes again, anxiously trying to scrub away the confusion lacing my mind. Elijah's voice cuts through the fog again as he stands up straight in the doorway.

"I'm leaving. Nathanial, you can bring her to my place when you're finished explaining everything. I have a few things I need to get done beforehand." Nathaniel's head whips towards him as he stands up.

"You are not leaving. You need to explain to her what's happened, Elijah." Nathanial moves toward his brother and I feel the tension building in the space between them.

"I *am* leaving. You've always been better with words than I have. You do it, I'll take care of the rest later." His flippant tone makes me feel like whatever it is, isn't a big deal. But the way his brother is so clearly out of sorts makes me wonder what exactly I've been dragged into.

"You can't leave. You know it will hurt her and you in the process." This time, I can barely make out the words. He said them through clenched teeth and in a hushed tone, but I decipher them all the same. It makes no sense. Honestly with Elijah's attitude the way it is, I'd rather hear everything from Nathanial anyway. I'm cold again, frustrated, beyond confused and all I want are answers. I have a feeling that hearing them from Elijah won't make it any less painful.

"Leave," I grind out. "If you don't want to be here, then leave. I won't stay long and I won't come to your place. I need to get a hold of my sister anyway. I just want to know what happened and then I'll get out of both of your hair. Thank you for helping me, now go." The words feel oddly painful as I choke them out. I'm angry and unexplainably hurt for no reason. Elijah's eyes meet mine in silence, showing no hint of what he is thinking before he turns on his heel and stalks out the door. Nathanial pauses for a moment, letting his fist reluctantly fall to the door frame before taking a breath and turning to face me.

I hear what must be the front door slam shut after Elijah's gone. Nathanial quickly steps back over the couch and takes a seat across from me, leaning forward and resting his forearms on his knees. Strangely, that mildly painful tick in my heart grows, becoming a sore throbbing that radiates across my entire chest. My breaths are suddenly coming in shallow inhales and a wash of panic runs through my mind. I'm confused and worried that maybe I'm not in the clear after all, maybe I'm still going to die, and they've somehow just prolonged the inevitable.

"Something's wrong," I begin as I rub a hand furiously across my aching chest. Nathanial's eyes are filled with regret and disappointment, but I don't see fear there. That's my only reassurance that maybe he knows I'm not going to die after all. "Seriously, something's wrong. I-I can't breathe and—"

"Slow down. Focus. I promise you're okay. Ah, it's hard to explain. It'll be like this for a little bit, but I promise it'll get easier. I'll take you to Elijah soon and—"

"No. No, I don't want to go to Elijah. I need to call my sister. Fuck, my chest aches. What the hell happened to me?" I ask, panic dripping from my tone as I wrack my mind for answers. Nathanial's hands fall to my shoulders as he tries to still me with his touch. It helps only mildly, but his calm demeanor seems to give me some sense of hope.

"Just tell me if I'm going to die. Rip off the damn band-aid and tell me. I don't want to be babied." I hate when people skirt around the truth. I'd rather just know what's going to happen than spend an hour trying to get to the point. Nathanial's face breaks into a small smirk, which I take as a promising sign to relax just a bit. But the aching pain and short breaths don't go away.

"You're not going to die. That, I promise, but we do need to talk about what's happened to you."

"Spit it out already. I feel like I'm choking here," I say, forcing my mind to focus on taking slower, deeper breaths.

"Well, I guess I'll start at the beginning. Tonight, you were taken by Angels."

CHAPTER TEN

Luna

I *HEARD HIM WRONG.*

Obviously, my mind was playing tricks on me or my oxygen deprived brain was hallucinating the words he just spoke.

"I'm sorry, I didn't hear you. Say that again?" I reply, dragging my hands through my entirely too tangled, matted hair.

"Angels. Well, Fallen Angels technically. It's a long story, but Amelia and Danner, myself and Elijah. We're all Fallen Angels, on opposite sides of an impending civil war, but Angels all the same." He speaks the words so casually, as if we're talking about the new restaurant that recently opened up in Times Square, or the weather outside on a sunny day.

I pause for several moments, processing and discrediting what he just said. Suddenly, an uncomfortable laugh bubbles up from my throat and spills out between us. It's bitter and sad and also amazed at the fact that he can say all of this with such a straight face. I'm not sure what has made him believe that now is the best time for a joke, maybe the truth is just so horrible that he needs to lighten the mood beforehand. That realization scares me the most.

"Wait, is the reality that awful? I wasn't kidding when I said to spit it out. I don't want to beat around the bush. Believe me, I went through some shit years ago and I'd rather know the truth now."

Nathanial watches me for a moment before speaking again, "This is the truth. I'm not joking or lying to you. I'm not hiding the facts from you. You don't deserve that, not after what you've just been through and what you're going to go through." His continued calm demeanor causes my heart to begin thundering in my chest at the idea that this could possibly be real. There is no fucking way what he's saying is true. No way. None of them look like Angels, where are their wings for fuck sake?

"Okay." I pause, "Let's just say I believe you. First of all, you all are nothing like the Angels I've ever heard about, especially Danner and Amelia. Secondly, where the hell are your wings? If you're Angels, you have wings." I lay out my rebuttals that clearly discredit his words as he watches me with intrigue written across his face.

"Fallen Angels, remember? Each of us has been stripped of our wings." I don't miss the pain lacing his features as he mentions this. It's undeniable and sends a wash of sadness rolling through me. "Second, just because we are Angels, doesn't mean we do the right thing. Amelia and Danner are perfect examples. Amelia has been after the throne of our Fallen race for a long time now. Danner is her bonded mate, together they are attempting to start a civil war to pronounce her as Queen."

Amelia's words crash back into my mind. "You unknowingly speak to your Queen with such disrespect, a fault I will choose not to hold against you. You have no idea, after all, the kind of blood that flows through your veins."

No. This is impossible.

"No, no, no. There has to be some logical explanation to this. Show me. If you were stripped of your wings, you have to some kind of scar, right? Prove to me you had wings." For a split second, I worry that I've asked something too intimate of him. Then I realize the fact that I've even worried about that notion at all means that in some space, I do believe him.

What the hell?

Without hesitation, Nathanial stands and turns his back to me. He lifts his long, strong arms in front of him and slowly unbuttons his white dress shirt. I feel my heart thundering in my chest, causing my already shallow breaths to shorten even further. All of this new and overwhelming information has briefly taken my mind away from the fact that my entire body trembles with a low ache. It feels like I'm missing something vital to my living.

He drops his shirt half-way down his back, exposing not only his sharp and impressive muscles, but also two long, red and raised scars. They start at the tips of his shoulder blades, very distinct wounds in which his flesh looks like it was torn and ripped where something permanent should have remained. His skin is healed, but the wounds were clearly not bandaged and cared for well. The scars aren't thin clean lines, they're rough and jagged, the skin puckered up around certain edges and flat in others. They disappear behind his lowered shirt and I gasp at the obvious pain he must have gone through.

I quickly realize somewhere deep inside of me, in a place dark and unknown, I do believe him. I don't understand why, and I don't believe it simply has to do with the fact that he showed me his scars.

I think it's because of the way he didn't hesitate or seem

surprised when I asked. He simply showed me, in honesty and vulnerability. He revealed something that has clearly caused him immense pain.

I can't deny what I saw happen in that cold, dark room tonight either. I witnessed Danner kill those women without laying a hand on them. I felt Amelia steal something fundamental from me when her lips landed on mine. I sense an innate and distinct pull when I lay eyes on Elijah. There is something uncontrollably supernatural about these people that I can't ignore and what's even stranger, is that I feel a vague taste of familiarity to all of this. As if this isn't such a farfetched possibility, which makes absolutely no sense.

When Nathanial turns to face me, I see the agony blazing behind his eyes. I feel badly for having him show me and relive those memories he so obviously tries to forget.

"I'm sorry," I say quietly, continuing my gentle massage over the pain in my chest.

He offers me a weak smile before rebuttoning his shirt and taking his seat again. "I understand the need for proof. I'm sure this is a lot to process."

"Do you know why I was taken? Amelia said something about my blood," I ask, hoping he has the answers I so desperately need.

"I don't know the details. But after what happened with you and Elijah, I assume you must have the blood of Angels in your veins. I believe he knows more than I do, so you'll have to get those answers from him." He looks at me with kind and sympathetic eyes, as if he knows Elijah won't give them to me. The mention of his name awakens a response inside of me, something that's currently painful and poisonous underneath my skin. Even the thought of his name elicits an ache in the pit of my stomach.

"What do you mean? What happened with Elijah and I?"

Other than the fact that he brought me here, I don't have an idea as to anything else.

Nathanial sighs, readying himself for whatever he's about to tackle. "In order to save your life, Elijah had to initiate a blood covenant with you." He pauses for a moment, letting his words sink into my already overwhelmed mind.

"A blood covenant," I repeat. "And what, exactly does that mean?" I say flatly, irritation suddenly building in my gut at whatever I have been pulled into.

"It's difficult to explain. It's something you'll honestly have to experience to truly understand. Hell, you're partly experiencing it now," he says as he dismissively waves his hand in my direction.

"Try explaining," I bark out, mentally preparing myself for his answer.

"The pain you're experiencing now, the way your breaths are shallow and rapid, the dull ache in your chest. It's because you are away from each other. Now that your blood has integrated and fused as one, you are literally each other's other half if that makes sense. You are stronger and more powerful together than apart. But it also comes with its own set of problems and complications." He speaks as if he's giving me a textbook answer and I hate it. I don't want the definition. I want the truth. The hard, nasty, emotional truth.

"You're saying the pain I'm in now, isn't one of the fucking complications?" I feel the anger welling in my chest.

"I'm saying it's one of the milder complications."

"So, lay out the others, Nathanial. What am I dealing with here?" I urge him forward, frustration leaking through my voice and infecting my words.

"Essentially, you'll both be privy to each other's emotional state, all of the time. You'll feel his emotions in the instant they manifest inside of him and he will feel the same for you. For actual couples, this is a benefit. It brings them closer and their souls work as one being. It's a blessing and a gift for those who are truly together. But for you and Elijah, it will be difficult. You've never known each other before now. Generally, blood bonds are initiated between committed partners who have found their soulmates."

I absorb his words, processing and dissecting each new bit of information. I wonder if the odd sense of possessiveness I felt towards Nathanial earlier was actually my own feeling, or if it was Elijah's? Was he feeling possessive of his brother?

"Earlier, when Elijah was here, and I had just woken up, I felt strangely greedy when I saw you for the first time. I didn't understand it. I don't know you but now I don't know if that was me or if it was—"

"Elijah. You'll learn to feel your way through the differences between yours and his emotions. Eventually, it'll be as clear as night and day. But right now, while you're adjusting to everything, it may be a bit confusing. And he wasn't feeling possessive over me, I'm sure he was feeling possessive over you," he explains gently. I can tell that he's trying to lay everything out in a way that I will comprehend but it's practically impossible. I'm one of those people who learn better in the midst of chaos, and I know whatever I'm about to experience will evoke plenty of questions.

"Elijah wants nothing to do with me," I state simply. It's true, I saw the way he watched me from across the room. I could almost feel the anger radiating from his body. He couldn't get out of here quick enough.

"Elijah doesn't know what to do with you," Nathanial admits.

"Why don't we break the bond? It can't be that difficult." It seems like a simple solution.

Immediately, Nathanial tenses at my suggestion. His brows

furrow deeply in the center of his smooth forehead and a scowl forms on his soft lips. "No. Severing blood bonds are a death wish. Especially yours and Elijah's. You can't, I don't think either of you would survive it."

"Why do you keep referring to Elijah and me as if we're different? What makes our bond unlike others? Other than the simple fact that we definitely don't know each and are not in any sort of relationship whatsoever." Sarcasm drips from my voice. It's a defense mechanism, one I've always used throughout my entire life. But it's true, why would Elijah and I be any different than your average Angel-initiated blood bond?

Wow, I can't even believe I just thought that. I'm losing it.

"Another answer you'll have to get from Elijah, I'm afraid. I promise, in the end it'll be worth it when he finally opens up to you." If he thinks I'll be sticking around long enough for that to happen, he's fucking kidding himself.

"I'm not staying, I need to leave. I need to get a hold of my sister. I have a job I need to get back too," I state as I move to slowly stand up from the couch. I want to test the weight on my legs, see if I'm able to get things moving again.

Nathanial immediately stands with me and offers his hand in a kind gesture. I take it, knowing I'll probably need assistance this first time. "Luna, I don't know how to break this to you, but you can't leave. The farther away you are from Elijah, the worse your state will become. You'll hardly be able to work let alone live your life away from him at this point."

I caution a step, a little unsteady at first but quickly gain my balance as I stretch with each movement forward. In a few quick strides, I'm feeling astoundingly better, aside from the shortened breaths and aching chest.

"Fucking hell, I can't miss any work and I can't not see my sister. You have to understand that," I plead with him, wondering why I'm in a situation where someone else holds so much damn power over me. I swore never to find myself in that place again.

"Come, let's go to Elijah's and we'll figure something out." At that, I reluctantly let Nathanial lead me out of his home as we climb into his blacked-out Mercedes G-Wagon and pull away from the house that uncovered few answers for me, but also raised countless more questions.

CHAPTER ELEVEN

Luna

UNFORTUNATELY FOR ME, THE MOMENT WE PULL INTO Elijah's long and expansive driveway leading up to a gorgeously modern home, I feel my breaths coming in a slightly longer pulls. Most of me didn't want Nathanial to be right. I didn't want to know any of this was true or that I would need to spend time with a man who wanted nothing to do with me.

I try to reason with myself, acknowledge the fact that the blood bond had to have been done in order to save my life. I am thankful for that, truly I am. But did it have to be Elijah that I bonded with? Why couldn't it have been Nathanial?

I'm not innately attracted to Nathanial in the way I am to his brother. Don't get me wrong though, he's unbelievably handsome. What with his movie-star, slick golden hair and immaculately tailored suit that screams *dominant*. I have a feeling he has a deliciously dark and commanding side to him that all the ladies love to play with. Hell, he would have been a lot easier to live with in dire circumstances such as these. But no, I have to be recklessly attracted to his sultry, angry, distant but sexier than hell, brother. They both are the most beautiful men I've ever laid eyes on for completely opposite reasons.

As we park in front of the entirely black and dark wooded home, all sleek edges and large glass windows, I try to calm my racing heart as I mentally prepare for what I'm about to walk into.

The front of his home is layered in dark walnut wooden planks, while the trim and details are lined in black. His front door is one of those large wide ones, also completely black with wooded trees lining the short walkway. I don't fail to notice that his large home is sheltered completely in the woods. In fact, it's the only home I noticed in this neighborhood that is so deeply immersed in forestry. It wasn't even visible from the street as we drove up to it on the way here.

I step out of Nathanial's vehicle and follow him up towards the front door. I instantly spot what I assume is Elijah's Jeep. It's big black Wrangler Rubicon. I can almost *sense* him on it, a gut instinct that reaches through my confused mind and tells me it's his. It's huge, lifted at least six inches with large, treaded tires that sit at a wider stance from the body of the vehicle.

I notice another small car is parked in the driveaway next to Elijah's, a silver Ford or maybe a Mazda. I catch Nathanial's eyes as they dart quickly to the vehicle, a scowl forming on his lips.

I'm thankful for the fact that with every step I take, the easier my breaths are coming and the ache in my body begins to fade. However, I can't help but notice the strangely apprehensive gnawing at my mind, working its way to the forefront when Nathanial knocks on the front door.

My first mistake was expecting it to be Elijah that would

greet us. My second mistake was not expecting the fact that there be obvious imperative pieces of information missing from Nathanial's brief and vague explanation earlier.

Such as an apparent girlfriend. That would rightfully be at his home, and that I would unrightfully experience mass amounts of hatred and jealousy towards. This fucking blood bond was quickly becoming the bane of my existence. When the little platinum blond bunny hopped up to open the door, my heart took an insane, uncalled for nosedive into the pit of my stomach.

He's not yours. He's not yours. He's not yours.

I recite the words inside of my head like they are a plea for my own life. The emotions that spiral through my heart and fill my gut are shocking. I have absolutely no basis for these feelings, no right to be territorial or possessive over Elijah. Nor do I want that right. I swore off men for the last seven years and I want to keep it that way. I don't want to want him, fuck, I practically hate myself for feeling this desire towards him. But I also can't control the way my mind and body are seeking him out immediately, for the simple need to be near him.

"Sam," Nathanial states in an agitated greeting as he reaches back and takes my hand in his. He stalks forward without invitation, leading us both inside the house and past blondie. "Where is Elijah?"

"In the kitchen, he's hungry after we—" Her chirpy voice rings out like a blaring siren in my ears, stinging and searing through my blood.

"Don't speak." Nathanial's sharp tone surprises me. I haven't known him long, but I can tell that he's furious. He pulls me through a narrow hallway that opens into a beautifully styled kitchen. It's filled with stark white granite counters and black cabinets on the bottom half of the room. The upper cabinets are white as well and there is a butcher block style walnut island in the center.

Elijah's shirtless and standing near the sink, casually leaning against it with a bright red apple in his hand. I immediately catch the way his body tenses as I step foot into the room. While he seems strained, I feel a full, refreshing breath of air fill my lungs for the first time since we've been apart.

I continue absorbing all of the oxygen I can while I have the chance, savoring the feeling of energy, and a strength I haven't felt before. Everything seems clearer, my hearing, my eyesight, my sense of touch, all of it. I fight the urge to try and decipher his emotions but truthfully, I can't feel them the way Nathanial had described. Everything is heightened but the barrier that stands between us is still firmly rooted in place.

My eyes uncontrollably fall to his stomach, and *fuck me why does he have to be so attractive?*

His tattoos cover the entire expanse of his strong chest, trailing down and seeming to highlight every dip and rise of his powerful, washboard abs. They're perfect. I may hate this bond and hate the fact that it's him I had to bond with, but I definitely do not hate his body or that sexy V that disappears under his low-slung, dark wash jeans. I glance back up as my eyes catch a quick glint on his chest as he tosses the apple core into the sink behind him.

Yeah, he has his nipples pierced as well. Two tiny straight silver barbells that aren't at all feminine. He is incredibly, indescribably masculine in all of the best ways. Ways that feel like they were designed exactly for me.

"Eyes up here, *mo dheaman beag*," that accented rough voice electrifies the air between us. I still can't place the language or the accent, it's so faint. He is probably calling me something horrid, but the words parting his mouth leave goosebumps erupting across my shoulders and my panties feeling wet. Heat floods my cheeks as anger bites at my chest when I remember that he may know every single emotion I'm currently feeling.

"What the fuck are you doing?" Nathanial interrupts our interaction, nodding his head back towards where Sam had met us at the door.

"I could ask you the same fucking question, brother," Elijah pointedly glances at our joined hands, ones I had completely forgotten about when we entered the kitchen. I'm the first to pull away, surprised at my own error. I shouldn't care what Elijah thinks, but a part of me feels loyal to him, for the fact that he saved my life and is bonded to me.

Sam comes hurrying in behind us, immediately moving towards Elijah and resting her hand on his chest as she comes up beside him. She's wearing a pair of short, denim cut offs and a sweet pink, flouncy top. In most ways, she's the literal opposite of me. Tiny, with a small chest and bleach blond hair. Her style is preppy and manicured while mine tends to lean toward a mix of bohemian and hipster. She lifts up on her toes, leaning into him and placing a quick kiss on his cheek.

His eyes never leave mine while she begins chatting and honestly, I can't hear a word she says. My head is rushing with an overwhelming amount of frustration at things I can't control. I was never this out of control anymore. I close my eyes to break our gaze, mentally taking several deep breaths to try and sort everything out internally.

"—not my girlfriend." I catch the tail end of his voice as it breaks through my self-induced trance.

"I'm sorry, what?" I ask, begging to hear the words I hope are true. God, I hate that I hope that.

"Sam, she's not his girlfriend. She's just a friend," Nathanial repeats Elijah's words. I notice the pout on Sam's lips as she hears it again.

"All right, not a girlfriend. But a damn good friend, that's for sure," she giggles, looking back up at Elijah and trailing her fingers across his shoulder. My eyes zero in on the subtle movement as I fight to force back any erupting emotions.

"Got a thing for blondes, yeah?" I bite out sarcastically. I'm aware of the fact that both women I have met, who clearly have had a past with Elijah, are small, slender, and blonde. I'm not heavy by any means, not even overweight. I make time for the gym after what happened years ago. I make it a priority to work on my strength and stay in shape. I do, however, have curves and a larger chest than the average woman. I used to think that was a blessing until everything happened.

Now, seeing these women who have clearly attracted Elijah's attention, I am suddenly self-conscious of all the ways I'm so drastically different. This couldn't have been a worse pairing if it had been fucking planned.

A flash of anger licks at my chest before it quickly vanishes, making me believe it had to be Elijah's. A small smirk lifts at my lips at the realization that I've gotten to him, even just a little. I'm not going to be the only one suffering through this.

"Yeah, I've got a thing for blondes. They do everything better, after all." My own smirk dies a quick death at his sharp response.

CHAPTER TWELVE

ELIJAH

THE SOUND OF SAM'S HYENA-LIKE GIGGLES GRATE AGAINST my ears but I refuse to let the mask of a smirk leave my face. Christ, having a blood bond with Luna is akin to drowning in the ocean, in the midst of a tsunami. Over and fucking over again.

Saying that her emotions are overwhelming is an understatement. Every glance towards Sam is filled with jealousy. Every time her rich, chocolate brown eyes met my own, I feel a symphony of clashing emotions. Hatred, anger, arousal, desire, confusion.

It's too much.

I left Nathanial's house, fully aware of what it would do to the both of us, but honestly not giving a shit about it. I needed the space. The physical discomfort of being apart is nothing compared to the mental shit storm I'm dealing with after bonding myself to another female.

70

I have one defense against letting this bond between Luna and I go too far. One I hadn't realized was going to be so beneficial until I found myself in this situation. When I Fell, my talent hadn't immediately manifested. I wasn't sure if one ever would, but I didn't necessarily care to discover it either.

After Amelia severed our bond, I was destroyed. I didn't think I would survive the physical aspect of ripping that part of my soul away, Angels rarely did. Which is laughable now that I think about it. It's incredibly unfortunate that at one point in my life, I believed we were made for each other. Ironic, right? The person I wanted all those years ago, wasn't intended for me and the person I don't want, supposedly is. Just another kick in the ass on the way down.

Either way, in the weeks following our separation, I felt a new wave of strength develop inside of me. It was odd, it came out mostly whenever I'd see Amelia. It aided me in getting over her so quickly but started manifesting in other situations as well. At the capital, when the Cambion's were attacking, or when I was on a mission to gather intelligence against Amelia's warriors. Until I realized I could call on it when needed. It acted as a shield, an invisible barrier that I could manipulate around myself. It didn't protect me completely, but it distracted others around me and manipulated situations in my favor. It also assisted me in shielding most of my emotions from my bond with Luna. It wasn't foolproof, if she really dug hard enough and learned to utilize the blood bond to its full capability, she'd be able to see right through it. Especially as my Fated, I could never truly hide anything from her. But thankfully, she is inexperienced and young. She has no knowledge about our race or what her possible capabilities are, allowing me to take advantage when I need too.

Did it hurt, being away from Luna already? Fuck yes. But

I'm able to control my personal shield enough to hide those emotions from her.

Nathanial sighs in frustration between the two of us, unsure of how to handle what is rapidly deteriorating. Luna chooses to ignore my heated comment as she anxiously runs her fingers through her long hair, still tangled and matted from earlier. Her clothes are a mess, covered in blood and torn in several places along her top. The girl needs a shower, badly.

"I need you to know that I'll be heading back to my own apartment now. I have a job I need to get back to and I need to see my sister. I'm not changing my mind, so don't waste your time trying to convince me to stay here."

I scoff, "Sorry sweetheart, I don't negotiate. You're staying."

"No, actually I'm not. Also? Awful effort there."

"Quit your job. Say goodbye to your sister. Whatever the hell you have to do to clear your life in the city and bring your things here. You can't stay away, it's not safe." In one sense, I'm lying. I would much rather her stay away. It would make things a hell of a lot easier for me. But I know if anyone catches word of a potential Fated, Luna will be taken out first. Especially if Amelia has any sort of idea after what happened in her mansion.

"Wait, why would she have to stay here?" Sam asks, an annoyed snarl resting on her lips. I glance down towards her, recognizing that she shouldn't be a part of this conversation.

"Leave," I state flatly as I dismissively nod to the door. A surprised yelp falls from her pouty lips.

"What? Why?"

"Because I'm telling you to go. You can come back later tonight, I'll call you." I clip the words out quickly and cross my arms over my chest. After watching me with disbelief for a brief moment, she turns on her heels and huffs out of the kitchen. I turn my eyes back to Nathanial and Luna who are watching with a mix of revulsion and sympathy.

"You're an asshole," Luna spits out. She's feisty, I'll give her that.

"One second your jealous of my non-girlfriend and the next your angry with me for how I treat her. Sort your feelings out, sweetheart. They're quite a pain in my ass." I turn my back on them, picking another ripe apple from the large wooden fruit bowl on my counter and sink my teeth into the flesh.

"If you think I'm staying here, you're out of your fucking mind." I hear her foot hit the floor in what I can only imagine is a childish stomp, but truly sounds more like a gently defiant refute.

Frustration fills my gut at her words. She has no idea what she's getting herself into if she stays away from me for that long. Twenty-four hours and she'll be sick as a dog and crawling back on her hands and knees.

On her hands and knees. The image sends a kick straight to my cock as I force it back.

Don't even go there.

"Get out, Nathanial," I demand as I place the half-eaten apple in the sink and turn back around.

"Brother, I—"

"I said, get the hell out. You can wait for her in the living room," I grind out the words and see Nathanial quickly turn and step out of the kitchen with a groan.

The instant he's gone, I feel a wave of fear roll through my chest—easily Luna's. I know how to separate her emotions from my own.

"Did you expect my brother to stay and protect you?" I say, closing the distance between us in two large strides. She shifts back and I follow suit, caging her in with my wide stance until her back hits the wall behind her.

"No. I'm not afraid of you." She tilts her chin up, bravely meeting my eyes. But I know the truth, I can literally feel her uncertainty, the fear lacing her blood and infecting my own.

"Try again, sweetheart." I dip my head down, my face hovering only inches above hers.

"Stop calling me sweetheart."

"Fine. *Mo dheaman beag*," I savor the words as they roll off my tongue.

My little Demon.

She has no idea how fitting the term is.

"What does that mean?" She speaks quietly, her words a breathy whisper. Her arousal courses through the air between us. I feel it in my blood, on my skin. I can smell it on her, every sense acutely attuned to *her* need. Like she was created for me. I choose to ignore her question— she isn't ready for the answer.

"Tell me, do you hate me? Or hate the way I turn you on?" I pause, "Do you hate how wet you are for me, without even knowing me?" My voice is low and rougher than I intend but it quickly breaks her from her own intrigue as she furiously shoves me away with her small hands.

"Fuck you, very much. Have a great life." Heat floods Luna's cheeks and I feel the embarrassment rush our connection. I laugh, sliding my hands casually into my jean pockets as I watch her hurry out to Nathanial.

"See you soon, sweetheart."

CHAPTER THIRTEEN

Luna

On the drive home, Nathaniel handed me a new phone that was already programmed with his number as well as Elijah's. I lost my phone in the midst of the abduction, so this was a godsend. After repeating himself no less than sixty times, I reiterated that I was to call immediately if I noticed anything suspicious. Nathanial finally dropped me off at the small apartment complex where I live. He also gave me one of Elijah's black sweatshirts that he luckily found buried in the back seat of his car after one of their outings. My bloody tank top was too obvious a sign for anyone passing by that something was incredibly wrong.

I finger brushed my hair and cleaned up the blood as best I could in Elijah's bathroom before we left. His sweatshirt was so large it fell to my knees, effectively hiding the mess underneath. I refuse to acknowledge the fact that it smells like him.

The sudden aching pain in my chest was becoming all too familiar of a feeling, and the shortened breaths I maintained while I was away from Elijah were increasingly mundane. But the rush of relief and comfort that washed over me at the sight of my own home was unmistakable. I walk forward, waving Nathanial off as he speeds away and turn my attention back to the small black gate that's hidden under the large staircase leading up to the building. My apartment is nestled in the very bottom, so I have access through the wrought-iron gate and door underneath the stairway.

I lift my brown nylon, *"I hope you brought wine"* door mat, searching for my extra house key and am thankful to find it exactly where I usually leave it. The little silver trinket sits in the exact same place, leaving a clear outline of dirt and dust that has collected around it. I quickly unlock the two deadbolts on my door and step inside. I attempt to inhale a long, deep breath, trying to absorb the familiar scent of my favorite Lavender Marshmallow candle and my usual Tide laundry soap. I'm always burning candles, so the scent has naturally become a part of the small space, a little reminder of home that I appreciated. But my breaths are a short and ragged disappointment, not fulfilling me to the depth I need.

"Luna?" My reprieve is quickly shattered at the sound of my sister's voice yelling from inside my home.

"Stella? What the hell, how did you get in here? The key wasn't touched," I say as I rush forward, feeling both excitement at seeing my sister and worry that something may have happened while I was gone.

I hastily round the entry way and find Stella nestled into the corner of my light grey, linen couch. She has a heavy throw blanket wrapped around her small frame but quickly jumps from her seat at my arrival. She rushes towards me, her long fiery red curls bouncing with each movement. The second she's close enough, she wraps her arms tightly around my neck and pulls me to her.

"Where the hell have you been?" she asks, her voice laced with anger and relief.

"Stella, it hasn't even been a day. I got caught up last night, stayed with a friend." I'm not ready to explain everything to her yet. I'm having a hard-enough time holding her up right now with my own lack of oxygen and physical pain. I feel dizzy as I hug her back, resting some of my weight on her before subtly tugging us down to the couch.

"You didn't show up to your shift today, your boss called me to ask where you were and when I tried calling you, it said your line had been disconnected. What the hell, Lun? You should have gotten a hold of me and your boss. It isn't like you to miss work for nothing important." She places her hands on my shoulders, gripping lightly as she pulls away and studies my face for any clues.

"I'm sorry. You're right, I should have told you both I wasn't going to be around today. I'm not feeling too well, I overslept, and I look like shit. Everything is fine though, promise." *I was actually abducted and almost killed by some psychotic supernatural beings, who are supposedly Fallen Angels. Oh, and by the way I'm also eternally linked to an asshole for the rest of my life. I can't really breathe without him and also—I fucking hate him.*

I caution a smile, knowing she can read me better than anyone else. Well, *almost* anyone else now. I can see the apprehension in her features, but she seems to buy it as her body visibly relaxes.

"Why are you here? Don't you have a shift to catch? Also, how the hell did you get into my apartment without a key?" I don't miss the fact that she intentionally ignored my question earlier.

"Sweet sister, you should know me well enough by now to

realize I have my own key. I got it made right after you put down the deposit for this place and started moving in. You didn't even notice when I took your key to go grab our pizza while we were unpacking your things." Her mischievous smirk pulls at her lips and rises into her pale blue eyes.

"It freaks me out how much of a planner you are, you know that right?" I lean away from her, casually trying to disguise the heavier breaths I'm attempting to draw in.

"Hell, one of us has to be. You run around like you have no care in the world. You scared me, Luna. Don't pull that shit again. I came over this morning and decided to stay here until you showed up before my shift." She stands, leaning down and kissing me quickly on the top of my head. I swear, sometimes I feel like she is the older sister. She's always had an older soul, always been more compassionate and understanding. She's an artist at heart, a truly beautiful person.

"Speaking of, I need to leave. I was already late to a shift two days ago. Thankfully the excuse that I had to pick up a stray kitten I found hiding behind my apartment is actually a valid reason for an animal shelter." She laughs as she steps away and begins collecting her things. As she picks up her phone, she glances back at me. "Wait, your phone. Why is it disconnected?"

Shit.

"I broke it last night after leaving the coffee shop. I accidentally dropped it and it shattered, but I got a new one today. I'll text you so you have the new number." It's a stupid lie, one that holds no weight or validity. But it's simple enough to do the trick and honestly, I'm ready for Stella to leave so that I can really try focusing on my breathing and take a shower.

She pauses for a moment and turns to study me, clearly reading the odd tension in the room. "All right, text me your

new number. I'm not kidding, Luna, don't pull this shit again."
She steps away, "And call your boss."

Stella waves a quick goodbye and hurries out, locking the
door behind her with her own key.

Relief washes over me at finally being alone and I stand,
immediately moving to the bathroom. I shut the door quickly
and turn on the shower, twisting the silver knob until it's practically scorching. I undress as the steam heats and fills the small
space around me. I take several shallow breaths, forcing my
mind to relax and the achy tension in my limbs to settle. It
doesn't work, but I relish in the feeling of hot steam lingering
on my skin, sinking in and finally giving me some warmth away
from Elijah.

I step into the water, letting it burn and redden my flesh. It
distracts me from the painful throbbing growing in my chest.
I've been home all of twenty minutes and I'm already feeling a
bit worse. I hate how true all of this is quickly turning out to be.
Everything Nathanial told me is coming to fruition and while it
seems absolutely ridiculous, I can't ignore the fact that I've
changed over the last twenty-four hours. My body has adapted,
and my mind has warped into something new, something a bit
angrier and more confused but also intrigued and attracted to
this unfamiliar life.

I lift my sore hands and rake my fingers through my long
hair, watching the red and pink stained water rush over my
body and swirl across the white ceramic floor of my shower.
The water slicks my skin as I draw my fingers across my shoulders, down my arms, rinsing and washing away the evidence
from my own abduction. I reach for the soap and lather it my
hands, skating them across my body again when a flood of heat
quickly builds in my stomach. My mind naturally drifts to
Elijah as I close my eyes, envisioning his broad bare chest and
the piercings that decorate his tanned skin.

Fucking hell, he is abnormally attractive. Truly otherworldly.

I can't stop my own thoughts as my mind conjures up images of his hands on my waist. His long fingers snake under the edge of my top and climb higher until his thumb brushes against the underside of my breast. His mouth falls to my neck and I physically release a moan as the blazing water slides across my lips and my own hand slips between my legs.

Pale green eyes pierce through my rapidly drifting thoughts and suddenly I need his lips against my own. My body is urging to claim his and be claimed by him in the same moment. I try to force my thoughts elsewhere, literally *anywhere* else. But the only slight relief I find is when my own slim finger circles my clit while the water flows over my naked body. My breasts are heavy, and my nipples are peaked, sensitive to the delicious sting of water as it falls over my skin. My finger continues working over me, playing and pinching until I finally slide inside myself on a breathless moan. I'm exhausted and physically in pain but this short reprieve is something I'm craving.

In my mind, Elijah tugs my bottom lip into his mouth as he devours me with both anger and that same need that I seem to feel for him. We're both furious. We're in a position neither of us wants to be in, but we find relief in each other. I see my own fingers scrape across his strong, tattoo covered back as his hips roll into mine. The long, jagged scars of his stripped wings sear my hands as I touch them. I feel his long, thick cock grind into my stomach. I need him inside of me, my pussy is agonizingly wet and slick between my thighs.

I slide a second finger inside myself, stretching and filling in a way that isn't nearly as satisfying as I'd like to be, but it's enough to send me over the edge with a shattering orgasm. Truthfully, it's far stronger than what it should have been and as my knees weaken when I fall to the floor of my shower, a terrifying thought flashes in my mind.

Could he sense that?

Through our connection, would it possible for him to feel or know what I was thinking over the last few minutes? Surely, we're far enough apart that it wouldn't be an issue. If so, however, I realize I've got absolutely no privacy and the insight throws my mind into a panic.

I rock back on my heels, securing my hands on either side of the shower walls to steady myself. My shallow breaths kick up as my heart rate skyrockets and I struggle to remain calm in the tight space. That painful ache is ten times worse and I furiously rub at my chest in hopes to relieve some of the sting.

Uncomfortably too soon, the water turns cold and it gives me the shock I need to get my ass moving again. I stand up, shivering as I turn the water off and slowly step out of the shower. My limbs seize and strain with each movement. I assumed a steaming shower would help my physical state, hell even an orgasm should have at least loosened me up a bit. But instead, I'm feeling even worse as anxious thoughts overtake my mind.

I can't go back. I have a shift tomorrow and I need to get back to work.

Somehow, this has to work away from him.

I'll make it work. I have no other choice.

CHAPTER FOURTEEN

CHAPTER FOURTEEN

Luna

AFTER CALLING MY BOSS, FRANNIE, AND PROFUSELY apologizing, I'd successfully secured my job for at least the time being. She wasn't happy I missed my shift but was quite forgiving when I mentioned not feeling well. She knew I never asked for time off and felt like it must have been serious for me to pull a no-show.

The bad news? It's 6:00am and I've spent the last four hours hovering over the toilet while dry heaving after puking everything I had left in my stomach up. Or I've been on my side with my arms tightly clutched around my stomach and my chest in pain. Everything hurts.

Everything fucking hurts.

Call me a believer, all right. I've never experienced something like this before in my life. That hypothetical addict? I've become a full-on user, wasting away without her fix and going through withdrawals. I couldn't sleep last night. I tossed and turned the second I got into my bed, discomfort pricking under my skin and settling behind my ribs. Things continued to get worse and sleep continued to evade me until I felt so nauseous, I had to race to the bathroom and throw open the toilet.

I've been here ever since, sitting up and laying down on the cold tile, in cruel cycles that wrack my body. Every once in a while, my mind uncontrollably drifts to Elijah and I briefly consider calling him or Nathanial, but I don't. I can't face them or put myself in a position to lose everything. My job, my sister, my little life I've built here. I settled for putting Elijah's sweatshirt back on and finding the only comfort I could in his faded woodsy scent.

I slowly brace myself on shaky arms and reach for the small counter in my bathroom, pulling myself up. I take deliberate steps to my room in order to find a comfortable—not fashionable, lord knows I can't do fashion right now—outfit to wear to work.

I pull on my very used, only pair of black, Lululemon leggings and decide to throw on a sweater. It's large and loose, my preferred shade of terra cotta and hangs off one of my shoulders. It's slouchy in that hipster chic way, and as I tie up my hair in loose buns on the top of my head, I know it'll *appear* as if I've tried to look decent today. When in reality, I chose the comfiest clothes I could find and pulled my hair up and out of my eyes in case I needed to make a quick run to the bathroom. Convenience would be my only friend today.

In the name of said convenience, I opt for an Uber driver instead of walking the seven blocks to work. It isn't far, I know that, but with how weak and exhausted I am both mentally and physically, I selfishly take advantage of the cab.

After driving the short distance and listening to the driver vent endlessly about how he had to wait an extra five minutes in the Starbucks line—ironic, I know—I climb out of the Uber as quickly as I can manage and slowly make my way inside the small shop I call work.

Barista.

Simple, classic, minimalist. The walls are covered in white subway tile and long, light wooden shelves. Each ledge houses countless plants, some long and green like ivy trail down the walls. Others, such as fiddle leaf figs or colorful ferns, are bigger and bask in the light from the corner of the little shop.

Frannie is currently behind the counter, knocking her grounds into the trash and preparing to pull another shot of espresso. She has a small line of customers, but they are all regulars and patiently wait as she tends to each of them.

I smile and nod a few polite hellos before rounding the counter and dropping my bag on the dedicated shelf underneath. Just as I'm about to take the next order, I feel Frannie's hand drop to my elbow and gently pull, urging me to look at her.

"Hi, I love you, but you look like shit," she says as she continues making drinks like it's second nature.

I meet her concerned gaze as it rakes over me, taking in whatever appearance I thought I really had done a good job of hiding today. Her short blond hair is pulled up halfway, her long bangs swept off to the side. She wears a cozy, floor length, olive green dress which is knotted tightly at the ankles. It shows off her brown leather slides and tiny gold ankle bracelet.

"So nice to see you too." I give her a sarcastic smile, one that doesn't reach my eyes.

"You look like you're going to die...beautifully?" She tries and we both laugh at her attempted kindness. Her giggle is infectious as it falls around us. Mine is weak at best, quiet and hoarse through my throat, but it's there.

Frannie's blunt, always straightforward. But I appreciate that about her, she knows how much I hate hedging the truth. Just tell me how it is so I can fix it.

"Seriously though, if you need to go home, tell me and I'll call someone else. You look like you need the rest."

"Thanks, but I'll stick it out while I can. I need the distraction and I promise it's not contagious." She eyes me warily but nods her approval and I turn to take the next order. Instantly, a rush of panic freezes me in place as I catch the quickest glimpse of snow-white hair. I snap my head to the side, seeking Amelia out but see no one. I anxiously scan the room for her, but again, see only our regular customers.

"Are you okay darling?" Karen, an older woman in front of me snags my attention. Her salt and pepper hair is piled high on top of her head and she dons a pair of thin framed glasses perched low on her nose.

"I'm so sorry, Karen. I'm fine, I just thought I saw someone I knew. What can we get for you today?"

And just like that I fall back into my rhythm, using every customer, every task, every drink as a way to distract myself from the pain coursing through my body. Sometime around ten a.m., I developed a consistent tremble and Frannie pulled me from making any more drinks, so I busied my hands by cleaning every square inch behind the counter. I tire incredibly too quickly, stopping every couple of minutes to catch my breath through a simple task of scrubbing the fridges. I can tell that she's is worried, I see her watching me with uncertain eyes when she thinks I'm not paying attention.

Throughout the rest of my shift, I continued catching quick flashes of Amelia's hair. It was by the bathroom, then coming in through the front door, she'd be next to the counter and then standing up from a small table. Each and every time I saw it, a piercing shot of fear sparked through my chest and every single time I had to remind myself that she wasn't here. But the anxious thoughts and my wandering eyes added weight to my already weakened body.

Now, I'm in so much pain that my vision is growing hazy and nausea is welling in the pit of my stomach again. I stand for a moment, taking a few of the deepest breaths I can manage when I relinquish my hold and tell Frannie I need to step out in the fresh air for a minute.

"Please go to the hospital, Luna. I'm not kidding. I've already called someone else in. You're almost set to be off anyway," she pleads as she gathers my bag from under the counter and passes it to me, all but shooing me out the back door of her little building.

"Okay, okay. Thank you, I appreciate it," I mumble a quick goodbye and stumble out the door. I don't even bother telling her I definitely won't be going to the hospital, or any doctor for that matter. The issues I'm experiencing can only be fixed by one solution, and that's something I don't want to think about now.

Walking a few paces away from her shop, I stop and rest a hand against the red brick wall. It's rough under my fingers and the gritty texture reminds me of that awful night seven years ago, as well as the night that happened all too recently. The back of Frannie's building is in a small alley way between the cute shops here in Brooklyn, so I've got some privacy.

I turn and rest my back against the wall as I slide down so that I'm sitting. My head falls back and I close my eyes, intentionally counting each breath that roughly works out of my throat.

Focus.

A wave of nausea rolls through me and I clutch my stomach, silently begging myself not to puke out here behind the shop. I want to stand up and order an Uber, but I need a few more minutes to catch my breath. I vaguely hear a few soft steps and pry my eyes open to look towards the back of the alley. Not surprisingly, but terrifyingly, I see another flash of snow-white hair as a shadowy figure stands at a distant. Immediately, my heart begins racing in my chest. It's thundering so loudly that the sound floods my head and rushes between my ears.

I try to breathe and calm myself so that I can stand and run but my natural instinct to inhale has all but vanished, making it nearly impossible. I close my eyes as my vision blurs and I fumble for the phone in my bag, feeling for it until I grasp it and bring it in front of my face. Opening my eyes again, I refuse to look in Amelia's direction. I focus all of my energy on unlocking and searching for Nathanial or Elijah's number, whichever comes first.

Unfortunately, the soft steps become too loud and the anxious thoughts paired with lack of oxygen become too much. Before I ever get the chance to call for help, my tired eyes slide shut as darkness overtakes me and I slump to the cold ground below.

———

"You are incredibly stubborn, Luna."

My name.

His voice.

Undeniable relief clouds my mind as I hope beyond anything that it truly is Elijah waking me up and not Amelia. I'm still outside, still slumped against the old brick wall as the chilly air dances across my skin and the cement below scrapes across my flesh.

I slowly blink my eyes open, letting my vision clear as his strong green eyes gaze back at me. For a split second, I think I see something other than anger shining in them. A quick glint of concern breaks through but disappears immediately.

"I hate how happy I am to see you," I mumble as I push myself up on shaky arms. The corner of his lips lifts just barely, and I'm rewarded with the tiniest of smirks.

He doesn't offer me a response, instead his strong hands slide under my legs and behind my back as he effortlessly lifts me into his arms. I'm too weak to do anything but allow it and as much as I hate to admit it, I'm beyond thankful for it. I sigh in relief as his warmth seeps into my body. God, it's like I'm the cold and he's my sun. It's an instant energizer, healing me and incrementally fixing everything I've been through overnight.

My breaths become significantly easier and I'm positive I sound odd as I force several long pulls of air into my deprived lungs. I can fully appreciate his scent while I'm this close to him, it's dark and smoky with hints of pine and fire like he's been out in the woods all night. He walks us out of the alley and towards his blacked-out Jeep, which is parked on the street.

"Where is Amelia?" I stammer out. I don't exactly want to know but I feel as though I need to. I can't help it, I burrow my face deeper against his chest, seeking out more of his blazing heat through the thin white t-shirt he's wearing. He immediately tenses, from my words or from the physical action of seeking more of him, I don't know. I try to ignore the pang of rejection by reminding myself that neither of us wants this with each other.

"Amelia? Was she here?" He halts his steps and pulls away just slightly so that he can look down at me. I meet his eyes by briefly tipping my chin up but honestly, I'm too tired to maintain it so I grunt out a quick *yes* and close my eyes again, wishing I could crawl under his skin and bury myself inside his sun.

His steps pick up as we quickly reach the vehicle and he instantly yanks open the back door. He gently places me on the seat but faces me towards him as he dips down low to put himself in my direct line of vision. My head slumps to the seat, along with the rest of my body as exhaustion rolls over me. I'm finally comfortable and all I want to do is sleep for the next decade.

"Luna. Pay attention for a moment. Did you see Amelia?" He asks the words clearly and deliberately. I realize in that instant, as I watch him from the open doorway, that he doesn't seem affected by our separation in the slightest. His chocolate hair is perfectly styled back, his tattoos shining against his healthy olive skin, he has no bags under his eyes because it seems he slept soundly through the night. How am I the only one effected by our bond?

"Why don't you look like shit?" I ask as the sting of how this is obviously different for him dawns on me.

"Excuse me?" His eyebrows shoot up and one of his large hands land heavily on the seat next to my thigh. He moves slightly closer, searching my eyes with his own.

I don't have the energy to explain it to him, I don't even think I truly want the answer. So, I close my eyes and utter a quiet, "Forget it."

"Luna," he growls my name out of his soft lips and my eyes snap open against the rough sound grating over my skin. Heat pools in my stomach, arousal coursing through my body. My addiction tempts me at the strong command of my simple name being spoken on his lips. "Goddamnit, fucking pay attention."

His large hand shoots forward and grips the back of my neck tightly, pulling me upright as a bolt of electricity ignites under my skin. I gasp at the touch and the feeling of his heat blazing in my own blood.

"Was Amelia here?" he asks again, the slightest bit of pain lacing his voice. I don't answer immediately, instead I watch him. My mind drifting to the countless reasons why he would be so interested in Amelia being here. I want to say it's because he cares about *me*, and I hate that I want that to be the case. But I'm not stupid, and I can clearly see they've had a serious relationship in the past. I feel more rejection at the idea that she very intentionally tried to kill me and he's still seeking her out.

When I don't answer, his other hand falls to the crook in my neck. His thumb gently strokes against my collar bone, through the sweater that's pulled up on that side of my shoulder. His strong fingers softly knead and work my muscles in a way that has me relaxing and tensing simultaneously at my stimulation to it all. Heat builds in my stomach, falling even lower and flowing through my limbs. My head tilts just slightly, allowing him more access when his voice breaks through my fog.

"Was Amelia here?" he asks again, this time softer, coaxing the answer from me in sync with his touch. I don't miss the intention there, and I suddenly understand how he's manipulating my half of the bond to get the information he needs.

I immediately straighten my back and reach for his hands, shoving them off of me. "Don't. Don't fucking manipulate what I can't control just so you can get closer to her," I hiss the words out through my teeth as anger boils inside of me. His eyes go wide for a moment, confusion pulls at his features until he understands what I mean and takes a step back.

"For fuck sake, seriously? Fine, don't tell me if she was here. I don't care anyway," he slams the door shut as I groan in frustration.

"You don't understand his relationship with Amelia.

Maybe if you asked, he'd tell you." Nathanial's voice speaks from behind and I whip my head around to find him settled in the far seat of the Jeep.

I scoff, "I have a pretty clear idea."

"No. I promise that you don't," he says and then turns his head to stare out the window as Elijah jumps in the front seat.

CHAPTER FIFTEEN

ELIJAH

LAST NIGHT WAS LITERAL HELL. AND BELIEVE ME, I HAVE
a pretty good idea on what Hell is actually like. I didn't sleep,
couldn't eat, and wanted nothing more than to climb in my Jeep
and drive into the city just so that I could be closer to Luna
without actually seeing her.

I'm internally torn in half. Part of me wants to be with her
all of the time while the other part wants nothing to do with her
again. She gets on my nerves, her emotions are too overwhelming and all over the fucking place, and then I find out
that Amelia is already looking for her again?

Fuck, I didn't want any of this.

I ended up sleeping out in the woods last night. The fresh
air helped, and I refused to come back inside and face Sam. I
felt too sick to give her anything she may have wanted. Sam is
not my girlfriend. She never will be my girlfriend and I've
made it pretty damn clear that's the case. However, she's a

consistent casual fuck and for that reason, sticks around a lot of the time without actually moving in. I'd kick her out now that Luna is around, but honestly, Sam makes it clear that nothing will be happening between Luna and I.

Though holy hell, last night while Luna was clearly touching herself, I couldn't keep my hands off my own cock. I don't know what had happened, but I could feel her relaxing for the first time since we had been apart. Relaxation turned to arousal, and before I knew it, I could practically see her touching herself. Her sweet, milky thighs spread wide. Her small hand circling and working her clit until she came. I pulled out my cock and stroked myself, gripping the thick base and squeezing hard before I came because I had already been that fucking close when I felt her. She doesn't understand it, but she could feel my own arousal while she got off, it's why her orgasm literally tore through her body when it shouldn't have been that intense. We came at the same time, and I rode out my orgasm with continued strokes as I imagined Luna on her knees in front of me, while I coated her creamy tits with my cum.

I spent the rest of the night in pain being away from her, while hating her all the same for making me feel this way. This morning, I held off as long as I possibly could before storming over to her and forcing her to come back with me. We can't stay away from each other. I am not going to deal with that bullshit for the rest of my life. Not until we find a way to manage it.

Thankfully, I was able find her pretty easily through our bond. I had to focus, but I basically felt my way to her while Nathanial drove, directing him through the city until we were near, and he jumped in the backseat. When I found her outside that little coffee shop, passed out against the brick wall, I wanted to yell at her for being so fucking careless. She shouldn't have let it get that far, and fainting in the middle of the city? Did she have no idea what could possibly happen to her? Who could take fucking advantage of her? That would destroy me. Then she mentioned Amelia and I about lost it all right then and there.

Rage burned through my veins at the thought that Amelia was already looking for Luna. I figured she would eventually, but by that point I hoped Luna and I would be on better terms, at least fucking living together so neither of us were in a weaker state. I also needed to have Nathanial start training Luna, teaching her defense tactics and how to fight if it was ever necessary. I had a sick feeling that ultimately, it would be.

Hell, the fact that Luna thought I was using her to get closer to Amelia for any reason other than to kill her myself, proves that she has no idea how to read our bond in the slightest. That's for the best though. She can believe whatever the hell she wants as long as she sticks close and simply doesn't die. I don't give a shit about the rest.

We pull up in front of my house and climb out of the vehicle, filing inside as I lead us all to my living room. Sam hurries in and greets me, leaning up and pressing her soft lips against my own in a kiss that's clearly claiming her property in front of Luna. I feel the spark of reluctant jealousy lick through my chest and I know that it's hers. Neither of them likes the other, but it makes no difference to me. Neither of them means much to me at all.

At least that's what I keep telling myself. I easily pull away from Sam, gently stepping to the side of her as I motion for Nathanial and Luna to take a seat.

"Give us a few moments, Sam," I say as I dismissively nod for her to leave the room. She looks disappointed, again. But no one knows about mine and Luna's bond, or the fact that we are Fated, and it needs to stay that way. She stalks out of the room a second later.

Luna takes a seat on the long, black leather couch, cozying

herself in the corner as she folds her feet up and tucks them underneath her. Nathanial sits down far too close to her, if I'm being honest, and lifts his hand to rest against the back of the couch, behind her head. My eyes zero in the nearness he's taking to her, but I know for a fact he feels nothing for her other than platonic affection. Nathanial has never been interested in dating. He's always focused on his work. He's one of the hardest working people I've ever met. He studied his ass off to get his doctorate in medicine for humans but also works as our race's healer after the attacks on the Capital.

It's not that he can't date, it's just that he'd rather have a one-night stand when he needs that connection, and then send them on their way in the morning so he can get back to work. Believe me, I know. He oddly attracts the wild ladies and I'm always the recipient of his crazy stories when he's done. Or I show up at his home and get the tail end of their insane arguments as he shoos them out the door. And I do mean them, as in plural, as in more than one woman at a time.

I take a seat on the arm of the gray recliner opposite them. Casually sliding my hands in my pockets, I cross my ankles and meet Luna's cautious gaze with my own. She's horrible at hiding the fact that she's attracted to me. The actual worst at masking her wandering eyes when they travel down my torso, or the feelings she experiences when I walk into the room. I get both halves of her, appreciating me and hating me at the same time. I can relate to that.

"You're staying here," I command. It's no longer a choice for her.

"You can't force me to stay, I can make my own decisions," she snaps back. I swear, she fights just to prove she can.

"Do you want to go through another night like the last? It'll only get worse the longer you're away."

She pauses before answering, I feel the uncertainty

clouding her mind. I know what she wants, and that's for none of this to have happened, but we can't rewind time. No matter how much we'd like to. That, I know firsthand.

"No. But I can't leave my job, or my sister. I need those Elijah. I can't come here and live in this house with you and do nothing, become nothing. I need something for myself," she pleads with me. Her eyes widen with both frustration and apprehension at the idea that she'd have nothing here. I contemplate telling her no, that it's not safe for her to be out in the city now, that I need to keep her hidden.

Fuck, she's a Fated. *My* Fated. But she doesn't know that, and it's not something she's ready to hear. As much as I hate to admit it, she'd go crazy living here without any outlet. I get that, so I compromise.

"Fine. You can keep your job and keep seeing your sister, but you get rid of your apartment. You don't need it anyway, and when you work, I'll head to the Capital and get my own shit done. That way we won't be so far apart that you're terribly uncomfortable." I state my terms clearly, my eyes not leaving hers, even though I'm tempted to look over her entire body. I feel the swell of acceptance and appreciation over being able to continue working, and the hesitation over leaving her apartment. I want to see whatever tick she's got going while she comprehends what I've just said. She absently tugs her bottom lip into her mouth as she thinks and I can't help but focus on the motion, imagining what that pouty lower lip feels like, tastes like in my own mouth.

I catch a quick movement behind Luna's head and realize that Nathanial has a stray lock of her thick hair twisted around his finger. He wraps it up tightly and slowly uncoils it, sifting the silky strands between his fingertips as a dark wave of rage builds in my stomach. My eyes dart to him, narrowing as I see a cocky smirk tug at his lips.

"Leave," I hiss.

"But why, brother?" he asks innocently. He's an intentional person, always making calculated decisions.

"Because you're doing this shit on purpose to piss me off and it's fucking working. We don't need you here anymore. Get out." I uncross my feet and stand, moving towards the door and opening it wide for him. I don't look at Luna, I don't want to see her face and the emotions I'm reading from her bond are more than fucking enough. Appreciation, frustration, confusion.

Nathanial's smirk grows into a full blown, shit eating grin as he releases her hair and stands up. He casually waves goodbye and saunters out the door. I let the door shut a little harder than I should and take a deep breath before turning around to finish our conversation.

Luna is quiet, which is rare I've come to realize over the short couple of days that I've known her. She's loud and argumentative. She tends to ramble when she's frustrated and confused. And even if I didn't have the bond with her, I'd be able to read her emotions all over her face. The chick is a wide-open book.

"I have one more condition. If you ever get so sick that you're going to pass out like this morning, or if you ever see Amelia again, you let me know immediately. Call, text, I don't fucking care, but you tell me. And don't pass out in a damn alley way, that was reckless and dangerous. You have no idea the kind of shit that could have happened had it been at night." I speak the words angrily, I'm on edge about Nathanial putting his hands on what's mine and I'm annoyed with even feeling this way. But I watch the color drain from Luna's face at my comment and I feel the way her heart begins thundering in her chest.

"First of all, don't fucking tell me what to do. I am my own person, Elijah. Deal with it. Second, I do have a fucking idea what could happen, believe me and don't think for one second that I haven't thought about that fact myself." She pauses for a moment, trying to reign in her anger as it spirals out of control. I let her words truly sink into my own mind. "You do realize, that prior to forty-eight hours ago, I had no idea what a blood bond was, right? Or believed that Angels were anything but winged figments of my imagination. I didn't know I was going to feel that shitty or pass out. I've had no intentions for the last seven years of feeling this way towards anyone, let alone an asshole like you." She stops talking, her chest rapidly rising and falling as she takes several deep breaths.

I'm silent for a moment, as I try to process everything she said, but only being able to focus on the first half of her words. "What do you mean, you already have an idea of what could happen?" The words come out of my mouth in rough, jagged syllables. I'm trying to keep calm but the fact that something may have happened to her, even years ago, rips my insides to shreds.

"It's none of your business, and it happened a long time ago. All I'm trying to say is that I already understand I should have gotten a hold of you sooner. You are right, I am stubborn. But I get that now. I'll call you or Nathanial next time." She stands up, brushing her hands down her thighs and tilting her head up to look at me. I stalk towards her until she falls back down on the couch and I'm standing over her tense chest, crowding her in dominance and security. I feel her heart rate kick up again, this time because of how close we are.

"It is my business. You're fucking mine, Luna. Don't mistake that. It'll always be my business, and you call me, not Nathanial." My knuckles whiten as I grip the back of the couch on either side of her body. The tension between us builds, my face directly in her proximity. I can almost feel her breaths against my lips and I definitely feel my cock thickening against the zipper of my jeans.

She surprises me again by leaning forward, bringing her lips even closer to mine as she places her hands directly on my chest and pushes me backwards. I let her, allowing her to stand and step into my own space.

"If I belong to you, then that would mean you belong to me. And that makes no sense to your sweet Sam over there," she nods back. "And I'll tell you when I'm damn good and ready. Maybe when you're ready to tell me why the hell you're still so into Amelia."

Goddamn, she has some serious fight in her. I would never tell her, but so far that's my favorite thing I've come to learn about her. She is right though; I won't tell her about Amelia, and she won't tell me about whatever the hell happened to her all those years ago. At least not yet, but at some point, I'll find out. However, I am done letting her believe I have any feelings more than hatred toward Amelia.

I step even closer to her, but she doesn't back up. Our bodies come flush against each other and the refreshing chill of her figure works to calm down the heated rage in my own. I'm constantly running hot, never finding comfort in the cool breeze that I so desperately want. It was why I preferred being outdoors when I wasn't feeling well, but the cold air just barely touches me the way Luna's chill relaxes me.

"Keep your secrets, but you will tell me eventually. As for Amelia, you're right, I'm not going to tell you about her. But if you think I feel anything for her more than complete and utter disgust, then you clearly haven't even tried to make use of our blood ties." My lips brush against hers as I speak the words harshly. Our thin tether being pulled so tightly it's about to snap. Her heart is racing in her chest, I can practically feel it thumping against my own. Her breaths are shallow and laced with so much heated arousal that I know I'd find her soaking wet if I just let my hand slip between us, inside her leggings and across her slick pussy.

Silence. She's caught off guard and truthfully, so am I. This angry dense air quickly turned into something so much more dangerous.

My cock is rock hard, straining against the denim and our bodies are so close that I know she can feel it. Subtly, I roll my hips against her stomach, just barely but enough to make her gasp at the connection.

"Tell me what you're thinking about, *mo dheamhan*," I demand roughly.

"You should already know," she whispers. I trail my fingers up her arm, over her sweater until I reach the tattered hem at her soft neck. I watch as little bumps break out across her chest and God, I want to run my fingers across them. But I don't dare touch her skin yet, I can only imagine how I'd lose control feeling her Fated flesh against mine.

"Is it what you were thinking about last night? When you were touching yourself after you left?" I shift my hand to take a bit of her hair in my fingers, rolling the strands and claiming them for myself after Nathanial foolishly touched her. The softest whimper escapes her lips and suddenly the need to demand her mouth overwhelms me. I have no choice, she draws me to her with an undeniable strength, chasing away any intentions I ever had of staying away from her.

I fist her wild hair roughly and she closes her eyes, fully succumbing to my touch and hold on her. I shouldn't cross this line, it's one I won't be able to get back. I tug her head to the side anyway, so that I can lean in and inhale her sweet scent. Delicious arousal and honeyed peonies fill my lungs, dragging me that much deeper into my need to devour her.

"Am I interrupting something here?" Sam's sharp voice

grates across my nerves and rips me back to reality. Luna immediately jumps backwards, tearing my grasp from her hair with a yelp and in her attempt to distance herself from me, falls back on her ass.

I meet her gaze for a moment longer until I let my shield slip back into place, successfully securing her behind the barrier I want her firmly behind. "Luna has to stay here for a little while and I thought you might as well bring your things over too, sweetheart." I plaster on a fake grin as I meet Sam's eyes. Like hell I want her here, but it puts another layer between Luna and I, so I'll take it.

CHAPTER SIXTEEN

Luna

YOU HAVE GOT TO BE FUCKING KIDDING ME.

We were *this* close, *this* fucking close to kissing. Not that I necessarily want that. Well, it's more like I don't want to want that. I wanted it. Shit, I really did. The way his hand pulled at my hair and the way I naturally submitted to his command. It was empowering, truly. Knowing, if even for a moment, that I affected him the way he affects me was well worth the risk.

It was also the first time I genuinely felt his emotions through our bond. It was like a thick blazing furnace, integrating with my blood and flooding my system with both of our emotions. We innately worked together, our bodies and minds in complete sync with what we needed from each other. I gave and he took, and in that moment, I wanted to give him everything.

Part of me still wants to give him everything. But the fact

that he invited fucking Sam to come live with him as well completely doused my fire like a bucket of ice water. That was a low blow and an intentional one at that. He was clearly giving me a warning, laying that barrier down thick between us as his emotions all but completely vanished from our bond.

Sam accepted, of course. So, she's currently gone while she packs up enough clothes for a damn week and will be back. Elijah, not so graciously, showed me to my room, careful to stay a solid ten feet away at all times, and then left to take care of his own business.

I text Stella, letting her know that some things have come up with my apartment and I'll need her help in packing and moving. I did tell Elijah that he had no choice but to let Stella help me move and come over here. He grumbled an annoyed acceptance on his way out the door.

Stella: WTF. Why are you moving? And where!

Me: It's a long story. There's black mold in my ceiling. I'm moving in with a friend, his name is Elijah. You can meet him.

Fucking mold? That was stupid.

Stella: Sounds like a short story, as in hell no. You'll live with me.

Me: I already paid a deposit for his place. I'm renting a room from him, it's nothing. I promise.

Stella: Wait, do you like this guy? Is that why?

Me: If by like, you mean hate, then yes.

Stella: I seriously don't understand you. But I'll help and I'll def be meeting Mr. mysterious.

Me: He has a brother if that helps.

Stella: Hot?

Me: In a rich boy, perfectly styled hair, ripped AF kind of way.

Stella: Oooh, my favorite. ;)

Me: So, Friday?

Stella: I'll meet you at your place. Well, your old place. Weird.

Me: Love you, thnx.

I FALL BACK ON THE BIG, KING SIZED BED IN MY NEW room. It's covered in a thick black duvet comforter, which has the astronomical sky subtly stitched throughout it in gold thread. I turn over on my side so that I can trace each line and star with my fingers, studying and wondering what it must have been like for Elijah before he Fell. What did he see? What did he do while he was up there? How do Angels communicate with each other? How did he Fall?

As if I was calling him, my door opens without a knock and

Elijah stands, filling the larger than average doorway. I halt my movements, my eyes meeting his in silence.

"I'm having a few people over Friday, after we get your things. If you want Stella to stay, she's welcome." He states the words flatly, as if it's a nuisance to waste his energy speaking them.

"Wow, so kind of you. I'll let her know." I drop my eyes back to the blanket and continue my dissection of the night sky. I expect him to leave, but he doesn't. He continues standing there, watching me as I trail my fingers across the bed. I glance back up at him, waiting for whatever it is he clearly wants to say. But he says nothing, still watching, still churning through whatever is going through his mind.

"We can't do whatever happened earl—"

"What did you do in Heav—?"

We speak at the same time and my face flushes at his painful rejection. It's not that I didn't expect it, I did. But hearing the words out loud make it more real. He tenses at my obvious question, but I choose to speak first.

"Don't worry, already forgotten. I got a pretty clear hint when you invited Sam to move in as well. We're going to be the happiest little family." I let a fake smile jump to my lips and my voice kicks up a sarcastic notch at the end. If I'm not mistaken, the corner of his mouth jerks humorously upwards. I think it's the closest I've ever seen him show a true smile.

"Are you going to answer my question?" I ask, taking us back in the conversation.

"Heaven is the neo-Christian preferred translation." He pauses, scrubbing a hand down his sharp face. "Arcadia. That's how we refer to where Nathanial and I came from. What I did there is nothing worth telling. It was a long time ago."

I blink a few times at his choice of words. *A long time ago.* Suddenly, a thought comes to mind about the age of Angels.

Elijah looks to be around my age, maybe a few years older. But I can't know that for sure. "Excuse me? How old are you?" I ask in caution.

"I don't pay attention to age anymore, I simply exist."

"So how old are you?" I pointedly ask again, and that subtle twitch of his lips happens for a second time. Hell, I'll keep being pushy if it gives me those little moments.

"Probably around five hundred and forty-seven, give or take."

Silence.

Deafening silence surrounds us as I try to process what he's saying.

"Five hundred and forty-seven," I speak the words slowly, my eyes wide in shock and disbelief. "You have been alive for five hundred and forty-seven years and you look like that. Do you know how old I am?" I press him, unable to fathom that length of time.

"No, but I have a feeling you'll tell me." I think he's making a joke, but I'm unsure because quite frankly, everything is blowing my mind at this point.

"Twenty-seven. That's a two and a seven. Meaning I've barely lived a thirtieth as long as you have."

"All right, don't say it like that. It's weird," he scoffs as he turns on his heel to head back downstairs. I leap from the bed and follow him to my door.

"That's because it is weird. We, this—" I point back and forth between the two of us as he glances over his shoulder from the bottom of the grand staircase, "—are weird, did you not realize that before?"

"Believe me, I fully understand." He steps away to avoid our conversation, but I call after him.

"Wait, you didn't tell me what you did in Arcadia?" I ask again. I'm not leaving this one alone.

He sighs in frustration before meeting my eyes, "I'm a Seraphim Angel. Which means in the Arcadia, I guarded the Throne. Nathanial and I both did together."

"Why did you Fall?" I'm getting more personal, I know. But I want to understand him better.

He flinches at my question, briefly closing his eyes before opening them again. "I chose to interfere in things I shouldn't have been involved in."

I pause, "Do you regret it?" My voice is quieter than I intend it, as if it might hurt to know the answer. His eyes bore into mine while strength and confidence quickly flash through me.

"Not for a second," his voice is firm, absolutely assured in his choice. An odd vibration of relief fills my chest as a small smile tugs at my lips. "Enough with the twenty questions. I'm going to get dinner, I won't go too far." With that, he reaches for his keys which hang on a black iron hook by the door before walking out of the house and leaving me alone. I hear the Jeep start and the fading of the engine as it drives away, taking my oxygen and heat with it.

I take a seat at the bottom of the stairs as I wait his return. I instinctually begin rubbing my chest in his absence, feeling like he took a piece of what's inside there as well.

CHAPTER SEVENTEEN

Luna

"Don't act so surprised I hid this from you. You're moving in with a man I have literally never heard about and you only told me when you needed my help to move." Stella bends over to pick up a small box. Her black, ripped skinny jeans cling to her legs and her long, red flowy Free-People blouse swooshes around her thighs. Her chaotic fiery hair is pulled up in one of the messy buns that look completely styled, even though she tied it up quickly and without a mirror, just to keep it out of her face.

"It's different. I'm not dating Elijah. We haven't been hanging out or spending intimate time together. You've been going on actual dates and building a genuine relationship with a guy. Also, you totally faked the possibility of being into Elijah's brother when I texted you." I follow her out of the apartment with the last box in my arms. Elijah stands by the open hatch of his vehicle as he takes each box from us and arranges it in the back.

"I couldn't tell you over text, that's ridiculous. You know I'm a planner, and I didn't want to say anything until I knew he was going to stick around for a while," she states dryly.

I brush off my hands and go back to lock my door for the last time. I pause and look up at what was once my home, a place I had made my own and earned by myself. It's bittersweet leaving, but something I've accepted rather easily now that I've felt how uncomfortable it is being away from Elijah.

"Hurry up, I've got places to go. People will be over soon." Elijah's voice yells from the driver side of his vehicle. I roll my eyes and turn, hurrying over to join him and Stella.

"You also didn't tell me that while Elijah may be more attractive than ninety percent of the male population, he's also a raging dick," Stella chirps as she jumps into the back seat. I can't help the laugh that falls out of my mouth as I shut the passenger side door and buckle up. Elijah's eyes dart back to her in the front mirror, an entirely unenthused expression on his face.

"Yeah you're a real peach too, sweetheart."

"Ew, I hate that pet name." She scrunches up her nose at his sarcasm.

"I told him the same thing," I say, smiling to myself.

"Why? Because it's generic? For nameless, unimpressionable women?" he asks.

"Yes," we both say in unison.

"Exactly."

My face drops at his admittance, and Stella rolls her eyes, but his lips are lifted just slightly with a conniving smirk.

"You sure you don't want to move in with me?" Stella pointedly asks and I tilt my head to rest against the window.

"Unfortunately, she's in a non-negotiable contract with me.

She's not going anywhere," he continues, his voice dripping with conceited sarcasm. It's been one week of living with Elijah and I'm already losing my mind.

For one, I've realized that he's a drinker. He drinks almost every single night. A decent amount as well, to where he's a bit tipsy but keeps mostly to himself and Sam. I hate that it seems he's so uncomfortable with me living here it makes him turn to alcohol. I wish things could be different, I wish Sam wasn't here. And I wish we didn't have this ridiculous blood bond that begs for me to be close to him, seek out his warmth and attention when he only seeks out Sam.

Sam.

She has become an ever present gnat, buzzing in my ear about all things her and Elijah. She drives me crazy, and when she doesn't shut up about their sex life, I find myself downing a few shots myself, just to fog out my mind. I already have to see them kiss, watch them spend time together, silently observe as her fingers trail across his chest and arms as they talk. I don't need to hear about him railing her at all hours of the night as well.

I actually did hear them once and I nearly threw up everything I had eaten for dinner. It happened recently too, just the other night after Elijah and I actually shared a decent conversation. He told me a little more about the Angel race. He explained the Capital to me, how it was that gorgeous cathedral in downtown Manhattan which doubled as the central base for Fallen Angels. He even shared that Nathanial currently leads their people, because Elijah had refused the role initially but was reconsidering. I hadn't felt closer to him than in that moment and I left the conversation feeling like maybe we could eventually be friends.

That night I had woken up from a rhythmic *thump, thump, thumping* downstairs. At first, I was worried that someone was trying to get in, so I jumped from my bed and slowly opened the door. That was when I heard her, Sam, moaning and crying out Elijah's name as he assumedly, slammed into her with enough force to break the damn wall down.

I couldn't help it, tears pricked at my eyes and I used all of my strength to force them back. But once I heard him as he groaned into her, clearly reaching his own climax, I truly lost it. I slammed my door shut like a child, in hopes that he heard me, so that he knew *I knew* what he was doing and surrendered to shedding a few tears throughout the rest of the night. I couldn't feel anything through the bond except disgust and hatred, and while I wasn't completely positive, I was pretty sure those were my own emotions. I had no claim over him, I tried to remind myself. But the warring blood bond between us said otherwise, and I had to force away those feelings.

We didn't speak the entire next day—which was yesterday —and today we were gathering my things and getting ready for the party he was throwing together.

"This isn't one of those, fifty shades type contracts, right? Because I don't know if I'd support that or if I might have to kidnap and hide you away, Luna." Stella's voice breaks through my thoughts as I force a sympathetic laugh at her remark. How funny, she could never hide me away from him and the fact that it both excites me and makes me miserable is the real problem.

"Wow, that was fake. I was just joking, promise. What's up?" Stella leans forward from the backseat and looks at me. I turn to assure her I'm fine when I see Elijah watching me silently, his soft green eyes piercing through mine, no doubt reading my emotions and putting two and two together.

Stella's small, pale hand suddenly smacks his chest as a scowl forms on his lips. "Dude, what the hell. Eyes on the road,

I'll take care of my sister." She turns her attention back to me as Elijah reluctantly focuses back on the road.

"Nothing is wrong, I promise. It's just bittersweet leaving that apartment," I lie.

She eyes me warily, trying to figure out if I'm telling the truth or not. Hesitantly accepting my answer, she leans back in her seat. "Alrighty then, if that's what you want to go with."

We drive the rest of the way in silence and when we pull up in front of the house, the tension has thankfully eased a bit. Stella's eyes widen with appreciation. "Okay, I can see why you would choose to live here rather than my little apartment."

I laugh at her comment as we all climb out and begin unloading the Jeep. We follow Elijah to the front door when it swings open and Nathanial bolts out. In his rush, he accidentally runs directly into Stella, knocking the box she's carrying from her arms and crashing to the ground. She topples over, bracing herself to hit the cement when Nathanial's hand darts forward and catches her elbow before she falls.

She looks down, straightening her shirt with trembling hands when Nathanial finally speaks. "Who are you?" he asks simply, but there's an edge to his tone that I've never heard before.

She finally looks up, meeting his eyes for the first time and I swear she's briefly stunned speechless. She quickly recovers and finally responds, "Nice to meet you too, asshole. Is this the rich boy you told me about?" she asks me, but her eyes never leave Nathanial's.

I laugh a bit to myself as Elijah's gaze shoots towards me. "Yes, this is Nathanial. Nathanial, this is my sister, Stella."

They don't shake hands—they don't even offer the sentiment. Nathanial clearly drags his hooded eyes up and down her body and she immediately tenses at his perusal. He takes a deliberate step away from her, putting distance between them and shakes his head before looking over to Elijah. "A few alarms sounded at the Capital, nothing serious though. I'm going to make sure things are okay and then I'll be back," his voice is clipped as he tries to sound vague enough around Stella and I suddenly realize that she is most likely going to be around others of their race tonight. I'm going to have to explain things to her at some point.

"Tell me if you need me, I'll be there. You know that," Elijah is tense, his body all hard lines and sharp edges. He nods for Stella and me to head inside and I quickly urge her forward. We leave the box on the ground, but I don't miss the way she quickly catches one last peek at Nathanial before we enter the house.

I motion for us to head up the staircase and towards my room. "Why are you acting weird around Nathanial?" I ask, phishing for her opinion. I know she supposedly has a boyfriend, but I'm curious what she thought.

"What? I'm not. He's a conceited prick, I can already see that, and I didn't even have a conversation with him. Hell, he's alright looking, I guess. But did you see the way he didn't even say hello? He just—"

A loud laugh rolls out of my throat, "Okay, okay. I get it. You don't like him. But he's not an ass, I promise. He just seemed a little off, stressed probably."

While a wave of mild anxiety courses through me over what could be happening at the Capital, and with no indication through my bond with Elijah, I choose to focus on unpacking and getting ready for this evening. Stella and I continued unloading boxes, having Elijah place them against one wall as he helped for a few more minutes before disappearing entirely.

CHAPTER EIGHTEEN

Luna

Stella and I still haven't left my room yet, and it's been a couple of hours since we first came up here. After unpacking almost everything, we began getting ready for the party. I want to say that I didn't care if Elijah noticed me, but I'd be lying to myself. I do care. I don't want to care, but I do. And that's just the simple truth of it right now.

I chose to wear a casual, flowy dress for the evening. A cream one that dipped low in the front and cinched at the waist with big tan buttons. They follow a straight line all the way to the bottom, where it parts the two sides just slightly. It cascades around my calves and has loose shorter sleeves that fall off of my shoulders in a wide neckline. I pulled half of my hair up in a relaxed top knot and opted for hardly any make up tonight, settling on foundation, blush, a few swipes of mascara and lined brows.

Stella, the ever-bohemian beauty, is wearing a floor length maroon dress. It's casual enough to look effortless, but absolutely enhances everything about her. Her wild, red hair hangs around her shoulders in loose, natural waves. The back of the dress is completely open aside for the thin straps that reach over her shoulders and fall to the material bunched up at the small of her back.

I was still worried about the possibility of Stella meeting other Angels in attendance, but Elijah surprised me earlier by sharing a bit of reassurance through our bond. It was the first time he had ever willingly opened up to me in that way and while I was thankful for it, I also knew I couldn't trust this development in our relationship. Or lack thereof. After that, he completely blocked me out and I knew I wouldn't read anything else from him tonight.

Stella has also been on edge since we got here. She won't stop rambling about her boyfriend or sending him quick text messages and reminding me how I need to meet him. I narrow my eyes at her suspiciously as she picks up her phone for the millionth time and obnoxiously giggles to herself over a text she's reading, I'm assuming from him.

"All right, let's get this over with," I mumble as I give myself one last once over in the long mirror I brought from my old apartment. I slide my hands down the front of my dress, turning to the side in order to check every angle.

"You look amazing, Lun. You hoping to grab Elijah's attention?" she asks as she wanders over to join me in the mirror. She drops her head to my shoulder as we speak to each other through the reflection.

"No. Definitely not. Besides, his girlfriend is here," I say dryly. I don't want to dislike Sam, but she makes it her mission to remind me of her and Elijah's non-relationship every time she can. It's hard to ignore that.

"She isn't his girlfriend. You told me that earlier."

"Semantics. They're basically committed fuck buddies," I say as I turn and move to open the bedroom door with Stella following on my heels. I'm not sure what to expect, but as we slowly descend the staircase, an overwhelming amount of chatter and voices fill my ears.

I glance to my left, looking over the iron railing and see that Elijah's living room is packed with party guests. There are a mix of red solo cups and traditional glasses in the hands of everyone below, some wine glasses occasionally scattered through as well. There's a long, farm style table nestled across the back wall of the room. It's filled with trays of food, vegetables, small cakes, some sort of pasta salad and other snacks. One end is also cluttered with an assortment of various bottles of alcohol.

At first, when we reach the bottom of the stairs, I don't see Elijah. I try not to look for him, but in a room filled with strange people, who could all be Angels or who knows what else, I end up seeking out his familiarity. I don't catch sight of him until my eyes firmly land on his, colliding together like two magnets finding their homes. A current of yearning and need crash through me. My body begs to step nearer to him, craving his touch on my skin and his voice in my ear.

His face is still, as well as his entire body, frozen in place while Sam clings to his muscular upper arm. She's telling him something, her mouth working at double speed, a few giggles thrown into the conversation as well. But he doesn't look like he's listening. It doesn't look like he hears anything or sees anything else. Sam leans toward him, clearly repeating his name several times before he finally tears his eyes off of me and turns to face her.

The widest smile I have ever seen on his lips is directed at her and I'm shocked in place by the beauty of it. I've only ever seen small smirks, or the tiniest lift to his lips. This is different, it's a full face, stunning smile that clearly has her forgetting the fact that he just ignored half of what she said to him. I bite my lip as the unjustified jealousy rips through me at the fact that Sam earned herself something so precious from him.

"Hey, earth to Luna. Forget him, he's not worth it, okay?" Stella's sweet voice fills my ears as her small hands land on my shoulders and she turns me to face her. I plaster a sympathetic smile on my lips and scoff at the comment, as if Elijah has no effect on me.

God, how I wish that were true.

At the same moment, the front door swings open wide and Nathanial saunters in with another man at his side. Several people look up and shout hellos or wave, but his gaze zeros in first on Stella, then quickly swings to me.

"Luna," he says as he steps towards us. His eyes politely fall to my sister with a nod, "Stella." I briefly notice the man at his side, similar to Nathanial in that pretty boy, immensely attractive kind of way. His hair is blonde, much blonder than his friend's and long enough to pull up into a small knot on his head. He has some scruff, nothing outrageous but definitely masculine enough to have me taking a second look.

I return my attention back to Nathanial and Stella, glancing back and forth between the two as her eyes burn into his and he refuses to break contact first.

"What the hell is up with you two?" I ask, stepping in between them and forcing them apart at my words. Stella immediately recovers, throwing an arm around my shoulders and placing a kiss on my cheek.

"Nothing at all, Lun. Nice to see you again, Nate-y." She smiles widely at him as she props her other hand on her waist. His eyes narrow at her nickname for him, but he chooses not to respond to it.

He swings his gaze back to me as he steps to the side, motioning toward the man next to him. "I actually wanted to introduce you to my friend, Camden."

I offer a polite smile and when Camden reaches his hand forward to shake mine in greeting, I'm surprised at the powerful grip he places on me. "Hi there," he says, his voice *much* lower than I anticipated. It rolls over my skin and wraps around me like a thick wave of heat from a fireplace, sparking and crackling from just two simple words.

"Luna. I'm Luna." I force out, uncontrollably smiling again. *Jesus, play it cool.*

He's intimidating, if I'm being honest. His arms bunch and flex with strength as he leans back and casually slides them into the pockets of his light denim jeans. He's wearing a cream, long sleeve sweater that hugs him tightly around his chest and shoulders. He has a narrower build, but still rippled with muscles and definition.

Stella introduces herself as well, taking his hand in hers and shaking it in welcome. Nathanial tenses at their interaction for a split second, and I can't help but wonder what he could be possibly thinking of my sister. They don't seem to get along, without even knowing each other. But there is something else between them, a tension that drags their gazes back towards the other, even if in anger and frustration.

"Nathanial. Who is your friend? Pretty sure this was a closed invitation."

A burning heat scrapes at the small of my back, working its way up my spine and enveloping my body in that sun I'm constantly craving. I feel the hairs on the back of my neck stand at immediate attention and shivers break out across my shoulder blades. I unconsciously sway back towards Elijah until his firm hand lands tightly on my waist, holding me steady and mere inches away from him. I glance down quickly and feel an intense heat build in my core and sink even lower, settling between my thighs where I'm already wet for him. The simple contrasting sight of his tattooed fingers against my creamy linen dress has me turned on and tuned into his touch.

Nathanial's smile widens as he rocks back on the heels of his brown, Brunello Cucinelli lace-up's. *Guy is attractive and has a sense of style.* "I figured she needed to meet more people, make a few more friends in the neighborhood since she's living here with you and Sam now. Speaking of—" he looks over his brother's shoulder until he spots whoever he's looking for. I refuse to turn around and meet Elijah's eyes, I refuse to see the expression on Camden's face. No doubt this is oddly uncomfortable. "Sam! Come meet my friend."

I inwardly wince at Sam joining us but make no expression to show that fact. She hurries up behind me and I step to the side, hoping to shrink away from the small gathering while they all continue chatting. Introductions continue to be made and I can't help but notice that Elijah is staying closer to me. Not close enough to be touching, sort of hovering around with Sam at his other side. I look to Stella, seeking her help in bailing us out of this group but her attention is locked on Nathanial with a slight scowl on her pretty face.

"You need a drink?" Camden's dark, deep voice fills my ears and I quickly turn towards him to realize he's speaking to me.

"Ah—Sure, I could use a drink," I stammer out and step back, putting space between myself and the small group. Camden steps away with me and takes the lead, reaching back to take my hand in his as he pushes us through the crowded room. I instinctively flinch and rub my chest as the tiniest spark of pain lances through it. Curiosity pulls at my mind and I turn my head to look over my shoulder, meeting the sharp eyes of Elijah at my back.

"Are you okay?" Camden pulls my attention back to him as he eyes the hand on my chest warily.

"Yes, of course. Sorry, just had a pinch." I smile weakly as we approach the wooden table with food and drinks. I release his hand, reaching for my dress and begin running the fabric through my fingers, just to give my hands something to do. Camden pours two drinks and I give him free reign on what to make me, I'm not picky and I'll most likely end up sipping on it through the night.

"Is he your boyfriend?" The question catches me off guard and I find myself looking back towards our group at the other end of the room.

"Who? Nathanial?" I ask, surprised at the notion.

Camden scoffs, "No. The tattooed one. I think Nathanial told me that was his brother?"

"Elijah. Yes, they're brothers but no, he's not my boyfriend. Far from it in fact. It's complicated." I turn back towards our friends and see that everyone has resumed their conversation, focused on each other while more of their friends begin mingling over. Stella is fitting in with everyone well and she doesn't seem to notice the fact that each person is a little different than we are. They're a little more perfect, a little more polished, their skin shines in a way that enhances their beauty. I have a gut feeling that Camden is an Angel as well but worry it's too personal of a question to ask.

"Are you—" I pause, readying myself to say the words, "are you an Angel?"

Camden laughs at my hesitation as he casually sips from his cup. "Fallen Angel, but yes. I am. I'm assuming you know almost everyone here is, right? Aside from a few strays of other beings."

I choke, my eyes widening at his casual tone. "A few other beings? Like what?" I ask.

"Well, Esme over there," he points to a woman who joined our group by the entryway. Her hair is incredibly long, falling down past her hips in thick blonde waves. She has a few beads tied into her strands, giving her a whimsical aura that is only heightened by the flowy multicolored dress she's wearing. It falls to her feet and literally sways around her as she turns and moves across the room. Her wrists are covered in gold and silver bangles as well. She's absolutely stunning and I notice her bright blue eyes as she turns to look at me over her shoulder. It's as if she knows we are talking about her and gives a little wave with her ring heavy fingers.

"She's a witch," he finally finishes, lifting his cup in hello to her.

"A witch. Like a real, actual witch?" I ask as he nods in agreement, a smile overtaking his handsome face. "Is it odd that a witch is hanging out with a bunch of Angels?"

"Not as strange as the Demon over there who is hanging all over James." He points to a couple that's cozied up on the couch in front of us. There's a beautiful girl with long caramel colored hair that falls across her shoulders in straight planes. Her arm is slung around the neck of a man with dreadlocks, all tied up and stacked on top of his head. His dark skin is a beautiful contrast to her pale white. The two are obviously with each other, their hands seeking out the contact of the other with each breath they take. She's either touching his hair or his shoulder, trailing her fingers down to his wrist while he plays with the frayed denim that clings to her thigh.

"Which one is the Demon?" I ask incredulously.

"She is. James is a Fallen Angel. They've been together for around a hundred or so years now." He says this so offhandedly, like it's just another day for him. Which it is, this is their normal.

"How does that work? Aren't you all at war with Demons?"

"Yes. But each of us is different, and just because her race is technically at war with us, doesn't mean she is. We accept people for who they are, not where they come from or were born from." His voice is tense with emotion and I can't stop myself from looking over at his thoughtful expression. He watches them with intrigued eyes, taking in their movements and passionate exchange.

"That's beautiful, you know," I say, and he glances at me, a kind smile tugging at his lips. That sharp pain prods at my heart again and I wince at the unexpected feeling. My eyes seek out Elijah's and we clash, again before he turns his attention back to Sam. I know he's watching mine and Camden's interaction. I can't help but feel loyal to Elijah, but as I silently watch him and Sam, I understand that he doesn't hold that same sentiment to me. I knew he didn't, logically. But it didn't stop the fact that sometimes I wished things were different between us.

"Do you want to go talk outside? You know, away from everyone watching," Camden suggests lightly. He says everyone, but I know he means Elijah. He's the only one who keeps nonchalantly glancing back at us.

"Yes, actually. That sounds nice." We both turn and walk towards the kitchen, where there is a small door that leads to the outside deck. I haven't been out here yet, but I've seen it through the windows. The long wooden platform rises above the forested backyard. There are black iron railings that line the entire deck in an elegant way, framing the edges softly and adding a bit of femininity to the feel of the house.

Stepping outside, I realize that I didn't know how chilly it was this evening. I wrap my hands around my upper arms, rubbing furiously to create some heated friction. Camden immediately notices and turns back around to head inside. He returns quickly, this time with a throw blanket that I know is

Elijah's. It was probably folded up in the wicker basket he usually has setting next to the couch.

Camden steps behind me, holding it up in offering and when I nod, he shifts forward to wrap the soft, burgundy blanket around me. His large hands envelope my shoulders as his chest frames me from my back. I tug the blanket closer around me as mixed sensations of Elijah's scent, but the feeling of Camden's unfamiliar body surrounds me.

He steps back and gives me space, sliding his hands into the pockets of his jeans as he watches me with curiosity. "Are you bonded to him?" his voice is lower, still kind, but with a hint of intrigue as it ghosts over me.

I glance away quickly and absently suck my bottom lip into my mouth, scraping my teeth across the thin flesh. I'm not sure how to answer him. Is it that obvious in the way I'm around him? Isn't this supposed to be a secret, in case Amelia and Danner find out?

"You don't have to admit it, truthfully. It's rather easy to tell," he continues as he scrubs his hand over the scruff covering his face. My eyes shoot back to him as worry courses through me. He laughs. "He watches you like you're the only person in the room. Even while Sam hangs off of his arm like it's her lifeline. You don't watch him, but it's only because you're actively seeking other places to train your eyes. Why is that? You said he wasn't your boyfriend."

"Is this twenty questions? I hardly even know you," I bite out. I'm not intentionally being rude but as fear builds in my stomach at his ability to so easily pick us out, I'm unsure if I made a mistake somewhere.

"Hey, I'm not trying to press you. I'm just trying to get to know you. If he's not your boyfriend, then maybe you'd be willing to get to know me. However, if you're bonded and he is, well that's quite a complication." He's being genuine, I can hear it in the slight lilt his voice takes on, as if he's trying to comfort me in this strangely complex mess I've found myself in.

I pull the blanket tighter around my shoulders, slowly breathing in the scent and using it to calm my nerves. Oddly enough, I do find it comforting. I find him comforting, even as I realize he's asking me out. While part of me is loyal to Elijah, I remind myself that he has Sam and has made it perfectly clear he isn't interested in anything other than a platonic existence with me. Maybe I could use a few new friends, or a distraction from everything going on around me.

"He's not my boyfriend," I state simply. A small smile pulls at his lips until it's stretched wide across his face. The tiniest flitter of hope dances across my chest as a small laugh works its way up my throat.

"Well then, I'm glad to hear it." There's a slight awkward pause of silence, where neither of us knows exactly what to say next. Camden breaches the tension easily, "So, tell me about yourself, Luna. How did you find yourself mixed up with Angels? I can tell you aren't one of us, or at least not fully."

I decide to trust him, maybe not with every detail. But with some, the vague outline of how I got here. So, I open up and tell him as he watches me with clear, focused intent, on every word that falls from my lips.

CHAPTER NINETEEN

ELIJAH

I SHOULDN'T HAVE DRANK. THAT'S FOR FUCKING SURE.

But I also didn't know that Nathanial was going to swoop in here with some blind date for Luna. That's not how this is supposed to work and definitely not in my own home. I assumed that when Luna moved out and moved on, we'd both have figured out a way to deal with this bond separately from each other. Now, I'm stuck, hardly feeling any of the bond between us because I stupidly chose to numb it away in frustration.

Hell, I can't even be mad. I'm fucking Sam in the same house as her all the damn time. But she doesn't know that I simply use Sam as a distraction from her. Every time I see Luna waltz through my house like this place is equally hers. Every time I walk into the kitchen and find her bent over in front of the fridge, usually in her tight jogger athletic pants and an even tighter work out top. Her perfect ass showcased just for me and

125

her tight nipples, peaked at the simple sound of my voice. Every time her and I have a new conversation and she digs just the tiniest bit deeper into my life. Every time we connect, I'm reminded that she was created flawlessly for me.

When she asked me about the Fall, the vaguest sense of déjà vu danced through my mind. Something pulled at my memories, begging to be connected with something that didn't exist. She pulls different aspects of my life together in ways I never anticipated and in ways that only leave me more confused, like I'm missing giant pieces of the puzzle before I gain the entire picture.

She grows on me every second of every day that we are together. My body craves her, but my mind seeks her out even more. When I need her more desperately than any addict could need his drug, that's when I look for Sam. She doesn't know that I'm only seeing Luna's tight body under mine when we fuck. She doesn't know how when I close my eyes and fist my fingers through her hair, I'm only seeing Luna's dark brown locks twisted around my fingers.

It's shitty. I know it is, but I'm a Fallen fucking Angel and I never claimed to be fair. My only redeeming factor is that Sam knows this thing between us is temporary. Every time she mentions being in a relationship with me or going out on a date with someone else, I make it clear that she is perfectly capable of doing whatever she wants and fuck whoever she wants.

Tonight however, Nathanial crossed a fucking line by bringing Camden here.

"What the hell is that about?" I grit out once Nathanial and I have a moment alone. Stella is busy talking with Esme and I painfully watched Luna leave to go out back with Camden a little while ago.

"I don't know why you're being such a dick. She needs to meet new people. You keep her in here like a prisoner while you flaunt Sam around like a damn trophy." Nathanial doesn't even look at me while he speaks, keeping that fake smile plastered to his face.

"Excuse me? Everything I've fucking done was to keep her safe. If she is a Fated—"

"She is a Fated. She's *your* fucking Fated."

"No one can know. They would hunt her down and kill her in an instant. You're risking everything I've worked for." I turn my body and step directly in his line of vision so that he has no choice but to look at me. He doesn't know who she came from, who her parents are. He hasn't fully comprehended that she's both Demon and Angel.

I'm a selfish prick and refuse to take her for myself but can't stand the idea of her being with Camden. If she was in danger, if she died, I wouldn't survive it. I hate the reality of this fact but it's true. Fated pairings live and thrive from each other, without the one, the other simply can't survive. Luna truly is my other half, one I hopelessly wish wasn't plaguing my life. But my Fated, just the same.

"No one will find out, Elijah. No one knows other than us. Hell, I doubt you've even told her. Have you?"

My house is currently crowded, yes. Filled with people who could find out about us. But every single person here is someone I've known for years, someone I trust or someone who is on our side of the war. I would never invite anyone I didn't know in immense detail. Camden, while my brother knew him, wasn't good enough. I don't know a damn thing about him.

"No. Of course not. I'm not putting her in danger like that. She only knows what she absolutely needs to." I glance back over my shoulder, willing her to walk back through that door any second now.

"No, but you'll torture her in the damn process," Nathanial says quietly, but so firmly that it radiates through my bones. I slam my fist on the wall behind him, catching everyone's quick glances as they try to interpret our interaction.

I drop my voice, "I drink. I fucking drink to drown out the bond so she doesn't feel all this bullshit. Okay?"

"Get rid of Sam," he demands.

"No. I can't." I bite the inside of my cheek until I taste the tangy bitterness of blood in my mouth.

"What the hell, why not?"

I pause, silent tension building between us. "If I get rid of Sam... if it's just Luna and I..." I trail off, forcing the words to stay glued inside my throat.

Nathanial laughs mockingly, as if he couldn't be more annoyed at my resistance. "You wouldn't be able to stay away from her. I know. You're a fucking idiot. So, Camden is here, and if anything happens between them, you don't get to say a damn thing about it." He moves to step around me and leave our conversation, but a quick thought worries my mind.

"Camden. How do you know him?" I ask quickly, before he has the chance to leave entirely.

"He works at the Capital with me. He's safe, I promise Elijah."

"What is his skill? His ability?"

Nathanial seems annoyed with me, rolling his eyes with a scoff before he turns in order to ignore my question.

"Answer me," I growl it out in a snarl, my lip curling back over my teeth at my brother's clear disregard. My tone provokes him and he turns on his heel before stalking directly up to my face.

"Since you can't seem to leave this alone and you're my brother, I will tell you. But not because he or Luna owes you a damn thing." He pauses, his chest heaving with angry breaths. I don't break eye contact, I'm not afraid of him and we both know that I could force him to tell me if I wanted him to. "He reads bloodlines. He can find ancestors, blood complexes, uncover blood bonds. That sort of thing. He specializes in DNA at the Capital."

I feel the blood drain from my face as the icy revelation hits me. He can find out who her parents are. He would be able to sense the kind of blood that runs through her veins.

"How? How does he read it?" I ask as countless thoughts come crashing through my mind.

"He can only read through touch, why? What—"

"Fucking hell, Nathanial. What have you done?" I grind out as I immediately push past him, rushing towards the deck on the back of my home. As I enter the kitchen, I move quickly towards the door, but stop abruptly when I catch their shadows only a few feet away from me.

Luna stands there, her back pressed tightly against the railing while Camden's larger frame surrounds her from the front. They're angled slightly, so I can see that his hand is clutched around her wrist, his thumb grazing back and forth across her soft skin. The simple fact that his hands are on her has my blood boiling, but the sight of his lips pressed tightly against hers as he grips her waist with his other hand, has me seeing red.

I break through the door so loudly, that Luna rips away from Camden in surprise. Her wild eyes fly to mine as she drops the blanket that was wrapped around her shoulders. Camden doesn't look phased, he simply turns towards me and steps ever so slightly in front of Luna, as if he's fucking protecting her. *From me.*

Rage builds in my chest and I have to use every ounce of strength inside of me not to rip his throat out. "How dare you fucking touch her?" I growl. Luna's gaze keeps jumping from Camden to myself and back. She is visibly trembling, and I ache to pull her to my side and away from the man in front of me.

"Excuse me?" he asks simply.

"Get the hell out of here." My hands are fisted at my sides, my fingernails digging into my palms.

"Elijah, stop. You can't—" Luna's voice is small, worry lining her words as she speaks. I've never seen her like this. Guilty. Apprehensive. As if I caught her off guard and her usual bold sass isn't in place to protect her.

"The hell I can. This is my home. I control who's here."

"I asked him to," she states, a little more loudly this time as she tries to find her self-reliance. The confession ripples through me in an agonizing reminder that I pushed her into this situation. She has no reason not to be interested in another man. But that doesn't stop the unjustified anger that rises in me at her words. I close my eyes briefly as I process what she says.

"He told me he could help. He could tell me who my parents were, where I came from, why I'm here." She's pleading with me to understand, to settle down in the face of reason. I wish more than anything I had the bond open between us so that I could literally feel what she's trying to convey.

"Have you told her?" Camden interrupts, a challenging tone coating his voice.

My eyes shoot to him in warning, threatening him with my stance to keep his fucking mouth shut.

"Told me what?" Luna asks, stepping forward to stand in between us. Her eyes swing back to me, searching for the answers she wants.

"Don't. She doesn't need to know," I caution.

"She definitely needs to know," Camden responds flatly, laying his hand on her shoulder in support. I instantly want to rip it off of his body. Bloody mess and all, I want him away from her.

"Tell me," Luna quickly turns to Camden for the answers and suddenly I hate everything about this moment in time, everything that's lead to this. The fact that she's learning this personal truth about herself from anyone other than me. I loathe him for offering it to her so willingly. I hate her for asking this of him, asking for his touch and I despise that I had to witness it.

I need Sam, my distraction—anything that would change the outcome of what's about to happen.

"You do have Angel blood in your veins," he starts. The rushing sound in my head is loud and I'm unsure how Luna will handle this which worries me even more. She's only recently learned that we exist in her world at all. "But you also have another's blood. You were born of both Angel and Demon. Both coexist inside of you." He hesitates for a moment before detailing her legitimacy. "You aren't human, Luna. Both you and Stella are half Angel and half Demon."

Silence. Luna stares back at Camden. His hand reaches up as he offers a sympathetic smile, brushing his thumb against her pale cheek. Her small body continues to tremble and her head whips back to meet my gaze. Her eyes are piercing, dark and wildly angry as she turns to face me. "You knew this?" She's quiet, her voice barely above a whisper.

Pain sears through me at the understanding she's coming to. Again, I curse myself for drinking on such an important night for her and yet I know, after all is said and done, that I'll still be angry with her for choosing him tonight. Irrationally angry with unjustified rage. But angry all the same. This is why I never wanted to bond again. It was a constant whirlwind of conflicting emotions.

"I knew," I reply to her, squaring my shoulders and readying myself for her wrath.

"When?"

I open my mouth to answer her but realize that I want this moment for us alone. "Leave," I motion towards Camden and notice the small smirk lifting at his lips. He glances down to Luna and squeezes her upper arm in encouragement.

"If you need me, call me. I'll be here," he tells her. I contemplate killing him now, in this moment for offering her the support I should be willing to give her. She nods in thank you and he walks past me back into my home, intentionally bumping against my shoulder on the way in. I'm *this* close to ripping the motherfucker's head off, but I force my attention to stay on Luna.

"Since I found you with Amelia and Danner," I admit.

"How? How could you possibly have known that?" she asks, taking a step away from me and back towards the railing. I follow her, step for step until I'm standing only a foot away. I take her agony and let it punish me. I absorb the pain she's experiencing, even if I can't feel it directly through our connection. I see it all written across her face and in her tense little body.

"Amelia said you were born of Archophys and Estera. I think you were nearly unconscious at that point. I don't know how much you actually remember of that night. They cut you, let your blood fall on her skin and it turned black against her flesh. That was how I knew it was true. Demon blood transforms against our skin," I explain as I place both hands on either side of the railing behind her, confining her to our private moment. I watch as tears build in her eyes and she fights them back. I can feel the war inside myself, begging me to reach out and lay my rough hands against her soft skin. Urging me to feel the cool breeze of her body against mine, to experience the touch of my Fated as we ride out this wave together. She craves me and everything in my soul is hungry to devour her.

"Who are they? My parents?" Her voice is even smaller in the space between us and my eyes selfishly fall to her rosy lips. I blatantly ignore her question. Few inches separate my aching body from hers and the need to suck her pillow like lower lip in between my teeth and bite is overwhelming. As if she knows this, like she can still feel my desire through the drunken haze of our bond, she sucks her lip in between her own teeth and away from me. A low growl breaks free from my throat as I sink closer to her, letting my nose drift across the fallen locks of her dark hair and inhale her scent.

For me.

Fucking floral peonies, the addictive smell of roasted coffee, and something sweet and bitter lying underneath. Vanilla bean and cacao.

Her arousal, perfectly tailored to infect my mind and electrocute my blood as it pumps through my veins. My cock is straining against my jeans, pushing and kicking to be closer to her.

Don't touch her skin. Don't touch her skin.

I feel her sharp intake of breath as I bury myself deeper into her hair, trying to curb the craving desire I have to touch her by breathing in as much of her scent as I possibly can. Her eyes drift closed, and her chest begins lifting and falling in strong, powerful breaths. She's taking everything she can from this as well, flourishing in the space between us. Even as the blood bond is numbed, I can feel the power and strength of our Fated connection growing. The fire blazes underneath my skin and mingles with the icy wisps of hers, coming together before stopping abruptly, just short of complete integration. I know the potential of what could happen if we took this Fate and made it ours. Luna has never shown signs of any sort of ability on her own, she isn't fully Angel or Demon. But together, there's a chance, a high fucking probability even, that we'd manifest something magnificent.

Luna lifts her hand and reaches for my face, intending to take this moment between us for herself. I tense, immediately straightening and stepping back, shattering the trance we had fallen into. A small, quiet whimper escapes her lips at the rejection and the separation between us. But I can't take it back, as painful as it is, this can never happen between us. I don't have anything left to give anyone. It will always be safer for Luna to go back to her own life when we can manage this, live out the rest of her existence as a human would.

In a split second, I watch as anger quickly replaces the simpering pain in her eyes. Her mind rapidly clears from the hazy daze we had slipped into. "What the actual fuck, Elijah?" she spits out, and honestly, I'm relieved at her anger.

Anger, I can deal with.

It's the possibility of fucking caring—loving again—that I can't do.

"You weren't ready to know, Luna. You still aren't fucking ready," I tell her, resentment laced in my harsh tone. "You were raised as a human. You were never around anyone from our race. You could have lived a traditional human life and been happy." I take another step back, creating the division between us that we so desperately need.

"It's *me*, for Christ's sake. I have the right to know about my own blood, my own family." Her small fists clench at her sides as she fights to keep her voice down.

"I don't give a shit, honestly," I scrub my hand down my face in frustration. "One day, you'll go back to your own life when we can manage this bond separately. You'll live out the rest of your days as a normal person, doing regular, ordinary things."

She laughs. A bitter, sadistic laugh that tears through her throat and poisons the air around us. "You think, after all of this, I'm going back? That I'll simply forget everything I've learned and everything I am?" She lifts her hands and rests them on her head, gripping her hair and clearly trying not to pull. "You made me get rid of my fucking apartment, Elijah! You bonded me and now I can't stand the fucking sight of you and I can't stay the hell away from you either." Luna turns and begins pacing back and forth across the deck.

Our bond is billowing between us. She doesn't realize that the pull of emotions flowing through her are pushing at my own simultaneously. We're like oil and water, refusing to mix even when our souls beg to do so.

The chilly air around us is ice cold one moment and blazing hot in the next. Our sentiments are riled and perfuming through the air, warring for control with each other when truly, they simply need to merge.

But neither of us will submit that easily.

CHAPTER TWENTY

Luna

I can't fucking believe him. The actual nerve he has to think he can control me? He's got another thing coming. Honestly though, it's no skin off my back. Camden has made it clear that he will give me the answers I want, and he's fucking hot. That's just a bonus.

My blood is frozen in my body, slow moving with an icy rage that's stuck in my throat. Elijah has completely shut down and placed his walls back in front of him. One second, he's breathing me in, feeding my desperate hunger for him, filling me in almost every way I want him too.

Almost.

Because holy fuck, in those moments, when we're so close that I can feel his heat radiating into my skin and warming my cold blood? That empty ache between my thighs is craving to be filled by his cock as well. I physically burn to have him inside of me, have his lips devouring my own. I need to feel his rough hands exploring my body, in ideally an even rougher way.

It surprises me that I instinctively know how I want it from him. I know how he would give it to me. Hard, demanding, dominantly harsh in ways that would complement my odd need to surrender to him.

"Fuck you, Elijah," I spit out, denying the quick turn my thoughts had taken.

"Not in your dreams, *mo dheamhan,*" his voice is thick with heat and irritation. But he isn't me, he isn't nearly as pissed as I am.

"What the hell does that mean?" I shout as I step around him. He grips my upper arm before I completely pass. His fingers bite through the sleeve of my dress as he drags me up against his side, close, but not close enough to touch.

"My Demon," he whispers the two words against my ear as his hot breath floods my body. A sarcastic bite lines his tone and I know he doesn't mean it as an endearing term.

A fucking Demon.

You've got to be kidding me. But how do I even deny it? We shouldn't have been able to bond if I didn't at least have some amount of Angel blood within me, or so I've been told. It should be no surprise I have Demon as well. It would explain my ability to attract outrageously shitty situations though, that's for sure.

"This can't be happening to me. None of it, it doesn't make fucking sense." I rip my arm from his grasp and stalk towards the back door leading inside his house.

"Believe it, sweetheart. You've already been here a week, you feel it in your gut. It sings in your blood, whether you want it to or not. I get it," he pauses for a beat. His eyes turning towards mine and meeting me head on. "I don't want you."

I don't want you.

It shouldn't hurt. God, I fucking wish it didn't pain me to hear him utter those words. But the excruciating confession feels like a knife slicing through my soul, tearing it in half and ripping off limbs I find essential to my being. I shut my eyes tightly, forcing back the stinging tears and refuse to show him that I actually care. No, I stopped begging a long ass time ago and I'm not about to start now.

I open my eyes again, letting a calm and casual smile fall against my face. A mask I should have put in place a long time ago but am just now trying to manipulate to my own needs.

"Say it again," I demand, knowing that hearing the words will internally shatter my little facade. I need to hear it though. I need to force him to say the words a second time.

His eyes widen for a moment as the smallest flash of pain sparks in his bright gaze. An inky darkness swims through them as he steels his callous expression back into place. *That's it,* I want that again. I want to see that pain in his eyes as he fucking rejects me. I can't feel it, he's blocked me out of the bond too much for me to read anything from him.

So, I'll push him this way. Make him say the words he promises he means yet agonizes over voicing.

"Do it. Fucking say it again, Elijah."

"Why?" His voice is deep and sinister against the night sky, making it seem even lighter than the darkness surrounding his large body.

"Because I fucking said so." I turn on my heels and stalk back over to him, stopping only inches away from his powerful chest. I feel the electricity buzz back to life between us, vibrating around our frames in a mix of lust and revulsion. "Tell me again. I want to hear you say it. Remind me that whatever this is between us, this blood bond *you* initiated, is nothing to you."

He leans down, his soft lips only breaths away from mine. My achingly hard nipples brush against his chest with every breath I take. I try to remain cool and apathetic, prove to him that I don't care if he wants me or not. The hairs stand on the back of my neck at our tense interaction however, every pulse inside my body is lighting up with our proximity and bond.

"I. Don't. Want. You."

He says it. Enunciating each word with a powerful punch to my chest. My skin feels like it's peeling off of my body, his fire licking through me as I burn alive in front of him.

But I see it, the hatred in his eyes as he watches me. It's not a hatred directed at me though. It's the way I can see him internally reflecting the words back at himself that really gets me. I don't feel this through the blood bond, I can't. But it's a knowledge that simmers just below the surface of what connects us. I don't understand it, but it's something else. Something deeper, a thinner wire that runs directly from his soul to mine, uniting us and throwing me off at the realization of how deep our connection is.

"I don't believe you," I choke out. I don't need the blood bond to see the way he watches me. I don't need to feel his emotions in order to see them written so clearly in his tortured eyes.

"Well then," he straightens his spine, sliding his hands into his pockets and leaning away from me. "I'll just have to change that, now won't I?"

Great. Just fucking great.

CHAPTER TWENTY-ONE

Luna

I spend the rest of the evening in my room, stewing over my own thoughts and trying to make some sort of sense out of this fucking mess. Eventually, I'm going to need to talk to Stella and tell her everything. How the hell am I supposed to explain what I've learned? What we are? She's my full-blooded sister, that's the only thing I know for sure. Other than the fact that we were abandoned when we were too young to remember anything. My memories are filled with new families, foster homes, foster siblings, and social workers until I was seventeen and filed the necessary paperwork to get myself and Stella out.

I was never given the names of our parents, no one actually knew. We were left at Safe Haven—a small refuge establishment in the city—until we were collected and taken to the hospital for routine checks before finally being filtered through the system. Thankfully, our social worker kept us together, insisting that we needed to go as a pair. She was kind, but it never stopped my need for us to be out on our own.

No one claimed us.

No one wanted us.

I don't want you.

The words seem to be repeated over and over again, throughout my entire life.

"No one wants you. You're good for one fucking thing."

The memory from seven years ago bites at my mind, clawing its way up to remind me of that horrible night. It started out just like any other, I was walking home from Stella's apartment and I took a detour, a quicker route to get home because it was so late. I just wanted to get off the streets sooner, but what a fucking mistake that was. Ironic too, trying to stay safe only placed me directly in the line of danger.

One by one, the four faces of the men that night spring to life inside of my head. Only their eyes though, because they all wore black cloths tied around the lower half of their faces. I shut my eyes, forcing the memories back down where they belong. In the darkness.

Thankfully, I'm distracted and pulled out of that night as a light knock sounds from my door. "You can come in," I say, knowing it isn't Elijah. I don't really care who it is as long as it isn't him.

Stella peeks her head in from behind the door and stumbles inside. She's been drinking, responsibly of course, but she's always been a little partier. "Well hello there, sunshine," her voice is chipper and I immediately know that she's happy. In this little world she knows nothing about, with these people who are so much more than she realizes. She's happy.

I smile back at her, patting the side of the bed for her to sit. "Having a good time?" I laugh as she complies.

"Oddly yes, more so than I thought I would when I first got

here." She smirks, taking another sip from the red cup in her hand. "But you aren't, I can feel it. What happened?" She pulls my hands into hers and leans back against the headboard, getting herself comfortable.

"Far too much to explain to you right now, especially when you're drunk," I keep my tone playful. I'm too exhausted to break the news to her now. I know it won't make any sense, and I need her completely present to absorb all of it.

"I'm not that drunk, just a little tipsy," she singsongs, revealing the fact that she's most definitely more than tipsy.

"Another time, promise. I'll tell you everything. Is your new boyfriend wondering where you are?" I ask, trying to change the subject. Her eyes shine with a mix of disappointment and excitement at the mention of him.

"No, he's sweet and knows I'm out with my sister and her friends." Her eyes fall to our clasped hands and I know something is bothering her. It's etched in the worried lines creasing her forehead.

"All right, spit it out. What's eating at you?" I push.

She laughs, but it's a bitter, hesitant sound that has me instantly anxious. "I've felt weird all day. Like something's waking up inside of me," she's whispering and trails off with a laugh like it's ridiculous. But my heart rate kicks up to a quicker speed and suddenly, I'm terrified for what she could be experiencing.

"What does that mean exactly?" I ask, giving her hands an encouraging squeeze.

"I don't know, but it doesn't feel good, Lun. Something's wrong. Like I'm missing something important, like something's being taken away from me." She laughs again. She's nervous and I can tell that she's afraid I won't understand what she's saying. She doesn't realize how much I do though.

"Stells, I think we should talk about all of this when you're sober. I believe you, okay? I think I even understand you." I give her a weak smile, but she brushes off my serious tone, standing up from the bed abruptly. It's as if she's frightened to confront whatever this is. I recognize that painful part too.

"It's okay. I promise it's no big deal, it's probably just because I'm drunk honestly." She paints a fake smile across her wide lips and turns to head back out the door. "I'm going to head home. Esme is driving me so don't worry. I just wanted to say bye." She turns around again and hurries back over to me, placing a soft kiss on my head before opening the door to leave.

"You can stay, you know. Here. You can stay the night with me." I want her to. I'm pleading with her to sleep here for the night. I feel the need to be closer to her while she's going through whatever this is.

"In a house full of crazy men? No thanks, both Elijah and Nathanial are assholes. Sexy, beautiful assholes. But assholes all the same." She winks and waves her little fingers at me before closing the door behind her with a giggle.

I drop my head back against the wall and close my eyes, willing myself to fall asleep, praying that tomorrow I'll wake up and realize that all of this was a crazy, wild dream.

But as always, that's just wishful thinking.

CHAPTER TWENTY-TWO

Luna

I LAUNCH UPWARDS IN BED WITH A START, MY HEART IS hammering in my chest, my breaths coming out as gasps as I try to regain control over my lungs. Everything hurts, fucking everything. My chest aches and my limbs feel heavy as I try to stand up out of bed.

Something is wrong. Something is so fucking wrong.

Wars of conflicting emotions crash through me and I realize my bond with Elijah is fully open, flooding me with a mix of hatred, rage, arousal, needy desire laced up with even more anger. I don't understand it and I stumble towards the door as I try to regain my balance. Everything feels off and I fight the waves of nausea as they course through me.

Opening the door, I'm slammed with a wave of heat that swamps the room. More of that blazing anger that's tearing through our bond and surrounding me. Moans escape all too familiar lips and rip through my ears as I halt at the top of the staircase.

"Elijah, let's go down to your room," she begs on raspy breaths.

"No," his voice is tense, strained and different than how I've ever heard him.

"Do you want to wake up Luna? She's going to hear us." Sam giggles, she fucking giggles. That high pitched, how-exciting-we-might-be-caught, giggle. And in that moment, I want her to fucking die.

"Good. I hope she does," he groans in a deep, husky sound.

A disgusting, inky darkness overwhelms my mind as I take a step down. Then another step, and another. I move slowly, listening to the clear sounds of what could only be a blow job, a slight gag every now and then in between sucks. I see red, I feel rage boiling through me as I intentionally look over the railing and find them on the couch below.

He's facing the staircase. Literally facing me as he's sprawled out on the couch, Sam tucked neatly between his thick thighs, her bright blond head moving up and down. Up and down. Up and down.

His heavy green eyes are fixed on my own, that inky black haze seeping through them and darkening his shade to a rich, forest green. His hand grips the back of Sam's head as he urges her back down, his eyes still locked on mine, as if *feeling* me this angry, this jealous, has him even more turned on.

I fucking hate you.

I don't mean it, but in this moment, I feel it. In all of its dark and distressed glory. The toxic jealousy growing between us. It's a vine snaking up my waist and around my neck, inching tighter and tighter until I'm standing there as an empty shell of want and need.

Needing to touch him.

Needing to be near him.

Needing to hear his voice in my ears.

Needing to feel his breath in my own lungs.

Needing his heat, to calm this raging icy storm inside of me.

God, why the fuck is this happening to me?

Good. He whispers, through our bond and it shocks me as I stumble back against the wall. Clear as day, I hear his voice in my own head and suddenly I realize he heard my own thought about hating him too. He was responding to my own anger, owning and claiming it for himself.

Enjoy that.

Always do, mo dheamhan.

I turn with a bitter smile tainting my lips and work to slowly pull myself back up the staircase. I fight every urge blazing within me to run down and tear Sam off of him, fucking destroy him for what he's doing to me.

I enter my room and slam the door shut behind me before racing to the bathroom and turning on the shower. I twist the knob all the way to cold, surprising myself at the choice. Instinctually, I need something to warm me up, fucking anything to break through this freeze inside of me. But I choose the opposite and embrace the cold instead. I tear off my clothes, fighting tears the entire time, forcing them back even as I choke on them.

I step into the icy water and sink to the floor of the shower, pulling my knees tight up against my chest. Letting my head fall back as each droplet crashes like a frozen piece of hail against my eyes, my cheeks, my shoulders. I surround myself in everything that isn't Elijah. I force the heat away through the chilling water, focus my mind on anything but the moans Sam made as she sucked his cock into her mouth, refuse to visualize his dark green eyes as they watched me glaciate in front of him.

All too soon, everything warring inside of me slows until

only remnants are left over. I don't feel things nearly as strongly and I know he's finally blocked me out of the bond. It's the only bit of mercy he offers me, and I hate how much I cling to it. Savoring in the ability he has to push me away.

My body begins to tremble as the cold seeps into my bones. My lips and teeth eventually start chattering in my mouth. My skin looks paler than usual and I know, without even looking that my lips are starting to turn purple and blue at the corners. But I can't tear myself away, I'm addicted to feeling the opposite of what Elijah elicits inside of me. The ice comforts me in an empty, negligent sort of way that I crave in the midst of my hatred and anger.

At some point, I fall asleep, my head lilts to the side and the water continues to fall and coat my naked body, bringing the chill deeper and deeper until it's the only thing I can feel anymore.

———

"Luna! Answer the fucking door!" His rough voice shreds through me, but I'm far too exhausted to care at this point. I don't even attempt opening my eyes. I'm numb and at this moment, numb is the best place for me to be.

"Luna, I will break down this fucking door if you don't let me in," he seethes. I don't even have to see him to know that his throat is tight and veined with tension. His eyes are shut firmly, and his tattooed fist is slamming against the door to my bedroom.

Do it, I don't care.

Just like that, I hear the door splinter from the molding as he crashes through my room, immediately knowing where I am and rushing into the bathroom. His heat infiltrates my space, breaking through the wall I've frozen around me.

"No. Go the fuck away," I try to speak, but the feeling of ice on my lips has me faltering. I attempt to open my eyes, but my lashes are coated with frost. I don't feel the water raining on me anymore, as if it's turned off without me realizing.

What the hell?

"What in the—" he starts, but in an instant everything changes. I feel the water sliding down my skin again, still cold while all the previously frosted areas have completely melted. Almost as if they were never frozen to begin with.

I *feel* it, his sun burning into my icy walls and I hate it. I want him gone. But I need it at the same time.

I hear the sink turn on before he's at my side. He quickly turns off the water and lifts a hot cloth to my face. I immediately try to shove him away from me but he's quick halt my movements with a rough hold of my wrist. He's careful not to touch my skin with his own though, intentionally using the cloth as a barrier.

I try to stop him again, but I silently struggle against his hold until he releases me. He knows that I'll keep trying however, and patiently waits for my refusal before moving to take care of me again. After several failed attempts to stop him, I give up, not in weakness but simply because I want to get this over with so that he can leave. He starts with my lips and cheeks, slowly warming my skin so that I can start regaining movement.

I open my eyes slowly and find he's moved to sitting in front of me, in the actual shower. I'm naked, he's completely dressed but strangely enough, I don't feel a hint of embarrassment over it. What he feels through our bond is far more private than anything he could ever see.

The cloth works across my eyelids, moving lower and down my neck as he works my tight muscles without even touching my skin. I close my eyes again, wishing to be left alone but afraid of what I just found myself in. My body was coated in frost, practically immovable as everything within me slowed down while I slept. How could that be possible?

"What happened?" I ask quietly, too tired to express any kind of surprise at the situation.

"I don't know," he says truthfully. I sigh a bitter sound of frustration, never any fucking answers.

"I hate you," I whisper the words, and this time I open my eyes to watch him as I say it. His hands stop moving against my skin as he looks up to meet my gaze.

"Liar," he states.

"I wish I hated you," I say, my voice cracking just the tiniest bit and betraying me.

"That I believe."

Silently, he stands and steps out of the shower, crouching in front of the cabinet under the mirror to retrieve a towel. I turn my head towards him, the curiosity of what he saw when he walked in here eating me alive.

"What did you see?" I demand.

He's quiet for a minute, refusing to look me in the eyes.

"Don't hide this from me, Elijah. You owe me that much," I turn to face him more forwardly as he comes towards me. He bends and wraps the massive towel tightly around my shoulders before sliding his arms around my waist and legs and picking me up with ease. I let him, simply because my entire body feels like a sheet of ice and I don't think I'd be able to climb out of here on my own as it is. The sooner he drops me on my bed, the sooner he can leave.

In his arms, his heat envelopes me in a thick wave that drapes and wraps all around me. I can't fight it away while I'm this close to him, but I attempt wriggling a bit, so I'm not so tightly pressed against his chest. It mingles with my senses and throws everything off balance.

Or begins bringing everything back into balance. I push that thought away.

"It looked like everything was frozen in midair. The water, your body, everything. Your eyes were frosted over, your skin had water droplets that had frozen in place, the shower water had frozen as it fell," he waits a moment as he kicks back my covers with his foot and instead of lying me down, climbs in to bed with me in his lap. "And then it was gone. It was back to normal, everything falling and dripping exactly where it should be."

Confusion races through my mind. I want to get away from Elijah's warm heat, but I'm so distracted by what he just said that I have to focus on which aspect to tackle first. Gently, I push away from his chest but his heavy arms cinch around my waist, holding me against him tighter.

"No. You need to warm up, Luna. You've been too cold," his voice is hard, logical as he speaks, and it almost hurts more to be reminded that this is such a clinical exchange for him. I push harder, forcing my body away from his as I climb to the end of the bed and keep the towel wrapped tightly around me.

"I'll keep myself warm, as I've done my entire life." Truthfully, I'm freezing. It's taking everything in me not to shiver in front of him. But I don't want him to see how right he is, see how I fucking need him even when it's the last thing I want. He's casually resting against my headboard, one leg propped up while his heavy arms rest against his knee. His other leg is laying straight in front of him and part of me wants to crawl up right between those thighs and prove to him that he was never meant for fucking Sam. I swallow the lump in my throat and return my thoughts to what just happened in the bathroom.

"So, what do you mean, everything was frozen around me?" I push, he has to have some sort of answers.

"Fuck, I don't know Luna. I've never seen it before. Everything was frozen. You looked like you were covered in ice and then suddenly you weren't. Everything was normal again."

"How do you not know, Elijah? You're the Angel, you're supposed to know what the hell is happening to me," I lean forward unintentionally, out of frustration and a bit of fear at the fact that the one person who should have some answers for me, doesn't.

"You think I don't wish I had the solution for you? I do. But you have to give me some fucking time to figure it out, *mo dheamhan*." He drops his head back against the headboard and shuts his eyes, annoyed lines begin creasing his forehead.

"Fine, then tell me something else. What language are you speaking when you call me that?" I was getting some damn answers tonight whether he liked it or not.

"Gaelic," he doesn't even look at me. It's a simple answer for him to give, something that isn't too painful.

"Gaelic? You don't look Scottish," I say, tilting my head to the side to observe him. The slight accent makes sense now. It's just the barest hint of it, hardly noticeable. The tiniest smirk pulls at his lips. I can't stop the immediate swelling in my chest at that view.

"I'm Scottish and Armenian. My Armenian roots run deeper. I lean to that side. But you can hear the Scot in my voice sometimes." Still, his eyes are closed, but his hands are clenched into fists at his sides.

"If you're an Angel, how do you have any sort of nationality?" I edge a little closer to that barrier between us, threatening to force a tiny crack into who he is.

He's quiet for a moment, clearly wavering on whether he should entertain my questions or not. "They were called The Original Angels. Each one was created in representation of every nationality, every race. They are a varying depiction portraying the masses of humans. We breed and birth new

Angels. But we aren't raised with the traditional roles of mother and father. The children are raised in the community by everyone. I never had stereotypical parents, I simply had every mentor surrounding and developing me. But I did have Nathanial, we were birthed of the same donors."

No parents. Ironically similar to my own upbringing. Whether I had been a full Angel or not, I still would never have had a mother and father to call my own.

I respond with a quiet nod, absorbing these small pieces of vulnerability he's willing to give me. "Do you all speak English in Arcadia? Or do you have a native tongue?"

He glances over at me, his eyes search mine as a tick flickers in his jaw. "Enochian is our first language, it's referred to as the Celestial form of communication."

"Enochian," I repeat. "Is that what you and Nathanial use to communicate?"

"Have you ever heard Nathanial and I speak to each other in another language?" he asks sarcastically, his voice tainted with clear disapproval at my prying. Sucks for him, I'm not backing down just yet.

I tilt my head to the side and settle my hard gaze on him. "No, but that doesn't mean you don't speak it with him, asshole."

Elijah drops his head back and shuts his eyes again, clearly surrendering to my questioning. "No. We don't speak it. I haven't in many years until I bonded you." He sounds dismissive, as if it isn't a bigger deal but something subtly tugs inside of me and lets me know it is.

"When you created our blood bond?" I ask, suddenly anxious to know exactly what he said. I want to hear his deep voice as he speaks his native language, however it sounds rolling off his tongue. "Can you say it now?"

Elijah's eyes snap open and meet mine. I can already see

the sturdy refusal forming on his mouth before it cracks around us. "No."

"Why? You've said it around me once. Technically I heard it then."

"Drop it, Luna."

I'm silent, contemplating my next move when I decide to settle into bed before kicking him out, but I have another question I want to ask before he completely shuts down. I climb up next to him, still keeping space between us, and curl up under the blanket. I let the towel fall to the ground once I'm covered and turn on my side to face him. He doesn't look at me, seeming to already know that I'm about to push that personal barrier between us even further.

"Fine, then answer a different question." I pause, "How did you Fall?"

CHAPTER TWENTY-THREE

ELIJAH

I don't think I'm ever going to be able to escape this. This uncomfortable, uncontrollable draw I have to Luna. She's pushing me farther than I've let myself go, let myself feel in seven years. I hate it but I fucking want it, and her at the same time.

That bullshit with Sam earlier ate me alive. I fucking burned with such hatred for myself through that mess that I felt my body go up in flames at the sight of her coming down the stairs. I hurt her, far more than I ever should and the most fucked up part about it is that I don't regret it. I still feel like I needed to do it, to put us back behind those lines we need to divide us.

But I couldn't get off, the second she walked away, I pushed Sam off and shut down the bond. Sam freaked the hell out, obviously. But I couldn't finish, I couldn't hurt Luna like *that*. If she was sick and in pain from watching me get head from another woman, having an actual orgasm with someone else would be fucking destructive.

Now here we are, in her bed, in my home, while she pushes to once again to blur those lines I work my ass off to keep between us. I couldn't speak the blood bond verbiage to her in Enochian. It's too intimate, too sensual in this moment while she's naked. Gloriously, sexually, beautifully naked and right next to me. I'm forcing every single ounce of restraint I have to the forefront in order to keep my hands off of her smooth, creamy skin and focus on what could possibly be happening with her.

She was frozen, literally frozen. I saw it—fuck I felt it—that's why I had to rush in there and make sure she was okay. But then everything changed in an instant, and now I have absolutely no idea what could be happening.

"Please," Luna's soft voice breaks me out of my thoughts as her small hand lands over the thin cotton of my black shirt, covering my abs. "Tell me."

Fuck. Even through my shirt I can feel her touch, the mild spark that's beginning to erupt under my skin. My blood is boiling in desire for her, reaching up and urging hers to come and dance. I glance down at her hand and then turn to her, she's watching the connection too, a small crease between her brows form in confusion. I need to change the subject from what she's feeling, but I'm too selfish to take her hand off of me.

"I got involved with a couple of children who were in trouble," I spit the words out quicker than I intend, catching her off guard. Her eyes dart back up to mine, searching me for more answers.

"And you can't do that?" She asks, her hand staying still against my abs. My cock is rock hard at the simple touch and I have to subtly readjust my sweats so that she doesn't see.

"No. We can't interfere with humans. We can be present,

share our aura and instill peace in times of hardship or fear, but we can't directly interfere," I explain, the memories of that day still haunting me. I try not to think about it anymore, it was the beginning of so much destruction.

Betrayal, love, anger, hatred.

"What did you do?" I know she wants the story, but I don't think I can give it to her. It's too much, too personal for what we have to keep dividing us.

"Luna, it was a long time ago," I try to end the conversation, but her fist immediately grips my shirt tightly her in hand. An electric shock rushes through me at the action and I instinctively move to pull her hand into mine but stop at the last second, keeping my touch at bay.

"Don't shut down, please. I get it. Neither of us wants this, you've made that absolutely clear. But that doesn't mean we can't, I don't know, at least know each other. Give me something, Elijah," she pleads with me, frustration lining her voice and I can tell she's actually holding herself back from what she really wants to say. I'm pretty sure she has a few unkind words to speak, but she's working hard to placate me into telling her.

I can't help it, I fucking laugh. I laugh at the fact that I can so clearly see that she's pissed but is working to fake her way through it in order for me to give this to her. She leans away from me, removing her hand from my stomach and immediately, I feel the loss spiral through my chest.

"Why are you laughing?" she asks incredulously. I see the waves of shock in her eyes as she watches in astonishment.

"Because, you're trying awfully hard to get me to tell you what happened. Including hiding your anger in order to appease me." Fuck, I want her to touch me again. I'd even settle for her leaning a little closer to me, give me something to hold on to while I cross this fucking barrier I've created between us.

Her knowing smirk lifts at my accusation, clearly agreeing with me and not feeling sorry for it. "Tell me," she says again.

I sigh in reluctance and lean back, staring up at the ceiling of the white room. "Nathanial and I guarded the throne in Arcadia," I begin, and I realize I'm going to have to tell her how I knew Amelia with this story. I don't want her to know that part of my life, any part that includes Amelia but it's instrumental to my Fall. "Amelia was our close friend. She was in a lower class than us, but she observed humans. We had known her almost all our lives, grew up together. She knew Nathanial always felt for the human race. He was always trying to help other Angels, and comfort people when he could step in without getting involved. Nathanial has always had a heart for taking care of others. It's why he makes such an amazing doctor now in this life. But Amelia had seen something, a couple of kids who needed help. There was no other way around it, if we hadn't stepped in, they would have died. Nathanial couldn't say no and the two of them came to me. We knew it would end with us Falling, we were directly interfering with two lives." I keep going, refusing to shut down at this point. I've come too far. But I'm not giving her intricate details, just the vague recollection of why we Fell. "We thought Amelia truly wanted to help, but she had other plans designed around her own quest for the throne. Either way, we did end up saving the children and it did result in us falling."

I turn to look at her after several moments of silence and am immediately taken back by the tears welling in her eyes. I've never seen her cry, not even when she almost died at the hands of Amelia and Danner. I search her eyes with my own, absently opening the bond between us without even realizing it until her emotions flood through my system and I groan instinctively. She's hurting, for so much more than this cursed blood bond between us.

I feel her pain over what she saw happen tonight with Sam. I ache at the anguish she holds over her childhood. I perceive the connection and relation she feels to my story, as if it resonates with her on some level. I know what would help, what would comfort the both of us, but I refuse to ask for it. Her simple touch would bridge this empty longing between us.

But I don't realize that I've already done exactly that, asked for it without verbalizing it. Because suddenly her hand is back on my stomach, her thumb stroking back and forth across my abs as a single tear breaks through her lashes and falls down her face.

"It was worth it, right?" she asks and the oddest sensation floods through me. As if she's seeking forgiveness. Guilt rides through her mind like a deafening ocean wave. She asks for absolution as if I could give it to her, even though it isn't mine to give.

"Of course," I say, giving it to her anyway. Because I fucking can't deny her this. I feel the pain lancing through her chest and ripping at her heart.

She closes her eyes and slides down on the bed so that she's tucked up against the pillows and nestles closer to my side. "Thank you," she whispers as I drop my hand to the silky strands her hair. I can't keep away from right now while she's so vulnerable and in so much pain from what I did to her. It eats at me, like a vicious poison that I both deserve and crave to feel the sting over.

I lean over her just a bit and click the bedside lamp off before returning my fingers back to selfishly tangle in her hair. I know this is wrong. This is a disaster waiting to happen. I know it won't be like this tomorrow. I lean my head back and close my eyes, reluctantly succumbing to sleep before I sneak out of here in the morning.

"You give her important parts of you," Luna's quiet voice tears through the darkness. Pain laces her tone as it works its way up her throat. Immediately, I believe she's referring to Sam and I on the couch earlier.

"Not that," she quickly adds, as if she knows what I'm thinking. "Although that does hurt like a bitch."

"Lun—" I start, because I feel it. I literally feel the excruciating pain she experiences when she thinks about it.

"No. I'm not talking about that," her voice is firm, effectively shutting down that subject as she pauses before continuing. "You gave her your smile tonight. You never give that. I've hardly ever seen it, but tonight you gave her all of it," she finishes on a whisper and I'm taken aback by her declaration. I've never thought about something so simple being so important to anyone else.

She's right though, I never smile. I've been through far too much shit to have anything to smile about. But she's wrong about me giving it to Sam. I'm fake around everyone else, a false personification of who I need to be to keep everyone around me in check. I smiled in order to manipulate my own relationship with Sam, so that she's not second guessing or nosing into my blood bond with Luna. I smiled because I knew Luna was watching. I smiled because I knew it would show her a fabricated representation of something I had with Sam that I didn't have with her. I smiled for the exact reason she's giving me now.

And it hurts. It's fucking destroying me on the inside to hear her say that it worked. God, I hate how this has to be between us.

"Every single thing I do, is because I believe it's what is best for you, *mo dheamhan beag*." This time, I don't call her *my little Demon* with any bite in my voice. I use it as I always intend it, how I hear it in my own head, before I taint it with unrequited logic and agonizing disdain.

As a blazing claim, staking my place within her heart.

Making her mine in every way she should be.

My little Demon.

CHAPTER TWENTY-FOUR

Luna

IT'S BEEN THREE DAYS.

Three days since I had the little freeze up in the bathroom. Three days since Elijah finally opened up, even briefly, and told me about his Fall. Three days since I woke up alone after falling asleep tucked into his warm side. Three days that I've been frozen cold on the inside, trying to stay as close to him but as far away as possible as I seek out his heat.

It's getting harder to ignore this blood bond between us. It's a constant voice in the back of my mind, reminding me that I need him, shouting at me to claim him, dragging me back and then punishing me when I don't. But I can't, because Sam is around, and she's on my opposite shoulder, prodding me with every detail she can about their relationship.

The bond is settling deeper than my blood. He's in my DNA now, every fiber and cell in my body. He's made home in every space of my mind. Even the darkest places that I refuse to enter, he's somehow infused himself there too. When we're in the same room together, it's like my blood surges and sings for him, a siren trying to lure her prey with only the simple act of being present.

And yet, somehow, I don't think he feels it. Somehow, I believe this bond is different for me than it is for him and that's what makes everything so much worse. I don't understand how that could be possible. How does every inch of my body crave him like he's the only oxygen I can consume, and yet he hardly glances my way when I live in the same damn house?

"Nathanial and Stella should be coming over tomorrow." Elijah's deep voice surprises me. It's the first time he's said a word to me in three days. My head darts up as I watch him enter the living room. I'm lounging on the couch, trying to occupy my mind with a good book, but utterly failing at the attempt. Nothing distracts me from Elijah.

"Why?" I ask. I'm glad Stella is coming, thrilled in fact. I need to tell her about the Angels and Demons soon. I'm also a bit worried about what she confided in me a few days ago.

He takes a seat on the arm of the worn leather chair opposite me and crosses his ankles in front of him. My eyes fall from his face, admiring his sinewy arms crossed around his chest and the way his charcoal grey T-shirt clings tightly to his large frame. My eyes linger on the veins that can't help but display themselves against his intricate tattoos. My mouth waters at the idea of running my tongue along every dip and rise of his forearms, working my down to his wrist, his fingers, sucking one into my mou—

"Because I believe you need to train, and Nathanial thinks we should get Stella started as well seeing as she is your full blooded sister and also half Demon and Angel." His tone is clipped, and my eyes shoot back up to see his jaw tense, moving subtly as his teeth clench and unclench inside his mouth. Which draws my attention to the hard slope of his neck, his tan skin covered in sexual tattoos that practically speak to my blood on their own. I don't even know what they mean, they're swirls and sharp edges of dark lines that disappear under the neckline of his shirt. I can already feel how wet I am through my panties. My legs tighten together as I absently seek out some kind of fucking relief to this need. Observing his powerful neck brings me back to his chest, and back to those fucking arms that I so badly want to wrap around me. My waist, my thighs, lifting my legs and spreading me open for him so he can—

"Fucking hell, Luna. Pay attention." He stands and stalks to the other side of the room, putting a solid amount of distance between us. He scrubs a hand up and down his face, mussing the light stubble he has shadowing his jaw. God, that's fucking hot too. I wonder what that would feel like against my skin, in between my thighs and—

"Go." He says as a hard edge laces his tone. He lifts an arm and points behind me.

I turn my head to look at where he's indicating, confused when I realize he's already moving towards the guest bathroom.

"What? Why?" I ask as I stand to follow him. I round the corner and see he's crouched in the shower, twisting the knob all the way to the cold side.

"Get in." His voice is demanding, leaving no room for argument.

"Are you serious?" No way. No way is forcing me to take a cold fucking shower.

"Yes. You fucking need it, and I can't focus on anything when you're like this."

A thought crosses my mind as I make myself comfortable in the small space with him. "Like what?" It's my turn to demand something. And I want to hear him say it. I cross my arms under my chest, lifting and drawing his attention to my breasts as they spill out of the top of my loose tank. His eyes immediately fall but shoot back up before he completely succumbs to ogling them.

"I will throw you in this shower myself, Luna. And it won't be fucking fun."

"Say it and I'll get in." I lift my hands and slowly untie my hair, releasing it from the messy knot I had on top of my head. The long tendrils fall down my back and around my shoulders. I watch as Elijah's entire body tenses, his hands fisted at his sides as that tick in his jaw returns in full force.

I push him farther, letting my hands slip to the button on my jeans as I begin to undo them. Fuck, I don't know what has gotten into me but I'm losing my mind to the nearness of him. I'm losing myself to the tiniest bit of vulnerability he showed me the other night, begging to have more of it.

Before I realize what he's doing, he's shot forward, caging me in without even touching me as he backs me up against the cool wall behind us. His foot kicks back as he slams the bathroom door, shutting us alone and inside.

"Do you think I won't?" he lowers his voice to a deep growl before pausing. "When you're horny and wet and practically coming over the sight of me." His lips drop down to my ear as he whispers the words. I gasp in surprise at his crude tone, realizing now that I didn't truly expect him to be so blunt about it.

"Are you, Luna? Are you wet right now?" His nose pushes into my hair, dragging it behind my ear as he breaths me in. "I bet you're fucking soaked. Do you want me to fuck you?" He leans in closer, his body flush against mine as he rolls his hard cock into my lower stomach.

I whimper as my legs naturally part for him, inviting him further into my space. My head falls back against the wall as he rolls forward again, this time grinding against my pussy and creating that friction I'm fucking craving. I moan into the space around us and his lips fall back to my ear.

"Say it," he whispers, throwing my words back at me. But I stay silent, lost in the trance of how my body is responding to him. Consumed by the way my blood is alive and rolling under my skin. Gone to the delicious heat that infects me while he's so close.

"Say it, Luna." His voice turns hard and grates against my insides. He demands something and I have to obey, submitting to the dominance he barks out through his tone and language.

"Yes," I choke on the words, my breaths falling in and out in quick, rapid movements. "Yes, I want you to fuck me."

Finally, my body literally lights up now that I've said the words to him. My need being voiced to the one person who has every ability to give it to me. The one drug tailored exactly for me, my perfect preference in every single way is him. It's everything about him.

His head falls on a malicious laugh as he steps away from me, taking his heat with him. A sadistic smile pulls at his lips, but I notice the way it doesn't reach his eyes. Whatever this is, it's a front he's putting on and I feel my heart sink to my stomach at the realization.

"Not in your dreams, sweetheart." The casual words fall from his lips like daggers directed at my heart. Piercing through the thick lust I had fallen into and shattering the little world I had let myself create over the last few days.

"Get the fuck out," I spit at him, taking a step into his space as he glares down at me. His bright eyes are dark again, that evil masque worming its way into his features. "I said, get the fuck out!" I scream the words, shoving him back as I open the door and push him through it.

I slam the door in his face as uncontrollable rage radiates and consumes me. I rush towards the shower, turning the water to the hottest setting and stepping inside, fully clothed. I let it burn me, feel the heat as it stings my skin, branding me as a reminder that this is what it will always be between us. Something I need to stop forgetting. But God, deep down I know it isn't real. I know he's lying to my face. I can feel the way it hurts him to say the things he does.

And that's the fucking vicious cycle of it. The fact that I *know* it's not real. The pain I see in his eyes when he's cruel keeps me coming back to him time and time again. Refusing to give up on what I know we can have if he would just bend a little bit. Give a little back to me.

Suddenly, the overwhelming need to stake my own claim takes over. The urge to remind him that he can't lie to my face and expect me to take it consumes me. I step out of the shower, soaking wet in my heavy clothes and move to the door, yanking it open and stepping out. I stalk to the kitchen and find him hovering over the sink, chugging a glass of water as his back lifts and falls in heavy breaths.

"I'm not playing this fucking game with you," I grind out through my teeth and he swings around quickly, clearly not having noticed my entrance through his own anger.

I lift the hem of my shirt and pull it up and over my wet hair, letting it drop the floor with a thump. "You can't lie to me. I'm over it," I unzip my jeans, yanking the wet fabric down my thighs as it clings to me. "I'm not fucking stupid and you don't get to make me feel like shit for wanting you while you lie to my face." I step out of my jeans and unclasp my bra, letting it fall off of my shoulders and to the ground.

"Jesus Christ, Luna. What the fu—" He scrubs his hands over his face again, forcing himself not to look at me but surrenders as I slip my fingers under the edge of my panties and slide them, soaking wet, down my legs as well. I'm already aroused again, it's ridiculous. But my own anger mixed with the surprise and clear arousal in his blood devours me.

"No. Stop lying. If you don't want to do this, fine. But don't fucking lie about it. Don't be cruel to get your point across."

"I'm not doing this with you," he states again.

"You realize, I'm the one person you can't lie to, right?" I step toward him, relishing in the fact that he can't keep his eyes off of me. They roam my body as flames lick across my naked skin, the heat within him envelopes me and draws me even closer, so that I'm only inches away from him.

For a split second, I think I see actual fear in his eyes before he completely shuts it down and goes back on lock. He leans back, resting his hands casually on either side of the sink.

"Stop keeping things from me. Stop refusing to teach me about the bond. I'll train, no problem. I want Stella to train too. But we need to tell her the truth about what we are." His eyes are hard and black as I state my demands, but he nods in acceptance.

"Fine."

"I want Camden here too." I push, willing him to go past his breaking point and claim me for himself. "He can help Stella and I with our past, and he can help train us."

I pause, waiting, begging him to fight back about the Camden point. His eyes search mine briefly and I see the flicker of pain that I wanted to see, hoping this is the line he's going to draw.

"Fine," he states again and everything in me collapses at the yield.

He won't even fight for me.

"Fine," I repeat dryly and turn around. I walk out of the kitchen, leaving my sopping wet clothes on the ground behind me and go up to my room, locking myself in for the rest of the night.

CHAPTER TWENTY-FIVE

ELIJAH

I TOLD SAM TO LEAVE. I HAD TO. THINGS ARE GETTING FAR too complicated and hostile between Luna and I. Even I know when things are becoming too destructive for her to continue being a pawn in my fucked-up game.

She cried, she yelled, she even hit me. Because despite the countless times I told her I didn't want any sort of relationship, she had grown attached. She lived here for a fucking week, one week. It was clearly the right move to kick her out, because things were about to get a whole lot worse.

We have been training the girls over the last few days without explaining to Stella the reason why. We chalked it up to self-defense lessons but were now going to tell Stella the truth and Luna was losing her mind over it. Nathanial and I told her we'd be there, well Nathanial said he would, and with Nathanial always came Camden. And there was no way in hell I was letting Camden be the one to partner with my brother to tell Stella the truth. He had already spoiled that shit for Luna, stepping up and taking my place. I wasn't letting him take this.

Speaking of taking, Luna had basically stolen every ounce of the hold I had over her after the little stunt she pulled in the kitchen. I left the bathroom feeling like shit, but also feeling like I had finally made my point clear. What else did I have to fucking do to her? She was killing me by forcing me to destroy her.

But no, she won that fucking round. Catching me off guard in all her naked, sexual glory. The literal Goddess of my dreams, every single thing I could ever want, dangled directly in front of me while I was forced into rejecting her.

How had I had the strength to do that? I reminded myself of Amelia. I thought of Amelia breaking our bond seven years ago. I remembered the way I loved her before everything had gone to shit.

I thought about us fucking, Amelia and me. I thought about her naked body in front of my eyes. It was so fucked up, and I wanted to throw up everything in my stomach. I hated the reminder, hated the fact that had even been me at one point in my life.

But it was the single, only way I could find the strength to push Luna away. I was damaged. I was wrong for her. I had given myself to something so vile in the past, to someone so disgustingly evil, that I could never be whole enough for her. I wasn't the same man I was back then, when I first fell. I would never be him again and who I was now, wasn't good enough for her.

"So, spit it out, whatever the hell it is. I can tell you all are tense as shit and it's freaking me out." Stella's spitfire voice broke through my thoughts and I brought my attention back to the room in front of me.

Luna and Stella were nestled together on the couch while

they faced each other. Luna was nervous as hell, her foot bouncing constantly while Stella looked bored at the fuss everyone was making. I glance over, watching Nathanial in the corner of the room. He stood in the back, putting a distance between himself and everyone else while Camden stood level with me, encroaching on my fucking territory.

"Okay, I don't really know how to start this but—"

"We're angels. Fallen angels. You and Luna have Demon and Angel blood inside of you. You both are targets, that's why we're training you." I speak the words in a casual tone, spitting them out just like she wanted them to be.

All eyes shoot to me, a mix of every emotion warring on all of their faces. Camden looks amused, Luna is livid, and Nathanial is anxious for her response. Stella on the other hand, looks relieved. As if she was just given an answer to a question she has been yearning to ask.

"What the fuck, Elijah!" Luna shouts, rage bridging through the bond between us.

"Luna and I are bonded through blood. It's a long story, but it's permanent," I continue, ignoring Luna's death glares from the couch.

"Well, it's not necessarily permanent..." Camden's voice confidently breaks through the chatter and my heated gaze swings to him. Luna's does as well, as if he's offering another fucking answer she needs.

"We aren't severing the bond. That would be nearly impossible," I grit out, anger coursing through me at him even suggesting the option.

"Why?" he asks, like it's no big deal.

Because she's my Fated, you fuckwit.

But I can't say that, no one can know that except Nathanial. "Because she's half Angel and Demon. She wouldn't survive it," I say instead, and an eerie smile slips onto his face.

"That's true, there is a probable chance that you wouldn't, Lun. We simply don't know for sure how it would affect your mixed blood," he starts, and I hate him for using a nickname with her. "But I've been working on something, a medication to temporarily numb the bond between those who don't want the effects. It's rare that people find themselves in the situation you're in, but it clearly does happen. I want to help those people," he finishes, his cocky demeanor back in place as he speaks.

A bitter annoyance simmers in my chest, spreading through my limbs at his attempt to offer her an out, a way for him to claim her for himself.

"Wait, really?" she asks and the genuine interest in her tone is a sharp blade straight to my heart. But I've done this to her, this is what I wanted.

"Yes," he says, smiling at her. "It's not ready yet, but soon. I'll have it available for anyone who wants it."

"She doesn't fucking want it," I snarl, stepping forward and in between Luna and Camden. He doesn't even hesitate, he stands and steps up to me, squaring his shoulders with my own, a challenge clear in his eyes.

Fucking do it. I'll destroy you.

Luna jumps up from the couch, rushing to stand between us and places her hands flat on each of our chests, attempting to push us back. Camden shifts a few inches, giving her the impression that she's in control of him.

What the hell, Elijah? This is good news. I hear her words as they bounce inside of my head. I clearly dropped my block on the bond without realizing it.

My eyes fall to hers and search her, filtering her emotions as I try to find what she really wants. I shouldn't be surprised when I feel that she does, that she wants something to take away the pain. I can't fault her for that. But I also want to punish her because of it.

It's a trap. I whisper back, there's no way he can create something like that unless he's using dark magic.

She rolls her eyes at me and turns to face Camden, "Thanks, let me know when you figure it out." She turns back to me, "If it does work, we'll decide how and when to use it together. This is good, Elijah. We can have our own lives back. You can have Sam move back if you want," she's placating me. Telling me what she thinks I want to hear when in reality, it's every single thing I fear the most. She knows I don't want Sam. I've never wanted Sam.

Before, there was no choice. Even if I didn't want it, we'd be linked for eternity. I glance over Camden's shoulder to see my brother, confusion lining his features as he watches our interaction. He didn't know about this little side project either.

"Well, honestly, I have a thousand questions, but it makes sense." Stella breaks through all of our tension and stands, coming to join us in the center of the room. "Especially with you two, watching each other like you want to tear each other's clothes off every second of every damn day." She points to Luna and I and I instinctively take a step back.

I watch as Stella's eyes glaze over for a brief moment, Luna notices too and I glance over to Nathanial, hoping he may understand whatever is happening. But for a second, his eyes are focused on Stella's, laser sharp and unmoving as the same fog washes over him. Stella suddenly shakes her head, clearing the haze that had taken them both over.

"Wow, seriously. The sexual tension is like a fucking ocean. I'm drowning in it and I don't understand why either of you are refusing it. Especially for Camden?" She turns to look at him and Luna's eyes widen in terror. "You're cute and all, but you aren't bonded to her. Sorry, dude." She pats him on the shoulder and looks past to Nathanial. "You. You have fucking answers that you keep hiding from me and it's pissing me off. So come on, let's go train and you can fill me in." She turns on the heels of her dirty black converse and stalks out to the back patio, waiting on Nathanial to follow her.

Surprise and curiosity wash through me at everything she just said. Something is clearly going on with Stella and by the shock on Luna's face, she doesn't understand it either. Camden looks disappointed and pleased all at the same time and as I try to decipher his motives here, I notice Nathanial moving towards the front door.

"Where the hell are you going?" I ask, turning towards him.

"I'm leaving. I have other work that takes priority," he states plainly, like he didn't just witness or experience the strange interaction.

What the hell is going on?

Luna immediately jumps in, "But Stella—"

"She's fine," he growls out possessively at her and I can't help but reach forward and throw him against the wall for speaking to her like that. I hear her gasp behind me and feel the presence of Camden as he steps closer to her in protection.

Fucking dick. I'm protecting her.

"Shit. Sorry, I'm going," Nathaniel says, clearly confused by his own actions. I search his eyes, wishing we were alone so he could explain whatever is going on.

"Get your shit together," I whisper as I release him with a jerk, opening the door and watching him walk through it.

CHAPTER TWENTY-SIX

CHAPTER TWENTY-SIX

ELIJAH

I WATCH IN PURE AGONIZING IRRITATION AS CAMDEN stands behind Luna, his arm locked around her throat while he teaches her how to pull herself out of his grasp. She kicks a leg back, unsuccessfully trying to catch him off guard and he laughs at the attempt, making her giggle as well. A low growl is grating against my throat and rumbling inside of my chest.

"Jesus, why do you keep pushing her away?" Stella laughs beside me, watching Camden and Luna.

"For a lot of reasons," I state plainly. "Trust me, it's better this way."

"Maybe for you." She pauses, inhaling a deep breath as she continues watching them. "But not for her. You don't know what she's been through."

"What the hell does that mean?" I ask, glancing over at her. Stella watches them with intensity as Camden throws Luna forward and pins her beneath him. His arm grips her around

174

the waist as he lifts her on her hands and knees. A knot forms in my chest as it burns my skin and rips across my bones. I hate seeing her with him, in this position no less. He looks like he's about to fuck her right here in the open and I want to kill him for it.

"She's been rejected her entire life, by everyone important. Except me, obviously." Stella keeps talking but her breaths begin coming out in short, ragged intervals and that hazy fog begins seeping back into her eyes.

"By who then?" I ask, trying to continue our conversation and observe whatever is happening in Stella unfold. I want to split my attention between her and Luna but struggle to find balance. I need to focus on Stella for a moment in order to gain any sort of insight on her condition.

Her condition. Shit, I don't know what the hell is happening with either of these girls.

"Our parents. They left us when we were young. I was a baby and Luna wasn't even two. They dropped us off in the middle of the woods and somehow we made it to Safe Haven." Stella's words slam into my mind and cascade through my body like a swarm of ants, overtaking and inhabiting every inch of space available. "Luna doesn't know the first bit though. I found out when I started digging around for information on our parents. Luna has never been interested in knowing about our family until recently. She never wanted to know why they abandoned us."

I turn to step between Stella and her line of vision to Camden and Luna. She shakes her head again, bringing her hands up to rub at her eyes before meeting my gaze. I watch her as confusion lines my features. "When was this exactly? How many years ago?" I press, trying not put pieces of my life together that should have no relation.

"A little over twenty-five years ago. Luna is twenty-seven. It happened right before she turned two." I stumble backwards, bringing my hands up to grip my hair as I turn to look at Luna. Her body is flush against Camden's and I see the tension building between them. Camden's hand drops to her waist as he yanks her tightly against him. They're facing each other as his other hand falls to the back of her neck and grips her hair.

Oh fuck no. I turn back to Stella and see that she's fallen into her haze again as she watches them. I feel everything spiraling out of my control as I try to understand what must be going on with Stella and I try to stop myself from tearing Camden away from Luna.

It's not my place. It's not my fucking place.

But I can't. I can't focus on anything else as I watch his head dip down and move towards her. In a flash, I'm behind her, wrapping my arm around the other side of her waist and tearing her away from him. I pull her against my chest, feeling her small body mold perfectly with my own as a growl bursts from my throat.

"Stay the hell away from her," I say as I try to reign in the rage that's flooding my system.

"You don't have that fucking right," he throws back at me, standing straight without an ounce of fear as his eyes bore into my own.

"I have every right. She's my fucking Fa—" I begin, but quickly cut myself off, releasing her in the process as my eyes narrow on him. Thankfully, I don't think Luna notices the comment. She's too concerned with the fact that I intervened like this.

But this is all part of his plan, I can feel it. He's trying to gain something here, knowledge, understanding, I don't fucking know what. Although, I know he isn't good.

The smallest smile tugs at his upper lip and just as I'm

about to launch forward and charge him, Stella's voice booms behind me. "Come on, Camden! Take me to Michael's."

Luna looks confused as she turns to Stella and pulls out of my grasp, hurrying over to her. I take a few more moments to calm myself, watching Camden as he follows the girls.

Everything is falling apart and I have no idea if I've just told Camden that Luna's my Fated.

CHAPTER TWENTY-SEVEN

Luna

"MICHAEL?" I ASK AS I CATCH UP TO STELLA. SHE'S turning quickly, a light flush working up her neck as we move through the house to the front door.

"My boyfriend, remember? Honestly, I need a good fuck. You all are a massive nest of raging hormones." She doesn't even look at me as she steps out the front door, like what she's saying isn't completely different than how she would usually speak.

"Stella, what is going on with you? How does Camden know Michael? You know everything now. I'm sure you have questions. We can talk about what you told me before." I say, reaching out and grasping her arm in my hand.

Stella stops to look at me, but her eyes linger behind my head as Camden comes up to stand with us. "I've met him a couple of times," he says casually.

A heat flares in her eyes for a brief moment and for the millionth time today, I'm feeling confused and surprised at every single person's actions.

Stella looks like she's ready to tear everyone's clothes off.

Elijah is acting oddly territorial again.

Nathanial was distracted and frustrated.

Camden is the only one who seems to be his usual, determined self. He's the only one who takes what he wants, when he wants it. I can't help but admire that trait in him.

If only Elijah did the same thing, because he wants me, I know he does. Especially after how he acted today.

Her eyes meet mine, an odd gaze staring back at me. She looks unsure, confused, apprehensive, but then her face breaks out into a grin and she nods back at Camden, "Come on, lover boy. I need Michael." She turns and waves goodbye over her shoulder while Camden nods in apology and follows her out.

I stand at the open doorway, trying to sort through the sequence of the day, everything that was said, everything that happened. I watch as my sister and Camden drive away, supposedly to her new boyfriend while I'm left behind with more questions than answers. Stella was the one who was supposed to have questions, but instead it feels like she was reassured, like it solidified whatever she was already thinking.

Suddenly, a sharp pain lances through my palm, like my skin is splitting and tearing along the flesh and I cry out. I lift my hand, expecting to find a bloody mess but see nothing except healthy, clean skin. Confused at the fact that I still feel the sharp pain, I turn and race through house, searching for Elijah. I quickly realize that it has to be him. Somewhere, he's hurt, and I need to find him.

I run through the kitchen and see that he's not there. He wasn't in the living room and I actually don't know where his room is. Well, I know it's below, on the bottom level but I've never seen it.

I look outside and notice he's still out in the yard where we were training, holding his hand as he looks it over. I race out the doors of his kitchen and across the patio, down the stairs and into the lawn until I get close to him. I launch forward, attempting to pull his hand into my own when he steps backwards, his eyes hard with resentment.

"No," he spits out.

"Why not?" I shout, the anxiety and frustration of today eating away at my patience.

"Because I don't need you." His tone is disinterested, bored at my question.

"What the hell is wrong with all of you today?" I shout, throwing my hands up in the air. Elijah's eyes meet my own and I watch as that inky storm begins wading through him. "Actually, you know what? I don't give a shit what's wrong. You're going to teach me. Teach me how to heal you with the bond," I demand and step closer to him, eliminating the distance between us.

He's silent, watching me with anger and desire warring in his eyes. "No," he says again. But instead of stepping away, he moves closer. I feel his heat slowly surrounding me, snaking around my body and drawing me towards him.

I glance up to his hand and see the dark blood slide down his forearm. It's a mess, and as much as he may not want to admit it, he needs me. "How did you even do that?" I ask, searching the ground for something sharp when my eyes land on a shattered beer bottle. The pieces in my mind quickly fit together. I can see the way Elijah probably smashed the bottle and then cut himself open trying to clean it up. When I look back at him, the answer is clear in his face and I know I'm right.

"Should I ask Camden to teach me?" I say quietly, inching

towards that boundary I know will affect him. He growls in response, his lip curling back over his teeth as he leans towards me.

"He'll never be able to teach you what I can. He could never show you what I can," he bites out, his breath lingering along my skin as his lips come closer to mine.

"Then show me. Teach me, Elijah," I respond, lifting my hand and moving to take his injured one in my own.

"Wait," he says, stopping my movements as he slides his other hand into his back pocket and pulls out a small switch-blade. "Take this and cut yourself open."

My eyes shoot up to him in hesitance and a ruthless smile spreads across his soft lips. "You asked for it, little Demon." His voice is tainted with a toxic pleasure that both scares and arouses me. I want the challenge, and I'm turned on by the fact that he likes it even more.

I slowly lift my own hand, taking the knife and slicing it through the flesh of my palm. I make a deep enough cut that blood easily flows out and I hiss at the sting of the pain. My heart is racing, hammering against my chest in both excitement and tentative fear over what we're doing. The connection we're about to make.

"When you do this, it's best if you bleed in the same place. Like now, palm and palm. It's not always feasible, but when you can, the healing process is quicker." He lowers his hand so that I can see where he's cut. His skin is flayed and pulled apart in two thick jagged lines running from the middle of one finger and down to the base of his wrist. Exactly where I felt the pain in my own hand.

I'm quiet, awaiting further instruction when he takes a deep sigh and continues, "Now place your hand on mine, blood to blood." I do as he says, laying my palm against his as I feel the warmth of our blood burn between us. At first, I'm surprised by the shock of it and jerk my hand away, looking up to him for confirmation that this is right. He nods, his muscles tense and his jaw hard as I return my hand to his.

He wraps his thick fingers around my small wrist, and I follow suit, locking our hands together in what I realize is the first time we've ever intentionally touched, skin to skin. In an instant, I watch as my blood turns black against our flesh and mixes beautifully with his deeper red. But worry courses through me as I observe, unsure if this is how it's supposed to happen.

"It's okay. It's black because of the Demon in you," he says, his voice turning just the slightest bit softer. My eyes are trained on where our hands are joined but his eyes stay concentrated on me. I can feel his gaze burning into me from above. "Focus on our blood, on the feeling of our bond. You know what it is, seek out that connection and draw from it."

I do as he says and in an instant, everything starts changing. Suddenly, I feel the actual merging of our blood as it comes together. I feel the way his body pulls strength from mine, from every cell in my being, to heal him and I immediately become addicted to the pleasure of it.

"When you bonded me," I start, my voice shakes with the heated feelings erupting inside of me. "Tell me what you said."

"Why?" he asks, a slight flicker of annoyance laces his voice as we propel through this new connection.

"Because I need to hear you say the words. I want to know what was so powerful, so influential that it created this between us." Ever so slowly, the bond in our blood continues pushing through my veins. It stretches through my body, lingering in places before infecting the next.

Elijah sighs in frustration before he speaks the words. His voice drops into a dark, throaty sound that I actually feel vibrate through my blood.

"*Ol, Elijah, seraphim Angel c arcadia, allar ol cnila de yours g sibsi.*

ol darbs de a etharzi c ge congamphlgh ca el."

It's impossible, I simply can't restrain the moan that slips from my lips as he speaks in a language that strangely feels so intimate. "What does it mean?" I ask, my voice falls out in breathless intervals.

"I, Elijah, Seraphim Angel of Arcadia, bind my blood to yours in covenant.

I submit to the harmony of our souls as one." This time, his voice his harder, stronger as it courses through the air around and us and directly links to the blood bond between us. My heart rate immediately increases, hammering against my chest as my blood suddenly experiences an electrical wave that pulses through me in thick, needy throbs.

I suck in a sharp breath and Elijah's other hand darts out. He snatches my wrist in his as he flips my palm upwards and joins our bodies at two places. His fingers circle around me while his thumb begins sliding back and forth across my sensitive skin, adding another sensation to the chaos that's overtaking my body.

It's compelling and potent, the words he spoke when he bonded me and the same words he says now feel as if he's initiating it all over again. I close my eyes, succumbing to it. Our bodies begin harmonizing together, seeking each other out. My icy frost to his blazing fire. They mingle and unify in a perfect alliance, drawing out each other's strengths and supporting the weaknesses.

My skin begins lighting up like a forest on fire, my blood continues to heat and desire pools in my lower stomach. I need to be closer, to feel his hard body against my softer one.

So, I give in. I step toward him and bring us flush together without opening my eyes. My chest rises and falls with each labored breath, my tight nipples graze against his chest in a way that elicits an uncontrollable whimper from my lips.

"Luna," his voice is rough, and I discern the pain warring through our bond. I feel his desire as it overtakes me. His fingers trail up from my wrist, slowly sliding against my soft body and up towards my elbow. They work over my sweet skin, burning his touch into my flesh like a brand.

Claiming me, marking me.

"Is this..." but he knows what I'm asking. If this is normal for people who are bonded. Because this can't be, it feels like too much, even for what I imagine a blood bond could create.

"No," he says as his lips brush the shell of my ear. "It's not normal."

I open my eyes and look to his injured hand as surprise washes through me. He's completely healed. Our skin is clean of blood and wounds, both our bodies having pulled the strength from each other to fix us. I look up to his bright eyes as they watch me with interest. His rough fingers trail up to my shoulder and across my exposed collarbone. His touch is a blazing fire warming me up where I've frozen over, working his way into the parts of me that I never intended anyone to enter. My eyes fall to his lips as his heated breath brushes my skin. My lips part instinctively for him and I crave them on my own more than anything.

"Ask for it, *mo dheamhan*. And I will give it to you. Right now, I can't deny you anything." His dark, husky voice drags across my ears, infecting me with lust and arousal that coats my inner thighs. I'm soaked, fucking disastrously wet and needy for him.

"No. I want you to want it too," I say, begging him to give it to me. I want everything from him, I want him to take it from me without having to ask for it.

"If you put as much effort into reading our bond right now

than you do into trying to piss me off, you'd already know how much I want it," he whispers as his hand grips the back of my neck and tightly pulls me toward him.

"Then take it, Elijah. Take what you want from me." I reach forward and slide my hand under the hem of his shirt, craving to feel more of his skin in any way that I can. A low snarl rips from his mouth at my words and he brings me closer to his face, our lips brushing against each other as he speaks. "Be careful what you ask for, *mo dheamhan*, because I'll take everything. And I won't be gentle about it."

Instantly his lips come crashing to mine, devouring me with every ounce of strength he has. But at the contact, something else wakes up inside of me and I give it back to him just as hard. Our bodies and blood are feeding from each other, pushing and pulling with an inconceivable wave of power as we fight to find our balance.

My mouth opens for his, inviting him in and he pushes forward without hesitation. His large hand grips my thighs as he lifts me and throws us both to ground, him landing on top as he rolls his hips into my own. His cock is hard, thick, and long as I feel him against my wet pussy, grinding into me as I open myself wider for him.

His teeth snatch my lower lip in a bite as he pulls and sucks it into his mouth. My head falls to the ground on a moan as I reach down to rip his shirt up and over his head. He lets me, sitting up just briefly as he reaches behind himself to pull it the rest of the way off. My eyes glaze over at the sight of him. His pierced nipples and dark tattoos, a mix of Angels and Demons warring across his muscular chest. His abs are covered as well, but I see every line and dip of his muscles, letting my gaze fall lower to the unmistakable V that leads under the black band of his briefs. But it's not enough, I need more of us together, more of our flesh crashing and uniting as one.

"Elijah, I need—" I don't know how to explain it. I don't know exactly what I'm craving for other than having him deep inside of me. But it's not just that, I need more of this connection that tethers us together.

"I know what you need, Luna," he says as he grasps the bottom of my own shirt in his hand and tears it over my head in one quick motion. He immediately reaches for my bra, hastily unclasping it and pulling it off as well. "I'm the only fucking one who knows what you need."

I moan as his lips fall to my right nipple, it's hard and aching for him as well. He pulls it into his mouth on a rough suck, but his tongue circles and licks until his teeth graze the tip before biting.

"Fuck, holy shit," I breathe out, harsh and ragged as more of our skin comes together. His head comes up as his lips claim my mouth again, his tongue demanding entrance and taking everything I offer him.

It's this, the fact that we're coming together even more that does me in. Both of us baring our flesh that unravels me. Our bodies find the addiction we've been searching for in each other. "Tell me what it feels like to you," I ask, my voice thick with desire. I need to know it's the same for him.

"You're cold," he says harshly, and immediately worry crashes through my mind. I'm blazing with heat for him. "But I'm too hot. I'm always too hot. It's an achy heat that consumes me while I search for anything to cool me down." His lips pull from my mouth and drop to my ear as he sucks my lobe between his teeth. His movements slow down entirely while his hand comes up to grip the base of my throat. His mouth works deliciously over my ear.

"But it's different for you, isn't it? You're too cold. You need my heat to keep you warm. Without it, you're freezing." His voice is a whisper, demanding my submission with every word he speaks. "Tell me I'm right."

"You're right," I say and the grip he holds on my throat tightens in a dominantly gentle way. I roll my hips up to meet him as his other hand moves between us. His thumb grazes across my nipple, sore from his previous assault. He laughs against my skin and lust rushes through me, wave after crashing wave in need of him.

"I've imagined having you every single night since I met you," he whispers, his lips moving down the column of my neck while he holds me still by my throat. "I've imagined taking your sweet pussy as mine. Licking and tasting you until you're screaming my name."

His words work through me, drawing moans and whimpers from my lips as if he was actually doing what he was saying. "But first I'll spread your legs wide open, little Demon, and watch you touch yourself before taking you myself."

"Fuck, Elijah. I'm going to come," I say, high on the sensual connection I'm pulling from the bond. Just his voice and his words have an orgasm twisting inside of me.

I've never felt anything like this before. Our bodies work together and worship each other as if we were created specifi-cally for the other. There's a deeper tie here, a powerful substance that serves us more than the blood bond ever could. I feel it working its way up, from our very souls while it gets ready to spill out of us.

"Not yet, Luna. You'll come when I tell you to," his hand leaves my throat and moves to my breasts as he takes my other nipple deep into his mouth. I arch my back, begging for more of his filthy words and dangerous touch.

One hand rolls my sensitive tip between his fingertips, pinching and pulling in a mix of pain and pleasure. His tongue traces circles around my other nipple, teasing me, tasting me until I'm writhing below him in achy need.

"Please," I say and immediately his teeth graze and nip, biting and then soothing in response to my request. His heavy body moves over mine, our hips in sync as he dry fucks me into the ground. He's hard and rough, devouring me in the exact way I want him to. It's like he already knows me, like we've already been here before even though we've never touched.

He speaks filthy words that twist up my insides. His teeth pull at my skin in every way I could want from him. His hands move across my body in deprived and painful grips that leave me whimpering in untainted pleasure. Every single thing he does has me seeking more but also leaving me the most satisfied I've ever been.

One of his hands dips lower as he slides it between my legs, feeling my pussy through the thin material of my pants. "Fuck, you're so wet, Luna. So fucking sweet," his mouth moves up to my jaw as he bites and nips down my throat. Gripping the waistband of my pants, he yanks them down enough to work his hand up against my lace panties. He drags a finger through my slit, feeling me through the delicate fabric as I try to grind against his hand.

"That first night you were alone. I could feel you getting off, feel you coming while you touched yourself," he whispers. "Tell me, were you thinking of me when you came?"

"Yes," I say, reminded of the fact that he knew. He groans into my neck as he pulls my panties aside, sliding a finger inside of me as I cry out. God, even his fingers are thick and long, filling me as I arch my back off the ground.

"Christ, you're tight. Cool even where I thought you'd be warm. You were made for me, Luna. Only for me," he pulls his finger from inside me and slides it up, taking my wetness and bringing it up to my clit in tight, destructive circles.

I can't think. I can't focus. All I can feel is the chaotic integration of our souls as they crash and connect with each other, begging and seeking, giving and fulfilling everything they crave from the other.

"I need to come, Elijah," I moan as I open my eyes and look between us, watching his tattooed fingers play with my bare pussy. I can see how wet I am from here and I watch as he pulls his finger out of me and lifts it to my mouth. He trails it against my lower lip, coating my flesh with my own arousal until I open up for him and take him inside of me.

"Taste yourself on my skin, feel your blood in my body until you know you only belong to me, Luna. *Mo dheaman beag*, and I will let you come." His voice is a command and my body's only choice is to listen and submit to his dominance. I run my tongue up the length of his fingers, tasting my wetness on him and pulling it into my own mouth. I moan, writhing and losing myself to the feeling of possessiveness he's engulfing me in. But also, to the claiming I put on him by having myself on his skin, putting my own blood into his body. It runs both ways. Elijah may be a distant prick, but he's mine and no one can claim him the way I can.

I sit up slightly, bracing myself on one arm while I slide the other around his neck, gripping the base of his head while my fingers tangle in the longer strands of his hair. I take his mouth with my own, sucking his tongue into me as our teeth clash and we consume each other. "Then you are mine as well, Elijah. My Fallen Angel, my addiction. My fucking obsession," I tug his hair harshly as he groans into my mouth and I brutally bite his lower lip. One hand grips my waist as his fingers dig into my flesh and I fall back to the ground, arching my body in offering to him.

"I could never be anyone else's," he grinds the words out as if they're difficult to say, but true none the less and then his finger slides back inside of my pussy. He moves deep inside of me as he pushes in another finger, stretching me and filling me while moans and cries fall from my lips. He fucks me with his hand, alternating between sliding in deep and then pulling out to pinch and circle my clit.

"Fuck, Elijah, God. I'm so close," I say in a breathless voice. My legs fall wide open for him and he grips the back of my thigh with his other hand as he lifts it up and spreads me even farther.

"That's right, Luna, this is all for me. Your voice, your moans, your wet pussy, your aching body, your fucking blood. It's all for me." He's pumping inside of me. I hear the sounds of his flesh moving inside of my wet core and even that has me even more turned on.

"Yes. Yours," I choke out, but I'm so wound up that I can hardly speak.

"Come, Luna," he says, and he dives down to hungrily take my mouth with his. His hand leaves my thigh and grips my throat as he holds me tightly for him while he fucks me even harder with his other hand and grinds his cock against my pussy at the same time. Fucking me dryly with his hard length and oh so fucking wetly with his thick fingers.

And just as he demands it, it breaks within me. This raging orgasm that crashes through on a loud and disastrous wave of emotions and tightly coiled desires snapping inside of my body. I've never came like this, never experienced anything remotely like it. It puts me on another planet while I ride the orgasm out on his hand as he continues to slowly fuck it through me.

I open my eyes to meet his and at first, I see the relief he's feeling at finally giving into this need for each other. I can feel it through our bond that's currently flowing wide open and feeding off of our connection. But suddenly, everything changes in his eyes and I feel the shift as it starts closing off between us. My body fights it, pushing back at him while he tries to force me out of the bond. But his eyes dart upwards, looking behind me as everything begins crashing around us.

Suddenly, I hear myself, words I'm not actually saying but have said before as they boom in the space around us. I'm crying, whimpering and begging as memories begin flooding the yard and instantly, we aren't at Elijah's home anymore. We aren't outside behind his house in the early evening.

We're in an alley in the middle of the night, in the city.

My heart begins hammering uncontrollably in my chest as Elijah sits up and frantically looks around us. I lean up on my elbows, not caring that I'm still naked, but searching for whatever is happening. We're literally sitting inside of my nightmare, living it as if it were happening all over again. It surrounds us in everything. The sounds, the vision, all of it as if we were really there. I can't see myself, but I hear my words as they spill out behind me. Elijah's eyes are wide with rage and pain as he watches, and I know he can see it all as it happens.

"PLEASE, NO. STOP. DON'T DO THIS," I BEG, TEARS FLOODING *my eyes as I'm shoved to the cement below me.*

"Shut the fuck up," one dark and masculine voice shouts as I feel his hard body come crashing against my back. His heavy hand holds me down while his friend helps him rip my jeans off of my hips and down my legs.

"I'm begging you, please let me go. I won't tell anyone," I cry, but the taste of gravel seeps into my mouth as my face is crushed to the ground.

"You can beg, baby girl. But it's not changing this. You're wrong. You shouldn't be here, shouldn't be allowed to exist. You're no good for anything but this." Another man crouches in front of me, bringing his face into my line of vision. He's wearing

a black cloth around the lower half of his face so I can't recognize him. All I can see are his piercing black eyes as they scorch through me, ripping me apart while his friends come at me from behind.

I shoot upwards and slam my hands around Elijah's ears so he can't hear them. So, he can't hear me. I never wanted to tell him about this, let alone have him see it for himself. I don't understand what's happening but it's everything I could ever be afraid of coming to light.

His eyes fall to me in excruciating pain as he grips my hands tightly and begins to pull them away. But he sees it, the terror in my eyes while he's experiencing this. He can feel it inside of me, so instead, he holds my hands tighter against him and keeps his eyes focused on mine. Intentionally supporting me. Deliberately not invading my privacy, even if it kills him not to know what happened to me.

Tears spill through my lashes and coat my face as everything continues behind us. I'm sobbing, uncontrollably and his breaths are coming out in ragged heaves as he trembles with rage in front of me.

Suddenly, everything shifts again and changes. We aren't in the same alley, but we've moved to another. It's still dark, and I can feel in my blood that it's near the same area that I was raped.

Only this time, I'm watching Elijah as he races through the city.

CHAPTER TWENTY-EIGHT

ELIJAH

WHAT THE FUCK IS GOING ON.

I'm destroyed, ripped apart at what I just saw happen to Luna. It was like I was living that moment with her. That horrible, agonizing night where she was violated and wrecked by four men that I now want to brutally kill with my bare hands. I crave their blood, I need their cries, I demand every single thing I can take from them for what they did to her.

But now we're living my nightmare and I know there is some tragic connection between the two. Luna's hands have fallen from my ears as she watches over my shoulder this time. I instinctively know she's seeing everything I've kept hidden away unfold in front of her, just as it did for me a few moments ago.

I'm running, I know exactly what moment this is. I'm searching the streets for the cries of the woman I heard just moments earlier. I'm looking for the man I heard grab her off the street and throw her to the ground. This is all just minutes before I'm torn apart by Amelia breaking our bond.

Fuck, Luna's about to see all of it. She's about to find out that I've been bonded before, to the one person who tried to kill her.

"Please, no. Stop. Don't do this."

Shit, shit. Fuck. Realization slams into my mind and I see it register in hers as well. Her eyes dart back to me, wide and fearful and understanding. Both of our nightmares start with the same words, in the exact same way.

I was looking for Luna that night, without even knowing her. And if what her sister told me earlier is true, then I've searched for Luna twice in her lifetime. She's been connected to two very important parts of my own.

SUDDENLY, I HALT MID RUN, SLIDING TO A STOP AND FALLING *to my knees on the cold ground. Amelia is in front of me, a manic smile gliding across her lips as she stands at the end of the dark alley. Danner stands behind her, his hands crossed tightly around his chest as he smirks.*

"Amelia, I need to go. Help me find her, she needs us," I place my hand on the ground to stand back up, but Danner uses his ability to shove me back down. I feel the weight of his invisible force on my back, holding me in place while my mind scrambles to create some sort of logical answer to this.

"No, Elijah. We have work to do," her voice is sickly sweet and terror rips through me.

No, no, no, no.

Instinctually, I feel her decision through our bond before she's spoken it out loud. She isn't hiding it from me, she wants me to feel it.

"Don't do this, Amelia. This is wrong and you know it. We

should be together," I cry out as I meet her icy gaze with my own.

"You no longer serve my purpose, Elijah. I'm sorry, but this is the right decision. I don't need you anymore," she lifts her hand, a long black dagger resting against her clutched fingers as she brings it to her own chest.

"Amelia, fuck! No. You belong with me. I love you," I beg her, because I'm fucking destructing inside of myself. My body is being called elsewhere, to someone I don't even fucking know who needs my help. But my mind is glued to this moment, logically convincing myself to stay rooted here. I have to fight for my bonded, it's the right choice to make, even if I'm being strangely drawn elsewhere.

"I don't though, I belong with Danner. I choose him, sweet Elijah. I'm sorry to hurt you in the process, but you were always a means to an end for me." The words rip through me as I try to remember every conversation we've had, every moment we shared since we were kids. This can't be true; I refuse to believe it.

"I sever this bond with Elijah, Seraphim Angel of Arcadia above. I sever the ties of blood between us and reject the unity of our souls as one." She speaks the English translation of our Enochian words loudly as she infects my body with the toxic elimination. Her hand comes down as she slices the blade across her chest, over her heart and effectively destroys everything we shared.

I yell out in pain, over the injury as it rips through my own chest, but also at the pain of the bond being torn apart. The metaphysical strands that had interwoven with each other rips and shreds throughout my body. I feel her being pulled from me as she crashes to her knees in the same pain I'm experiencing. But she has Danner, who immediately pulls her into his arms and comforts her while I begin falling apart at the seams.

I look down, watching my own blood soak through my shirt and spill over the ground beneath me. I feel the strength leaving my body and exhaustion overwhelming me while my mind strays to the girl in another alley nearby. Even in the midst of my destruction, I'm looking for her. In my mind, my body, I'm seeking her out.

But Danner catches my attention as he stands and lifts Amelia in his arms. She's collapsed into him and he turns away from me. He takes her with him as he stalks in the opposite direction, leaving me alone as I bleed out in the abandoned space.

My vision goes black and every bit of energy I held escapes my body. I fall to the ground as the excruciating pain engulfs me and takes over, leaving me to die alone as the cries of an unknown girl surround me.

INSTANTLY, EVERYTHING SHIFTS AGAIN AND WE'RE BACK IN my yard. We're on the ground, still half naked and I'm crouched above Luna as everything clears around us.

She moves first, immediately pushing herself backwards as she rips her panties and leggings back up her thighs. She turns over and searches the ground for her shirt and bra, finding and clutching them up against her chest to cover herself.

"Luna," I urge, shooting forward to reach her. Any part of her, anything she'll let me grasp on to.

"No, don't say anything. I can't—fuck. I can't process anything right now." She stands, turning quickly and moving to hurry back inside. I sit back on my legs, a catastrophe of different emotions running through me. I bring my hands up to my head, pulling at my hair as I try to understand what the hell just happened.

"You were bonded to her?" Luna's voice cracks around the yard and I immediately look up to find her stalking back towards me. I feel the betrayal burning through her. I feel what she believes is now completely false between us, just another blood bond like any other.

But she doesn't know how wrong she is.

"Yes," I say quietly, unsure of how to handle this.

Tears fill her eyes as she fights to let them fall. She hates crying, I haven't known her long, but I know this.

Actually, I'm now realizing that I may have known her all her life.

"So, everything we just did. Hell, everything I felt. Everything I thought you felt, it's the same as it was with her." Her voice cracks, betraying the strength she's struggling to portray.

I'm silent. I don't know if I should tell her about being Fated. That fact may fix the impending disaster that's about to unfold, but it would complicate things going forward. She would be in danger. If it became known that we were Fated, she would never be safe, and I could never live with that.

She laughs, a bitter, painful sound as she takes my silence as agreeing with her. But I'm not, nothing with Amelia could ever begin to compare with how I feel being connected to Luna.

"Luna—" I start, deciding to try and explain myself to her.

"No. Shit, no. You loved her. Do you still love her? Is that why this has been so fucking difficult for you?" she asks. The struggle to keep her tears at bay finally fails and I watch as streams begin coating her cheeks. Pain lances through me, this started out so well and now we're falling apart.

The hardest part about all of it though is wondering if this is how it should be. Wondering if this is actually better for her in the long run. Because at the end of all of this, she would be better off living her own life on her own terms.

"No. I don't love her. That, I can promise you." I force the truth out at her question. No matter what happens, I can't have her believing I could ever love Amelia like that. How could I when every ounce of my being has always belonged to Luna?

"Don't lie to me, Elijah. I'm the only person you can't fucking lie too."

"Luna. Listen to me, use the fucking bond to your advantage and read it. I'm not lying to you. I don't love Amelia," I grit the words out as frustration and anger over this entire situation builds inside of me. I stand, reaching for my shirt and pulling it over my head.

Stepping closer to her, I slide my fist through her hair and grip the back of her head so she can't move away from me. "I don't know what the hell just happened. I don't know how we saw what we did. I have no idea what it fucking means. But we both went through that shit, clearly on the same night and at the same time. We just went through it again, right now. Together." She whimpers in my hold as she closes her eyes, refusing to acknowledge it on her own.

"When we figure it out, we can work on living our separate lives, even with the bond. We can focus on separating ourselves and you can go back to your own life." I pause as her eyes snap open and shoot back up to mine, realization crashing into her at what I'm saying. God, it's tearing me apart, but I've already blocked her out of the bond, and she knows it.

"What—" she starts but I cut her off with harsh tug at her hair.

"No. This doesn't change anything. We aren't doing this. The only good thing that came of this is having some sort of idea at what our potential ability is together, maybe we can use it to our advantage in living apart."

"Wait, you're saying we did that? We created that?" she asks, her eyes frantically bouncing between my own while her brows crease in disbelief.

"I think we did, somehow we managed to pull our darkest

secrets out of each other and alter the space around us." There's no use in keeping that part from her, she experienced it all for herself.

I release my grip on her with a gentle shove backwards, forcing distance between us. She stops herself, standing still as her eyes fill with pain and rejection. She hates me, but she also craves me in the same breath.

Instead of turning and running away, she steps forward and back into my space, pushing herself at my boundary like she always fucking does.

My hand shoots forward and grips her jaw, holding her back while my body fights the instant need rising in me at simply touching her. "No," I grit out through clenched teeth.

"Yes," she bites back, trying to push against me. But my strength is no match for her, and she doesn't make any progress.

"Fuck, Lun. No." I growl, tightening my hold on her in both torment and desire. God, I want to drag her lips back to mine, make her come against my fingers again, make her come on my cock as I spill inside of her and mark her as my Fated. "I don't fucking want you." The lie burns my throat as it painfully claws its way out. It poisons her mind and her heart, and I watch in silence as it eats her up.

Misery tortures me, feeds me and then punishes as I hurt her. I can't stop it. I can't fix it. Because this is how it has to be. She may be the Demon, but I'm the Devil disguised as an Angel. Eternally created to ruin her in every way I can get my filthy hands on.

CHAPTER TWENTY-NINE

CHAPTER TWENTY-NINE

Luna

I'VE LOST COUNT OF THE DAYS. HONESTLY, I DON'T REALLY bother trying to tell them apart anymore. I don't sleep well, because now that my body knows what Elijah feels like, it refuses to settle for anything less.

I'm constantly cold. I've never noticed how cold I was until I experienced my true heat for the first time. Every once in a while, I can convince Elijah to at least sit near me on the couch so I can catch a couple hours of sleep while he watches TV or reads a book. He never reaches for me, never seeks out my own touch, and sometimes I wonder if I'm the only one going through withdrawal. It was one hit, one fucking hit off of him and I'm addicted.

Believe it or not, I still have my job. Although I'm rarely scheduled. I think Frannie knew that I was going through something I couldn't really explain. So, we talked and she keeps me on for call in shifts or busier events. At those times, Elijah does exactly what he said he would do. He goes to the Capital, where I still haven't been, and gets some work done while I finish my shift. When I clock off and step out of the little coffee shop, he's always waiting on the edge of the street, his eyes on me while I walk towards his big Wrangler and climb inside.

We generally don't talk. I take advantage of the nearness of him and fall asleep. Sometimes, if I'm lucky, he'll carry me inside and up to my room, tucking me under the heavy comforter. Unfortunately, he always sneaks out before I have the chance to ask him to stay.

Tonight, I'm thankfully distracted by my wild sister, who has turned from a sassy bohemian pixie, to a free-spirited sexual goddess. I don't know what has gotten into her, but she's become someone new. She's incredibly confident, in love with her curvy body, and flaunts it without shame like the queen she is.

It's moments like this, when I'm achy and craving Elijah that I wish I had her strength. I wish I could just move on to someone else, like Camden, who has shown every kindness and interest in me since we met.

We're all going out tonight, to some bar that Stella has picked out. She also picked out our outfits and honestly, I'm not sure where the fuck she got this shit. I'm about to tell her she can pack it up and toss my outfit in the trash because there is no way in hell I'm leaving the house like this.

I look in the mirror, turning myself around to inspect the skin-tight, black latex dress she got me. That's right, it's fucking latex and clings to every single curve on my body. It's short, ridiculously short and cuts off right underneath my ass. The back is cut down to a deep V and the straps cross into an X in the front before shaping and framing my large chest.

"Stella. What the fuck is this?" I ask, turning around and

around as I try to process what I'm wearing. She's in the bathroom, getting into her own outfit, so she yells out the door at me. "It's a fucking dress, Lun. What does it look like?"

"It looks like lingerie. Spank me lingerie, whip me kind of lingerie," I state dryly, but the description has my mind instantly drifting to Elijah. Imagining his tattooed hands around my neck and in between my legs while I'm wearing this.

"Exactly. And you'll pull it off like the icon you are." Stella steps out of the bathroom casually, like it's just another day but suddenly, I'm all too thankful for the clearly modest dress she picked out for me.

"Holy, fuck. Stells," I breathe out as she glances up at me innocently. Her bright blue doe eyes sparkle with mischief, like she knows exactly what she's doing.

I take in her outfit, observing the flashy, fire engine red latex. It's a series of thick and thin straps that cross and tie up and down her frame, showing peeks of her alabaster skin underneath, over various parts of her body.

She walks to the mirror, looking herself over with mild interest. She knows she looks amazing. And with all the training we've been doing with the guys, our bodies have tightened and toned in all the best places. I can definitely appreciate that.

"No way. You're not wearing that around Elijah and Camden," I joke, but in all truth, I am a little nervous about them seeing her like that.

"Please, I could walk out completely naked and Elijah wouldn't even glance my way. And Camden is just a distraction for you. Admit it," she scoffs as she turns around to gather her things so we can leave.

My heart selfishly swells at her clear dismissal of Elijah, but guilt pools in my mind over her Camden comment. "I like

Camden," I say quietly, as if I'm trying to convince myself more than Stella.

Her head shoots up and she smirks at me, she knows I don't feel the same way about him as I do for Elijah. It's impossible, I simply can't. Especially after what we both saw from each other a couple of weeks ago. He witnessed my darkest moments and I experienced his. As much as I hated the fact that he saw everything, he knew now and I couldn't take it back. Whatever this is between us is bigger and more powerful than I anticipated.

Stella saunters over to me and lays a complacent kiss on my cheek, "Whatever you say, Lun."

She steps towards the door, holding it open for us both to leave and I pause for a moment, considering changing my outfit.

"Don't even fucking think about it, you're about to drive those men crazy." With her harsh demand, she reaches forward and grabs my hand, pulling me out before I have a second chance to change my mind.

"Stella, shit. Wait—" I start as I try to maintain my balance on the glossy black heels she brought me.

"Hello, boys." Her voice turns silky sweet and mesmerizing as my head shoots up to glance down the staircase. Nathanial, Elijah and Camden are all standing there, eyes turned up towards us with gazes that are literally on fire. Every single one of them. I feel a hot flush work its way up my neck and into my cheeks, my skin breaks out in goosebumps all across my shoulders and my arms as I avoid their stares.

"I should have changed," I mumble to Stella as she takes my hand and we both step down the staircase. Stella is all lethal grace and sexual charm while I'm nervously watching the floor and refusing to make eye contact. God, when the hell did Stells get like this? How did I miss this part of her?

"They want to eat you up, tasty Luna. Believe me, it was well worth it," she mumbles back, a playful giggle in her tone.

"What the hell are you wearing." It surprises me that its actually Nathanial's voice breaking the tension first. I glance up at him and see that he's watching Stella, directing his demanding remark towards her. I can't help it, but a quiet laugh falls from my mouth at his bold declaration.

"Wearing whatever the hell I want to wear, Daddy," she shoots back, her hand lifting to twirl one of her fiery red locks around finger. "You have a problem with that?"

Nathanial takes a menacing step towards her, crowding her space as he dips his head to speak. "Unless I have you bent over the railing while I'm fucking you from behind, don't call me Daddy."

"What the actual hell is happening right now," finally Elijah speaks. And it's not even to me. Nathanial takes a step back, a tiny smirk playing on his face as he turns and stalks out the door. Stella is frozen still, in shock and also with that hazy fog that's been washing over her lately. I reach out and place a hand on her arm, trying to shake her from the trance but when her eyes turn to me, they're blazing white with a fiery heat.

"Hey, you okay, Stells?" I ask, stepping closer to her. Elijah comes to stand behind me, watching our interaction as well.

"I'm fine," she says, but her voice is thick with need and lust. Even I can hear it and I'm taken aback by it. Elijah tenses behind me, and instantly I'm self-conscious that he's attracted to her. I glance back to look at him, to see if there is any heat reflected in his own eyes but I'm thankful to find a sense of pure curiosity, like he's uncovering an important piece of information.

"Come on Stella, let's get to the club." Camden steps up to her other side, taking her arm in his hand as he gently pulls her along. Just as he's about to pass me though, his hand reaches up and grasps the back of my neck as he lands his lips against my ear, "You, little Luna, look absolutely demonic. I'd like to taste you right here."

A shiver breaks out across my spine at his words, and while they don't affect me as much as Elijah's filthy tongue, I appreciate them for what I can manage with someone I'm not bonded to. I offer him a playful smile and step up behind them, while Elijah follows closely after us.

My body naturally draws his heat out of him and I try to calm my nerves at his presence, focusing on his warmth while I attempt to understand Stella. I wish we knew what was going on. I'll have to remember to ask Elijah about his reaction to her earlier. Maybe he notices something I haven't pieced together yet.

We all climb in Elijah's Jeep and head downtown. Stella is chatting everyone's ears off while Nathanial ignores her. I think she keeps talking because she knows it's grating on his nerves. All the boys have dressed up tonight as well, none of them in latex, unfortunately. But each in their own style of fashion.

Camden is the most clean cut in a pair of dark denim jeans with a simple white t-shirt. It clings nicely to his broad chest, while his longer hair is pulled up into a knot and his light beard trimmed attractively.

Nathanial is always in a pair of incredibly tailored, black slacks and a button up. Tonight however, he sports a slightly different look. His dress shirt is stark white, unbuttoned and without a tie at the top so that it parts nicely and shows a bit of his muscular chest. The sleeves are rolled tightly up his thick forearms. His long golden hair is slicked back on top, while the sides have trimmed up a bit closer to his scalp. He's still his dominant, wealthy self, all hard jaw line and sharp features, but he's leaning a bit towards the reckless side tonight. A little more dangerous, a little more erotic. He's incredibly sexy, if I'm being honest. But not my drug of choice in the slightest.

Elijah on the other hand, draws my attention like there is no one else in the room. His black distressed denim hangs low on his hips, tucked loosely into a pair of black biker boots. He wears a simple black t-shirt, but I swear it was made to fit his chest and torso perfectly. It hugs his thick arms tightly, stretching thin across the expanse of his shoulders and tapers inwards as it goes down, showing every single person the work and dedication, he's put into his body. He's fucking powerful, strength and vitality radiate off of him in waves that both suffocate and feed my hunger for him.

He's driving and I try to keep my eyes off him, attempting to focus on other things but it's a struggle. I hope that when we get to the club, I can separate myself from him and find a distraction.

"You guys are going to love this place," Stella says as she leans forward, and I can't help but notice the way the latex squeaks when she moves. I can't stand it, it grates against my ears and from the look of it, it's driving Nathanial crazy as well.

"What is it called again?" I ask, turning my attention out the window to gain a sense of direction as to where we could be.

"You'll see when we get there, I don't want to spoil the surprise." She laughs and then instructs Elijah to take a right turn at the light.

"Here! Here!" She jumps up and down in her seat, that sexual squeak invading the small space when Nathanial whips his head around and lands his heavy hand on her latex covered thigh.

"Stop. Fucking. Moving," he grinds out, and she leans forward to get in his face.

"Make me." Her tongue slides out to slowly trace the line of her bottom lip and Nathanial's eyes drop to the action. She's never been like this, never this sexual or aggressive with men.

Don't get me wrong, I'm not judging her for it. She can absolutely do whatever she wants with whoever she wants, I'm just surprised. And I know she's never been this way so I'm not sure what could have changed in her.

"Come on, let's get this over with. If Stella's weird, sexual appetite is any indication, I have a feeling I know what kind of club she would have brought us to." Elijah sounds tense, his jaw hard and ticking as he climbs out of the Jeep and we all follow suit.

"I knew I always liked you, Elijah," Stella chirps as she reaches for my hand and hurries me along. I look back over my shoulder and see Nathanial whispering something in Elijah's ear, but I can't hear what they're saying. Elijah has shut me out of the bond for so long now that I can't even try to dig for the information. Camden steps up between Stella and I, dropping his arms over our shoulders and tugs us tightly against his sides.

"Stay close, girls. I see you brought us to *Pandora's Box*, Stells." He's excited, I can hear it in his voice and feel it in every step he takes. Stella glances up at him and laughs with anticipation of what we're walking into.

I look ahead, reading the giant red neon sign that flashes the clubs name in bright letters. There's a long line outside the door, with a bouncer that's refusing to let anyone in. It looks like he's telling each person that they're full tonight. A slight wave of relief washes through me at the thought that we won't be able to gain entrance either.

Stella walks straight up to the bouncer, waving her fingers in an innocent hello and it looks like he immediately recognizes her. *What the hell.* The guy is massive, like as tall as Elijah and Nathanial but maybe even bigger. He's straight machine and muscle and it's clear why he would be the one standing guard outside of this place. His forearms are covered in tattoos, not as intricate as Elijah's, but plenty of them all the same, and his wide body relaxes at the sight of my sister. "Hi, Hawk," she says as she jumps forward and wraps her small arms around his neck in hello.

"Stells, we weren't expecting you, but it's nice to see you here." He lifts her up in a big hug before setting her back down gently. "You playing or watching tonight?" Stella's eyes flash with heated interest.

"A little of both I think." She pauses and points back to me in introduction, "This is my sister, Luna. She'll be doing the same. These guys are with us, I don't care what they choose to do."

Just as I'm about to interrupt and tell her I won't be participating in anything until I know what this is, Elijah steps up to my back and cuts in.

"She's not playing. She'll watch." His voice is firm as he answers for me and instantly, I feel the need to do the opposite just to spite him. He hardly says a word to me, refuses me, and then decides what I can and can't do without even talking to me about it? No fucking way.

"Actually, I have a voice and I'll speak for myself." I pause, hesitant to commit to something I don't understand yet. "I'll play."

"Oh, hell yes." Stella laughs.

"Luna. You're not playing. You have no idea what kind of club this is." Elijah's tone gives no room for argument. Good thing he's not the fucking boss of me.

"Hey, Eli. Have you always ruined all the fun? Or just when it comes to my sister?" Stella turns and steps into Elijah's space, coming flush up against his chest as a wave of jealousy and frustration courses through me. She's in that tight little dress, outrageously sexy, and stepping into my fucking territory.

Elijah stares down at her, her head tipped up to him and for a brief moment, my heart begins hammering in my chest. I hate seeing her so close to him and I don't understand what angle she's working.

"I'll play." Nathanial cuts through the tension, effectively stealing all of Stella's attention as her gaze flies over Elijah's shoulder and back to him. I step forward, intentionally placing myself between Elijah and Stella as her eyes turn milky and white in front of me.

"All right, rich boy. We'll see if you can handle it." With that she turns around, taking a red wrist band from Hawk and stalks towards the club ahead of. "Hawk, can you have my viewing room available in case any of us needs it?"

"Sure thing, baby girl. Are you staying the night?" he asks.

"I don't plan on it, but if any of these guys decide to crash here, I want them to have the space." Stella quickly nods in farewell and disappears through the darkened doorway.

Who the hell sleeps at a club? No way am I staying here longer than I have to.

I turn back to look at Elijah, but he won't meet my eyes. He's watching the empty space where Stella left, and it burns through my blood in an angry blaze. "What are you thinking, Elijah?" I ask pointedly. But when his eyes flick down to mine, they're dismissive and disinterested.

"I'll play too," Camden speaks and steps up to stand next to me. As a jealous heat washes over me about Elijah and Stella, I decide to try my hardest not to think about it anymore. Not to think about Elijah or the bond at all. I'm going to go in there, face whatever kind of club this is and take it straight on.

I reach up and slide my hand through Camden's arm,

offering him a smile as he steps forward to lead me into the club. We both take red wrist bands, while Nathanial steps in behind us doing the same. The bouncer asks for an answer from Elijah, and I hear a grunt as he pushes past him, refusing one.

I follow Camden's lead, focusing on him and forcing all thoughts of Elijah to the back of my mind.

CHAPTER THIRTY

Luna

AHEAD OF US ARE THICK VELVET BLACK DRAPES, BLOCKING out any vision of what we're about to uncover. A shiver of anticipation rolls through me and Camden laughs at the obvious nerves he picks up through my body language.

"Don't be nervous. I have a feeling you're going to enjoy this," he whispers against my ear as he reaches forward to pull the drapes back.

My eyes widen as he steps ahead, taking my hand and pulling me along behind him. The club is dark, with black walls and red velvet drapes coating every surface. It's huge and crowded with a variety of different people. Some are wearing latex as well but revealing far more than Stella and me. Some are covered head to toe, not showing any skin whatsoever, masks cover their faces as they waltz through the room.

Camden easily pushes through the crowd, confident and

sure of himself as he walks. I stay slightly hidden behind him, my eyes straying from one side of the room to the other as I take everyone in.

The closer I look, the more I realize exactly what kind of club this is. There's a woman to my right, bent over the back of a black leather couch, while a man roughly holds her hips and fucks her with not his cock, but a massive red dildo. Her breasts are exposed, swaying with every thrust he gives her, but her moans are drowned out through the chaos of the room.

I falter my steps and Camden looks over to notice what I see. He laughs and tugs me in front of him, his arms wrapping around my shoulders as he directs me forward.

"Have you ever been to a kink club before, sweet Luna?" he whispers in my ear. His lips brush my lobe and my heart races in my chest.

"No," I answer honestly, scanning the crowd for Stella. I'm afraid of what I'll find but I also want to make sure she's safe.

"I'll ease you into it," he responds, his voice dark and husky over my skin. "Red wrist bands are for players. Black wrist bands are for watchers." His words filter through my mind and my heart kicks at the idea of *playing*. Of course, I wish I had opted for the black wrist band but I'm not turning around now.

For an instant, I look over my shoulder, searching for Elijah. I quickly try to feel him out through the bond but find that I'm still blocked off. If he really wanted to, he would open it up and seek me out, but he hasn't. And at some point, I need to fight for my own sanity.

"All right," I whisper back, succumbing to Camden and the desire he actually shows me. He relaxes at my back, snaking an arm around my waist as we break through the crowd and find the bar. He asks if I'd like a drink, but I decide against it, I want to be present for everything tonight. I want experience it and choose it for myself without the influence of alcohol.

"Do you see Stella anywhere?" I look over the club, trying to focus on finding my sister but keep stopping at every new couple I cross along the way. Some women are being fucked against the walls, covered in leather and masks. Some men are being paraded around on leashes and collars, with either other men or women baiting them along.

So much sex.

So much kink.

Things I didn't even realize existed surround me and I feel the heat work its way up my chest and pool between my legs.

"She's usually on the dance floor," Camden shouts over the music.

"You've been here with her before?" I ask, curious about what has been happening with my sister and him.

"Only when she comes with her boyfriend," he quickly adds but an uncomfortable hesitance crosses my mind.

"Hey," I place my hand on his arm, feeling his warm skin under my touch. It's nothing like Elijah's. No heat. No sun bursting through me. "If you like Stella, that's okay. I get it," I say, and the tiniest spark of disappointment flashes inside of me. I want a distraction. I need this diversion from my bond.

Camden brings both of his hands to either side of my face, tilting my chin up so that I'm staring straight into his eyes. "I'm not into your sister. I'm here for you, Luna," he dips down, bringing his lips to brush against my ear. "And that sexy little outfit you have on has me wanting to do dangerous and dirty things to you."

I'm unsure of how to respond. I don't feel the same way I felt when Elijah spoke to me like that. But I try to remind myself that Camden isn't Elijah, we aren't bonded, and nothing will feel the same as it does with him.

And that's okay.

So, I let my lips rise in a smile as I wrap my arms around his neck and pull myself against him. I let my body feel his, let myself appreciate and accept his warmth, even if it is different.

"Besides, I've got a gift for you." Camden's words catch me by surprise, and I lean back, seeing the excitement dance in his eyes.

"What? Camden, you don't have to—"

"Hush. You already knew it was coming, you just didn't know when."

He reaches into his pocket and pulls out a tiny, clear plastic bag. It holds a single, white and round pill.

My eyes dart back up to his, disbelief raging inside of me. It can't be. It can't be ready yet. He just told us about it a few weeks ago. But the huge grin spreading his lips has me hoping otherwise, silently begging for it to be true.

"No. Is this it? Is it ready?" I ask quietly, refusing to let the hope root itself in my gut.

"It's ready, Luna. You're the first to get it. It's been tested, reformulated, tested again until it was perfect. It only lasts six or so hours right now, but I promise I'm working on a longer trial. It'll give you both a break. You'll be able to leave and breathe on your own, you won't be trapped in a bond you never wanted." His hands slide around my waist, gripping my hips as he pulls me against him. Our chests crush together and my heart races against the idea that I could actually have a moment of peace without begging for it from Elijah.

"Camden. I don't even know what to say." Tears well in my eyes but I force them back, this means so much to me and he can see that already. "Thank you," I finish, resting my hands on either side of his neck.

"You're welcome," he says quietly. There's a tension building between us as his eyes drop to my lips. I watch as heat flares within him and I know he wants to kiss me. Instinctively, I reach out through the bond one last time, looking to see if

Elijah has opened anything between us. But he hasn't. I'm cut off and for that reason, I take advantage of what I have in front of me.

I don't wait for him to make the first move, I take it myself. I pull his head down towards my own, taking his lips in a kiss as my fingers move up and tangle in the fallen strands of his hair. But it only takes that invitation for him to take control of our kiss. He quickly flips us around so that my back is pushed up against the bar top as he leans into me. His hand tangles in my dark hair as he fists my head, roughly holding me still for his hungry kiss.

For a split second, my mind shifts back in time. Seven years, to that awful night so long ago, but just as quickly Camden's grip relaxes and I'm brought back to this moment. Something strange tugs in my memories but I return my focus to Camden's soft kiss and gentle touch now that he's reigned himself in.

Honestly, I'm actually turned on by the fact that he has to hold himself back. That his need for me is so strong that he has to maintain control.

I pull away for a second, trying to catch my breath as Camden watches me with fire in his eyes. "Are you going to take it?" he asks, holding the little baggie up for me to take from him. I do, I reach for it and slowly slide it into the top of my dress as he watches, his eyes focused on my tits as a low groan erupts from his throat.

"I can't, not without talking to Elijah first. I just can't throw him off like that without at least telling him," I explain, knowing he'll be understanding about it.

But I'm surprised when I notice the slightest tick in his jaw over my words. It's barely noticeable, I doubt he even realizes he's doing it. It has me second guessing his intentions over giving me the pill. I know he has feelings for me, he's made that perfectly clear. He'll have to be patient with me though. He knows I'm bonded.

"Absolutely, I agree. I'm sorry, I just hate the way he treats you. I hate the way he hurts you." His thumb comes up to softly brush against my cheek and I lean into his touch. He's always been kind, and I know better than to not trust him. He's always protected me when he was around, stepping into any situation he felt compromised me. He's been teaching me how to fight, how to defend myself against Amelia and Danner. And Nathanial clearly considers him a good friend.

"Come on, let's find Stella. I just want to make sure she's okay." I lay my hand against his cheek and lean up on my toes to place a soft kiss against his lips. Stepping back, I take his hand in mine and move us through the crowd and toward the dance floor.

We both search the room, looking for anyone in our group, but don't see any of them at first. Camden steps forward and pulls me deeper onto the dance floor, we're surrounded by countless bodies when I finally spot Nathanial.

And holy shit I've never seen him look like that. He's dancing, with two girls pressed to either side of him. One in the front and one up against his back. His eyes are completely glazed over, milky and white like Stella's were earlier. One girl has red hair, just like Stells, but she's taller and leaner, lacking the curves that the other brunette he's dancing with has. However, it's their hands that have me surprised. The girl in front of him has her hand down the front of his pants, while his shirt is pulled out and wide open for her. His strongly defined abs on full display and she grinds against him while she works his cock, clearly getting him off in the middle of the dance floor.

Nathanial's hand is actually behind him, up the skirt of the girl who's dancing at his back. He's playing with her while the two girls kiss and make out around him. But Nathanial isn't watching the girls. His eyes are trained on someone else across the room and I follow his gaze until I find Stella, surprise and confusion taking over as I watch their interaction.

Stella is sitting back on a red leather couch, her dress hiked up around her thighs while a guy is crouched below her. Her legs are loosely draped over his shoulders as he clearly eats her out. I immediately turn my gaze away so that I don't invade her privacy. Which is ridiculous, I realize that. Seeing as we're in a kink club.

"Is that Stella's boyfriend?" I ask, noticing that Camden is watching the same exchange in front of us.

"No. But he doesn't mind, he knows she has needs," he explains, as if he knows something about Stella that I don't.

"What does that mean?" I ask, turning to face him and drag his attention away from them.

Camden glances down at me briefly, but quickly looks back up until a sympathetic expression crosses his face. "It looks like Elijah's getting his needs met as well," he says softly, and I whip my head around at his remark.

"Where?" I demand as Camden gently turns my head to the right, until my eyes crash with Elijah's. He's back against the wall, with a tall, leggy woman donning purple hair. Her head is yanked back against his shoulder as he towers behind her. His lips are moving down the side of her neck until he looks up to meet my gaze. His eyes are on fire with anger, as if I have something to be sorry for. As if he's punishing me for something I've done.

I watch as she arches her back and pushes her body into his, reaching a hand up to grip his neck as he goes back to devouring her neck. I quickly turn around and push Camden back out of the crowd.

"Come on. I want to see the rest of the club," I urge as rage fills my stomach and spills outwards. I can't be angry. I can't be upset. He made it clear he didn't want this and now he's showing me that. He's doing exactly what he promised me he would do. I shouldn't be surprised at this point.

Camden steps forward and takes the lead, pulling us to the back of the club where new hallways begin splitting off in different directions. This is what I want, this is what I need. A distraction, an impulsive night to do whatever it is I need to do. And tomorrow, I'll tell Elijah about the pill, I have no doubts that he will be thrilled about it.

Then I'll take it and give us six hours of fucking freedom.

CHAPTER THIRTY-ONE

Luna

CAMDEN BROUGHT ME INTO A SEPARATE ROOM IN THE
back of the club. It's dark, and one wall is completely glass. He
shuts the door behind us, closing us in so that we're alone and I
finally feel the smallest wave of relief at being away from
everyone else.

I crave the privacy now, crave the ability to truly be alone
now that I know how plausible that reality actually is. Camden
takes my hand and leads me toward the glass wall. Once we
reach it, he steps behind me, his hands slide down to grip my
hips as he gently tugs me against him.

In front of us is another room, one we have a clear vision
into as three people enter ahead of us. One woman, two men.
There's a large bed in the center. It's perfectly circular without
any headboard and covered in thick red blankets and pillows in
all different shades. On one of the walls behind them, there's

countless objects hanging in rows. Chains, whips, masks, dildos, and several other pieces I don't recognize.

"What is this?" I ask quietly, worried they will hear me through the glass. Camden's hands slide up my arms as he trails his fingers across my skin.

"It's the viewing room Stella has available for us. People come in here who want to watch and people who want to be seen go in there." His fingers run down the length of my neck as I tilt my head to the side, allowing him access to more of my skin.

The three people climb on the bed while the woman stands on her knees in the center. One man comes to her back, running his hands through her hair and pulling it off to the side so that he can trail kisses across her shoulders. She relaxes back into him as the second man comes to her front. His hands start lower, working their way up her thighs and brushing lightly between her legs.

"So, they know they're being watched?" I ask breathlessly. I feel my panties getting wet at the mix of sensations moving through me. Camden's hands move to my stomach as he flattens his palm and rolls his hips into my ass. He's already hard and he's eager to let me know, showing me how much this is turning him on as well.

"Yes," he whispers as he drops his lips to my neck, sucking and kissing my sensitive skin while the woman in front of us continues playing with her men. The one at the back of her slowly raises her shirt, tugging it up and over her breasts enough to release them, but not pulling it off of her completely. The man in front immediately takes one of her nipples into his mouth as he sucks and nips at her hard peaks. Her moans fill the space around us, and I feel my body relax into Camden's touch as it inches lower than my stomach.

"Do you like this, Luna? Watching them while I touch

you?" His other hand moves to my hair as he wraps it around his fist, holding my head straight so that I can't look anywhere but at them. The man in front unzips his jeans and then pulls out his cock, it's hard and ready for her as the man behind her pushes her forward so that she's on her hands and knees.

Do I like this? Shit, I think so. It's not what I crave though. He's not fulfilling my every need with his touch and kiss, but I don't expect it to. I don't expect anything to be like Elijah.

"Yes," I say honestly. Because I genuinely believe this is as good as it's going to get for me.

The man behind her grips her hips as he slams into her pussy. The one in front holds the back of her head as his cock slides in between her lips. She's taking them both, pleasuring them both while she's filled and fucked in front of anyone who wants to watch.

A whimper escapes my lips as my thighs begin rubbing together, creating a subtle friction to relieve some of the ache inside of me. But Camden is quick, and his hand is right there, working its way under my tight dress until he finds me soaking wet and needing to be filled.

"Fuck, Luna. You want this, don't you? You want me slide my fingers inside your wet cunt?" He grinds the words through his teeth as he pulls my panties aside and slides inside of me without waiting for an answer. My knees weaken as I stretch around him, but he holds me up and against his chest while I lose myself to everything around me.

The woman in front of us is pulled upwards while both men come flush against either side of her. One man angles his cock at her ass while the other slides in from the front and she cries out at being filled by both, each one finding a rhythm and working inside of her.

I feel it, the orgasm building within me while Camden circles my clit before plunging back inside of my pussy. Truthfully, it's not necessarily him that's so close to getting me off, it's the entire situation that's turning me on. This taboo idea that I'm watching strangers fuck, while Camden distracts and touches my frozen body is too overwhelming to ignore.

"Give it to me, Luna. That's it, baby." He speaks the words as another voice barrels into my mind a second too late.

Where the fuck are you, Luna. He's shouting the words through my mind and I collapse to the ground as my body tries to ride through the crashing orgasm. It wasn't huge, and the three in front of us are still going at it. I'm not satisfied in the slightest, in fact I feel needier now than I did before we even came in here, but I think that may have more to do with Elijah's voice invading my head at the last second.

Immediately, Camden surprises me by backing up and moving towards the entrance of our little viewing room. I look over to him, confused as he casually opens the door to step out.

"I'll be right back, Luna. Don't go anywhere, I just need to check on Stella really quick," he says as he quickly hurries out and shuts the door behind him. I'm suddenly exhausted and confused. An irritating pain radiates through my chest and begins throbbing throughout my entire body. Something's wrong and I'm alone, without anyone I can trust in this stupid fucking kink club. On top of that, I can't escape the now outrageous moans of the fucking happening in the room behind me.

Answer me, Demon. Elijah's voice is hoarse and filled with hatred in my head. The fact that he just referred to me simply as Demon evokes an entirely new sense of rejection that I've never felt before.

Fuck you. Don't call me that. I whisper back and I fall to the floor as rage flows through our bond and into my own body.

Tell me where you are now, Luna. I can't fucking find you.

I groan and rub my hand across my chest, the throbbing

pain turning into a severe sting that lingers and intensifies. *I'm in a room, in the back of the club.*

Not even a minute later, Elijah comes crashing through the door, falling to the floor as soon as he enters. He kicks his foot back and slams the door shut so that we're alone.

"What the fuck have you done, Luna," he spits out, his voice rough and cracking as it breaks in the space around us.

"What are you talking about?" I shout, climbing back to my knees as I slowly make my way closer to him.

"Stay the hell away from me," he says, anger and pain burn in his eyes as they set me on fire. God, even his stare pulls more from me than Camden's touch did.

"What's going on, Elijah? I don't understand and I can't fix anything if you don't fucking tell me!" We're feet apart, close enough to touch but I hold myself back, even though everything inside of me is imploring me to bridge the distance.

"You got off with him," he shouts as pain slashes through his voice. For a second, I'm too surprised to speak. A furious lump builds in my chest at his words, as if he can do whatever the fuck he wants and I can't. How many times had he fucked Sam since we've been bonded?

"You're kidding, right? You've gotten off a thousand fucking times with Sam since you bonded me. You were out there, practically fucking another woman in front of me while I watched." My heart is racing, thundering in my chest as fury courses through my blood and my breaths come out in rapid releases. "How dare you try to control me when you have never offered me the same respect." I pray these rooms are soundproof because my mind is spiraling out of control as our emotions come crashing and colliding together in a raging storm around us.

"I numb the fucking bond, Luna. Every goddamn time, I numb the fucking bond by drinking so that you don't feel it."

He launches forward and I fall back against the ground while he towers over me. In being this close to him I can see how sickly white his skin has become. I can see the thin layer of sweat that has broken out across his forehead. I feel the seething heat emanating from his body and scorching my own.

"How was I supposed to know that, Elijah? You never teach me about the blood bond! You haven't told me anything other than how to heal you, weeks ago, and you haven't said anything to me after what happened to us." I pause for a moment as I try to catch my breath. Both of us are ragged and harshly inhaling the air between us. "How the hell was I supposed to know?" I finally whisper, searching his eyes for the answers I so desperately want.

I slowly lift a hand and tentatively reach it forward, hoping that he'll allow me to rest it on his forehead and check his temperature. He's blazing hot and I'm actually worried for him.

He looks at me for a second, pain and agony fill his eyes as he drops his head against my hand. His skin is on fire, literally fuming against my icy touch and I instinctively pull my hand away before it burns me.

An awful snarl rips from his lips at the absence of my touch and I immediately shift forward, placing my hands over his sweat soaked shirt and push him backwards so that he falls to the ground. He needs my freeze, my wintry touch against his blazing skin and I know I need to give it to him. I want to give it to him.

I climb over his huge body, hiking my tight dress upwards so that I can straddle him and rest my cold form against his. His breaths are harsh and rapid as he tries to regain the control he needs over his own body.

I lean forward and rest my hands against his neck, stroking my fingers along his skin and dragging my touch down to his chest. Sliding my hands under the neckline, I inch as far as I can before I drop them to the hem of his shirt. I slowly drag it upwards so that I can move my touch to the hard expanse of his stomach. His skin torches my own with a painful reminder of what I did to him without even realizing it. I take the burns willingly, accepting them and giving whatever I can back to him.

"I didn't know," I whisper again as tears break through my eyes and fall down my ruddy cheeks. I hate crying. I fucking hate it and I can usually keep it under control around everyone. But I can't now, not as Elijah's tortured gaze rakes over my body and his labored breaths continue to crash between us. Not as his sickly pale skin lights up against my own and my blood seethes under my flesh in anger at what I've done.

I don't regret taking something for myself. I wasn't wrong in enjoying myself with another man. However, I do wish I had known how to block this from Elijah so it wouldn't hurt him to this extent. I never wanted to physically inflict pain on him and while he never taught this to me, I'm being ripped apart while I watch him suffer.

Elijah's hands shoot upwards and tightly grips my own, halting my movements along his skin. I'm sure he's going to push me away again. "I'm sorry," I choke out the words as I try to regain my movement along his body, but he resists. His jaw is hard and tense as he silently refuses me.

"I'm sorry, Elijah," I say again, anger and frustration nipping at my tone. I try again, pushing my hands forward, making only an inch of progress before he silently stops me. "I'm fucking sorry," I cry out and this time I pull my hands away and out of his grasp before I try again for the next connection. But he's quicker than me, stronger than me even while he's weakened and sick from what's happened.

I push forward again as I taste the unfamiliar salty tears slide over my lips and into my mouth. My vision blurs and then clears with each attempt I take at connecting our flesh. He keeps pushing me back, keeps holding my hands together so that I'm bound and forced away from him.

"I'm sorry," I say the words out loud and then I whisper them in my mind. I flood our bond with regret and apology and as I shift forward again, he grips my wrists tightly between his thick fingers and yanks them up over my head. He holds me tightly, painfully, silently and sexually as I'm stretched out above him.

I try to pull my hands from his grasp so that I can attempt touching him but he doesn't let go. Instead, my hips shift forward at my failed effort and I unintentionally grind against his hard length. He rips my hands back even further so that I'm arched, and my legs are forced farther apart. A selfish whimper slips from my lips as I try again, moving against his thick shaft and taking my own pleasure from him again.

"I'm sorry," I say, but this time it's on a moan as he continues to hold me in place. His other hand falls to my thigh as his fingers dig into my flesh and his hard eyes turn silky and black. He uses his grip to shift me back, and then drag me forward, back and forward again and again as I move against his cock. I try to pull my hands from his grip, try to give us more than this but he refuses me.

His hips begin rolling up to meet my own and my breaths become labored and anxious as my pussy grinds against him through his jeans. Elijah sits up even farther as his hand slides to the back of my thigh and he yanks me forward. He positions himself so that he's sitting up while he maintains control over my body.

"Say something," I beg him, seeking his thoughts on where his mind is while we ignite around each other.

"Fuck you, Luna," he growls the words out as his lips come crashing onto mine, taking me and slamming my body backwards into the ground as he launches forward. His teeth bite into my lower lip, making me bleed and beg and crave him all the more. I taste my blood in my mouth, that tangy metallic flavor that he's feeding off of through our bond.

His hips roll and fuck into me as I shift upwards on each thrust until my head smashes into the glass wall behind us. Everything's dark, the room is empty, the threesome must have had finished a while back.

"Say something," I plead, looking for his words to punish and destroy me. Everything inside of me burns for his pain, taking it as my own and absorbing the sting.

"I can't stand the fucking sight of you," he grips the sharp hem of my dress and yanks it upwards as I lift myself and try to help pull it off. The latex stretches and tears in places, but I don't care, I need it off of me so that I can fix this.

"Say something," I demand angrily, and I rush forward to tear his shirt from his chest as more of our skin clashes together. Power and strength build between us, pulling and giving to each other as we clash through this together.

"I hate you, *mo dheamhan*," his words fall from him on a tortured voice and rip through me as new cries claw out of my own throat. Elijah's lips fall back to mine and he swallows every sound I make, every tear that falls as he takes them for his own. His lips move against mine in a furious demand of passion and war. He claims my pain and I claim his, shouldering each other's burdens as we fight to become one.

His hands work to quickly tear off his own jeans while I reach for my panties and yank them down my thighs. His hard cock rolls against my pussy and he groans into my neck. The only thing separating us is the thin material of his tight, silky briefs. I arch my body into his as he continues thrusting into me.

He's rough and demanding, his huge cock begs entrance

that neither of us are giving in the moment, torturing ourselves with the inevitable as we work through the betrayals and rejections of the last several weeks.

I run my hands across his shoulders, slowing my movements so that I can focus on how hot his skin still is. He's working through a fever that's high and dangerous and I know my touch is the only thing that can bring it down.

I trail my fingers down his chest, brushing my thumbs across his pierced nipples, focusing on our blood the way he had instructed last time. His lips take mine again and I give it to him, opening as his tongue slides in and sucks my own into his mouth. He tastes every inch of me, stroking inside and savoring the connection. He pierces me in sync with his thrusting hips and I let my hands fall down to his abs. I trace the lines and dips of his muscles and then bring my hands around to his lower back before working my way upwards.

His mouth devours me, hungry and starving for what only I can give him. I'm the same way though, my achy body craving to have him fill me. He nips at my jaw, biting harshly before kissing and soothing the sting of his punishments. He moves even lower, sliding the tip of his tongue across my collarbone and down through the valley of my breasts.

I moan and writhe underneath him as he pulls one of my nipples into his mouth. At first, he bites down, rough and angry as he reminds me why he's livid. Then he sucks and licks, tastes and forgives as his hands fall to knead and grip my ass.

He sits back on his legs as his hands reach for the outside of my thighs and he pulls me around him. I watch as he slides his hand into the band of his black briefs and shoves them down, releasing his heavy cock so that it falls between us.

I uncontrollably moan at the sight, his hand sliding down to his pierced tip and back to the base. My hips inch up to meet him, feel his cock against my pussy but his large hand quickly spreads wide across my stomach and holds me down.

"This wasn't supposed to happen to me again," he grinds out, anger and resentment coating his tone. "I wasn't supposed to bond again. I wasn't supposed do this again, Luna. You ruined everything the night I found you at Amelia's."

My eyes are locked on his length as he continues stroking himself, playing with his piercing at the tip before moving back down to tightly squeeze the base of his cock. Fuck, I'm so turned on, even while his painful words work through me. I know he needs to process this, hell, I need to process this. So, I let him talk. One way or the other, at least I'm getting his truth.

"And then you wouldn't bond Nathanial. Fuck, I tried. I knew he was the better choice for you. I knew I'd never be able to give you anything you needed. Nathanial would always be the better option." He shifts forward just slightly, letting the tip of his wide cock slide through my slick slit and I gasp at the sensation. His piercing hits my clit on a cold touch that spirals through my body in need.

"I don't want Nathanial," I say, determination heavy in my voice.

"No, you want Camden," he spits back, pulling his cock away and resuming stroking himself.

"No, I don't want Camden. It's only ever been you."

"Lies," he snaps tightly and sits back so that he's even farther away from me.

"And what about Sam? I listened to you fuck her, I watched her suck you off. I get that you numbed the bond but that doesn't stop everything. I felt that shit Elijah. You found me frozen in the goddamn shower after that shit." I sit up and force myself closer to him as I reach up and grip his neck in my hand, yanking him down so that he's on top of me.

"What do you want to hear, Luna?" He taunts, sliding his cock through my wetness and coating it over my clit.

"The fucking truth, Elijah. For once, give me your truth." I wrap my legs around his waist and dig my heels into his ass as I lift my hips to meet him. He fists my hair with one hand as he thrusts forward and slides into me with one movement. I gasp out as we come together, joining our bodies in perfect unity. His cock thrusts deep inside of me, hitting places I know only he can fill. Our bodies move and mold together as one while our blood meets through the bond and integrates, igniting an uncontrollable storm within our bodies.

It's a mix of my blizzard no longer warring with his raging fire. Instead they come together in perfect alliance, joining as one force that awakens a power within each of us. I feel it billowing around us, electrifying the air and injecting into our veins. We pull from it, from the power coursing through our bond and what's leaked out into the air.

"You want the truth, Luna? I fucked Sam when I needed to be inside of you. She was my distraction when I felt like you were getting too close. When you were breaking down my walls and forcing your way into places I swore off years ago. When I needed to remind myself that I could never have you," he thrust inside of me, over and over as our bodies slam together. His hand moves between us to pull and roll my nipple as I moan around his mouth. He swallows everything, my sounds, my cries, my pleas for more.

"Then you know what Camden was to me," I force out in between my heavy breaths.

Elijah sits back and pulls out and I immediately feel the painful loss of him inside of me. But he quickly flips me over and pulls me up so that I'm on my hands and knees. Instantly, an uncontrollable worry rushes through me at the position, but I force the tainted memories to the back of mind.

Elijah leans forward, over my back as he slides back inside of me, thrusting forward with a much slower, intentional rhythm and I feel the heat rip through my chest. He eases me into this, taking my flash of fear and reminding me I'm safe. His body temperature has fallen slightly, which is good and I'm immediately a little more at ease.

His hand slides up to my throat as he pulls me up and against his chest while he continues moving inside of me. He tugs my head backwards as he crashes his lips against mine. His cock rocks forward and stretches me open, my pussy clamped tightly around him as I milk everything he's giving me.

I feel a shift in the air around us, as it settles and balances out the power that's been chaotically warring. His thrusts drag into torturously delicious draws on my body, slowly pushing back in as I feel every stretch and yield I give to him.

"Say something," I brush the words against his soft lips again.

"You're perfect, Luna" he whispers back as he sucks my bottom lip into his mouth and nips at me gently.

"Say something," I arch my back and push into him as his hand falls in between my legs and begins circling my clit.

"You were created for me, and only me." This, he says on a possessive growl that thunders through my chest. His lips fall to the nape of my neck as he trails kisses along my shoulder and we fall forward.

"Say something," I beg one last time as the orgasm builds and twists inside of me, ready to snap in the next second.

"I need you, *m'aingeal*," he whispers in my ear and every bit of anger or distrust melts away inside of me. He suddenly replaces that night seven years ago with this refined moment. Flawless and immaculate even while I'm in this position that had been ruined for me before now.

I release a breathy moan as his thrusts become more frantic

and his fingers soak my clit in my own wetness with every pinch and stroke he gives it. "Come for me, Luna. And give me what only I can take from you, what only belongs to me. Give me everything."

I do. I break around him in the strongest orgasm I've ever felt. I pull and clamp around his thick cock while he comes inside of me, meeting my orgasm with his own as our blood rises and unites through the bond.

Completing us. Drawing us together and feeding our addictions with our personal brand of heroine.

My Demon and his Angel, tainting and purifying each other with each consuming kiss.

CHAPTER THIRTY-TWO

Luna

I'VE SHIFTED TO MY BACK, STILL WONDERFULLY NAKED AS Elijah's soft lips trail slowly across my jaw line. He works his way up to my ear, grazing his tongue along the thin shell before sucking my lobe into his mouth and then releasing.

"So good, *mo dheamhan agus mo aingeal*," he whispers, dark and husky against my skin. His voice draws more needy moans and whimpers from my lips. We've just finished, basking in the lusty satisfaction that surrounds us but I'm already yearning for more.

I intentionally tilt my head closer to him, seeking his lips against my mine. He gives it to me, willingly and roughly as he works to satiate the desire inside of me. He's working to quench the thirst of his own as well.

His tongue slides across the soft skin of my lower lip as he urges me to part for him. I immediately respond, opening while lifting my head and pressing myself harder against his body, taking him for myself as he matches my aggression with his own. We consume each other, simply and perfectly.

"I don't think I'm ever going to get enough of you," he says as he rolls to his back and pulls me along with him. I'm tucked into his side, my thigh draped over his waist while one of his hand's rests possessively on the back of my neck. We continue to explore each other's mouths, refusing to part just yet.

"Good," I mutter against him before I lean back, searching his eyes and our bond for his true feelings in this moment.

I relax slightly at the realization that he genuinely seems happy. I don't believe he regrets anything we've done. God, I hope he doesn't. I feel whole for the first time in my life, satisfyingly warm as I'm pressed against his hard body. I don't want this to end.

I do notice the slightest tense coil that remains inside of him, but I'm thankful that he isn't hiding that from me. He watches me as I try to read our blood bond and lifts his thumb to brush across my cheek.

"We have a lot we need to discuss," he says, and I notice the strain he has lining his voice.

"I know," I answer honestly. "But I'm not ready yet. I just want to stay in this moment for a little while longer."

Elijah rolls his heavy body towards me, so that my head rests on his bicep and his hand grips the side of my face. "I understand, it can wait. But Luna, there's something else I need you to know," he pauses, focusing on his touch coasting across my skin. "That night, seven years ago—"

"Elijah," I start, closing my eyes and refusing to revisit that memory.

"I was trying to find you, Luna."

His words cause my eyes to snap open. I felt the possibility of that notion when we saw each other's memories. I remember considering how that could even be a possibility, we didn't know each other then. "We don't know that for sure," I explain, trying to find logic in the impossible.

"It's true. I know it. I know it in my head, I know it in my heart, I know it in our bond." He speaks roughly, but an urgency is evident in his tone. "I should have found you. Fuck, I should have been there, Luna."

Suddenly, I realize what he's trying to do. He feels guilty over that night and is taking the blame on his shoulders. It's the last thing I want, for that night to taint anything we have together.

I lift my hands to his face and try to convey every ounce of the passion I'm feeling for him through my eyes and through our blood. "Don't. Don't do that Elijah. You were going through something horrific as well. You have no reason to feel guilty, or sorry for anything. It was never your fault. It was never my fault. It was their fault. But those men can't take anything else away from me, or from us. I won't let them." I speak the words frantically as I press my lips against his and claim them once again. For us, for this moment. For everything we have together.

"It's always been you, Luna," he says as he bites my lip and releases it. "Even before, when I didn't know you." His lips collide with mine again in a possessive mark to my skin. "Even after, when I tried to deny it and push you away."

His words send waves of warmth burning through my body with a delicious flood of desire and devotion. I feel our potent energy pooling around us as I let my fingers trace patterns across his chest. It's heavy and dense and I don't quite understand it, but I let the air bathe us both in its effect. My mind wanders back to his words earlier, about Nathanial attempting to bond me first.

"Why couldn't Nathanial bond to me?" I ask, thankful that he couldn't but curious to know why as well.

"That's what we need to discuss. There is a reason, but it's a long story. We can talk about it later when we get back to the house," he explains, and I look into his forest green eyes for any signs of deceit. I don't find them, so I relinquish the pursuit of my answer and let him roll back as I rest my head against his chest.

"All right," I whisper and instantly the exhaustion of the last several weeks catches up to me. I have Elijah, finally and entirely. My body is satisfied and while I'm still hungry for more of him, I'm relaxed in the nearness of him and open acceptance of our bond.

"We'll rest, but only for only a little while. I think Nathanial and Stella can keep themselves busy out there." He yawns and pulls me tighter against his body. I naturally mold myself to him, every one of his hard lines matching my softer ones perfectly. Another reminder of how he genuinely feels like the other half of me that's been missing my entire life. Two pieces of a puzzle finally fitting together and creating the final image of power and beauty.

I let my eyes fall closed as I surrender to sleep, my hand clasped tightly around the side of Elijah's neck while his rests greedily on my thigh.

———

I SLOWLY BLINK MY EYES OPEN AS I TRY TO REMEMBER where I am. The carpeted floor is hard beneath me, but my body is entwined around heavy, hot limbs and I instantly know it's Elijah. I can feel his presence in every part of my body. It's a welcome feeling and I relish in the moment briefly before trying to slowly pull myself away from him.

The lights to the room behind us have turned on and a couple has taken their place on the circular bed in the middle. I can hear them, which is what woke me from my sleep, but Elijah seems to have no problem sleeping through her heated moans and his masculine grunts.

Hell, he even slapped her ass and Elijah still hasn't moved a muscle. I laugh, realizing how heavy of a sleeper he is. But I shift away from him and quickly search the floor for my dress. I find it tossed a few feet away and swiftly pull it over my head so that I can go look for Stella before waking Elijah. If I can get everyone together, then we can all head out soon. I don't think we've been asleep long, probably only forty-five minutes or so.

My eyes glance to the floor as the small white pill Camden gave me catches my attention. I reach for it, holding it up in front of my face before sliding back in my dress against my chest. I need to tell Elijah about it, I doubt we'll use it now. But when we talk later about why I couldn't bond to Nathanial, we can cover this base as well.

Strangely enough, I don't feel any sort of anxiety over my relationship with Elijah moving forward. I'm connected to him, on so many different levels now that it seems we've completely merged. Our bodies, minds, and souls belong to each other in a catastrophe of power and destruction. I love it. I crave it. I'm no longer afraid of it.

I slowly open the door and sneak out without waking Elijah. I'll be back to him in a few moments after I find Stella. I hurry down the hall, unsure of what direction I need to go but try to follow the music and voices I hear drifting in from the main club.

I take a series of turns down the dark hallways, surprisingly not passing another person until I'm relatively certain I'm getting to closer to the crowd. A couple stumbles past me, two women who are clearly drunk and giggling as they hurry down the hall. I consider asking them which way to turn next but ultimately decide against it, not wanting to interrupt their fun.

Instantly, a large hand snakes around my shoulder and slams over my mouth as I'm yanked back against a hard chest. Hot lips brush against my ear as stiff hairs tickle the side of my face.

"Are you lost, little Luna?" Camden's quiet voice fills my ears as my heart races against my chest.

"Jesus, Camden. You scared the shit out of me," I say after pulling his hand from my mouth. I turn around quickly so that I can see him. His hair is down, a sweaty matted mess as it clings to his skin. His eyes are wide, frantic and slightly bloodshot as he looks me over. "Hey, are you okay?" I ask, lifting a hand to rest on his shoulder. Confusion races through me, and suddenly every muscle in my body tenses in preventative alert.

"I'm great, baby. I was wondering when you were going to come and find me," he says as he dips his head forward and brushes his nose down the length of my cheek. I take a step back, placing my hand on his chest so that I can put a little space between us.

"Camden, listen—" I start, but suddenly I'm thrown back against the wall as he pushes his body roughly against my own.

"I'm sorry, sweetheart. But we don't have time. See, I thought this was going to go a little differently. I assumed Elijah would be so furious with you—" he pauses, trailing his tongue across the skin of my throat. "—coming against my fingers that you'd feel your only option was to take the fucking pill." His hand darts forward and crams down the front of my dress as he plucks the little baggie from where he knew it would be. I try to push against him, but his other hand comes forward to bind my wrists together while he tears the bag open with his teeth.

"No, Camden. I'm not taking it. I don't—" But I fall silent as he puts the pill in his own mouth and then crashes his lips against mine. I fight against him but his tongue pushes and invades my mouth while he shoves the pill as far back as he can reach. He bites my tongue and lip while I yelp until I'm gasping for air and have no choice but to pull away and swallow without choking.

Luna. Where are you?

Elijah's voice breaks through my mind but I'm too frantic to respond. I swallowed the goddamn pill and I don't even know where I am.

"What the hell, Camden!" I shout, trying to shove him backwards. His heavy hands grip my waist as he turns me around and slams be back against the wall. My chest and face are crushed against the black paint.

LUNA.

I don't know. It's my only response, because I'm trying to fight against Camden and sort through the mess I've suddenly found myself in. I have no idea where I am, or how to explain it to him, but I know the bond will cut out at any moment if everything Camden claimed is true.

"Fuck, you're so sweet. Always so sweet against my body," he says as his lips press against my ear again. "Good for one thing, baby girl. Only one fucking thing." Instantly, terror and memories come flooding back at the same time the blood bond goes black. Completely dark. I don't feel anything. No presence. No indication of Elijah even being alive. No vague notion of where he is within the vicinity. Nothing. Even when I was blocked from the bond earlier, I at least *knew* Elijah was around. I could feel the thin wire that connected us even if there weren't any emotions or energy flowing through it.

Six hours. I can handle this. Six hours and the bond will be back, and I will be able to communicate with Elijah. I just need to handle Camden for that long.

CHAPTER THIRTY-THREE

ELIJAH

IT HAPPENED IN AN INSTANT. THE QUICKEST, LOUDEST AND yet all too silent separation I had ever felt. It was barely noticeable and left my blood screaming and searching for her.

LUNA.

I shout again, out loud and through the blood bond that I no longer feel. I lift myself off the ground and race out the door while I'm still yanking my jeans back up my thighs. Every single door I pass I throw open, shouting her name and stalking the halls. But I have no inclination of where she is. I have no idea if she's alive, no clue if she's hurt.

I have nothing.

It wasn't painful in the same way my break from Amelia was. No, this was far worse. It's a silent killer of toxic poison that tore us away from each other without anyone's consent.

"Luna," I yell through the halls as I feel my pockets for my phone in order to call her. I try. She doesn't answer. So, I move to Nathanial next, urging him to pick up and pray that he has somehow seen Luna.

"Elijah," his voice is hoarse, and music blasts around him through the speaker.

"Where the hell are you?" I shout over the line.

"The bar. You?" he asks dryly.

"I can't find Luna. I need your help," my voice cracks in fear and I hate the betrayal, but I need him.

"What do you mean you can't find her? Use the bond and—"

"Yeah, I fucking get that, I can't fucking find her Nathanial. It's gone." I grit through clenched teeth as I finally break into the main area of the club and hastily move towards the bar until I spot my brother. I hang up the phone without waiting for an answer as I come up to stand with him.

"How is it gone, Elijah?" Nathanial asks as he meets me immediately and rests a reassuring grasp on my shoulder.

"I don't know. I don't fucking know. But I can't feel anything, it's gone. Like someone cut it off without breaking it. Like something's blocking it from—" Immediately, Camden's promise comes back to my mind, reminding me of what he told us he was creating. "Call Camden. Find out where he is," I say quickly as my eyes start scanning the crowd for him as well.

"Fuck, do you think it's the pill he was making?" he asks, pulling out his phone and lifting it to his ear.

"I know it is. We need to find him." I begin moving through the crowd, working my way back to the front of the club while Nathanial follows behind me.

"He didn't answer. Shit, I need to get Stella. I'll meet you at the Jeep," he calls out before veering off and looking for Luna's sister. I'll fucking leave them if I have to, but I head outside and scan the streets for any sign of Luna and Camden.

Rage builds inside of me at the thought that he might have

her, but I don't understand why he would want her, other than some sort of sick obsession. I don't know his motives for pulling a stunt like this.

Stella and Nathanial race out of the club and rush up to the Jeep as we all jump inside. I throw Nathanial the keys so that I can focus on finding Luna.

"Where the hell is my sister?" Stella shouts frantically from the back seat.

"With Camden, I think." I drop my head into my hands and close my eyes, pushing outwards with the bond that I logically know still exists, but is absolutely invisible to me.

Where are you, Luna?

"No, Camden wouldn't make her take the pill if she didn't want to do it," she refutes and rage boils in my chest at the underlying assumption.

"She didn't take it willingly, I can fucking promise you that," I say, trying to ignore her comment. It tugs at my mind though, making me wonder if she actually did take it on purpose.

No, she wouldn't do that. Not after tonight.

"Elijah, you need to focus. Feel it out even if you don't know it's there. Focus on your blood, on her blood. You know the bond exists, it's just hidden from you right now."

I lean back in the seat, and drop my arm over my eyes, blocking out any streetlights or distractions as I try to focus on everything Nathanial instructed. I search and search, begging for the slightest sign of her location or the tiniest whisper that she's still alive.

But I come up with nothing, again and again over the next several hours while we drive around aimlessly searching for my Fated.

CHAPTER THIRTY-FOUR

Luna

I'M COUNTING DOWN EVERY SINGLE MINUTE UNTIL WE HIT six hours. Thankfully, we're fucking close. I'm pretty sure I've got twenty-three minutes left before this pill should dissipate and I can tell Elijah where I am.

Which is ironic, because I actually have no fucking idea. My head throbs, a bloody mess in the back after Camden smashed me against the cement outside the club and knocked me out briefly. He threw me in the back of a white Escalade—where I caught a glimpse of the clock when I woke—and I've been here ever since we left.

We've been driving, and I vaguely felt us slow to a stop for several minutes while someone else climbed inside the vehicle. But no one has said a word, and I'm afraid to sneak a second look and let them know I'm awake. I'd rather wait out the next twenty minutes and have a moment to talk to Elijah without any of them realizing it.

I continue counting down, always trying to reach out and feel the bond ahead of time, in case Camden's calculations were incorrect and it shorts out sooner than he planned. God, I hope for that. But I also worry that things could spin the other way, and it lasts longer than the potential six hours. I push that thought to the back of my mind though, refusing to let that fear fester.

Camden's words flow through my thoughts again, *"Good for one thing, baby girl. Only one fucking thing."* An icy shiver races up my spine as they connect to another horrible part of my past. I'd like to believe that there's no way Camden could have been there that night, been a part of the four men who attacked me. But I also thought it would be impossible for Elijah to have any connection to that night either and it turned out he had been searching for me.

My mind spins and twists with all of this new information, connecting so many different people to various parts of my life that I've tried to forget. Who the hell were my parents anyway? That this was the life I was born into, that they felt the need to abandon me and Stella when we were just babies.

I don't fucking get it.

"I'm telling you, they're Fated." Camden's quiet voice suddenly breaks through the silence and I hold in a breath while I try to listen.

Fated? Elijah and I?

"We don't know that for sure yet," a female voice responds. One I'm unfortunately too familiar with. Amelia must have been the person he picked up earlier.

"He all but screamed it at me when we were training, trust me." Camden sounds annoyed. I can imagine his jaw is tense as he angrily forces the words out of his mouth.

"Fine, then we kill her. Elijah will be nothing without her," Amelia says casually, like this conversation is nothing but a nuisance.

"You're letting your emotions for Elijah cloud your judgement. If we're going to kill one, we need to take out the other." He pauses before a low laugh ripples from his throat. "Or kill Elijah and give me Luna."

Fear courses through me at the realization that either myself or Elijah might not make it out of this alive. I need to warn him, but the bond is still internally blocked.

"Find someone else to play with, Camden. If they are Fated, Elijah will find her, and we'll know for sure. At that point, we will decide which course of action to take." Amelia's voice becomes slightly more tense, frustration fills the space around us, and I have a feeling it's due to Camden's clear disapproval.

"What does Danner think?" he pushes her, and I feel the vehicle take a swift turn to the left.

"Danner is not the fucking King. And you would do well to remember who rules over this fucking race." Her voice turns icy and cold as she suddenly loses her temper. Camden immediately falls silent at the harsh rebuke.

My heart rate picks up several notches as the vehicle comes to a stop. Before Amelia and Camden step out, he quietly speaks up one last time. "You're right. I apologize, I serve you and you alone, Amelia."

She doesn't offer him a response, or even an acknowledgement to his apology. Instead, she simply instructs him on what to do next. "Take Luna to the tree. Get her ready, and I will meet you shortly."

I listen as both doors open and shut loudly. I scramble to prop myself up against the back of the seat so that I can immediately kick either of them back with my legs. My chest heaves with each passing second as I wait to hear the click of the back-door unlatching.

I race through my mind again, quickly reaching out in search of Elijah before my situation becomes more chaotic. But there's nothing, and I know we're past the six-hour threshold. A hesitant fear builds in my stomach at the thought that maybe I won't be able to reach him in the midst of this.

The definitive click of the door lock sounds in the tense air and I pull my legs back towards my chest. As soon as the latch lifts enough for me shoot forward, I launch my feet into Camden's groin, and he stumbles backwards on a growl.

"What the fuck, Luna," he says with a laugh as I dart out of the back of the vehicle, but he's far too quick and launches his fist into my hair, gripping and yanking me backwards against him. "It's a good thing that I've been the one training you over the last several weeks. I know exactly what to expect." His teeth graze my ear as he shoves me forward and I fall to the ground where gravel scrapes into my palms.

I glance up, quickly trying to determine where I am. But we're surrounded by unfamiliar scenery. Tall, thick trees and a mix of grass and gravel are layered in the darkness of the night. The only light provided is from the glossy moon. Stars are scattered above, and I have the strangest sense of finding comfort in them. Finding contentment in the fact that at least some of the stories I heard as a kid, of Angels above, are partly true.

But it's the Fallen who have captivated my attention now. A warring race of incredible creatures. Some who have taken the worst of me and others who have brought out the best. Yet I've found myself in the middle of their battle, another piece of collateral damage in their wicked game.

Camden shifts forward and begins dragging me down the dirt path ahead of us. He's taking me further into the demoni-cally shaded woods, dark with uncertainties and hidden sins.

No one will be able to find me in there and anything Camden does will be easily buried under the depths of the night.

I fight against his hold, pulling myself back and digging my feet into the uneven ground, but he's strong and he rips me harder against his body. His fingers dig in the flesh of my arms and the thin skin at the nape of my neck.

"Be a good girl, little Luna and this will end far quicker," his sickly voice scrapes and grinds against my skin while his body presses tightly to my back. He pins one of my arms behind me, strictly between his thick fingers and I do everything to hold back the whimpers of pain that are threatening to work their way out of my throat.

We walk deep into the woods, the farther we go, the darker everything becomes. Sounds of the creatures around us should scare me, but I force myself to find comfort in the fact that I won't be entirely alone out here. We make our way to a small clearing, where a single grand tree sets in the center. It's dead, the branches bare and thin as they stretch out in a tumultuous mess towards the sky.

He shoves me forward until I hit the ground against the tree and turn back to face him.

"Why?" I demand, eager to know why he would spend so much time teaching me how to fight, how to defend myself when he planned all along that this is where we would end up.

Camden crouches down to my level, his piercing eyes bore into me and a wave of nausea settles in my stomach in anticipation. "Because of what you are. Who you are. You shouldn't be here. You're a genetic mistake between supernatural creatures that should have never mingled. You're a threat to all of us. You and Elijah are too big a risk to take, little girl." His voice is clinical, as if this is just another day at the office. No hard feelings, not personal.

But it is.

He may sound bland and disinterested, but I can see the anger raging in his eyes. It's barely there, professionally contained but simmering all the same.

I slowly lean forward, lifting a hand to hesitantly rest on his cheek. I catch him by surprise and let my thumb brush against his lower lip. "I thought this was different," I whisper the words as bile rises in the back of my throat. "I thought we were different." For the first time, I let the tears I've been holding back spring to my eyes as I spit out the lie between us.

I can tell he's suddenly uncertain, confused not because he wants me, but because he didn't expect this. I take advantage and I close the distance between us. I crush my lips to his and launch forward so that he falls back before he has a chance to fight me off.

I kiss him, for only a second until I suck his tongue into my own mouth and bite. Hard. Really fucking hard. I bite until I feel my teeth meet again, taste the awful metallic flavor fill both our mouths as he yells out in pain.

I shove myself off of him as quickly as I can and turn, scraping my hands and knees through the dirt until I catch my balance to stand and run.

And I fucking run as far as I possibly can into the sinister woods ahead of me. I'm swallowed by the darkness and soon even the stars above are hidden by the wide expanse of the tree-tops. I see nothing as I become blind to everything around me.

Camden is quick to react, and I hear the faint falls of his footsteps as he tries to follow me. "Luna, you won't be able to hide from me," he calls out. His voice is disturbingly closer than I'd like it to be.

I scan the area around me quickly and find a tree that has a large trunk. Something I can hide behind as he runs past. I crouch behind it, holding my breath as the heavy hits of his steps hurry past me.

Thank God.

I take a moment to catch my breath, reaching out in the bond as I inwardly beg to find Elijah. But there is still no response, no hint to our connection being there and I fight back the anxious rise of panic as my heart rate increases and a sour pain hits my stomach. I'm missing a vital piece of my existence. An agonizing ache sits in the center of my chest and radiates through my blood. I can't help but worry that it's gone, permanently. That I've lost everything I had with Elijah.

But I can't deny the fact that even without the blood bond, I need him. It's ingrained into my soul, in every fiber of my being that he's it for me. Even in the midst of our fighting and raging anger, even when we're pushing each other away and refusing to acknowledge this force between us, I want him.

Now, I wish for the bond if only to be able to tell him how I feel. If I die tonight, he will never have known that I don't actually need the bond to need *him*. Because I do, I need Elijah like he's my last breath. I need his sun because I'm frozen in a winter storm without him.

I need his presence like a Demon needs an Angel. To balance and harmonize, to feed and thrive off of, to bleed together as one strength.

Instantly, everything around me flickers. The scenery, the woods. It all shifts to the night I was attacked seven years ago. I'm thrown back to that horrible moment and I'm terrified that if Amelia and Camden are around, they're seeing this too.

The vision keeps flashing, the woods are transforming into the alley and then back to the woods again. Over and over in quick flashes of pain and agony while I try to settle my disordered mind. I can't let them see this strange ability that was forming and building with Elijah.

Even though my back is pressed against a tree, I see the face of one of those men crouch in front of me again. The memory playing for me like a movie as he stares into my eyes, the black cloth still tied around his face when he speaks.

"You're wrong. You shouldn't be here, shouldn't be allowed to exist. You're no good for anything but this." The words etch themselves into my subconscious all over again.

His eyes pierce into me, dark and malicious, as the words and the tone of his voice seeps into my skin, reaching my memories and pulling something familiar to the forefront. Instantly, everything flashes back to the woods and I scream uncontrollably as Camden's face replaces the one from my memory. Exactly the same eyes, exactly the same stance.

"Remember me?" he whispers, a sick smile spreading across his face as I scramble backwards but hit the tree behind me.

He grips my legs and yanks me forward until he can flip me on my stomach. His hand falls heavily to my neck as he shoves my face into the ground and lands on top of me.

"I should have fucking killed you that night. After we were all done taking what we wanted. I should have killed you. You shouldn't be alive, you're a twisted disgrace of perfection. A mistake in the world we come from. A failure. Worthless. Forgettable. Nothing." He grinds the statements out across my ears. I feel his breath and spittle land on my cheek as his filthy words taint my mind. He rolls his hips forward, crushing his erection against my ass as he groans.

"You're fucking disgusting," I say, tasting the dirt as it fills my mouth.

He laughs but rolls forward again. I won't beg him this time. I won't ask for mercy or to be freed from his grasp. I know what he plans on taking from me, but I refuse to give him the pleasure from my cries and pleas.

I mentally detach myself from the moment, hiding in my own mind and refusing to be present for what he's going to do to me. I'm surprised to watch as everything around us changes again, only this time I'm still in the woods. It's during the day, and I watch as two little girls are left alone. One is a baby, new and crying as the other, kneels to hold her little sister.

"OKAY, OKAY." THE OLDER ONE SAYS. SHE'S BARELY TWO *years old, a toddler who's face is pinched with fear and confusion.*

She rocks the baby as she looks around. "Ma! Da!" she yells out, but no one is around to hear her.

CAMDEN HAS PAUSED HIS ASSAULT, WATCHING THE SCENE unfold around us as well. I hear him muttering something above me, like he doesn't understand how I'm able to do this. Joke's on him, I have no idea how to control it either.

THE OLDER GIRL BEGINS TO CRY NOW, BOTH OF THEM SEEM *afraid as she tries to stand and hold her sister at the same time. But she's small, and her little legs and arms aren't strong enough to carry them both. She falls back to the ground and pulls her sister close, crying and saying "Okay, okay, okay," over and over again through her tears.*

I'M SOBBING AGAINST THE GROUND, TEARS FLOWING FROM my eyes, dampening the dirt below me. I'm lying in a muddy mess I've made on my own and my heart is cracking wide open inside of my chest.

. . .

"It's okay, little ones," a familiar voice whispers, and I watch as Amelia steps in front of the little girls. She's wearing a long, white, silk dress that wraps around the back of her neck as she picks up the smallest baby. She softly coos until the child stops crying, then bends forward to brush her thumb against the older girl's cheek, wiping away the tears.

Shock and confusion flash through me as Elijah enters the scene with Nathanial. Both large men walking up behind Amelia. They are wearing the same silky white cloth, but as long pants and completely bare on top. Elijah is still covered in tattoos, less than he has now, but that's not what has me completely mesmerized by the three of them.

I'm lost to the stunning beauty of what's on their backs. Each of them carry a set of massive, white, feathery wings that span above their bodies several feet and fall almost to touch the ground below. They're a heavy array of iridescent wisps, thick feathers that look dense and full against their smooth skin. They're absolutely magical and my tears suddenly stop as astonishment replaces any fear I've been experiencing.

God, they're beautiful. Fucking striking and hypnotic.

The older girl slowly ambles to her feet and pushes past Amelia. She looks up and lifts her tiny arms to Elijah, who immediately takes a hesitant step back as he watches her with curiosity. But she follows him, and I hear Nathanial's confident laugh as he observes their interaction.

"Whoa, whoa, whoa, little one. Don't touch," he jokes, but he crouches down to her and she stops in front of him as they eye each other warily. Elijah tilts his head just slightly, as if he's confused by the little girl in front of him.

She puts her arms out to him again, and this time he slowly inches forward and pulls her against his chest. Her tears have stopped completely, and a beautiful smile overtakes her features as she looks over his shoulders and notices his wings.

I notice Amelia watching as well while she holds the smaller baby, her eyes shifting back and forth between Elijah and the little girl. I can see that she loves him, even if she chooses to hide it at this moment. But there is something else lurking in her eyes.

Manipulation, speculation, fear.

The little girl reaches a chubby hand forward and grazes it across Elijah's wing as the they all turn and begin walking through the woods. Elijah shudders at the touch and his eyes dart back to her sweet face. "Yeah, get a good feel now, little girl. I have a feeling I won't have them much longer," he whispers, and suddenly he steps back and away from the group for a brief moment. Amelia and Nathanial stop and turn to watch him as he lifts his wings and spreads them wide behind his back in one majestic motion.

The little girl giggles and Elijah laughs as he watches her, so he does it again. Pulling them together and then spreading them wide as she becomes enthralled with his wings. She's laughing hysterically now, and her little arms wrap around Elijah's neck.

"What are their names?" Nathanial asks as he quietly watches the smallest baby in Amelia's arms. She offers the baby to him, but he steps back and shakes his head, a wary expression crossing his face.

"This one is Stella," Amelia says as she glances up to watch Nathanial's reaction curiously. Then she nods back to Elijah and the little one he's holding. "That one is Luna."

"Luna," Elijah whispers as he resumes walking with the other two. "Why do I feel like I'm going to see you again?"

· · ·

"Enough." Amelia's sharp voice echoes behind my head and the vision shatters like glass around us. "Get off of her Camden and take her to the fucking tree like I told you too."

CHAPTER THIRTY-FIVE

Luna

Camden launches off of me and grabs my shoulders, yanking me upright as he turns us to move back towards where we came from. My mind is too busy racing through everything I just witnessed as if it were my sister and I in the vision. Was that true? Had the three of them saved Stella and I when we were abandoned?

All I knew about our past was that we were dropped off at Safe Haven. I have never wanted to know the details behind our births, not until recently when I learned about the blood in our veins. Even then, I wasn't necessarily concerned about the facts. They rejected us, didn't want us. And left us to learn about our true identities alone without any help or support. They didn't seem like people I wanted to know.

We make our way back towards the tree in silence and Amelia shifts to stand in front of me while Camden lifts my arms above my head and secures them tightly to a branch. I can see the blood that's spilled from his mouth and dried against his face. It gives me a small swell of satisfaction, knowing I hurt him. I'm stretched upwards so roughly that my toes barely touch the ground and I struggle as the pull on my shoulders becomes grossly painful.

"I think I may have underestimated you, little Luna," Amelia starts as she steps forward and brushes a single finger down the length of my cheek.

"You definitely underestimated me," I spit out while I meet her icy eyes with my own.

She smiles sympathetically, like she's breaking the bad news to me, "I won't do it again. I can promise you that." She bends slightly, keeping her eyes locked on mine as she pulls her familiar black blade from her thigh and places the tip against the thin skin under my jaw. She drags it downward, not piercing my flesh but threatening to do so.

"Your little trick back there was impressive. I doubt you even know what you're capable of. Something I'm thankful for because you're actually quite powerful. And seeing as you won't be alive after tonight, I'm not afraid to share that with you." She drops the blade to my thigh as she speaks, and slices straight through my latex dress, burying the blade in my skin as I cry out. "I've been keeping an eye on you and your sister since the three of us found you both in the woods that day. See, your mother was an Angel and your father was a Demon. They were the first of their opposing kinds to come out as a Fated pairing."

I stay silent as she continues speaking, absorbing the new information she's offering. The pain in my thigh is insurmountable and I have a feeling that things are about to get worse. But I bite my inner cheek and force the tears back as I continue meeting her stare in defiance.

I refuse to die tonight, but I'll play along with her games until I can escape.

"You don't know what that is though do you? The Fated of our kind." She drags the blade to my other leg and repeats the same motion, slicing through my skin and muscle as the scream rips painfully from my throat. "No, Elijah wouldn't share that with you. Because at the end of all this, he knows he shouldn't want you. He knows you won't be together because you shouldn't exist in the first place." Her voice becomes tight with anger and resentment as she slices my dress down the center, exposing my body to her completely. She places the blade in the center my stomach, trailing it to the right and towards my hip until she's only inches above my pelvis. In one quick motion, she buries the tip until it's fully penetrated through me.

My heart hammers in my chest as I try to maintain the energy I need to survive being tortured. But already in the mere minutes I've been strung up, I'm beginning to lose hope. I try to focus on her words, absorb what she's telling me but the agony ripping through my body is a heady distraction.

"A Demon and an Angel will never be together. It's an utter disgrace to our kind, to accept someone so tainted and possessed as a partner. But your parents fought that truth to be together, effectively muddying up our genetics and creating abominations like you and your sister."

Amelia skulks in closer to me, bringing her sadistic smile to my face as she whispers the words against my skin. I close my eyes at her declaration, slowly letting my head fall backwards before I pull the strength I need to shoot it forward and smash it clear against her nose. She rears back in pain as blood spills across her lips and I muster the energy to actually laugh at her reaction. At least I got one good fucking hit in.

Amelia's hand flies back and crashes against my face, whipping me to the side as I taste my own blood flowing into my mouth. I savor it though, because it's her weakened response to my rebellion. I feed off it, thrive off of her anger towards me. I get to her and as I die by her hand, I relish in the absolute truth that my presence affects her.

"Elijah could never love you. He could never give you everything you'd want from him. Even if you are Fated. Do you know why, sweet Luna? Have I made it clear enough to you?" She grips my jaw tightly in her small hand and breathes the words into my ear. Her blade enters on the other side of my stomach, as she twists the blade and digs it into my flesh.

I cry out, the scream scorching my throat on the way out. For an instant, I feel the flicker of the bond and suddenly it's more painful than any physical agony I'm enduring. Because it feels like it's severing. As my life and strength flow from my body through blood, the tie feels like it's crumbling between us.

And it's for that reason, that pain alone that the tears fall from my eyes and down my face. "Do you feel it? The blood bond falling apart in your frail body? It's beautiful. The destruction of something so pure, so powerful between two people." Her blade moves to my back as it pierces me again, but my body is quickly becoming numb to the outside pain as everything inside me begins collapsing and failing.

Elijah.

I try to reach out again, I'm aching to feel anything from him in this moment. I need him to know that I'm here. That I'm fucking trying. That I love him. But God, it's hard. I'm losing the fight and I don't know how to fix this.

"Does he tell you how beautiful you are?" She stabs again, another wound to my back that I hardly feel.

"Does he make love to you like you're the only air he breathes?" Another slice, this time across my upper stomach. A shallow marking that still draws blood.

"Or does he fuck you like it's a punishment?" Another slash through my numbed and destroyed flesh.

"Like you're something he should never want, something he shouldn't indulge in?" Again, across my stomach like a brand.

"Amelia. We need to leave." Camden's hard voice is barely recognizable, my ears are filled with too much pain and agony to decipher how close he is.

"Because he doesn't. Want you, that is. You could never be me, and he knows that," she spits the last words as she lays a kiss against my lips, using her ability to drag a little of my life force out as a souvenir.

"So, goodbye, little Luna. And know that I'll take care of Elijah for you. And your sister too, because she's just as toxic as you are." She steps away from me as I finally lose the strength to keep my eyes locked on hers. My head falls forward and my eyes rake over my red and ruined body. I don't hear them leave as I struggle to reach out one last time through the bond, try to break through the haze and failing ruins of what we shared together.

I tried, Elijah.

CHAPTER THIRTY-SIX

ELIJAH

I'M A FUCKING WRECK. UNCONTROLLABLY SHOUTING AT Nathanial as we race through the back streets to a forest I'm all too familiar with. I caught the smallest glimpse of where she is. It was a minuscule flash as I felt the blood bond start crumbling between us.

I'm in so much fucking pain I can hardly breathe and Nathanial and Stella are officially losing their minds over what's happening. Stella is sobbing in the back seat while Nathanial tries to calm both of us down. But I can't stop yelling and searching for her in my mind. I can hardly sit still in the vehicle as my body begs to be freed so I can be near her.

I'm losing her. I can feel her slipping away, and I haven't even had her for twenty-four hours.

I suspected I wouldn't get the bond back after the supposed six hours Camden mentioned as the efficacy of the pill. He had to have used dark magic to create it and he clearly had ulterior motives that neither Nathanial nor I picked up on. I had an instinct, a nasty feeling in my gut that something was wrong. But I ignored it and let Luna get close to him. Like a fucking idiot, I put my Fated directly in the line of danger. I will destroy every single thing in my way to get back to her.

It's quickly becoming early morning, and the sun is rising in the distance as we finally get to the place where Luna and Stella were abandoned as children—if it was indeed them all those years ago. The location can't be a coincidence and I have a suspicion it truly was them.

It's an open forest, and I see no signs of Luna anywhere. I jump out of the Jeep and rush into the woods having no idea of which direction to go, but I move anyway.

"Stay in the Jeep, Stella," I hear Nathanial call back as he races up next to me. He grabs my shoulders and turns me so that I'm facing him. His face is a mix of apprehension and sympathy, his eyes filled with only a sliver of the pain I'm feeling.

A possessive growl rips from my throat but he pushes forward and into my space with a snarl of his own. "Listen to me, Elijah. You need to focus on your Fated. Search out that connection like you did in the vehicle. Take a moment to breathe and find her in your mind, in your soul. Because she's there. She's always there." He reaches in his pocket and pulls out a small blade, anticipating that I'll need to heal her. The acknowledgement sends new bolts of pain through my chest. He shoves me back and toward the forest as he adds, "I have to stay with Stella."

I nod in agreement and turn to rush into the woods ahead. I want to do this alone anyway. I do as he suggested and close my eyes for a moment, mentally reaching out into the space ahead of me. Everything is dark, it's angry and evil with odd pockets of light that shine through in sporadic places.

Luna.

I beg for her in my mind as I call out her name. But I get nothing in response, just as I haven't since she disappeared, and rage burns through my chest with the excruciating reminder.

I push farther, deeper in my mind, into the depths of my soul and the places I haven't visited in years. I focus on the pain, accepting it and consuming it as my own until I find the tiniest flicker of her particular sting. Her pain, her acceptance and her need to survive sparks through me and tugs me instinctively to the left.

I have no idea where I'm going. But I shut my eyes and simply feel for her, struggling to bury myself deeper inside of our integrated souls. I move, without opening my eyes, step after step as I let our Fated connection build and draw me toward her.

I keep moving, stepping over branches and through trees that I don't anticipate but naturally avoid in this state. I force long breaths in and out of my lungs as I let my mind fully succumb to the agony of losing her. I groan out as the blood bond continues slowly crumbling between us.

A constant sharp ache throbs in my chest, directly over my heart as I draw nearer to her. I refuse to open my eyes, I can't shatter this pull to her. This is the only connection I've felt in the last several hours and as painful as it is, I don't want to let go of it yet.

I walk for several minutes, completely blind to my surroundings but visualizing through the rest of my senses. I smell the earthy blend of dirt and trees around us, feel the icy breeze that grates against my skin. I'm too hot, my body overworking itself to seek the chill I need from Luna. I can hear the birds chirping as the morning rises in the sky, as if nothing is wrong. Even though everything is.

Finally, I feel it. The highest peak of pain that stabs my

chest and radiates through my limbs. It tangles in my mind, like a toxic vine that chokes and suffocates me. I stop my movements and smell the thick scent of blood as it wafts over me. I let out a painful growl that surrenders to an agonizing cry as I force my eyes to open and am met with a vision directly from my nightmares.

Luna hangs in front of me, her strong arms now weak and worn from holding her up against the branch of a single tree. She's almost completely bare, her dress torn down the center while her body is covered thickly in her own blood. Her once vibrant and wild dark hair hangs limply around her shoulders and down her back, matted together in dirt while clinging to her sickly white face.

I launch forward immediately, intending to quickly to free her from the tree and bring her into my own arms. But my feet drag and trip through the dirt as my body weakens in torture. My soul is dying with her, climbing inside of her and refusing to let her go alone.

I immediately lay my hands on her cheeks, hissing at the frozen temperature of her skin. I brush my trembling thumbs across the stray strands of her hair, naturally trying to make to her comfortable even though I know it may not matter at this point.

"Luna," I whisper, my voice cracking as I reach up to untie her delicate and blue hands. "Luna," I say again, as I free her and she falls against me, completely limp and weightless while I carry her to the ground.

I press my ear against her lips, trying to slow my own breath as I search and beg for her own. A wave of relief crashes through me as I'm met with small, shallow gasps when our skin finally meets. Her soft lips part and her eyes make the barest of movements under her eyelids.

"I'm here, Luna. I'm here," I say again as I pull her small

body tightly against my own. I let my eyes travel across her ragged skin, trying to determine what's been done to her. She has multiple stab wounds, knife lacerations across her legs and back. But my eyes drift to the injuries intentionally positioned on her stomach.

An uncontrollable rage burns through me at the word that's been carved into her milky skin. It means I screwed up along the way and revealed our secret. It means I put her here, without giving her the knowledge to defend herself. It means I gave her to our enemy, blindly and disastrously because I fought to deny what was so clearly in front of my face.

Fated.

"I'm so sorry, *m'aingeal*," I choke on the words against her cheek and move to speak them over her ears and then her lips. I push through our bond and beg for it to stimulate between us. I reach for the knife in my pocket and shift Luna in my arms so that I can access my own skin.

I quickly grip the hilt and drag the tip down the inside of my forearm with shaking hands. The cut is rough and deep, but I don't give a fuck about it as I do the same thing to my other arm. I lean forward, laying Luna down gently on the soft ground as I tear my shirt and jeans off of my body. I use the blade to slash my flesh in several different areas, welcoming the sting and pain as my own blood spills and flows over my skin.

Sitting back down, I pull Luna back into my arms as I lean against the tree. I close my eyes tightly, absently rocking her as I beg and plead for this to work. I feel my blood soak her skin as ours merges together in painstakingly slow increments. Hers doesn't answer mine, instead the blood simply flows together in a disoriented mess of blood and dirt.

"Come back to me, Luna. Come back to me," I say as I nudge my face into the crook of her neck. I let her darkness consume me, lose myself to the smell of her sweet skin, let my heat work its way into her frozen body. I trail my hands along her arms, trying to warm her and breathe life back into her weakened state.

I drag my fingers painfully across her carved stomach, cursing Camden for what he's done and for Amelia's participation in this. Because I know, without a shadow of a doubt that he's working for her and Danner. Camden is a follower, he's no leader. Amelia would want the Fated flushed out so that she would have no retaliation to the throne.

Camden must have told her about my slip while we were all training. When I almost called Luna my Fated. He caught it. Christ, I hoped he didn't, but he fucking did and now here we are. With Luna practically dead in my arms as I struggle to use everything inside of me to bring her back.

"My Fated," I whisper the words as I brush my lips against her jaw. "My Demon," I say as I move to the soft skin under her ear. "My Angel," I claim her as I breathe against her skin and softly kiss her shut eyes. "My Luna," I declare as lay my lips against her blue ones, feel her icy breath against my own.

"*Ol boaluahe, ol allar ol cnila de g,*" I let the Enochian words rolls off my tongue in an indestructible vow to her. *My love, I bind my blood to you.*

I continue chanting them like a prayer, I profess and demand the words into the silent space around us. Because I can't do this, I can't let her go. I'll never be able to let her go. I pull her body even tighter against mine and wrap my arms around her weakened figure so that every single inch of us is touching and connecting with one another.

My voice becomes rough and angry as I continue claiming her as my Fated, affirming her as mine and no one else's. I get louder, shouting the words as I feel the power between us grow incrementally bigger. It's barely reacting, but if I can get enough of our Fated connection to respond, maybe it will consume us and heal her enough to save her life.

I feel the soft gasp of air as Luna takes a quick breath in. She takes another, and another one. Each of them swift, rapid draws as I try to give her more of me.

"That's it, Luna. Breathe, just breathe *m'aingeal*," I urge her to continue as I lift my hand and clasp her jaw so that our foreheads are pressed tightly together. My lips brush against hers as I breathe into her, giving her everything she can take from me. She's devouring my scent, my breaths, the feeling of our skin pressed tightly together. Her blood slowly begins to merge with mine as my familiar call beckons to her and she finds her way home.

"Elijah," she whispers the words and while they're barely audible, they explode around us and inside of me as if she's shouted them out.

"I've got you, Luna. You're safe," I say to her in a low, ragged voice. Her hand slowly lifts and I reach for it, pulling it up the rest of the way and anchoring her hand behind my neck. Her fingers softly move against my skin as her body begins the slow process of healing everything that's been done to her. My own body naturally doesn't attempt drawing from her yet, my wounds and cuts still freshly giving her everything she needs from me.

"It's ruined, isn't it?" she asks, her eyes still shut while her heart begins hammering strongly in her chest. My own mimics hers, thundering loudly as our bodies continue joining together. "The blood bond."

Disappointment blooms around us, a joined emotion that is evident without the covenant responding. It's true, I still don't feel what we once shared. Her body draws from mine on a completely separate connection even though our blood reacts just the same. It's as if it's working and operating clearly, but we simply don't feel the effects of it any longer. I know it's there though. It no longer crumbles between us in agonizing division. It's simply mute.

"No, nothing is ruined sweet Angel. We'll fix it."

That, I promise. Because I will never lose my Luna. And I will destroy anyone who gets in the way of us again.

CHAPTER THIRTY-SEVEN

ELIJAH

LUNA AND I STAYED IN THAT SPOT UNDER THE TREE FOR over an hour while her body slowly regained the strength it needed to at least superficially heal the injuries scattered across her wounded torso and legs. Mine eventually pulled minimally from her, as she took the time to gently trail her fingers across each cut, giving back to me anything she could manage.

Now, I refuse to let go of her. Which is why I'm laid back against the door of the jeep while Luna stays nestled tightly in my arms and between my legs. She's wearing my shirt and my eyes linger over every inch of her. Physically, she looks healed. Her skin has taken some of its color back, the abrasions are gone with only minimal scars left behind. Eventually, they'll disappear as well but I know it's going to take more connection through our bodies and our bond before everything is fully restored.

Stella can't take her eyes off of Luna as she sits in the front passenger seat with her head resting in one of her hands. Her eyes are swollen and red, her cheeks stained from the salty tears that keep flowing down her face. Nathanial keeps glancing towards Stella, he knows Luna is safe now, but can't seem to ignore the fiery red head sitting next to him. His hand rests on the back of her chair, and I can't help but notice the way he remains close to her without touching.

It reminds me of myself, before when I insisted on fighting to stay away from Luna.

My attention falls back to her as she burrows her head deeper against my chest. I rest my heavy hand on the side of her face, savoring the connection of her body against mine. I can't stop myself, when her head tips up and her soft pink lips angle toward me, I take her. Gently, and slowly as I memorize the feeling of her lips moving against my own. I taste her, and she willingly opens for me as I slide my tongue between her lips. My fingers tangle in the strands of her hair but I don't grip or hold her tightly. I simply cherish the sensation of her skin against mine, of my heat melting her frost. Our Fated tie creates an intense flood of energy that gently consumes us.

"Stop," Stella's voice is a quiet whisper and Luna and I both glance her way as we pull apart. Her eyes are ghostly white again and her chest rises and falls on rapid breaths. "Please."

"We need to figure out what's happening with you," Luna says, as she turns to rest her head against my shoulder. My fingers shift to twist her sweet locks around them, dark and delicious against my tattooed fingers.

Stella watches for a moment longer, until her eyes clear and she turns around without another word. I can feel the tension surrounding her, and I'm surprised when I see Nathanial hesitantly drop his hand to the back of her neck over her hair. His thumb grazes back and forth in support of her and I notice the way her shoulders immediately relax at his touch.

I turn my eyes back down to Luna and see as she watches the same curious interaction. It's a discussion we will have to address sooner or later, I think it's obvious that Stella is drawn to sexual exchanges. And Nathanial seems drawn to her especially.

Luna and I continue subtly touching and connecting with each other. Living in the moment of finally accepting what our relationship is meant to be. But my mind is racing with thoughts of what happened to her. I need to know who exactly was responsible for this.

"Can you talk to me about last night?" I whisper against her ear as she takes a ragged sigh against my chest.

"It was Camden and Amelia. He forced me to take the pill at the club when I left to find Stella. He and Amelia drove me out to the woods," she pauses, collecting herself before she begins to explain what happened. She glances toward the front of the vehicle, noticing that both Nathanial and Stella are listening to her as well. "There's a lot. About all of us. I saw people, things that happened when we were children." Her eyes turn back to me, "Like when we were at the house, in the back yard. It happened again, quick flashes that showed me parts of our pasts."

"What happened at the house?" Nathanial asks, trying to catch up to speed on what she's talking about. We hadn't told anyone, hell I hadn't even told Luna about the ties that run deeper than our blood bond.

"We should start at the beginning." I interrupt, needing to explain where all of this starts. "Because Luna needs to know about the Fated."

"Amelia told me. Well, at least partly. I heard Camden tell her that you and I were Fated. And then she mentioned it as well. She said a lot of things that don't matter, but I want to know why you didn't tell me." Luna sits up slightly, so that her eyes can meet my own. I don't see anger or irritation in her, but I do see the flashes of pain at the memories of whatever Amelia said.

I lift my hands to her face and hold her still so she can hear each word I say to her, "I didn't tell you because I wanted to keep you safe. That is the only reason. The Fated were couples of our kind who were destined to be together. They were rare, but incredibly powerful. They have been slaughtered for centuries until the Fated no longer existed. We haven't seen a surviving Fated pair in countless years. And if any do step forward, they're quickly killed and destroyed. That's why I didn't tell you, I didn't want anyone to know." I speak the words truthfully, enunciating each sentence.

I can see her relax in both her eyes and her body. "How did you know we were Fated?" she asks. She has no idea how different it feels compared to a blood bond.

"Because you wouldn't bond to Nathanial when I brought you home that first night." Stella visibly tenses in front of us but shows no reaction in her expression. "And because of how different this feels compared to anything I had with Amelia. You asked the first time we touched, if what we felt was normal. It's not, because we're so much more than simply bonded through blood. It was the only way I was able to find and heal you today."

Luna accepts my answer with a gentle smile as she leans forward and quickly places a soft kiss against my lips. God, I want to take her right here, show her how much she means to me in more than what just words can provide. Then her face suddenly falls, and hesitancy pulls at her eyes.

"I saw something else," she begins, and I urge her to continue as I brush my thumb across her lower lip. "Stella and

I, when we were young. Stella was only a baby and I was barely a toddler." She's whispering, like she's sharing a secret that I already know. Disbelief washes over me as I instantly know what she must have seen. Nathanial tenses as well and I instruct him to pull over on the side of the road.

"Show me," I insist. But I glance up to Stella who is watching us intently. I nod pointedly at Nathanial as he gently turns her to face him. If this works, they'll both see the vision anyway. But I need Stella in her right frame of mind to truly understand it.

"I don't know how, Elijah. It just happened in flashes earlier," she explains, but she does know by what means this can be initiated. We both do, we just haven't tried to access it intentionally until now.

I take her hands and place them on either side of my face as I rest her forehead against my own. I lay my hands gently on her cheeks as our lips brush against each other with each breath. "Relive the memory, call it up in your mind and I will meet you there, my Luna." I hungrily take her mouth with my own, easing her lips apart as we fall into a day that happened so many years ago.

Instantly, I'm thrown back in time and Luna pulls away in a rush as we find ourselves back in the middle of the woods. Stella gasps in surprise and fear as she watches the memory unfold around us. Nathanial takes her neck in his hand again, reassuring her safety as we find the two little girls left abandoned so long ago.

It plays out, and I feel the wave of nostalgia ripple through me as we see ourselves with wings again. But I would never take this moment back, never regret this decision in the slightest. However, I'm surprised at a portion of the memory I don't recall. When Luna reaches her small hand forward and touches my wing. Reliving the memory like this sends an electric shock across my back where my scars now adorn me as flaws. I don't remember Amelia telling us their names and by the look on Nathanial's face, he doesn't remember this part either.

Just as quickly everything shifts back around us, placing us each back in our respective seats in the Jeep and on the side of the road.

"How is that possible?" Stella asks quietly, and for the first time, I have a somewhat decent answer to her questions.

"From the very beginning I was drawn to Luna. It's as simple as that for the time being." My eyes don't leave Luna's as I speak the words and fall deeper into my Fated. Quiet tears fill her own and I brush them away before they can break free. Pulling her back into my arms, I press a soft kiss against her head as Nathanial drives us the rest of the way home.

Home.

CHAPTER THIRTY-EIGHT

Luna

I'm finally home. Finally comfortable in Elijah's house, knowing there is nowhere else I'd rather be. Although, I don't feel *complete*. I know there's a piece of us missing. Something instrumental to our connection, the basis of us first coming together.

We just got back a few hours ago and the blood bond is still muted. It's a silent tether that forcibly divides us by simply not giving us what we crave. My drug is being dangled in front of my face, held against my blood but never fully given into. It tempts me and arouses me but doesn't satisfy the need I have for him.

I know he feels it. He's twitchier than usual, constantly moving his hands across my skin in search of that fix we both need. Our only option was to call Esme and hope that her magic would be able to restore this disconnect within our blood.

"This is going to hurt," the tall blonde says as she steps forward in front of the couch. Elijah and I are both sitting next to each other, his hand is wrapped possessively around my thigh as I lean into his side. I'm comfortable in long jogger pants and his sweatshirt which hides the scars that haven't fully healed. I hate the sight of them, the markings she left me with to remind me of the poisonous words she said.

The painful comments about her and Elijah gnaw at my mind and fester in my chest. Without actually being able to feel what Elijah is truly thinking, I can't help but question the validity of what she said. I believe everything he's told me, I really do. But it's different when I don't have his resolve flowing easily through our bond.

"It can't be worse than everything I went through last night," I say sarcastically, and she offers me an apologetic smile.

Nathanial and Stella stand in opposite corners of the room, reinforcing the separation they generally maintain now that we are back in familiar territory. Stella is visibly nervous, chewing on her nails and fidgeting restlessly in the corner. I smile at her, conveying my confidence in what we're doing with my eyes.

"Thank you for this, Esme." Elijah's voice breaks through the tension in the room, solidifying the fact that we truly are going through with this complex spell.

She nods and motions for both of us to rise. "Elijah, you stand behind Luna. Go ahead and wrap your arms around her waist. You will want to hold on to each for this."

I feel Elijah's heat as it wraps around me and I sink back into his embrace. I rest my hands against his arms and focus on the touch of his skin against mine.

"Everything over the last eighteen hours will hit you at once. All of it. Elijah, everything you missed while she was gone, every ounce of pain she went through, every spike of fear

275

will course through you. The same goes for you Luna, any terror or anger he experienced, you will feel as well. I know you both experience flashes of visions at times and there is a chance that will happen again. It's something you need to be aware of if you're ripped into that moment."

My heart begins hammering in my chest at her warning, the last thing I want to do is relive anything over last night again. But if this is the only way we can restore the blood bond, then I will give anything to have it back.

"Nathanial and Stella, I suggest you both leave. Elijah and Luna will need the time to find their balance again." She turns towards us, "As soon as I know the spell has worked and your blood is cleansed, I will leave as well. You will both be left alone, which is exactly what you need."

I can see the hesitation in Nathanial and Stella's eyes, neither of them wants to leave us but they have know it's for the best. Nathanial nods to the front door as the two of them quickly leave the house.

Esme begins once we're alone by lighting a small bundle of sage she has tied together with twine. She steps closer to us and immediately I feel the undeniable strength that surrounds her. She's powerful, and even alone, without a Fated mate, she's incredibly strong. I can't begin to imagine what she's capable of.

She starts slowly walking around us, chanting words I vaguely recognize as what I believe may be Enochian. They filter through my ears and begin pricking at my blood. I feel it, the way her magic is strangely seeping in through my skin.

My heart rate kicks up and I close my eyes, focusing on Elijah's warmth surrounding me. My breaths quicken and I forcibly slow them to try and calm the rising force inside of me. Elijah tightens his arm around my waist and wraps his other around the front of my shoulders and chest as he pulls me against him.

Esme stops in front of us, I can tell because all of my senses are enhanced. I keep my eyes closed but I feel her presence directly in front of me. Her voice grows louder and the pull in my blood grows stronger. It feels like the spell is literally withdrawing from me—my strength, my essence, the toxic poison of the pill. It's infected me far more than I realized because every one of my organs is responding in a sudden stretch of pain and panic.

I can't hold back the sharp whimper that falls from my mouth and I feel Elijah stiffen around me. My lips fall open as I try to maintain the pace of my breath. My chest falls and rises in heavy motions and Elijah has to hold me together as he suddenly begins trembling around me.

"Support each other. Focus on each other. Feel the blood bond as it comes rising back to the surface. Pull it out of the blood that flows between you both," Esme shouts over the loud chaos that begins invading the space around us. Everything seems louder. Our breaths, the rushing of blood in our veins, the sound of our bodies moving against each other with every exhale.

I hear Elijah groan behind me, a painful and dark sound that transforms into a dangerous growl at the back of my neck. My knees weaken and everything becomes too overwhelming. Elijah tries to hold us both up, but we surrender to the fall and slide to the ground as I collapse against his chest. He keeps us tangled together, and my hands seek his skin as I lift them and cling to his warmth.

I sense when Esme leaves the room. She does it silently, her presence is no longer here. Her magic, however, is in full force as it continues ripping through us and everything begins shifting in the room.

I don't want to open my eyes because I know what's happening. I feel the anger and fear that doesn't belong to me, rising in my gut. It's Elijah's, his emotions from last night shredding my flesh as the memory is relived around us.

But just as I'm experiencing his nightmare, he's reliving every moment of mine. Our clashing visions come colliding around us. I pry my eyes open as my fingers dig into the skin of Elijah's arms. His body is rock hard behind mine, a dangerous mix of volatile rage and fury at what surrounds us.

It's a deadly storm of chaos and revelations. I hold on to him for my life, because if I let go, I know I'll drown in a sea of anguish. Everything mixes in two messy visions. I see myself pressed to the ground as Camden climbs my back and reveals his involvement in that night seven years ago. I watch as Amelia takes her blade and slices through my skin, hear the words she spewed into my ears about Elijah.

I feel the blazing anger burn through him and into me. I uncontrollably arch my back as the pain pierces through my blood and the bond begins restoring new life. I watch as the vision shows Elijah rushing through the club, breaking down every door he passed as he shouted my name into the empty spaces. I feel his pain and regret as they drove endlessly without any idea of where I was. I see Stella crying in the back of the Jeep and watch as Nathanial fails to comfort either of them.

Suddenly it's there. Thriving between us. Pumping so strongly it's nearly bursting at the seams with our heavy emotions. The blood bond is at full force as the vision shatters around our bodies. Elijah's trembling hand grips the side of my face as he tears me back to press his forehead against my own.

His thumb drifts down the front of my throat, touching, connecting, absorbing the feeling of my skin against his while both our Fated and blood bonds pulse with new life. My head falls back as the pain flows from our bodies, leaving us with a new energy that demands the same attention.

My body shifts from the messy pain into a needy desire to claim Elijah once again. I feel the change in him as well as he frantically drops his hands to the hem of my sweatshirt and rips it up and over my head. I'm leaning back against his chest and his hands fall around me, his rough fingers grazing over every inch of my skin as he explores my body.

"More," I choke out, reaching back to grip his shirt so that he knows I need to feel him as well. He responds quickly, ripping his own shirt over his head and dropping it the ground beside us. I lean back again and consume the heat of his flesh against my colder torso.

My hand rises to the back of his neck as he presses his lips against my ear, sucking my lobe in between his teeth before his tongue slides out and down the length of my jaw. He presses hard, hungry kisses against me, tasting me and eating at me while my body arches against his.

"Fuck, Luna," he growls and I turn my head towards his in search of his lips. He takes my mouth harshly, savoring me while we're alone and can finally give in to each other on our own terms. "Everything she said was a lie. Feel that, know that in here," his hand slides to rest over my heart as he takes my lip and sucks it into his mouth before deepening the kiss even more. His tongue slips inside, clashing with mine in a hungry battle for satisfaction.

"I want every part of you. The Angel. The Demon. Every dark and dangerous corner, every bright space that claims you. I take them all and demand each piece as my own." His hands slide to the thin straps of my bra as he slowly tugs them down my shoulders and exposes my breasts. His thumb brushes across one of my nipples, pulling and rolling it until I'm moaning against his neck. "I want to consume every inch of you. Devour you and destroy you until you're writhing beneath me and begging for what only I can give you."

His other hand slips to the waist band of my pants as his fingers slide underneath and find my bare pussy, soaking wet and aching for him. He groans against my shoulder as his teeth nip and pull at my skin. His tongue slips against the same space, dragging up the side of my neck until he's whispering against my ear again. "Life. Passion. Energy. Satisfaction."

He dips his finger down to my opening, slicking through my wetness and bring it back up to soak my clit. My legs fall apart for him as my hips roll against his hand, seeking to be filled in any way that he'll give me.

"I fuck you because I need you. Because your body calls to me in ways I've never felt before. I fuck you because my blood calls out to yours, demanding the fix it craves from what only you can give me." He plunges two fingers inside of me, going deep as I cry out and succumb to his hold. His other hand leaves my breasts and grasps the base of my jaw as he turns my head back to him. His lips graze mine as he continues speaking in that dark, dangerous voice that affects me just as strongly as his touch. "But I fuck you in the same breath that I make love to you. Because I do, Luna. I love you. More than anything or anyone that came before. More than anything that could ever happen in the future. I belong to you. You own me in every way that could ever exist."

An orgasm quickly erupts inside of me as my pussy grips his fingers. He continues sliding inside of me while I ride it out against him. He's quick to pull out and twist us so that I'm on my back on the floor beneath him and he hovers over me.

"I love you," I say the words as his lips fall to mine and he rolls his hard cock against my aching core. His hands grip my pants and panties in one motion as he yanks them down my body. He lifts my legs by the back of my knees and spreads me wide open for him as he sits back. I watch while his eyes hungrily fall to the apex of my thighs and his fingers drop to my wetness.

He lets one finger slide through my slit, slick and hot as his eyes lift to watch my reaction. I whimper at the slight touch, begging for more as he gently pulls my thighs even further apart and slowly slips his finger inside me. He's pacing himself, agonizingly slow as he begins building me back up in need and desire for him. His thumb rubs against my clit as he pumps that one finger in and out, in and out.

"Give me more, Elijah. I need more," I say as I roll my hips against his hand in search of that friction. He plays with me, continuously taking me incrementally closer to an orgasm, but not nearly enough to throw me over.

His lips fall to my ear as he comes above me. "Beg for it," he demands and suddenly the air around us turns hot and thick with a darker desire. He halts his movements, slowly pulling himself away as I'm left painfully empty.

"Please. I need you. Fuck me Elijah," I plead on a breathless moan as his lips move to the center of my chest and work down my body.

"Not yet, *m'aingeal*. I'm taking my time with you." He lifts my legs and drops them over his shoulders as his mouth roughly takes my pussy. I feel his tongue slide through me, tasting and eating me before he trails it up to my clit. He sucks the sensitive bud into his mouth, biting before soothing the sting he intentionally gave me.

"So good, Luna. You taste so fucking sweet. Like my own personal poison."

My hand slides into his hair as my hips uncontrollably start grinding against his face. His tongue dives into my pussy, going deep as he fucks me with his mouth. His hands grip my hips tightly as he pulls me against him, shifting and moving me so that we're working as one to draw out my orgasm.

"Fuck, Elijah. God, more. Please," I beg him, needing to feel his thick cock inside me.

"Soon, *mo dheamhan*. Soon." He tugs my clit between his teeth as he slides two fingers inside of me and begins working me over while new sensations rush through me. The painful bite of his teeth and soft stretching of my pussy around his fingers is overwhelmingly delicious.

But I'm greedy, and now my body is begging for his rough touch and hard fuck. So, I reach down to his head and tangle my fingers in the strands of his hair as I pull him up back up to my face. I take his mouth with my own as he groans into me. I lick his lips and delve into his mouth, tasting my own wetness on him and becoming that much needier to have him inside of me. I lift my lips to his ear, brushing them along the shell as I speak.

"I need you to fuck me. Hard and dark like only you can do to me," I whisper as I push him back and throw my leg across his waist. I quickly unzip his jeans and roughly tug them down his thick thighs. His black briefs are tight and hold back his long, heavy cock which begs to be inside me.

I grind myself against his length, my wetness soaking through his briefs and coating his cock like I want it too. "Please," I beg again, letting my moans fill the air as I dry fuck him against the floor.

Elijah shoots up, pinning my hands behind my back as he yanks his briefs down and releases his thick shaft. "Sit up," he demands, and I do as he says. He drags the wide tip through my slick pussy and I immediately move to sink myself on him when he pulls it away. "Not until I tell you too," he growls, and I whimper at the loss of him.

"You'll fuck me when I say you can. And then you'll ride me hard and fast while I watch you take my cock. Say yes, Luna."

Fucking hell. I'm so turned on.

"Yes," I obey him, submitting to his dark tone and dominating demeanor. He drags his cock back through my pussy, holding me still with the bind he has on my hands.

"Touch your clit," he instructs as he releases one of my hands but maintains his grip on the other. I slide my hand forward and in between my legs, circling my clit as his cock continues torturing me slowly.

"Fuck, you're killing me," I say, moaning and writhing as I touch myself for him.

His eyes stay glued to my fingers while I pinch and roll my clit. His hand begins fisting and stroking his cock at the same time as he moves it against me, working us both up and into needy messes.

"Destroying you," he corrects plainly and then his eyes find mine again as finally gives me what I want. "Now, fuck me."

I immediately sink down on him and we both suck in a breath as his hard cock stretches and fills me. I mold and fall around him while his fingers harshly dig into the flesh of my hips. "Put your hands over your head," his voice is deeper, huskier as he begins lifting and dropping my hips to a rhythm that rips into both of us. I lift my hands and stack them on my head, stretching myself out and arching my back into his touch.

"God, you're stunning," he says as his eyes move up and down my body. They fall to where we are joined and linger there, watching as he stretches me open and then pulls out. He moves me quickly over him, up and down in a fast and rapid pace. I feel the coil twisting tightly inside of me. Low and heavy as the orgasm begins building intensely.

Suddenly, Elijah lifts up and flips us so that I'm on my back. He hovers over me as he pulls one of my legs up and around his hip. He's spreading me even wider as he plunges into me deeper than ever before. He grinds the base of his cock against my clit every time he fills me, and I know I'm close to coming.

"Come here, Luna," he whispers and lifts us both so that he's sitting up while I straddle his broad stance. Our chests are pressed tightly together while I lift and fall against his cock. My hands fall down his shoulders and trail over his biceps. I move them to his back, feeling his skin until my fingers brush over the clear scars where his wings used to be. I graze against them as his head falls to the crook of my neck while I continue to ride him.

"You're everything I could ever need," I whisper in his ear as his body shivers with my touch. "You've always been everything I've ever needed."

His head turns to take my lips and I give them to him. He kisses me with an eager passion that crashes through my head. An orgasm rips across my body while his hips lift to meet mine on every thrust.

"My Fated," he whispers as his hips crash into me and he finds his own release. We lose ourselves to each other, to the blood bond and Fated connection that flows powerfully through us. We consume each other with every breath, love each other with every thought, and I realize that for the first time in my life, I feel whole again.

CHAPTER THIRTY-NINE

ELIJAH

IT'S BACK. EVERYTHING IS BACK AND THRIVING BETWEEN us. The blood bond was restored, and I've spent the last two days buried so deep inside of Luna that I want to forget my own fucking name.

She's perfect. And I can't help but hate myself a little for pushing her away for so long. I swear, I gave an inch and fell the rest of the damn way into her. As soon as I let myself accept Luna, my entire being consumed her and she devoured every inch of me.

I can't fucking get enough.

We have a lot to figure out though. Which is why Nathanial and Stella are coming over today. Luna wants Stella to move in with us, and I as much as I don't want anyone to interrupt my time with my Fated, I do agree that Stella needs protection. Especially as we try to understand what has been happening to her lately.

I have an idea, but it's highly unlikely. It would mean that the Demon in her veins has essentially taken over the Angel. That she leans more to the Demonic side than Angelic. But in order for that to happen, someone would have to have pulled it out of her. Essentially, fed and nourished the Demon while they effectively starved her Angel.

We've already asked her how much time she's spent with Camden away from all of us, but she swears it wasn't often at all. I know she isn't lying. She hates him for what he did to Luna. Despises him and wants to kill him herself. She doesn't know that she'll have to fight me for that honor. Because the next time I lay eyes on Camden, he's fucking dead.

We're taking the girls to the Capital today. It's time they see the place for themselves and start getting comfortable in our world. They're forever linked to this now.

I'm lying on my side in mine and Luna's room. I decided to move into hers rather than move her downstairs. My room was filled with too many memories of bad mistakes and angry nights. Her room has only ever been for her. It's remained empty all these years until she moved in, and I like the idea that it was intentionally that way without me realizing it.

Luna is quietly sleeping next to me, her peaceful self nestled tightly into my side as I watch her. I lift my hand and trail a finger across her cheek, gently pushing back some of the dark strands of her hair that obstruct my view of her sweet face.

"Are you going to lay there and watch me all morning?" Her quiet voice is thick with sleep as she cracks one eye to look at me. I can't help but smile at her. She's been doing that to me lately, drawing out more and more smiles and laughs. I can't remember the last time I've genuinely felt happy like this.

"No," I reply as I roll over and pin her face down underneath me. I drag her hands up above her head as she pushes her sweet ass into my hips. "Now that you're awake I'm going to fuck you until you're exhausted and you fall back asleep. Then I'll watch you this afternoon until you wake up and we do it all over again." I nip at her shoulder as a tired laugh escapes her. She writhes beneath me in desire and all I want to do is fill her tight pussy up.

My hard cock pushes against her as I hold her in place and slide my hand to the front of her naked body, snaking it down between her legs and feeling her slick heat. "God, so fucking wet," I groan, and she moans in response as I fist my aching cock to slip inside of her from behind. Since Luna and I are officially together—and because we absolutely couldn't get enough of each other—Luna informed me that she's been on birth control for the last ten years. Truthfully, I didn't care if she was or not, because I know without a doubt that she is it for me. It's going to be us from here on out. And I plan on making her a mother at some point in our long lives. But that'll come when she wants, and I'm not ready to share my time with her yet.

Just as I'm about to take her sweet body, we tense as the front door to the house flies open and swings shut on a loud slam. I pause for a moment, my mind instantly racing with possibilities of who would just walk in. Logically, it's Nathanial and Stella. But after everything that has happened, I've been on edge.

I quickly pull away from Luna and tug the blankets up to cover her naked form. She sighs in frustration as she rolls over and I hurry to the door of our room as I yank a pair of pants up my legs.

"All right, stop screwing and get down here. We have a lot of shit to get done today." Nathanial's voice booms from the bottom floor and I pound my fist against the door in annoyance.

"Mother fucker," I growl as I pull it open and step out onto the landing. "I should kill you for what you just interrupted." I glance back at Luna and find her smiling as she watches from our bed.

Our bed.

Her hair is mussed, and her skin is flushed in arousal. One leg is propped up over the blankets while she clings the thin fabric up to barely cover her chest. One of her rosy nipples peeks out from behind the sheet and fuck, I just want to pull it into my mouth and taste her sweet skin all over again.

"Get dressed, *mo dheamhan beag*. Before I come in there and decide we're never leaving this room again."

Luna laughs as she climbs out of bed, gloriously naked and begins getting dressed. I leave her to it as I move down the staircase and meet Nathanial at the bottom.

"Stella here yet?" I ask as I move past my brother and into the kitchen. I put on a pot of coffee, pulling down four mugs from my cabinet as we wait for the girls to join us.

"I don't know. I'm not her fucking keeper," he snaps, and I twist my head back in confusion.

"What the hell? What's your problem today?" I ask, ignoring his comment and pressing him for answers.

"Fuck. I don't know. I've been on edge lately. Like there's this constant itch under my skin that I can't reach. And Stella annoys the hell out of me, she makes it worse," he answers as he slides into a chair and takes a mug for himself.

"Are you sure the itch isn't Stella herself?" I ask tentatively. They have an odd interaction, the two of them.

"I'm fucking sure. I just haven't been sleeping well, and we have a lot to discuss at the Capital. We need to decide if you and Luna are coming out as Fated. And if that's the case, if you both will step in and take the throne."

He's right. It's a thought that's been nagging at the back of mind since I met Luna and the possibility of her being my Fated presented itself. Initially I didn't want anyone to know about her. I wanted to keep her safe and hidden from our kind. But clearly, that did nothing except make things worse, and I know Luna will want to share her input on this as well. Before I can answer him, however, Stella's voice sounds from the front door.

"Please tell me we have coffee," she shouts as she slowly makes her way into the kitchen. Her hair is a mess, wild and pulled into a feral bun on top of her head. Her white skin is looking even paler today, with purple bags settled under her eyes.

I don't miss the way her and Nathanial's eyes meet for a brief moment before both of them ignore each other and she ambles her way to the coffee pot. She takes a mug from me without a word and pours it herself before taking a seat on the opposite side of Nathanial.

"What happened to you?" I ask Stella before lifting my eyes as Luna enters the room.

"Can't sleep," is all she offers in response, but my attention is fully focused on my Fated now. Through our blood bond I can feel the energy of apprehension moving through her. She's worried about her sister and confused by what's happening to her. I'll need to talk to her about what I think could possibly be going on.

Luna stops next to Stella and presses a soft kiss to her hair before walking over to stand in front of me. She leans back into my chest and I rest a hand possessively on her hip as the four us settle into the morning.

"So, we're going to the Capital. We'll show you guys around and we have a space there where we can discuss every-thing. We have a lot of possibilities we need to nail down, decide where we are going from here, whether Luna and I are going to reveal ourselves as a Fated, and a few other things." I lay it out, hoping we can go and get this over with quickly. I'm eager to get Luna back home where I can continue laying out every other term in a very different form of nailing things down.

Stella rubs her eyes as she groans in exhaustion. "Fine. But my boyfriend has been bugging me to meet you all. He thinks we've been together long enough to meet each other's families. Can we do something tonight? Go out somewhere for dinner?"

"Tonight? Can't he wait a week or something? I think we're all a little exhausted," Luna offers. She's reading my mind, or the bond because going out and meeting Stella's boyfriend is the last thing I want to do.

"Believe me, I don't want to do it either. But he's been fucking nagging me, and if everything goes poorly, I can break up with him afterwards. Please, give me a great reason to break up with the poor guy." Stella lifts her doe eyes towards Luna, silently begging her to agree. Nathanial seems tense as he silently glowers in his own chair, and I'll put up with anything as long as I know I'll have Luna at my side.

"Fine. But just have him come here, I don't want to go out tonight." Luna pauses, and I know without her saying the words, she's thinking about mentioning Stella moving in now. "Speaking of, why don't you just stay here tonight?" she adds coyly.

"Sure, that sounds like a good idea. Maybe I'll sleep better being closer to you guys. I always worry while I'm away."

"Well if that's the case. Why don't you just move in?" Luna says it like it's a casual question, but Stella's head shoots up and her eyes widen between us.

"You're kidding right? Staying the night is one thing.

Moving in is something completely different." Stella's voice is tense, unease dripping from her tone at the idea. I can't understand why she would be so worried about it, but I notice the way she glances at Nathanial for a split second, as if she's looking for his opinion.

"Shitty idea, honestly," he offers and her face pinks up in irritation.

"What the hell does that mean?" Stella turns to face him, defiance spreading across her features.

"Wait. Christ, you two are ridiculous," Luna interrupts them. "First of all Stella, I'm serious. We've already talked about it. Honestly, with everything that's happened to me and the fact that you have both Demon and Angel blood as well makes me feel like we should be together. You live alone, in the tiny apartment, go to work alone, you only see your boyfriend outside of us. Who none of us know. We'll meet him tonight and you can move in here. Maybe get some better sleep? Then we'll go from there." Luna lays it all out for her, and I watch the wheels turn in Stella's mind. She's processing things, considering her options while she chews on the inside of her cheek.

"Fuck," she says finally. "I guess we'll try it out. But—" she pauses, dropping her eyes as she decides what to say, "—I've been having these dreams. Nightmares really. Sometimes I wake up in the middle of the night. I just want you to know ahead of time. Just in case." She speaks quietly, clearly not wanting to admit that to us. But Luna is quickly crouched in front of her and holding her hands.

"I'm always here, Stells. No matter what, we'll figure it out together." The girls embrace each other, and I watch as Nathanial visibly tenses in his seat. Curiosity and worry line his features as he watches the two of them and I can't help but wonder if he's thinking the same thing I have been about her.

"All right, enough with the sentiments. Let's go get this over with so we can get home and drink." Stella stands up as Luna steps back and the two girls turn and walk out of the kitchen, their arms wrapped around each other's waists while Nathanial and I follow them.

CHAPTER FOURTY

Luna

"Holy shit this is beautiful," I mumble under my breath. Elijah leans in to whisper against my ear while his arm snakes around my waist tightly.

"I don't think you're supposed to curse inside of a church, *mo dheamhan.*" He plays, a quiet smirk tugging at his lips as he speaks.

"I don't think Fallen Angels or Demons are supposed to be in churches either," I whisper back as I move deeper into his warmth and he laughs quietly in my ear.

The church is massive, long and narrow with towering ceilings that drip with gothic designs. Angels and Demons, saints and sinners are all hand carved into the white marble while every window is decorated beautifully with stained glass.

There are gold accents on each pew, and the head of

church holds a stunningly beautiful organ in the center. There are smaller carved terraces towards the front, where the priest or speakers can stand and address the congregation.

I can almost feel the tangible history in the cathedral. The walls themselves declare their beauty and importance. There are several people walking about, either admiring the delicately carved details, or kneeling in prayer towards the front of the church. Everyone glances our way in admiration of Nathanial and Elijah. Which I can hardly blame them for, the two men that stand with Stella and I are just as stunning as the building we stand in.

Only they're slightly more intimidating and demand more attention even though they never ask for it. I silently claim Elijah for myself as I slide my hand into his, interlacing our fingers as he leads us to a small door at the front of the sanctuary.

He opens the narrow entrance, allowing Stella and I to enter in front of him before Nathanial quietly shuts it and the boys follow behind us.

"Up ahead, take your first left. We'll pass a few rooms before we get to our office," Elijah instructs as we keep moving down the dark hallway. It's just as beautiful as the main floor of the church, but this passageway seems much less used and not as easily accessible. As we take the left and begin passing rooms, I glance inside them to see a few people in each. Immediately, I know they're Angels. Each of them incredibly beautiful in a different way than the average human. The men are larger and more masculine, with a strong beauty that radiates through the space.

The women are healthy and powerful, their skin glows with a peaceful positivity that truly takes my breath away. We're offered polite smiles and cautious waves, until they see Nathanial and Elijah and truly relax in our presence.

The brothers receive a dense respect that I've never witnessed before. Both Elijah and Nathanial are attached to the throne in some way. Elijah, because he's denied the position thus far as ruler. And Nathanial, because he's stepped in to take that place. Everyone nods or bows to them as they pass, and while both of the men are kind, they don't offer words or greetings as we quickly make our way to our own space.

We pass a room on the right that has been covered in caution tape and dons clear signs that say not to enter. I look up to Elijah in curiosity and he nods, acknowledging my thoughts that it was Camden's office. "It's under investigation now. We're going through all of his records, his trials, anything that can give us more information on the drug he created, or his intentions."

I nod silently, squeezing his hand in recognition as we finally come to Nathanial's office. The room is larger than all the others and, in the center, sets a grand black desk. His computer and files are neatly stacked on top and on the other side of the room sits a hospital bed with scattered cabinets. Stella observes the room surprisingly, and I suddenly realize that she doesn't know what Nathanial does for a living.

"He's a doctor. And he rules over the race of Fallen Angels," I speak quietly as I take a seat across from the desk in one of the two large, black suede lounge chairs.

Stella's eyes widen in surprise. "Like you're the King?" she asks. "And a doctor? As in, you help people?"

Nathanial's eyes narrow as he watches her make herself comfortable in the large chair behind his desk. She's small, and the chair practically swallows her tiny frame.

"Yes, is that surprising to you?" he asks, an edge lacing his tone as he leans against the hard desk in front of her.

Stella scoffs, a wicked smile playing along her lips. "No. I guess not. I just didn't think someone as saintly as a King or a doctor would want to be called Daddy while he fucks," she replies as she kicks her tiny feet up on the edge of his desk, intentionally pushing him slightly out of the way in the process.

Elijah laughs. A full blown, harsh laugh that falls out uncontrollably and I can't help but join him while Nathanial's eyebrows furrow in annoyance at Stella's comment.

"Maybe little Stella has no idea how a real King would fuck his subjects senseless. Maybe little Stella won't ever have an idea of how good I fuck them." He leans forward, venom and lust dripping from his words.

Stella meets him halfway, challenging him in every sense of the word as she stands against him in defiance, "Good thing I'm not your fucking subject then." She backs up and steps away from him, shaking that milky fog out of her eyes in a split second before coming to sit in the other chair next to me.

A tense silence fills the room briefly, so I interrupt to go over the details of what we know. "Okay, so let's lay it out. What do we know for sure and what questions do we still have?"

"Firstly, we know your parents are Archophys who was a Demon, and Estera, who was an Angel. They were one of the few public couples from different races. We don't know anything about them other than they didn't survive. Amelia mentioned that they were Fated, but that would mean they were the first Fated pairing that we know of in thousands of years. Let alone the first Fated from different races." Elijah speaks sympathetically, explaining one piece of the giant puzzle we're working through. I never thought our parents were alive honestly, so the news of their death doesn't surprise me, and Stella doesn't seem horribly affected by it either.

"We know that both you and Stella have Demon and Angel blood. And we have an idea that Camden and Amelia, probably Danner as well, believe you are a disgrace to the race, that you shouldn't be allowed to exist," he continues, anger lacing his tone and filling the bond as he speaks.

"Fucking assholes," Nathanial adds as he sits back in his chair and rests his elbows on the desk in front of him.

"We also know that Elijah and I are the first Fated to come out in decades. But we need to decide what that means for us," I interject, approaching the subject I know Elijah is the most uncomfortable with.

"If we don't hide the fact that we're Fated, we will suffer attacks from all angles. Both Demons and Amelia's army will find ways to come after us," he states, trying to convey the most dangerous aspect to our relationship.

"But if we do, we offer a new sense of hope and peace amongst the Fallen Angel race, right? It would be beneficial to those who aren't at war with us?" I offer the other perspective. This is the side that's been nagging at my mind since I learned of the wars within the races.

"Yes. That is inarguable. Those that loyally serve us and support our race would be a new force to reckon with if they learned that Fated connections were resurfacing. Especially if you both decide to take over the throne," Nathanial speaks this time, tentatively supporting my point of view.

"But is that worth the potential loss of either of us? I don't think so. I can't fucking lose you, Luna. And this doesn't mean I want the throne." Elijah snaps the words out as he crosses his arms tightly against his chest. He props one leg up against the wall as he leans back, but I can see through his tough exterior now. He's losing himself, collapsing on the inside as the control he fights to maintain slowly unravels.

I stand up and cross the room to meet him, lifting my hands to rest on either side of his face. "You could never lose me. And

I'll never lose you. We will train and learn from other's past mistakes so that we don't suffer the same losses. We become stronger and better together. We fight to protect each other and this race against people who have set out to destroy it. We don't have to take the throne if we decide not to. Nathanial is doing a wonderful job as it is."

Elijah searches my eyes painfully, wanting desperately to convince me otherwise. I can feel it inside of him, but something else springs up within of our bond that excites me. It's the smallest glimmer of hope, the smallest inkling that maybe this could work. That maybe we could change the direction that this war is headed.

He leans down and takes my mouth with his, fisting his hand in my hair and holding me tightly against him. "I love you," he whispers against me and I melt against his hold as the world slowly slips away around us.

"All right. Next on the agenda, when do we kill Camden?" Stella chirps in, effectively breaking our trance as I turn around quickly to address her.

"No one is going after Camden," I say pointedly to both her and Elijah who tenses behind me.

"No one said anything about going after him, my Luna. But he is going to pay for what he's done. In blood." Elijah's quiet but dangerous words elicit a shiver across my spine as he leans down to kiss the soft skin at the nape of my neck.

"I don't want anyone getting hurt by seeking revenge," I say quietly, wishing I could change their minds on this point.

"When it happens, it'll be the right time and the right place, *m'aingeal*," he says finally, leaving no more room for discussion.

Nathanial clears his throat, drawing our attention towards him. "We also know that Amelia somehow stole parts of our memories from the beginning. I don't ever remember learning Stella and Luna's names when we found them in the woods years ago."

"How is that even possible?" Stella asks.

"Amelia can absorb the life of a person. Their strength, their essence, and their power. It may be possible that within her skill, she can manipulate or take parts of memories," Elijah explains. "That's the only possibility I can think of."

"And yours and Luna's ability is seeing visions of the past?" she pushes into another subject that has been plaguing my mind.

"Sort of. I think I have an idea of what we can do together. My ability alone, is sort of like a shield. I can manipulate situations to benefit me. I can mostly block my feelings from the blood bond, which is what I was doing before. But I've never tried strengthening the ability, I don't necessarily use it often. I believe Luna can affect the mental state of things, whether it be through visions as we've seen, or her surroundings. I found her once, seemingly frozen in the shower as she slept. But as soon as she woke everything shifted and changed back to normal." Elijah's voice is hesitant as he reveals what he's been researching over the last few days. "Together, I think we can manipulate our surroundings entirely. We can potentially affect others in the manipulation as well, possibly use it as a weapon if need be in the future. It's something we need to practice and enhance, especially if we come out as Fated."

Nathanial and Stella watch us intently as they process everything Elijah explained.

"Well, that will be helpful in defending you both against any attacks," Nathanial finally speaks. "We should also move. Into one big home, truthfully. Until everything settles and we know you both are safe."

Elijah groans behind me, adamantly against the idea. "No," he says dryly.

"I know you don't want to, but we need to keep the girls safe. We need to keep you and Luna safe, and we need a location that is completely off the grid to everyone's knowledge. Too many people know where you are now." Nathanial is the voice of reason, quickly offering points that are too strong to refute.

"Shit," Elijah's voice rumbles behind me as he lifts a hand and scrubs it down his face.

"All right, so we find a new place and you don't come out as Fated until we're already moved. Deal?" Stella finally says, laying it out plainly.

"Fine," we both agree reluctantly.

"Things we don't know. Why Stella is an irritatingly raging sex addict," Nathanial tacks on sarcastically at the end.

"Ha ha. We also don't know if Nathanial is always an asshole, or if the saint is just deliciously tempted by my sinful nature." She smirks maliciously as she stands, "Can we go find some food now? I'm horny and starving and honestly, I want to get this dinner with Michael over with. Maybe we can just do lunch."

"Yeah, call him now and see if he'll meet us at home. We can grab food on the way," I add as I step forward and pull Elijah's hand into mine.

"I assume you're going home, King Nathanial?" Stella asks mockingly.

"No way, there's no chance I'm missing the meet and greet for your loser boyfriend," he replies dryly. But a possessive growl rips from his throat at the last second when Stella suddenly stops mid-step, her eyes ghosting white as she looks back over her shoulder at him.

Elijah and I stop as the two watch each other, Nathanial's eyes mirroring hers in a lusty haze. Neither of them makes a move towards the other, they just simply watch as their breaths become heavy and labored in their lungs.

Finally, Elijah steps in between the two, effectively cutting through their trance as they return to their normal state.

"Come on, you two. Let's figure out what the hell is going on."

CHAPTER FOURTY-ONE

CHAPTER FOURTY-ONE

Luna

STELLA STILL DOESN'T KNOW THE DETAILS OF HOW intricately Camden is involved in my life. She doesn't know about the attack all those years ago, and I'm not sure I want to tell her about it yet. She's going through so much as it is, and I can see that she's afraid. She does a damn good job at hiding it with sarcastic comments and crude humor. But every time her eyes go milky white and she falls into this uncontrollable trance she has to fight her way out of, there's that flash of confusion and fear lingering there.

"Are you okay?" Stella's voice quietly cuts through my thoughts as she comes up to stand behind me while we fix food together in the kitchen. The guys are in the living room, trying to put something on the television that we all agree on, which is practically nothing.

"Of course, sorry. Just thinking about everything. It's a lot, honestly," I say as I begin stacking assorted sandwiches on a tray. Suddenly, Stella sways where she's standing, reaching quickly for the counter before she falls to the ground.

"Shit," she says, confusion pulling at her features. "That was weird, I felt dizzy all of a sudden." She offers me a casual smile, brushing off the odd sensation that washed through her.

"Are you sure *you're* okay?" I offer her words back to her, concern coursing through me and a strange feeling of familiarity wafting across the room.

I glance towards the door, immediately noticing Elijah stalking through it and over to us. "What's going on?" he asks as Nathanial quickly comes up beside him.

"I don't know," I start, entirely confused by how Stella and I are feeling. "Stella was dizzy. I feel like something's coming, like something is wrong."

Instantly, Stella's eyes glaze over again as she stands, completely balanced and steady on her feet while she turns and walks out of the kitchen. Nathanial is hot on her heels, his body strangely not responding to her like he usually mirrors when she falls into a trance.

I look to Elijah, concern reflecting back in his eyes as he takes my hand and pulls me behind him. We move into the living room and watch as Stella steps towards the front door silently, Nathanial keeping a safe distance between them but still following her protectively.

"Stells, where are you go—" I start, but as soon as she opens the door, everything inside of me freezes as a terrifying panic consumes me.

"Well, hello everyone. It's about time I met my girlfriend's family."

Danner stands in the doorway, his narrow figure towering over little Stella as she moves beside him, her eyes ghostly white and completely unresponsive.

CHAPTER FOURTY-TWO

Luna

A SNARLING GROWL RIPS FROM NATHANIAL'S THROAT AS he lunges forward to grab my sister. But she was already too close to Danner and his arm snakes dangerously around her throat as he pulls her against him.

He uses his ability, simply nodding his head backwards to throw Nathanial against the staircase effortlessly. Elijah immediately steps in front of me as Danner drags Stella into the living room. Fear engulfs my heart as it hammers against my chest at the sight of them together.

Suddenly things begin spiraling out of control even further as both Camden and Amelia enter the house and come to stand on either side of Danner.

"What the actual fuck," Elijah roars, anger and apprehension bleeding through our bond and seeping into me. I can already feel the power begin to merge between us, the way our bodies are going on alert in every sense of the word.

Nathanial quickly comes to stand next to his brother, both men towering over the four bodies in front of us. Unfortunately, though, the unwelcomed guests hold the upper hand with my tiny sister at their mercy.

"Surprised? It's been a long time coming, Elijah," Danner remarks, and Camden laughs at his side when his gaze meets mine between the two men in front of me.

"Missed you, little Luna." Camden's voice is sick and scrapes across my skin in all the wrong places. Elijah's lip lifts in a growl as he moves to step towards Camden, but Danner is quick to reign everyone in.

"Now, now, let's take a moment to lay out the ground rules." His hand tightens around Stella's throat as he twists her head towards him and captures her mouth with his own. At first, Amelia doesn't look phased, but I notice the tiny flicker of jealousy in her eyes when Danner deepens the kiss and Stella sags in his arms.

"First of all," he starts as he pulls his lips away from her. She seems hungry for whatever he's giving her, and she whimpers at the loss of his contact. Her eyes stay that same milky white the entire time he's near her. "At the end of all of this, I'm leaving with either Luna or Stella. I do have a preference, but either way, one of them is coming with me."

"No fucking way," Nathanial grinds out, his body trembling with an uncontrollable rage that Elijah mimics exactly.

Danner laughs, "Second, let me explain to you what has been happening over the last several weeks." He shifts Stella forward and grips the back of her neck in mock offering to us. In actuality, he's dangling her possessively in front of our faces. "While you all have been engrossed in Luna and this disgusting blood bond between her and Elijah, I've been taking the time to get to know our sweet Stella. You may have heard of me as Michael, her newly acquired boyfriend who has been dying to meet all of you." His lips pull up into a sick smile as his thumb grazes up and down the side of Stella's neck. He could easily snap it if he wanted to.

Nathanial is practically seething with hatred and anger at what's ahead of us and my own mind is racing with the possibilities of what she's been enduring without any of us realizing it.

"See, I've had my own work to do. In creating the perfect little Demon that would lead us to you all. This little pixie suffers from the traits I've successfully pulled out of her. They were buried, far deeper than I initially thought. But after a lot of sexual awakening, she's become quite the little Succubus."

Succubus.

I wish I knew exactly what that meant, but I vaguely remember old myths of the kind of creatures they were. They fed off sexual energy and as much as I want to believe Danner is lying, I have a sick feeling he's telling the truth. My heart sinks at the realization that Stella has been manipulated and abused over the last several weeks right under my nose.

"Come show them," Danner instructs Camden, who saunters forward and wraps his thick arms around Stella's little waist. I immediately step forward, the protective need rising inside of me to keep him from my sister.

Danner clicks his tongue in a disciplinary tone at me, urging me backwards before he hurts someone I care for. Rage boils inside of me as I step back to stand level with Elijah and Nathanial. The heat radiating out of both of them is dangerously high. It consumes every inch of me in seconds and poisons my blood with a heavy blaze.

Camden's hands snake into Stella's hair as he drops his lips to her neck and begins slowly kissing a trail down to her shoulder. She turns for him, tilting her head and giving him more of her skin for him to touch. Her lips part slightly, and her breaths become heated and quick as he moves farther down her chest, trailing his tongue across the swells of her breasts. Stella whimpers in an achy need and instantly things around us begin shifting as hatred burns inside of me.

Watching one of the men who attacked me all those years ago, and then who manipulated me again just recently, forcibly touch and influence my sister without her consent is too much. I can't control the power as it rises between Elijah and I and begins spilling out into the area between us.

Danner laughs as Amelia steps forward to separate Camden and Stella. I know she isn't intending to help any of us, but I do see the wary expression in her eyes as she watches Camden use another woman without her permission. For some reason, I have a feeling that it crosses a line for her as well. No matter how evil and ruthless she can be. She kills recklessly, she mutilates and poisons others with her words and actions. But she doesn't want to be a part of this portion of the plan.

"Get back," Danner's voice is a hard command as it washes over Amelia and he uses his strength to forcibly pull her away from them. Camden continues his assault over Stella, moving lower to her breasts as she relaxes in his arms.

"Danner, this is enough. Stop them and take what we fucking need. I will not ask again," Amelia speaks the words in dominance as she stands before him, and I notice Nathanial take a slow step to the side in the moment of distraction. Elijah laces his fingers between mine and tries to communicate with me through our bond.

We can change the surroundings.

His voice is quiet in my head. It's difficult to communicate this way while our emotions are running so high and the stress overwhelms the room.

I don't know how, or what to change it to. I respond to him as I watch Nathanial slowly make his way towards Camden and Stella.

Danner laughs as he draws his attention back towards Amelia and suddenly things start falling out of control at a different level. "You are nothing but a pawn in my game, Amelia. I am done with you," he lifts his hand slowly, but it's enough to drop Amelia to her knees in front of him.

Confusion races through me as I try to decide what I need to do next. But Danner shoots his arm forward and drags Stella back to him and away from Camden, who laughs at the sight of Amelia on her knees before Danner.

"I knew Luna and Elijah were Fated. It was clear from the moment he took her away from you at the mansion. You fool. You let him because you've always been so distracted by his presence. My only question now, is if Stella is Fated to Nathanial. Because truthfully, I want her for myself."

Nathanial's entire body tenses at Danner's words but he stays silent, refusing to acknowledge his accusation. I would never have thought they were Fated, their interactions with each other are always distraught and negative. However, I can't help but notice how innately protective Nathanial has always been over her.

Amelia moves to stand but Danner's imperceptible weight crushes her back to the ground again. I can see her body shake in fear and uncertainty as she watches the scene unfold in front of her. I want her to suffer, but not at the expense of my sister.

"See, this little slut has become quite the good lay. And she needs someone like me to truly satisfy her. She needs an Incubus as her counterpart to feed that natural hunger she can't live without."

Confusion washes through me at his words. How could Danner be an Incubus when he's an Angel? I thought they only derived from Demons. "I know, it's confusing isn't it? It actually shocks me that that no one picked up on the trace amounts of Demon blood in my system. All this time Amelia, you've been fighting against the mutts of our kind when you've been bonded to someone of the same supposed genetic flaw. But I've got a surprise for you too my dear." Danner pulls a blade from his back and lifts it over his chest. I feel the familiar terror rip through Elijah and course into me.

The blood bond.

Nathanial is still inching forward, doing his best to maintain his quiet approach while a storm rages around us.

"We're stronger. By leagues and bounds. Even Luna and Stella, who have only recently learned of their blooded roots. They are still stronger than you, and they have a larger claim to the throne than you do my darling. I was only lucky enough to not have black blood in my body. A minor flaw that I picked up on at a young age so that enabled me to blend in easily with the other Angels.

Now I did worry, that bonding to you would give you the insight no one else had. But you've always been blind, my Amelia. Blinded by the demented and false theories your father indoctrinated you with. You've been programmed by lies that have clouded your judgement. But you've gotten me here, and that's an honorable enough achievement so I will let you live if you survive this." He lifts the blade and slashes it across his chest, spilling blood across himself and my completely absent sister.

"I sever this bond with Amelia, Throne Angel of Arcadia above. I sever the ties of blood between us and reject the unity of our souls as one." Danner collapses to the ground while Nathanial launches forward, aiming to pull Stella into his arms, but he's a second too late as Danner's blade slashes across her arm and he begins chanting a new line of words.

Ones I instantly remember as the Enochian phrase Elijah spoke to me when creating our blood bond.

"Don't you fucking dare," Nathanial grits out as he shoves Danner away from Stella. But their blood has already mingled and Danner's voice drifts through the air over the cries of Amelia as she self-destructs in front of us.

Camden is above her, sliding his arms under hers and dragging her across the floor away from the commotion while Elijah and I rush forward. Danner is weakened by the severance of his own bond, hindering him from using his own ability but he finds the strength to stand and move towards Stella.

Nathanial beats him to her, yanking her into his arms as her limp body falls against him. He begins speaking something else above her, drowning out the words of Danner's chant as he tries to initiate their bond.

Now. Elijah shouts the words in my mind and I immediately spring into action. I run off of instinct, shutting my eyes and reaching out into the space around us, willing everything to change and depict something else entirely. I feel the power flow between Elijah and I as we both manage the same image in our minds.

When I pry my eyes open, everything is different. Sculpted into a reality that doesn't make sense but far outweighs what we were just witnessing. We're back in the middle of the woods, in the place where Amelia, Nathanial and Elijah found Stella and I when we were young.

Danner is on his knees in front of Nathanial, while he stands and holds Stella clutched tightly in his arms. At first, Danner looks confused as he glances around and tries to comprehend where we are. But Nathanial's knee catches him off guard as it comes crashing against his face. Blood flows from his nose and he laughs maniacally at the observation. But Nathanial isn't done, and while he won't let go of Stella, he comes forward again by launching his foot into Danner's chest, sending him colliding with the ground. Danner stares at him with wide eyes and begins chanting the blood bond again, desire and entertainment flaring over the sight of Stella's white empty eyes.

Nathanial crouches in front of him, keeping his hold on Stella's frail body and begins saying something of his own. Danner looks down at Stella and apprehension crosses his features when he realizes that Stella's blood is no longer integrating with his. Instead, it naturally moves towards Nathanial, seeking him out rather than Danner.

He reaches forward to snatch Stella out of Nathanial's arms. But Elijah's brother is quick, and his fist comes forward and smashes across Danner's face, whipping it back as more blood flows and falls from his features.

I maintain my hold on the vision, drawing the strength and power from mine and Elijah's combined efforts. I glance to my left, expecting to see Elijah next to me but panic overwhelms me when I realize he's gone.

I'm here, m'aingeal.

His words drift through me and his voice is the peaceful tenor I need to calm the fear inside of myself. I look around for him and see nothing until Camden's body flashes in front of me. He's alone, on his knees as he gasps for air and his hands come up to pull at the snake that wound itself around his neck. I know this isn't me, I have no idea how to control different aspects of the vision. I've only been able to create them around us. I look behind him and see Danner's eyes widen at the sight of Camden and then in a flash he's gone. His figure whipped into a small spark before it vanishes entirely.

"What the fuck!" Nathanial shouts as he watches the empty space that Danner previously occupied. He whips his head around to find me, his eyes searching me for answers that I don't have. Stella's eyes suddenly clear and she gasps for breath in his arms, dragging his attention back to her.

"I should have killed you," Camden's hoarse voice captures me as his hands continue gripping the thick black snake around his throat. It won't budge, it pulls tighter and tighter as satisfaction roots itself in my stomach. My eyes fall to him wholly, now that I know Stella is safe, I offer him my complete attention.

I step forward slowly and crouch in front of him as my eyes rake across his now blueish face. Tilting my head, I observe him, slowly and fully while he struggles to catch his breath. I notice the veins pulling in his forehead and the way his once powerful hands now look thin and frail against his own skin.

"I feel sorry for you," I say quietly. "That someone has done you so wrongly, that you allowed the poison to fester inside of your mind and soul. It coats your skin and spills from your cells. I can feel it, begging to be freed but you don't release it." I slide my hand up to the snake, letting my fingers skate across its scaly flesh and admire it. Appreciate it. "Because it doesn't want to be there. The darkness. You could have let it go and become something more than this." I let my fingers wrap around the thick body, adding to the strangle it offers Camden's throat. "But you didn't, and you took parts of me I will never get back. So, this is where life ends for you."

I pull. Pull the snake tighter around his throat as its efforts join with mine and Camden chokes on the lack of oxygen. He tries to speak, to fight, but the strength has left his body and he succumbs to death with eyes wide open, a sad unity of fear and fulfillment shining through them.

Suddenly the vision shatters around us and I'm left in front of Camden with my hands wrapped tightly around his throat. It's in that moment that I look around and see that the snake around his neck was actually Elijah, who's rough, tattooed fingers are laced tightly with mine.

I fall backwards, releasing my hold as Camden crashes to the ground between us. Elijah rushes forward and immediately wraps his arms around me, pulling me against his chest in that blazing sun that I need to warm the freeze taking over me.

"I'm here, Luna. You're okay. Stella's okay," his soft voice breathes into my ear and I force my mind to target the bond between us. I focus on the warmth he instills in me, the peaceful strength he gives me when I needed to pull it from him the most. I absorb his scent and his power until my own heart rate falls enough to clear my mind of everything that just happened.

Well, holy shit.

CHAPTER FOURTY-THREE

ELIJAH

My blood is pumping vigorously through my veins as I come down from the adrenaline high we were just riding. Nathanial is on the couch, an unconscious Stella tucked safely in his arms as he refuses to let anyone come near her. Amelia is weak and frail in the corner of the room, covered in her own blood from the severance of her bond. Tears stream down her face and even while I hate her, I feel for the pain she's currently in.

Betrayal. The loss of someone so important to you. Finding out that everything you've come to believe is a lie.

I've been there. And I wouldn't trade any of it if it meant I didn't end up with Luna at the end of all this. But I never wish to experience it again.

Luna is leaning against my chest as she attempts processing what happened. After the vision shattered and I calmed her, I pulled Camden's lifeless body out of the house. I will go outside to burn him and bury his ashes as soon as we figure out our next move.

I don't regret it. Killing him that is. Does that make me a monster? Probably. But I've never claimed to be anything more. In fact, at the beginning of all of this, I was never certain that I was truly the Angel in my relationship with Luna.

In fact, I believe I said I was most likely the Devil.

CHAPTER FOURTY-FOUR

CHAPTER FOURTY-FOUR

Luna

"Where is Danner?" I ask aloud, hoping any one person in this room will have an answer for me. But everyone remains silent, aside from Amelia's continuous cries and whimpers of pain.

I should be happy as I watch her crumble piece by piece in front of us. But honestly, something pulls inside of me at what she just went through. Suddenly I'm looking at a broken girl no older than myself.

Pretty, but abused and broken.

It hurts, knowing everything she did to me but still feeling this way about her. I should hate her. I want to fucking hate her.

But I don't. Instead, I foster the idea that maybe there's a chance we can save her.

"I'm going to kill him," Nathanial's hard voice scrapes against my skin as his hatred leaks into the air around us.

"He didn't bond to her, right?" Elijah asks as his hands wrap around my arms and move along my skin in a delicious reminder of who he is to me.

Mine. My Fated. Bonded, for eternity together.

"Hell no," Nathanial says as if there is no other possible answer. "She wouldn't accept him."

"Thank you," I look to him, offering every ounce of gratitude I have for him saving my sister.

"You and Elijah are a force to reckon with. I couldn't have gotten her away from him without you both," he responds quietly. But my attention falls to back to Amelia as she listens to every word we speak. Nathanial follows my gaze and his body tenses at the sight of her. "What are we going to do with her?" he adds, disgust lacing his tone.

"I don't know," I say truthfully, and I search the bond for any indication of how Elijah is feeling towards her.

He must know I'm searching, because his nose grazes the crook of my neck as his lips gently kiss across my skin. "I trust you," he says, and I know in that moment that he would support any decision I made.

"I want to hate her," I whisper to him, turning my head to meet his eyes. They're filled with respect and admiration; with a love I could have never imagined experiencing. "But I don't."

"I know you don't," he says back, brushing his lips across my own. "That's what makes you different than the rest of us. Stronger. Influential. A leader."

My body melts into his heat as his hand grasps the base of my jaw and pulls me against him, devouring me with his touch and kiss. Heat courses through me and I lean into him, taking his lip between my teeth before pulling away gently.

I look back to Amelia, who has now fallen asleep from exhaustion on the other side of the room. I tear my eyes away from her and bring them back to Elijah and Nathanial. "I think we can save her," I whisper the words carefully, trying not to wake her.

Nathanial groans in frustration and drops his head to Stella's worn body. He's already wrapped and patched the wound Danner left on her arm when he tried to initiate a blood bond.

Elijah laughs quietly as he pulls me snugly against him. "All right, little Angel. If that's what you would like, then I'm here for you."

"We have to leave, which means Amelia comes with us," Nathanial states, bringing logic back into the reality we've found ourselves in.

"I agree, and we can't tell her where we are. She can't have knowledge of the information. If Danner truly is an incubus, he'll have access to her dreams," Elijah adds as he shifts back and stands, pulling me up along with him.

"Wait, doesn't that mean he has access to Stella's dreams as well?" I wonder out loud. I hope it's not true, but we have to acknowledge the fact that it may be.

Elijah and Nathanial glance at each other with uncertainty in their eyes. But it's Amelia's weak and strained voice that suddenly breaks through the tension.

"Yes. He's been visiting her in her dreams for several weeks now. Wherever we go, neither she nor I can know the location." She slowly sits up and leans back against the wall, pulling her shaking knees up to her chest.

"Well, I guess things really have come full circle, haven't they?" Her words are frail and filled with regret as she speaks. Self-hatred is evident in her eyes as well as a clear anger towards everything surrounding her. She hates each of us, I can see it. Hell, I can feel it radiating off of her in thick waves of that toxicity that leaks from her pores. She hates what we are, mutts of her kind, or those who willingly accept and love us.

"We don't trust you. We don't owe you anything. In fact, I would have no problem killing you, Amelia. But my Fated refuses to let you go, and for that reason alone, you're coming with us," Elijah speaks firmly and finally from behind my shoulder.

She looks to me, her icy eyes meeting my own in undeniable revulsion. "You're making a mistake, mutt. I'm far too gone to be saved now." The cold words graze over my skin, but my own frost is too strong for hers to root itself within me now.

Because I've changed. I'm not the same girl I was all those nights ago. Not when she had me in the mansion, or when she tied me up in the tree.

No. I'm a powerful mix of both Demon and Angel, I accept both parts of me wholly and thrive in either place. Both darkness and light have claimed me, and I willingly surrender to both sides.

Uniting what can be evil and what is naturally good, and with my Fated, we're far more indestructible than we've been given credit for.

EPILOGUE

EPILOGUE

Luna

"ELIJAH, WAIT," I MOAN BREATHLESSLY AS HIS LARGE hands tightly grip my thighs and lift me onto the counter.

"No," he growls as he spreads my legs apart and then drags me up against his thick cock. "I told you what would happen if you wore this fucking dress."

"Jesus, do want everyone in the damn house to hear us?" I gasp as his teeth graze my collar bone, drifting further down to the swell of my breasts. I'm wearing a sun dress, it's a short, flouncy yellow one that hugs my chest and waist tightly and then flares over my hips. It's got thin straps that cross in the back and honestly, I wanted to tease him with it.

"Yes," he says plainly as he quickly tears the straps down my shoulders and chest until my breasts are completely open to him. He drops his head, skimming his teeth across every inch of me and then biting in sporadic places. One of his hands falls to my ankle as he lifts my leg and hooks it around his hip.

"Fuck," I moan uncontrollably as his fingers slowly slide up the back of my calf and then shift to brush the inside of my thigh.

"Come on Angel, spread those pretty legs for me." His voice is low and husky as it glides over my sensitive skin and settles low in my pussy. I do as he demands, always. Because I can't fucking get enough of him.

He laughs darkly and he takes my mouth with his, "That's right. Tell me how wet you are, Luna." He sucks my tongue into his mouth before releasing and diving into my own. His other hand lifts to the back of my head as he fists my hair and drags me even harder against his body.

"We're in the fucking kitchen, Elijah," I say harshly, but secretly I love playing this game with him. Where he corrupts me and seduces me even though I think it's a bad idea. He feels me out still, always and every time through our bond. He never pushes me to do anything I'm not comfortable with.

He takes care of me. Genuinely and completely. I fucking love him for it.

"Yeah, I know. I've been dying to fuck you on these counters since we moved in," he responds and his head dips to suck one of my nipples into his warm, wet mouth. They're hard, stiff and aching for his touch to sooth them. His tongue slips out and across my chilled skin. His fire blazes me with every lick and suck he gives them.

Elijah and Nathanial quickly found us a new home after everything happened three weeks ago. We moved in the middle of the night, without telling Amelia or Stella when or where we were going. We can't risk them telling Danner. Stella has completely lost herself to the condition. She's either partying hard and fucking anything that moves, or she's hidden and reserved inside of herself while Nathanial silently watches her from a safe distance.

Esme came and placed a barrier spell around the house. So, if we leave, Amelia and Stella can't actually decipher the directions to and from wherever we go. It's like the spell scrambles the turns inside of their head, fogs over any words or numbers that could hint as to where we are.

The truth is that we aren't that far from where we were before. But we're in a secluded portion of those woods that have made home to so many of our memories. Nathanial and Elijah bought the mansion together. It's roughly 27,000 square feet and filled to the brim with countless rooms and spaces where we can all keep to ourselves.

But Elijah wants to fuck in the kitchen—the communal fucking kitchen—where anyone could catch us.

He grips the hem of my panties and yanks them down my thighs until they fall to the floor below. The cold counter shocks my bare ass and I absently arch my back to run from the sensation. He's quick though and his hands immediately slide under me as he grinds his hard cock into my pussy through his jeans.

"You feel so good, Luna. So fucking tight and ready for me," He groans the words as he slides his finger into my pussy, going deep and hard as I whimper around his lips.

"Shit, yes. Please, Elijah," I surrender. Giving him what I know gets him impossibly harder before he decides to slam his cock inside of me.

"Quiet, Angel. You don't want to wake everyone, do you?" His voice is low but demanding as he fucks me with his hand. Going faster and harder while I bite my lip to hold back my moans.

He quickly pulls me from the counter and my knees weaken as I fall to the ground in front of him. His hands are immediately at his jeans as he unzips himself, but I take his hands in my own and pull them to his sides. I want to finish undressing him.

He pulls himself away from my touch as he crouches down in front of me. He drags his thumb across my lower lip, tugging it downwards as his broad chest flexes with each movement. He's shirtless, and his fucking body is something I could never get tired of.

"Do you want to suck my cock, *mo dheamhan?*" he says darkly, and a flash of that inky obscurity whips through his eyes.

Wetness pools between my legs and coats my thighs as I think about tasting him, having his cock slide through my lips and across my tongue.

"Yes," I whisper, arching my back and willingly lifting myself towards him.

"Try again," he demands harshly as goosebumps break out across my shoulders.

"Please, let me suck your cock." This time, I voice the needy desire through both my words and through our bond, letting the ache flow through me and into him. I watch as his hard cock kicks back against his tight briefs and I can't stop the smirk that tugs at my lips.

"Yeah, yeah, you've got me Luna. Every fucking part of me," he laughs against my lips as he stands again and quickly releases his cock from the waistband of his briefs. It falls long and heavy between us and my tongue naturally slips out to wet my bottom lip at the sight of him.

I whimper in need as his hand tangles in my hair and he yanks me forward. "Part those soft lips, Luna. Let me fuck that pretty face of yours," his cock pushes against me, spreading me open as I take him in as far as I can manage. I let my tongue lick across his pierced tip, lightly pulling on the silver bar before I move to lick up the underside of his shaft from base to tip again.

"God, fuck. So good, Luna," he chokes the words out as his hand fists the back of my head, gripping my hair and setting a rhythm that I fucking love. It's hard and fast as his hips thrust forward to meet me. I take him, every single inch that fits, and then I fist the rest of him with my hand.

I feel the salty taste of his cum as it pearls at the tip and I drag his cock across my lower lip. He watches, his eyes flaring with surprised heat at the sight of his cum on my face.

"Shit, shit. Holy shit, that's fucking hot." He holds my head still, just barely above his cock as he watches me, and I dart my tongue out to lick at the taste he left on my skin.

"Then fuck me and I'll let you cum wherever you like," I say the words quietly, but let that sultry tone dances across my voice. He suddenly yanks me up by my hair and turns me around so that my back is against his while I'm pressed up against the counter.

"Make it a promise and I'll fuck you anyway you like," his tone bites against my skin as he rolls his hard cock against my ass.

"I promise," I whisper softly. "Now fuck me, Elijah. I need you," and just like that I'm gasping at the sudden stretch of him as he fills me, inch by delicious inch he consumes me. "Oh my god, so deep. So good," I mumble the words as his hand slides up to the base of my throat and he holds me against him.

He thrusts into me, deeper and harder as our bodies slap every time they come together. I'm soaked, incredibly wet and the sweet sounds fill my ears and turn me on desperately. He keeps thrusting, meeting me match for match as my skin licks against his own. Our blood rages between the bond while an even deeper connection keeps us grounded together.

Suddenly, everything shifts around us for a brief moment and we're surrounded by a stunning mountain scape. We're outside, large trees and soft grass envelopes the large area while wildflowers are scattered across ground below. I glance behind me and watch as Elijah takes in the scenery as well.

This has been happening lately, our minds and bodies throw us into a new beautiful location that we've never been to before. I love it and appreciate it for the quick reprieve it gives us. I love the home we live in now, but the size of the house doesn't change the fact that we're essentially hiding. And Amelia lovingly refers to herself as our hostage.

We're struggling to find answers for Stella while Nathanial refuses to share the exact reason why Stella didn't accept her bond with Danner. I have a feeling I know, and Elijah believes it as well. But we both know better than anyone that you can't force a Fated bond until they're ready to accept it.

The visions aren't what truly capture my attention anymore when we're like this. No, my favorite part is how Elijah sees himself in these moments. Because in these visions, he's in his true form. Far from a Fallen Angel and much more than what he was born to be.

His large white wings span the length of his back and wrap around us as he continues thrusting into me again, and again. He claims me and consumes me with every breath while I run my fingers across the soft texture of what he used to have. But I swear he feels it, these visions are becoming sturdier and stronger every time we create one.

We're growing more powerful, fiercer together with each passing moment and even now, while we're losing ourselves to the passion between us, I can feel the influence thickening the air.

Elijah's thrusts grow more frantic and his hand falls to circle my clit as he continues that drag of his cock in and out of my tight pussy. I cling to him, milking his body and craving what he gives me as my orgasm erupts around us. It swallows me and I drown in it happily, relaxing in his arms as he pulls out at the last minute and strokes his cock as he rides out his own orgasm on my back and down my thighs. I feel the silky streams of his cum coat my skin and then feel his warm hands they skim across my body, marking me and branding me with his essence.

He leans down and rolls into me one last time, slipping more of his cum back inside my slick core. His lips drop to my ear as the vision shatters around us and we're suddenly back in the dark kitchen and against the counter. "Mine," he growls, resuming the act of feasting on my skin with his dark touch and caress.

"Yours," I whisper back. "Always."

He lays another soft kiss against my lips as he turns me to face him and slowly straightens my dress back down my legs. He lifts the thin straps up to my shoulders and we both work to rightfully return my state to something presentable.

Elijah pulls up and zips his jeans and then picks up my thin panties from the floor, dangling them in front of me on a single finger as a smirk pulls at his lips. I laugh and quickly snatch them from him, turning to stalk out of the kitchen when a piercing scream rings through the house.

Stella.

It's the middle of the night and I know everyone is asleep, but as soon as we hear her voice, several sets of feet leap from their respective places and race towards her room. Elijah is right on my heels as we hurry up the grand staircase and down the hall. Her room is near ours, but directly next to Nathanial's and of course he's the first one to find her as we break through the door.

He has Stella in his arms as she screams in the small space, her fingers digging into his flesh as she holds on for her life. He gently coos in her ear, his hand grasped protectively around the back of her neck as she clings to him.

Her eyes are completely white, and it looks like she sees something that terrifies her, but none of us can see what she's looking at.

Suddenly, Amelia is standing behind Elijah and I, watching the scene unfold with boredom and disinterest. "It's Danner," she states plainly, and Nathanial's gaze snaps up to her in bitter anger.

"He's an Incubus, and he's trying to find his Succubus."

THE END

THANK YOU
THANK YOU

HUGE THANK YOU. To so many people.

First of all, if you've made it this far then you have officially been subjected to the full extent—almost—of my filthy language and I commend you. Seriously, this book pushed my boundaries when it came to sex, language, and more sex.

Elijah and Luna played on repeat in my mind, over and over again until I finally sat down and worked their story out on paper. It was all consuming, developing and progressing in my mind in ways that surprised even me as I wrote it. Believe me, not everything that happened in Fated was intentional or planned out. But I think I love it even more because of that. It came out raw and unscripted, deliberate but accidental.

I want to give a massive thank you to my girls. Allison, Brie, Karlie, Jessica, Chelsea and Natalie. You guys are always the first to get your hands on my stories and you all keep me in line or push me even further when I need it. I appreciate you all more than you could ever know.

Brianna Jean. You crazy fucking friend, you're amazing. Seriously. You were the first to truly reach out in the community and really explain things to me. I was so lost on so many different avenues, but you cleared things up and guided the process. I appreciate you so much and am so glad to have you in my life now.

Amy Briggs. My editor and life saver. I literally could not

have done this without you. You transformed Fated into something so much more than it was when it got to you. It's powerful and such a stronger version of what it was at first. I have you to thank for that.

Readers, Bloggers, Bookstagrammers. You guys are amazing. Fated was the first book I was able to put out into the community and you all have absolutely rocked my world with how supportive you have been. Fated wouldn't be what it was without you guys, so THANK YOU. For absolutely everything. All of you.

Stay tuned for Stella's story next. You don't want to miss it.

CONNECT WITH

LIZA JAMES

Website: www.lizajames.org

Printed in Great Britain
by Amazon